THE BEAST

Jonathan Fast comes from a family of writers – his great-great-uncle was the Yiddish writer Sholom Aleichem, and his father is the novelist Howard Fast.

Born in New York City in 1948, he attended Princeton University. He has written extensively for the theatre, motion pictures and television, and is the author of four novels. He lives in Connecticut with his wife, poet-novelist Erica Jong, and their daughter, Molly.

'I found THE BEAST an engaging Hollywood fairy tale, consistently witty and inventive.' Ira Levin

'THE BEAST is the most original new novel I have read in ages. Jonathan Fast has had the clever, crazy idea of taking a fairy tale and transplanting it to contemporary Hollywood, and the result is . . . well, enchanting.' Ken Follett

JONATHAN FAST

The Beast

METHUEN LONDON LTD

A Methuen Paperback

THE BEAST
ISBN 0 417 07060 8

First published in United States 1981
by Random House Inc

Copyright © 1981 by Jonathan Fast

This edition published 1982
by Methuen London Ltd.,
11 New Fetter Lane, London EC4P 4EE

Acknowledgments

Oxford University Press: Adaptation of *Beauty and the Beast*.
Adapted from *The Classic Fairy Tales*, by Iona and Peter Opie, ©
Iona and Peter Opie 1974, by permission of Oxford University Press.

Random House, Inc., and Faber & Faber Ltd: Excerpt from *In
Memory of W. B. Yeats*, from *W. H. Auden: Collected Poems* by
W. H. Auden, edited by Edward Mendelson. Copyright © 1940 and
renewed by W. H. Auden. Reprinted by permission of Random
House Inc., and Faber & Faber, Ltd.

Made and printed in Great Britain by
Richard Clay (The Chaucer Press) Ltd,
Bungay, Suffolk

For Rachel Fast

In the desert of the heart
Let the healing fountains start . . .
—W. H. Auden

The
Beast

·1·

There was once a merchant with three daughters. These daughters were extremely handsome, especially the youngest; when she was little everybody admired her and called her "The Little Beauty," so that, as she grew up, she still went by the name of Beauty, which made her sisters very jealous.

While Beauty loved nothing better than hard work and walks in the country, her sisters slept until ten and sauntered about all day, imagining the rich princes they would marry; in fact, they cared for little but money.

One day the merchant was called away to a distant city on business. When the two eldest daughters heard the news, they begged him to buy them new gowns, headdresses, ribbons and all manner of trifles; but Beauty asked for nothing, since she felt she already had everything a girl could want, except a husband to share her life.

But the merchant insisted and presently Beauty asked him, more for his pleasure than her own, to bring her a rose, for none grew thereabouts, and were a kind of rarity.

The merchant went to the distant city and completed his business and soon set off for home again, his fine horse weighted down with new gowns, headdresses and ribbons for his elder daughters. But as of yet he had been unable to find a rose for Beauty, and that saddened him grievously, for it was she he loved best.

He was only thirty miles from home and thinking of the pleas-

ure he should have from seeing his children again, when he rode into an enchanted forest. It grew dark all around him, and the trees took on horrid faces, while lightning made their branches look like the hands of demons spread against the sky. A clap of thunder so terrified his horse that the animal reared, throwing him from the saddle, and ran off into the night. The poor merchant continued through the forest on foot, cold and hungry and tired; just as he was despairing of ever finding food and shelter, he noticed a light far ahead . . .

Leslie Horowitz's big white Lincoln Continental broke down about two hundred miles from Los Angeles on a seldom-traveled highway known as California State 127, in the eastern end of the Mojave Desert. He had been driving south at ninety miles an hour when suddenly a noise like machine-gun fire had roused him from his reverie, and black smoke billowing from the edge of the hood had filled him with dread.

He pulled to the side of the road, cut the engine, climbed out and waited for the smoke to clear, then lowered his head, like a lion tamer, into the gaping mouth of the Lincoln's open hood, hoping to diagnose the malady even though he knew nothing about automobiles. After probing and poking and burning his hands, he came up with a frayed length of rubber he took to be the fan belt; he threw it on the ground in disgust and walked to the side of the road to thumb a ride.

He didn't expect to wait long; he had passed several cars and trucks since leaving Death Valley and Rebecca earlier that afternoon. People were bound to stop here in the Friendly West, where every man seemed to actually enjoy being his brother's keeper. However, after a whole hour without sight of another car, Leslie began to wonder, and after two hours he became positively perplexed. Then he recalled that today was the day every decent citizen was home with his family, gathered around the dinner table, carving the turkey, dishing out the stuffing; with typical luck he had chosen Thanksgiving afternoon to break down. If he was determined to wait for a ride, he might have to wait all night.

He got the map out of the glove compartment and spread it

on the hot metal of the trunk. There was a town called Baker some thirty miles south. Twenty miles to the north was Shoshone, but he remembered, passing through it earlier that day, nothing but a few wooden shacks bleached white as skulls, and wind blowing through the power lines until they sang, like violins, of their loneliness.

Could he walk thirty miles? When was the last time he had walked even a mile? Despite the exercises he did every morning—well, not quite every morning, perhaps twice a month was a more accurate figure—and his infrequent excursions to the Beverly Hills Health Club, where he rarely did more than soak in the whirlpool and cruise the locker room, Leslie was not in good shape. He ate too much, smoked too much, drank too much and slept too little. As a result, his good looks were fast deteriorating, his body growing pudgy, his complexion sallow, the skin around his eyes as crinkly as puff pastry. From time to time, catching sight of his nude form in the bedroom mirror, he would vow to lose those extra pounds, and then he would visit the gym three days in a row, jogging, working out with the Nautilus machines, jerking and pressing the weights. But his resolution would soon waver, for the single passion in his life was his work, which he did superbly, and his single concern was his clients, whom he loved like father and mother combined. As for his body, as long as he could get laid he would let it go its own way.

He was thirty-six years old, a few inches under six feet, curly-haired, swarthy, with olive eyes and a sensual lower lip. Rebecca Weiss often teased him about being a great big sexy teddy bear, and indeed there was something nonthreatening, motherly even, about his sexuality that made him attractive to men and women alike. He was a flashy though tasteful dresser, and the white suit he wore that afternoon, with red silk shirt and canvas loafers, was his favorite summer uniform.

He turned to the map again and tried to reach a decision. Walk thirty miles to Baker? Take a chance on finding help in the ghost town of Shoshone? Stay put, hoping somebody might roll along this Godforsaken road? Had the problem belonged to one of his clients, Leslie would have solved it instantly, but since the problem was his own, he was stymied. Baker, he decided, finally, fearing permanent paralysis from indecision. He took his brief case out of the trunk, locked the doors, and started down the highway.

The desert stretched before him in a great gray plain speckled with creosote bushes of green and rust, and white burr sage bushes as white and lacy as ice crystals; further on there were low mountains the color of slate and then the clouds, like taller mountains, and finally the sky, so clear and blue that it wrenched the heart. The power lines, strung along the highway, went on forever.

He had walked barely half a mile when shortness of breath overtook him; his heart began to palpitate irregularly, and the dryness of the air seemed to burn holes in his throat. He trudged back to the car, collapsed in the front seat and listened to the patter of a Las Vegas D.J. on the car radio until the symptoms passed.

When evening came, he got out of the car again and sat on a fender, hugging himself for warmth, watching the sky darken, the stars appear. That was when he saw it, a light in the mountains, a single beacon not more than five miles away as best he could reckon it. He heard the throbbing of a helicopter engine overhead, and spotting the enormous dragonfly of a machine, began to jump up and down, screaming and waving his hands. When the helicopter made no sign of noticing him, he got in the car, honked the horn, flashed the lights. Then, grabbing his brief case, he ran after it, ran as fast as he could; but in moments the helicopter had vanished behind the mountains. He slowed to a walk—a stitch in his chest was agonizing—and continued in the direction of the beacon, assuming that it was a home, a ranch, even a fire tower; in any case there would be food and shelter and a phone, and perhaps the pilot of the helicopter could be persuaded, for a price, to fly him back to Los Angeles. Leslie was phobic about almost everything; the idea of flying in a helicopter terrified him, but not so much as spending a night alone in the desert.

He walked for an hour across an arid plain etched by flood and drought, tripping on bushes that snared him like rolls of barbed wire, twisting his ankles on rocks and crevices. Then suddenly the beacon blinked out. Leslie stopped and looked back, but the car and the highway were hidden by the wavelike roll of the desert, and the landscape was everywhere the same, plains and mountains, mountains and plains. He had no idea from which direction he had come, nor where he wished to go. He turned around and around again, trying to find a landmark he recognized, but all he succeeded in doing was confusing himself more thoroughly. In desperation he looked at the sky, remembering vaguely from Boy Scouts something about locating the North Star with the help of the Little Dipper, but the night was so black, the stars so brilliant that he found it impossible to recognize any constellations; even if he had, his sense of direction was so poor it wouldn't have done him much good. If only he had stayed in the car and waited for morning, surely help would have come. But no, impatient idiot that he was, he had to go get himself lost in the largest and least populated desert in the Western Hemisphere. He was shaking from the cold, terrified by the eerie song of a poor-will, the hooting of an owl, the howl of a coyote. For an instant the air was black with bats, like a section of badly scratched film. A few feet ahead he heard a rustling he took to be a rattler and tiptoed away, heart banging in his chest, icy sweat running from his armpits, when actually it was nothing but a tiny kangaroo rat emerging from his hole to forage for mesquite beans. He who could lead others, like a native guide, through the perilous swamps of Hollywood, identifying all species of poisonous producer, of venomous journalist, of fatal deal, was the most helpless of tourists here in the desert.

He would build a fire; anything to stop the shaking. It shouldn't be hard, he thought, with all the dry brush around. He came to a bush of tiny white maplelike leaves, which he assumed flammable because of its ashlike color, and began to tug on it, not realizing that this white burr sage, like the ubiquitous creosote bush, had an enormous root structure—filaments stretching for hundreds of feet underground in their search for moisture—and a stem like steel. He felt something warm and moist in his hands, brought them to his mouth and tasted his own blood. The branches, slipping through his fingers, had made cuts which even now he couldn't feel, he was so numb from the cold.

Burn the fucking bush where it is, he decided. He reached in his jacket pocket and took out a gold Dunhill lighter, pressed it once and was delighted by the wavering yellow flame. When he got back to Los Angeles, he would write a letter to the Dunhill company: "The lighter that saved my life." Perhaps they would use it in an ad, along with a picture of Leslie. Maybe there was a TV movie in it: Hollywood type lost in desert, survives through own resourcefulness, gains new self-respect. He could package it with all his own clients, pitch it to Colby at Universal . . . Leslie laughed at himself, how even here, lost in the Mojave, he could be thinking deals. He pressed the lighter again, and knelt beside the bush, but before he could bring the flame to the leaves, the lighter slipped from between his fingers. He got down on his hands and knees, searching for a glint of gold as prospectors had, in this very spot, a hundred years ago. Again and again he examined the ground, unwilling to admit his loss.

Presently, he lay down on a bare patch of ground, curling himself into a fetal position, covering himself with his thin jacket; but he couldn't sleep. The cold was invading every joint of his body, chilling his blood, making his teeth chatter. When he could bear it no longer, he stood up and started to walk toward a black peak outlined by stars, hoping that it was the same mountain where he had seen the beacon, though any mountain would do as long as it was a destination, a reason to keep walking. Weariness was a poison in his body but motion kept him warm, and given a choice between the two, he'd sooner be weary than cold, anything rather than cold. When he reached the foot of the mountains, the climbing became easier—the ground was a smooth alluvial plain, bare of plant life—and more difficult because at times the steep clay would crumble beneath his feet. Then he would fall to his hands and knees and crawl until he could stand again. Now that he had a rhythm to his walking, his heartbeat evened and his breath grew regular, though heavy; disaster, like a lover who brings out the best in one, was revealing surprising resources of strength and endurance. Nature might be conspiring against him, but he vowed to do all he could to survive.

His clients needed him.

Three days earlier Leslie had received a letter from his favorite client, Rebecca Weiss, a plea for help if ever he'd seen one.

Dear Leslie,

I'm so miserable I want to kill myself (is that why they call it Death Valley?) Everything that can possibly go wrong has. John Guilford's smoking so much marijuana he can't remember his lines, and they have to give him drops to get the red out of his eyes. Yesterday Tony Corelli, one of the grips, passed out from sunstroke. Then when we were just about to shoot, it started to rain! Can you imagine? Here's a place where the annual rainfall's 1.4 inches, and it's rained twice since we got here. And when nature isn't out to get us (is it possible God read the script and wants to "eighty-six" the whole thing?) the fucking tourists are doing their best. I mean, you imagine Death Valley and you imagine desolation, right? Forget it! This place is Grand Central Station. I guess we're the most interesting thing to happen here since they discovered Borax. Every morning the Winnebagos start showing up about 7 A.M. They line up for miles and everybody climbs out and crowds around, trying to get a look at me, and shoving autograph books under my nose, which would be pretty flattering if I hadn't overheard somebody explaining that I was the girl (girl? I'll be thirty next week!) who played Princess Leia in *Star Wars*.

But the thing that is making my life a living nightmare is Mr. Mack Gordon. He is definitely of the Donald Duck School of Dramatic Arts. His favorite directions are "Can't you scream a little louder?" and "Let me see fear, real fear!" (That's easy, all I have to do is think what this movie will do to my career.) His real passion is the giant mechanical spiders. He spends hours fooling with them, like a little boy with a new set of trains. He also loves long, complicated tracking shots, the kind that go on for ten minutes and if one little detail's wrong you have to do the whole "take" over. (All the time he's setting them up I can see he's dreaming about his Museum of Modern Art retrospective.) He loves the car chase sequences and he loves to blow things up. Whenever he thinks that the film might be getting dull, he blows something up. If he ever leaves the film business, he can always become a demolition expert. The only thing he doesn't much like are actors, but I guess he can't figure out how to do the movie without them.

Leslie, I don't have to tell you how depressing it is to be treated like a prop. I mean, I'm not like other women. I don't even have a husband and children to validate my existence. I don't have a boyfriend at the moment. I don't have a terrific body like our friend Ms. Dunbarr and *Vogue* isn't after me for a fashion spread. My knees are knobby and my hair is frizzy. The only self-respect I have comes from my acting skills, and from doing the best possible job I can. Without that I feel like nothing, and all I want to do is crawl in a hole and pull the dirt on top of me.

So I'm trying to make something special out of this role, I'm trying to give some breadth and depth to the character, and Mack Gordon is doing everything he can to stop me. He insults me and calls me names. Sometimes he makes me so miserable I just want to curl up and die. And the terrible thing about location shoots is there's no place to go, nobody to talk to. We're stuck in Death Valley with all the frustration of delays and broken spiders, and hot weather and frayed nerves, and I feel like I'm in a pressure cooker that's going to blow up any second. I could get out of here in a couple of days if Mack would just shoot my scenes first. But he won't talk about it. You'd be doing me such a favor, Leslie, if you could call him. I know you could convince him, you're so good at that sort of thing.

> Love you and miss you more than I can say,
>
> Becky

Leslie received the letter on Tuesday the twenty-first of November and promptly postponed all his meetings for Wednesday, except for a lunch date with an important agent, which he laid off on his partner, Sheila Gold, a plump, fast-talking girl from New York. Thursday was Thanksgiving and Friday was a holiday; but he had left the four-day weekend free to catch up on scripts he was supposed to read. He wouldn't let a client even consider a project until both he and the actor had read the script personally;

as a result, because he read so slowly and his actors were so much in demand, the pile of scripts by his bed grew ever higher, swelling in recent months to a mountain, a paper Everest, with periodic avalanches that threatened to engulf his bed and spill into the other rooms and finally, he feared, drive him out into the street. To ease his conscience he threw a few scripts into his brief case, although he doubted he'd find time to read during one of Rebecca's crises.

The next problem was telling Tommy Troy, a young actor friend he shared his apartment with, that he might not be back in time for Thanksgiving, that he might have to stay on with Rebecca if she was in very bad shape. Tommy had invited a number of their friends, both social and professional, for a special Thanksgiving dinner and he had been planning menus all week, debating goose versus turkey, chestnut stuffing versus prune and raisin. He was from the Midwest, from a big family that always celebrated Thanksgiving together, and he was trying to gather a surrogate family to ease the loneliness he always felt at this time of year. Leslie hated holidays, but he adored Tommy, and considered him a last hope for a lasting relationship before the loneliness of middle age closed in about him. After all, in a few years he'd be forty and life would be over.

That night, when Leslie told him the news, Tommy turned away, trying to hide his disappointment. He was only twenty-one, a handsome sandy-haired boy with a dancer's body, so slim that the tendons in his arm stood out when he reached for something on a high shelf.

"Can't you understand?" Leslie said. "She needs me. She sounds like she's on the verge of a nervous breakdown."

Tommy smiled sadly. "Well, I'll be sure to save you some turkey—even though you don't deserve it."

"Thank you for understanding."

"What makes you special," Tommy went on, "is that you'll give up your vacation and drive ten hours to help a friend in distress. You're one of the most beautiful people I know."

Embarrassed, Leslie tried to make light of it. "It's business. She's my client. Can't ignore a client in distress."

"Bullshit. It's one of your children who needs her daddy. And thank God for her she's got you."

"So you'll be all right without me?"

"I'll be fine."

"You'll have the dinner anyway?"

"I don't know," Tommy said, thoughtfully. "Maybe I'll call it off and go to a restaurant instead."

"Alone?"

"Larry and Vince and Bill asked me if I'd go with them."

"You didn't tell me," Leslie said.

"I didn't think I had to report to you on every phone call I got."

"You don't have to do anything. You're a free agent. Go out with anybody you want. I don't care."

"You are the most jealous, controlling person I've ever met in my life," Tommy said. He sighed. "Tell you what. I'll stay home all alone on Thanksgiving and watch television. Would that make you happy?"

"Why do we always get into these stupid fights?" Leslie wondered.

Tommy shook his head. "I don't know. It's so hard when you really like someone. You're on a tightrope and you know that sooner or later you're going to fall, so to make yourself less nervous, you jump."

"That's it exactly," Leslie agreed. "But knowing it doesn't make it any easier, does it?"

Next morning Leslie picked up two pizzas at Tony's in Hollywood, stowed them in the back seat, hoping the oil wouldn't soak through and stain the blue velour upholstery, and was on the road by ten, his huge white Lincoln speeding east on Interstate 15. He stopped in Barstow for lunch and joined the Las Vegas traffic, the high rollers and slot-machine stuffers, as far as 127, where he turned off for Death Valley Junction, then over a ridge and down into the sun-scorched scab of land which was his destination. Romantically, he had expected endless vistas of golden-sanded Sahara and he was disappointed by a terrain not substantially different from the monotonous miles of Mojave he had driven through all morning.

The Furnace Creek Inn appeared on a cliff above him, a rambling stucco hacienda with clay tile roofs, surrounded by date

palms, tennis courts, a big swimming pool. This 1930s luxury resort was housing the actors and the director (in addition to the
usual clientele, whom Rebecca described as "newly wed or nearly
dead"); the rest of the film crew, that is to say, the Production
Manager, the Assistant Director, the Second Assistant Director
(they needed two to control the crowds of tourists), the three
Production Assistants (including the Producer's teen-age daughter,
who wanted, someday, to direct), the Script Girl, the Director of
Photography, the Camera Operator, the Assistant Operator, the
Sound Recorder and the Boom Man, the Gaffer and his Best Boy,
the Key Grip and his Best Boy, the Key Make-Up Lady and the
Special Make-Up Man (who did all the spider-inflicted wounds,
not to mention the spiders themselves, who needed special pow-
dering to make them look less mechanical), the Wardrobe Mistress
(who hardly did anything, but was having an affair with the Production Manager), the man who designed and operated the spiders
(an old-time special-effects wizard who had once built seventeen
giant mechanical alligators for *Tarzan in the Valley of Death*, one
of the best of the series) and his three Apprentices, not to mention
the Generator Operator, the Teamsters, the Still Photographer, the
Publicist, the A.F.I. Observer, and a spy sent up by the studio to
find out why Mack Gordon was running so far over budget—all
of these skilled technicians were being housed in the Furnace Creek
Ranch, a dreary motel two miles down the road, thereby saving a
few dollars and reminding everybody Who Is More Important
Than Whom, always a basic concern of Hollywood.

A good-looking college boy carried Leslie's overnight bag to his
room. Their eyes met and they instantly recognized each other as
members of the same underground. The signs they exchanged were
so subtle neither could have enumerated them had they wished to:
a motion of the hands, a lowering of the eyes, an inflection of the
voice. Passwords between friendly spies.

"What brings you to this neck of the woods?" the college boy
asked.

"I've got to see a friend who's working on the movie."

"Yeah." He smiled. "I guessed you were from Hollywood."

"I hope I see you later," Leslie said, placing a five-dollar bill in
his hand.

"I get off duty at midnight. Might be down in the bar." He laughed. "No place else to go."

Perhaps it wouldn't be such a bad trip after all, Leslie thought, opening the curtains. The pool was visible from the window, cool, blue and inviting to his car-cramped body, but he was shy about parading his fatness in front of strangers; instead he showered and changed his shirt and returned to the lobby to ask for Rebecca Weiss.

The man at the desk said that the entire company was shooting at Ubehebe Crater, some sixty miles north, and weren't scheduled to be back until ten or eleven that evening. Leslie groaned—the last thing he wanted to do was drive for another hour—but he took directions and climbed back into the Lincoln.

Soon his wish for dramatic scenery was satisfied: as he neared Ubehebe Crater, the earth turned black, like a mountain of shiny coal rippled by strips of iron-gray, desolate and lifeless as the dark side of the moon. He came around the side of the mountain and saw the equipment trucks and the cinémobiles and the trailers, and he turned another corner and saw the cameras set up at the peak of the mountain, aiming down into an enormous crater, a crater so vast that he was seized by a sudden vertigo contemplating it. He parked his car among an assortment of campers and recreational vehicles and joined the crowd, which stood gaping from a respect-ful distance. He could see, at the bottom of the crater, a three-quarter mock-up of a flying saucer. Clever, he thought. For all the bad things he had heard about Mack Gordon—and Lord knows he'd heard little else but bad things about him, about his drinking, his bursts of violence, his cruelty toward actors—the man could make visual magic. By placing a few hundred dollars' worth of painted wood and plastic at the bottom of this huge geological funnel, he had created the impression that the former had caused the latter, that the "flying saucer" had blown an enormous hole in the earth while landing.

Rebecca Weiss and John Guilford, clothes torn, hair matted, faces smudged with black grease paint, were scrambling up the side of the crater, dislodging rocks, kicking up dust, then slid-ing back down, evidently fleeing the passengers of the saucer, two big mechanical spiders which, out of camera range, lay slumped inert on the ground.

An operator with an Aeroflex hung over the side of the crater, recording all this on film while an assistant held his legs; Mack Gordon stood a few steps behind them, shouting orders through a bull horn, reminding Leslie, for some reason, of a coach at an athletic event.

"*Gimme fear! I want to see fear on those faces! The spiders are breathing up your asses, they're going to take over the earth and you're the only ones who can stop them. . .*"

Donald Duck School of Dramatic Arts indeed, Leslie thought.

Gordon was a small, energetic man (five foot four including his high-heeled cowboy boots), with steely little eyes and a salt-and-pepper beard trimmed close to the face. He wore a straw panama, aviator sunglasses, a denim shirt open to the solar plexus, faded jeans with a big-buckled belt.

The rest of the crew wore blue T-shirts that said "Beware the Web" in gold letters, with a picture of the planet earth caught in a spider's web, the film's logo; and they wore white track shoes with three black stripes across the arch, as though the uniforms were official issue. Actually, the crew had chosen to dress alike, probably through an unconscious need to emphasize the distinction between themselves and the local folk. Location crews always enjoyed feeling like barbarian hordes who had placed a small town under siege, raping the women and drinking the wine, and one morning vanishing as suddenly as they had appeared.

Leslie knew most of the actors and a few of the crew, but he remained hidden among the tourists because he wanted to see how much of Rebecca's feelings about Mack Gordon was the usual actress' paranoia, and how much was justifiable outrage. He didn't have to wait long. Climbing the inside of the crater, Rebecca banged her knee on a rock and howled with pain, lost her footing and slid about twenty feet before she could stop her fall.

"*Keep it rolling,*" Mack screamed to the cameramen, "*this is great, this is the best footage we've got all day!*" He shouted down to Rebecca: "*You're dying from the pain, but you start to climb again, you've got to reach the top . . .*"

"Fuck you, man," Rebecca screamed back. "I think I busted my goddamn kneecap. Somebody help me, please!"

John Guilford slid down level with her and offered his arm, and together they began to hobble up the steep, crumbling wall. Meanwhile three crew members dropped over the side of the crater to help, and others crowded around the edge, eager to lend assistance.

Mack Gordon's power had momentarily eroded and, short man that he was, it drove him into a frenzy.

"Get away from her," he yelled, and, "Keep those cameras rolling! I want to see all of this on film! I want to see Guilford—all alone—saving the woman he loves!"

The crew members hung back; Mack was the captain of the ship and disobedience was mutiny.

Finally John reached the top of the crater and helped Rebecca onto level ground.

"All right, cut," Mack said.

The crew members crowded around with words of sympathy. Two of them helped her to her feet and, supporting her by the shoulders, steered her back to the trailer.

Mack stood apart from the rest, arms folded across his chest, tapping his foot, watching a vulture swing across the clear blue sky.

"Where do you think you're going?" he called to Rebecca.

"Back to my trailer."

"I'm not done shooting."

"I am."

"If you're not in front of these cameras by the time I count five, you're going to be in big trouble with the Guild. One . . . Two . . ."

"Stick it up your ass," Rebecca said, regally.

The crowd of tourists cheered.

Mack spun at them. "Go to hell!" he shouted, and stomped away.

They booed him as though he were Richard the Third.

And Leslie thought, Who says the American Public hasn't got any taste?

Rebecca Weiss slammed the door of her trailer, limped to her daybed and, lying down, allowed herself the luxury of crying. She had wanted to cry all day, all week for that matter, ever since she had met this awful man named Mack Gordon, but crying was a weakness, and she would not permit herself to show weakness in front of him. She liked to appear strong, tough, a dirty-mouthed street kid, when actually she was an upper-middle-class Jewish girl from Manhattan, educated at The Brearley School and Sarah Lawrence College. It is difficult, it has been said, for an actress to play the part of herself.

Now, a week shy of her thirtieth birthday, she was a woman of alabaster skin and delicate beauty. People who thought her voluptuous after seeing her films were always surprised by how slight she was in person. Her hair, which she had stopped straightening in the last few years, was black and frizzy and reached almost to her waist. She wore the front braided, to keep it out of her face, a style evolved by her hairdresser, who thought she should look like the princess in a fairy tale. Her eyes were dark brown, almost black, her teeth small and sharp, her chin pointed. Seeing only her own faults, as women are apt to do, she thought she looked like a rodent, and believed that all those who said she was beautiful were trying to raise her spirits or curry favor.

She was wearing tight jeans and hiking boots, a plaid wool shirt that had been ridiculously tapered to show off her figure, and a push-up bra to create some cleavage between her small breasts. The pants were torn to show an expanse of pale thigh, the shirt ripped (cautiously, by Olga, the wardrobe mistress) to reveal more of the bra ("A shame to hide that nice lace," Olga said).

As she cried, her tears dissolved her make-up, forming rivulets which spilled on the pillow, staining the white linen gray. Rebecca noticed it and got mad at herself for making a mess; then she got mad at herself for caring about making a mess (after all, she was the star, she could dirty anything she damn well pleased!) and then she got mad at herself because she couldn't act like a star, didn't feel like a star, but rather like an actress who had managed to trick them into giving her a part. An actress who had never worked before and would never work again. An actress who was not really an actress at all.

Indulging in this line of thought she became more and more miserable, wept harder and harder. She had no friends, she decided. Victoria Dunbarr, the woman she shared her house with, had sent her one post card, to tell her that the cat wasn't eating and ask what she should do. Her father hadn't written at all. And Leslie—Leslie, whom she counted on when everyone else failed her—had ignored her letter altogether. Nobody cared about her, nobody loved her; if she were to die right then, nobody would know the difference, not the fans, not the critics or the columnists.

Certainly not Mack Gordon.

Least of all Mack Gordon.

Somebody was knocking at the door.

"Go away!" Rebecca shouted.

A strangled voice said, "Tony's pizza. I got one for Miss Weiss, extra cheese, pepperoni, anchovies . . ."

"Tony's pizza?" Rebecca sat up and wiped her eyes with her hands, spreading the grease paint into deltas across her cheeks. Tony's was her favorite pizzeria. They delivered—but not 350 miles from L.A. Or did they?

She opened the door and Leslie grinned at her and held out the pizza. Rebecca opened her mouth, but couldn't speak. She looked as if she were about to cry. Then she threw her arms around him as though he were the last standing mast of a storm-beaten ship.

"Easy," he said, balancing the pizza with one hand, worrying he'd drop it.

"Leslie," she gasped. "Oh Leslie, Leslie, Leslie. With a pizza!"

"Brought it all the way from Hollywood."

"You lunatic. I'm so glad to see you I could cry."

She released him and stood back, grinning.

"This is a minstrel film?" he asked.

"Huh?" She glanced at herself in the mirror. "Oh God." Then she stuck a washcloth in some cold cream and wiped away the black grease paint which, spread by hands and irrigated by tears, covered most of her face. "I thought you weren't coming. I thought nobody cared if I lived or died."

"I got here as soon as I could."

"Leslie, I need your help."

"It's that bad?"

"Remember the old joke, *Who do I have to fuck to get out of this movie?*"

"I hate to say it, but I told you not to take this job."

"Oh, you did, you did. I'm such an idiot. Why don't I ever listen to you?"

"Because you haven't worked in a year. Because you're insecure and you're scared that if you turn down a job, people will hate you and nobody will ever hire you again. So you wind up doing shit like this."

"How do you know me so well?"

"That's my business."

"Next time I promise I'll . . ."

"Next time you'll do exactly the same thing."

"But you'll still be my manager?" she asked anxiously.

"Where else can I get paid for doing nothing?"

"Oh Leslie." She hugged him again, and again he found himself balancing the pizza with one hand, like a waiter in a comic opera, and embracing her with the other. Gently he disentangled himself.

"Is there someplace I can put this to warm up?" he asked, referring to the pizza.

"Right outside the door."

They both laughed.

"Actually," Rebecca continued, "the Forty-Niners always used to eat their pizza cold. It's an old Death Valley tradition. Like sunstroke. And scorpion bites."

"If it was good enough for the Forty-Niners—whoever the hell they are—it's good enough for me."

They sat cross-legged on the floor of the trailer, the oil-soggy box between them, eating slice after slice of cold pizza, wiping their fingers on Kleenex, gulping down cold Coors beer (the trailer was equipped with a small fridge), enjoying themselves like two college girls on a late-night study break.

"There's cheese on your chin," Rebecca said.

Leslie felt around for it, located it, popped it in his mouth.

"I've got two things for you," he said, drying his hands with

Kleenex. He reached for his brief case and took out a magazine. "*American Cinema* thinks you're one of the three most interesting young actresses of the year."

"Let me see . . ."

Rebecca grabbed the magazine out of his hands and opened it to a dog-eared page.

"That awful picture," she said. "It makes me look ninety years old."

"Why do I bother?" Leslie said, half-humorously. "If I gave you an Oscar, you'd say, 'Oh, look, the gold's chipped on the base.'"

"I would not! I'd say, 'I want to thank all the little people who made me . . .'"

"All the horny dwarfs and gnomes . . ."

"No! Let me finish. '. . . who made me what I am today'—you've got to say that part, to show your humility and appreciation—and then I'd say, 'But most of all I want to thank my manager, Leslie Horowitz, for keeping me from killing myself with an overdose of Valium.'"

"That's very poetic."

"Thank you, thank you."

"Are you finished?"

"I guess."

"Okay, take a look at this."

He removed a script from the brief case and passed it to her.

She read the gold print on the cover. "*The Other Woman*, by Harriet Klaus. Is it good?"

"Quite simply, the best screenplay I've read in years. Becky, it's a real old-fashioned woman's movie, in the best sense of the term. Jacqueline, the lead, is a sensitive, intelligent young woman trapped in a hopeless marriage. Her husband leaves her and she has to support the kids, so she starts designing dresses. Before she knows it, she's a fabulous success. Suddenly she has to cope with a whole new set of problems, becoming a public figure, competing with other women, falling in love with a man less successful than herself."

"Sort of Mildred Pierce on Seventh Avenue?"

"A hundred times better. Billy Rosenblatt is producing, and you know what kind of work he does: quality every step of the way. He wants you to play Jacqueline."

"Oh?" Rebecca raised her eyebrows and said nothing more.

Leslie continued quickly. "It's a once-in-a-lifetime part, a real showcase. It's the kind of part Bette Davis would have done as a girl, or Kate Hepburn." (He named these two women intentionally, knowing they were Becky's idols.) He looked her in the eye. "Will you test for it?"

"Test?" Rebecca said, uneasily.

"Just a videotape. Billy loves your work but he's never seen you do anything like this."

"I shouldn't have to test anymore. He knows how I look on the screen."

"Rebecca . . ."

"Anyway, I want to go back East after I finish this."

"Rebecca . . ."

"Will Roach is doing an Off-Off Broadway production of a new play by . . ."

"Rebecca, you are not going back East, you are not doing off-off anything, you are testing for the part of Jacqueline and I don't want to hear anymore about it; you've fucked up enough things in your career and I'm not going to let you fuck up this, I'm simply not going to allow it!"

"I'll think it over."

"I'll give you ten seconds." Leslie looked at his watch. "Time's up."

"He probably won't want me after he sees my test. I can't do tests anymore, I've forgotten how."

"Don't be ridiculous."

"Oh, all right, you win. God, you won't even let me be self-destructive anymore."

"Sorry. Now, what's the situation with Mack Gordon?"

"Hideous. Today I practically fractured my kneecap and he made me . . ."

"I know, I saw it."

"He's a fucking monster."

"He is," Leslie agreed.

"You've got to get me out of here."

"I'll do my best."

"There's one problem."

"What's that?"

"We're having an affair."

"You and . . . ?"

"Mack Gordon."

"But you said . . ."

"I know."

"Oi," Leslie said, expressing dismay beyond words.

"That's how it is on location. You're stuck with the same group of people day in and day out, until you feel like they're family, only you've never seen them before and in a month you'll never see them again. No movies, no restaurants, no parties, no dancing, nothing left to do but sex, and sex with Mack Gordon is really something. It's better than that, it's great, it's cosmic."

"Sex is always great with the bastards."

"Oh Leslie." Rebecca sighed. "Why do we always love the men we hate?"

"I guess because we hate ourselves," Leslie said, and poured another beer.

It was close to midnight when Leslie drove Rebecca back to the Furnace Creek Inn. He took her to her room and put her to bed (she would have liked to stay up and drink with him but she had a 6 A.M. call) and then he went to the cocktail lounge.

The boy who had helped him with his bag that afternoon was sitting at the bar, drinking a gin and tonic, reading a paperback in the insufficient light. His name was Greg and he was broad-shouldered, clean-shaven, with smooth black hair and a smile full of sparkling teeth. He was taking a term off from the University of New Mexico, trying to find himself (Sure picked the wrong place, Leslie thought, do better in San Francisco). His family raised cattle. He played football and wanted to be an architect.

They sat at one of the tables surrounding the small dance floor, listening to three middle-aged men make disco music on an organ, bass and drums, while two elderly couples who should have known better did the hustle.

"Aren't they good?" Greg said. "The band, I mean. They had a free week, so they came up from Vegas. Usually it's some teenagers from Lone Pine who think they're the Stones. Like to dance?"

"I've got three left feet," Leslie said. He ordered a Margarita. "What's it like here?"

"A solitary cell at Sing Sing."

"Come on," Leslie said. "There must be some interesting guests."

"Well . . . those two couples at the bar? They're into swapping, I think. And there's an eighty-year-old woman who goes out every day and hikes ten miles. A couple of men got drunk last week and made obscene suggestions to their chambermaid."

"A regular Peyton Place."

Greg laughed. "See that girl over there?"

He nodded at a skinny blonde, homely but not without a certain appeal, wearing an off-the-shoulder Mexican dress; she was sitting with another couple at a table across from them, talking busily, unaware that she was being observed.

"I can't figure out what her game is. She's pretending to be a tourist, but every evening she calls some guy at World International Pictures and gives him a rundown on the day's shooting. At least that's what the hotel operator tells me."

Here was the missing term in the equation: like some champion chess player who could see ten moves into the future, Leslie suddenly knew that he would have Rebecca Weiss back in Los Angeles by Monday, knew it beyond a doubt.

"What's her name?"

"McDougal . . . no, McDonald. Cynthia McDonald."

"Will you wait a minute? I need to talk to her."

Leslie approached her table. "Miss McDonald?" he said with his best smile.

"Yes?" She was friendly but apprehensive.

"Could I speak to you for a moment? *Alone?*"

The couple she had been sitting with excused themselves with elaborate politeness and began to circle the dance floor, and Leslie sat down in a freshly vacated seat.

"I'm from the studio," he said confidentially. "They asked me to check in with you."

"Thank God, somebody to talk to! Did they say when I could go home?"

When Leslie didn't answer, she rushed on, her voice high and reedy, her tone intimate.

"I'm sorry, but I wasn't cut out for this kind of work. See, normally I'm in the secretarial pool, but my boss asked me if I'd like to spend a month at a resort in Death Valley, and all I'd have to do was keep an eye on Mack Gordon, make sure he wasn't getting drunk or wasting time, phone in a report every evening, and he'd give me a hundred-dollar bonus! It sounded perfect, but you know what? I haven't got the conscience for it. Every time I see Mack Gordon I want to take him aside and tell him what I'm up to. I never could lie. Please, how much longer do I have to stay?"

"Another week or two," Leslie said. "Relax and enjoy it. You want to move up in the business, don't you?"

She nodded eagerly.

"Well, you can't become a movie executive until you can lie comfortably for periods of three or four months at a time."

It sounded like a joke and she searched his face for a clue that would okay her laughing out loud; but Leslie was as serious as a priest.

The music ended, the couple returned and Leslie departed, promising to tell the boss what a good job she was doing.

Later that night, back in the hotel room, the two men shared a "popper" and still later they lay naked together on the carpet, each with his cock in the other's mouth, like an Escher etching that falls in upon itself, a snake eating its own tail, a human conundrum. Yet despite the excitement of sex with a stranger, despite the annihilating drug rush, Leslie could not abandon himself to orgasm; his mind had fixed on the sorry figure of Cynthia McDonald and on the similarity of their situations. Like her, he was a spy, an outsider in a rigidly heterosexual world, aping the manners of those about him, copying their dress and their styles; but unlike her, he had no reprieve, no homeland to escape to, no flag or anthem (except, as he liked to joke, Judy Garland singing "Somewhere Over the Rainbow").

Early next morning Leslie stopped at the production office, a suite at the Furnace Creek Ranch which had been equipped with electric typewriters, desk calculators, a Xerox machine and lots of phones. A production board, like some incredibly complex train schedule, hung on the wall, and people in blue "Beware the Web" T-shirts ran every which way answering phones, delivering messages, typing memos.

Leslie examined the production board: vertical cardboard strips identified each scene, while horizontal columns represented each actor; a black square at the intersection of vertical and horizontal indicated an actor's presence in that scene. While planning a shooting schedule, the production manager would move the vertical strips around, in the attempt to group together as many black squares as possible, thus minimizing the time an actor had to spend on location (and the money he had to be paid). It was obvious to Leslie, after studying the board for only a moment, that Rebecca was being kept on unnecessarily: the horizontal column representing her location time was completed with the exception of one black square, a scene to be shot a week and a half hence. Nor were there any other actors in the scene whose presence would require it to be thus scheduled. In order to double-check his own analysis, Leslie called over one of the young production assistants and asked why Rebecca Weiss's last scene was being thus delayed.

"Mack wants to keep her around and torture her," the production assistant, a pretty girl in her twenties, replied. "I don't know how she can stand him. He's such a bastard and she's so nice."

Apparently their affair was common knowledge.

Leslie drove on to Ubehebe Crater expecting to find shooting in progress, finding instead the crew gabbing idly, playing poker on makeshift tables, while the tourists watched with rapt attention (proving that even people doing nothing were more interesting to observe than the most elaborate formations of rock); among them Leslie noticed Cynthia McDonald making notes in a steno pad.

Rebecca was in her trailer, lying on the daybed, drinking a cold Coke.

"Happy Turkey, Turkey," she said, hugging him.

"What?" Leslie said.

"It's Thanksgiving, you Communist."

"I forgot completely."

"We're having a big dinner. I hope you're going to stay."

"I'm sorry, I promised Tommy I'd try to get back."

"Creep. You love him more than you love me."

Leslie sighed. Why couldn't the children behave when he had so much to do?

"I love you all equally," he said. "Now, why aren't you shooting?"

"Well, we started to shoot and then the camera magazine jammed. So the operator said, 'Mack, can I have a minute to fix this?' and Mack said, 'One more delay and I'm walking off the picture.' So I said, 'If you really mean it, I'll go break the other camera.' So then all the tourists started applauding like they did yesterday, you know? And Mack called me a big-mouthed cunt—which might not have been entirely inappropriate—and stomped away."

Leslie tried not to laugh because he didn't like to encourage Rebecca to play the bad girl—quite simply, it was bad for her career—but he couldn't resist smiling.

"Where's Gordon now?" he asked.

"Shooting jack rabbits."

Leslie cringed.

"That's what he does when he gets pissed off," she explained.

She led Leslie out of the air-conditioned trailer, into the oven-like outdoors and, from their vantage place atop the crater, pointed out a lone figure with a shotgun standing in the middle of a plain of crazed, crackled earth.

Moments later a shot fractured the still air, echoing off the mountain on either side of the valley. Leslie strained his eyes to see the form of a wounded jack rabbit, but the distance was too great. Rabbit must have gotten away, he told himself, to make himself feel better.

"I'm going to talk to him," Leslie said.

"Not while he's so angry . . ."

"See you," he said, kissing her on the forehead. He climbed into his Lincoln and drove the spiraling drive down the crater, then along level road until he came to Mack Gordon's jeep. He parked behind it and walked a few hundred yards to where Mack was standing with his rifle poised at eye level, the twin barrels moving slowly from right to left and back again, scanning the terrain like radar.

"Hi," Leslie said, coming up behind him.

"What do you want?" Mack said without turning around.

"How's the hunting?"

"Shitty."

"I'd like to talk to you about my client. I'm not happy about . . ."

"Shhh," Mack whispered, "there's one."

A jack rabbit appeared from behind a rock about five hundred feet away. It was not, Leslie noted with interest, anything like the pink-nosed bunny he once owned as a child; it was gray, dark-spotted, long and lean, with enormous ears that lay flat against its head when it moved, and move it did, almost at the speed of light.

"This time I got the little bastard," Mack whispered.

Leslie watched the trigger finger whiten as Mack applied pressure, and just as he fired, Leslie slapped him on the back; the shot went wild and the animal vanished, like a rabbit in a magic trick.

Mack spun around. "What the fuck . . . ?"

"Scorpion." Leslie crushed something under the heel of his shoe. "Think I got him." He smiled. "Like I was saying, I'm not happy about the way you've been treating my client."

"Isn't that too damned bad."

"She's a fine actress and a sensitive person, and she simply can't work under these conditions. I want you to promise to treat her respectfully from now on. Furthermore, I'd like you to reschedule the shooting so she can be out of here by Sunday. I was just over at the production office, looking at the board, and I see no reason why she should stay another week to shoot one little scene."

Mack stared at him in disbelief. "I heard you were an asshole, but this beats everything." He raised the shotgun from his hip, casually, until the barrel was level with Leslie's stomach. "Listen, man, I'm the director of this movie and no Hollywood faggot is going to tell me how to shoot it, understand?"

"You're in big trouble," Leslie replied without the slightest sign of fear or discomfort. "You're a half-million over budget and the studio's thinking of pulling the plug. They're scared of you because you drink and you're crazy and violent. Your last two pictures have bombed. If you screw this up, you're finished."

"Bullshit! I've got deals. I've got a mini-series at CBS, the life of Mark Twain . . ."

"They just hired Walter Pollack."

"Who gives a shit? I've got deals. The studio's behind me."

"They sent a spy," Leslie said, calmly.

"Bullshit. Who?"

"Can we make a deal?"

"Can we make a deal? Can we make a deal? You guys are all the same." Mack sighed. "What do you want?"

"One: change the shooting schedule so Rebecca can leave by Sunday. Two: treat her with kid gloves until then. Three: break off the affair you're having."

"Listen, pal, she came after *me.* Get her to lay off and you'll be doing *me* a favor."

"Do we have a deal?" Leslie said. He offered his hand.

Mack showed signs of internal struggle; reluctantly he agreed, but he pulled his hand away quickly after shaking, as though Leslie's brand of sexuality might be passed like a virus.

"Cynthia McDonald," Leslie said. "She's staying at the Inn."

"I'll bust her fucking teeth in," he muttered.

"If I might make a suggestion? This is a poor, unhappy girl from the secretarial pool, who's been forced into the job against her will. She spends a considerable amount of time in the cock-tail lounge. If you were to meet her there 'by chance,' and turn your charm on her—without ever letting on that you know who she is—then she would file favorable reports. On the other hand, if you expose her, or commit another violent act, she would re-port it, and not only would the studio pull the plug, but you would probably be sued or at least have criminal charges pressed against you. It would be a shame to end your career like this. I thought some of your early films were marvelous."

As Leslie was walking back to the car, Mack called to him:

"Hey! You represent any directors?"

"Call me when you're back in Los Angeles," Leslie said. "We'll have lunch and discuss it."

As soon as Leslie was inside Rebecca's trailer, he started to shake and his legs turned to jelly. Rebecca fixed him a Scotch and soda —he downed it in a gulp—and then another, and even then he couldn't forget the feel of the shotgun barrel pressed in his belly.

When it came time to leave, Rebecca walked him to the Lincoln. She punched the car with her fist and it banged hollowly.

"Why do you drive this piece of shit?" she said.

"Are you kidding?" Leslie raised his eyebrows. "This is the finest car made! I'll take one of these over a Mercedes any day."

"It's like the *Queen Mary*," Rebecca said. "And furthermore, it's an environmental menace. I'll bet you don't get more than ten miles to the gallon."

"With a tailwind," Leslie laughed.

"Drive carefully, darlin'." She kissed him. "Sure you can't stay for turkey?"

Leslie shook his head. "But I'm taking you out to dinner next week."

"For what?" Rebecca said.

"Don't be coy. It's your birthday."

"I was hoping you'd forget."

"Why?"

"Leslie, it's the big three-oh. *Thirty*. You know what that means for an actress? The beginning of the end. I'm washed up, finished, over the hill. I'll sit home until I'm sixty and I can start doing character parts."

"You might learn to crochet."

"You're so cold-blooded, you never have any sympathy for me."

"It's true. Now, what can I get you for your birthday?"

"A rose," she said, without a moment's hesitation.

"A rose?"

"A rose."

Leslie nodded. "A rose."

He kissed her and climbed into the car and drove away.

Leslie reached the top of the ridge and was staring down into a small valley, ringed by mountains on every side. There seemed to be a structure in the valley, but the moonless night was sharing no secrets. Could this have been the helicopter's destination? A place to beg a meal, a bed and a bath, a phone to call L.A.? Even if it was just a shelter with a couple of blankets and a jar of water, even that would be a blessing.

Leslie started down the mountain, descending too quickly in his excitement, forgetting how little strength was left in his muscles; he thought he had a foothold but the slope was too steep and his foot slipped away and he began to fall. Grabbing for a purchase, for rocks that came loose in his hands and sand that slipped through his fingers. Falling faster now, tumbling over and over again, head over heels, down the mountain to a black oblivion.

No, not dead. There was the morning sun piercing his eyes, penetrating to the back of his brain like a red-hot wire. He was a marionette with severed strings, lying in the dirt. He tried to move and whimpered from the pain. His tongue was so swollen it filled his mouth, strangling him. He heard a cawing noise and, straining to see past the sun, distinguished three vultures circling above him. Vultures! It was so corny he started to laugh, and his own laughter was a frightening rasp.

My life was a B-movie, he thought, and this is my B-movie death.

With what strength remained, he raised his head. A mile away he saw a Palladian-style manor, a massive stone structure of extraordinary balance and symmetry, simplicity and refinement; a sweep of steps leading to a portico with fine Grecian columns; two floors, each rowed with tall windows; an orange roof penetrated by eight dormer windows and eight massive chimney stacks; and, at the very top, an eight-sided cupola with a brass lightning rod.

A man in livery was coming to greet him.

B-movie heaven, Leslie thought ruefully, and passed out.

·2·

Rebecca lay stretched out in the back of the limousine, her feet on the jump seat, watching the palm trees and stucco mansions of Beverly Hills glide past the window. Soon she would be back in her cozy Benedict Canyon house surrounded by all the familiar décor of her life: her books, her records, her antique costume jewelry, her marvelous fat tabby, Charlemagne. She was even looking forward to seeing her roommate, Victoria, despite the back rent she owed Rebecca and her habit of eating all Rebecca's food.

Although in the past few years Rebecca had come to think of Los Angeles as home, she was born in New York City, on the Upper West Side. Her father, Aaron Weiss, the famous sculptor, whose career had suffered in the fifties because of his leftist leanings, was a charismatic character. He had made the top floor of their brownstone into a studio by tearing down walls and adding skylights; and Rebecca could actually remember lying in her crib, watching him chisel massive figures into luminescent marble. Rebecca's mother would appear, warning timidly that the stone dust could not be good for the baby, and Aaron would simply laugh at her; Rebecca was his girl, his muse, his mascot; he liked to have her around. And yet he was never really there for her; even when he made her paper jewelry, his mind was more intent on the paper, the way it bent, the forms hidden within it, than with the big-eyed little girl who watched him so worshipfully.

Her childhood was a succession of promises—presents he would give her, places he would take her—promises he made and forgot as soon as the chisel was in his hand and the marble dust had begun to fly. His egocentricity was such that at times Rebecca felt he was using up all the air in the house, leaving herself and her mother nothing to breathe.

In 1962 the Museum of Modern Art held a retrospective of his work in the sculpture garden, returning him to prominence, identifying him as a Great American Artist. One by one commissions came tumbling in, a sculpture for the reflecting pond in Lincoln Center, a piece for the courtyard in front of Columbia Law School, a small one for the downstairs vestibule of the White House (ordered expressly by Jackie Kennedy), a larger one for the collection of Nelson Rockefeller. Aaron Weiss became a very rich man and moved his family to a carriage house on 63rd Street between Park Avenue and Lexington, one of the poshest pieces of property in the city. The old Communist friends, folk singers, labor organizers, blacklisted screenwriters and the rest, were replaced by art collectors, millionaire Republicans whom they wined and dined without a trace of bad conscience. Rebecca was transferred to The Brearley School, where she enjoyed shocking the teachers by talking dirty and causing mischief whenever possible. Senior year she and her best friend, Bunky Collins, were suspended for making out, flagrantly, with two Trinity boys at the school dance.

Sylvie, her mother, had gone to Sarah Lawrence years ago to study dance (during the rare moments when Aaron didn't need her to cook him lunch or clean his tools, she snuck away to the bedroom and, putting on an old leotard, leapt about, not without a certain grace) and this was the only reason Rebecca could think of to explain why that college had accepted her with her lousy grades, her poor "board" scores, her history of causing trouble. For the first two years of college she stumbled about the campus high on drugs, concocting excuses for "contracts" (so they called term papers) late or never completed. Fortunately Sarah Lawrence had a tradition of nervous breakdowns, and a simple plea of "emotional problems" accompanied by a tearful sniffle were usually enough to get out of any assignment. She never even considered being an actress until junior year when, quite by whim, she signed up for Will Roach's theater arts class. He was a dapper little homosexual who shaved his head and affected wire-rimmed spectacles rectangular in shape. Being a quirky sort of genius, he recognized Rebecca's talents the first time she ever read in class, and devoted himself to her, making her stop taking drugs (except for a little grass now and then), steering her into the proper theater classes, spending hours coaching her personally.

It was no coincidence that the two most important men in her life were homosexuals. She felt she couldn't trust straight men; straight men were the Establishment, the wielders of power, and Rebecca saw herself as a criminal. Exactly what her crime was she could not have said, except that it had to do with defiance of authority and with being an outcast. What was the sign they used to post in boardinghouses during the days of vaudeville? NO TRAVELING SALESMEN, ANIMALS OR ACTORS ALLOWED. In that order. Even today, when show business was a source of such high revenues that it showed every sign of becoming respectable, an actress was still only a step above a prostitute in most people's minds.

Many of her gay friends shared this alienation and when they got together with Rebecca, they were as happy as a bunch of expatriates in a foreign land, free to make fools of themselves, to be outrageous and behave like clowns. Having no standing in society, they had nothing to lose. When she was angry, Victoria would call her a "Fag-hag," and Rebecca would argue that she wasn't, not really, because she loved having sex with straight men, and she slept around a lot. But gay men were her soulmates.

After she met Will Roach her life took on a direction it had lacked until then. He began giving her supporting roles at the Proscenium, a theater club on the Lower East Side where he was artistic director; after graduation, he starred her in several plays, and that was how Leslie found her. He was based in New York at that time, and every night he would visit the small theaters and workshops that flourish around the city, looking for talent he could nurture and cultivate. He saw Rebecca three times before he went backstage to talk to her. It was almost as though she was too good and he didn't trust his instincts.

Now a bitter rivalry broke out between Will Roach and Leslie. Roach wanted Rebecca to stay with him and devote herself to experimental theater. A few of his plays had gotten to Broadway, so there were prospects. Leslie, on the other hand, wanted her to do all kinds of theater and film, and even television, provided that the show was of a certain level of quality. He believed that a career had to be built taking advantage of whatever medium was at hand, as long as it didn't involve too much artistic compromise. Unfortunately an actor's freedom was granted in proportion to his earning ability—that is to say, how big an audience he could draw. Television was unparalleled in its ability to expose actors to vast audiences—as many as fifty million viewers at one time—but it could also trap an actor in a part, killing his opportunities for anything else, or make him so mannered and broad and full of tricks that he could no longer recognize a good role when it came along, much less play it.

Rebecca understood the risks, but she knew she would also take a risk joining the Proscenium ensemble. At best, Roach used his actors like a fine violin on which to realize his ideas, at worst he set them up like toy ducks in a shooting gallery, venting his rage and frustrations (he felt he had never achieved the recognition he deserved). And if any of them became well known outside the Proscenium, Roach would ask them to leave, claiming that their interpretive abilities had been damaged by "exposure."

Rebecca chose her present path not through any desire for fame or fortune; these things meant little to her. What did matter was acting. And while the Proscenium offered a certain security of quality and employment, the price seemed to be atrophy, stagnation. Instead she would take her chances with the world of commercial entertainment, she would run the gauntlet of film people, of avaricious agents, high-rolling producers, writers with barely the skill to endorse their pay checks; and of the hangers-on, the sycophants and drug dealers and hairdressers, and hope to emerge like those few lucky ones with talent and body and soul intact.

So she signed with Leslie and from that day on, the funny little man named Will Roach who had discovered the actress in her, and teased it to the forefront, and taught it to spread nets of enchantment over an audience, refused to speak to her.

Another splinter in her heart.

"Miss Weiss?"

The limousine had stopped, the chauffeur was holding the door open.

"Thank you," Rebecca said, climbing out, her step unsteady after such a long ride.

They were parked on West Wanda—a side street off Benedict Canyon, high enough to be above the smog yet still low enough for Rebecca's pocketbook—in front of the wood-shingled ranch house were she lived. It was a small house, a humble house by Beverly Hills' standards, of the kind that had been built back in the canyons during the fifties, before real estate speculation and emigrant Arabs had driven prices to the sky. Unhappy with the drab brownness of it, she had painted the shutters and the front door robin's-egg blue and, to further spruce it up, she had planted (to her neighbor's dismay) a pink iron flamingo, a housewarming present from Leslie, amidst the iceweed and sharp cactus shrubbery that was her front lawn.

She fitted her key in the door and stepped inside, shouting "I'm home!" while the chauffeur, carrying her bags, staggered up the path behind her.

Victoria Dunbarr leapt to her feet—she had been lying on the living-room floor in her leotard, stretching her long limbs in time to the organ music and false pregnancies of a daytime soap opera—and ran to the hall to embrace her.

"I'm so glad to see you!" Victoria gushed.

"Oh, me too, me too," Rebecca agreed.

"I thought they'd never let you go."

"One more day in the desert and they would have brought me back in a strait jacket."

The chauffeur cleared his throat. "Where should I put these, Miss Weiss?"

"I'm sorry," Rebecca said, letting go of the other woman. "Leave them there."

She looked through her old black beaded handbag, found a five-dollar bill and put it in his hand. He thanked her and left, and the two women stood there, smiling at each other.

"You look great," Rebecca said. "But you always look great."

And indeed Victoria did. She was nearly six feet tall, with the figure and carriage of a Las Vegas showgirl. Her hair was jet-

black, smooth, reaching nearly to her hips when she wore it down;
now she had it in a thick braid, more convenient for exercising.
Her face was the face of a child, smooth of any wrinkle, eyes
spaced far apart, a small mouth which tended to pout, a pert little
nose. This baby face made a shocking contrast with the rest of
her, her breasts, which everyone assumed to be siliconed because
of the extraordinary way they stood up (in fact, they were all
her own, she had never gone near a plastic surgeon except for
one time, after her ex-husband broke her nose), her slim waist and
flat stomach, her lavish behind and long legs.

"And you look wonderful too," Victoria said, "except for those
bags under your eyes."

"I know. I didn't sleep much."

Victoria turned her so she faced the light and inspected her
face more closely. "And you seem to be developing crow's-feet."

"It was the dry air and the sun."

"Well, it's lucky that you can play those *down and out* sort of
parts. If my skin looked like yours, I'd never work again."

Rebecca peered at herself with concern in the hall mirror.

"Is it that bad?"

Victoria laughed. "No, darling, of course not! It's nothing a
little moisturizer won't fix. I've got a wonderful new cream from
Sweden . . ."

"Please, not now, Vicky. Where's Charlemagne? *Charlemagne!
Charlemagne!* Did he eat?"

"Well, he wouldn't touch the Tender Vittles, so I tried baby
food, liver, like you said. That worked for two days and then I
switched over to imported sardines. You owe me eleven dollars."

They drifted into the living room, where someone in the soap
opera had just been stricken with amnesia. A friend had once told
Rebecca that her home looked like a junk shop, in a good way,
of course, and there was some truth to the observation. In one
corner of the living room an old dentist's chair stood covered
with a red silk shawl, to hide the cracks in the upholstery, and on
the table next to it a gum-ball machine boasted a globe full of
costume jewelry. More jewelry of colored glass had been hung
across the window because Rebecca liked the way it broke the
light into rainbows on the opposite wall. She had a milk can filled

with peacock feathers, a coffee table made out of an old sewing-machine stand, and a coatrack draped with Christmas tree decorations (she'd done it for Christmas in lieu of a tree one year and let it stand, thinking it looked so pretty).

"Charlemagne?" Rebecca said, looking behind the sofa, one of the few items in the room being put to the use it was designed for. "He's pissed at me for leaving him alone. He'll never talk to me again. Oh God, what am I going to do? *Charlemagne!* Vicky, will you keep an eye out for him? I'm going to take a bath."

Rebecca gave a cursory look around her bedroom—Charlemagne wouldn't be found until he was good and ready—then went into the bathroom and turned on the water in the tub, adding a handful of bubble bath. This hot bubble bath, this was what she had been dreaming about all day, all during the five-hour drive home from Death Valley.

She slipped out of her blouse, a gauzy thing of lace and floral appliqués, and laboriously worked her way out of her much-too-tight French jeans, appreciating her freedom to breathe afterward as much as women a hundred years ago must have enjoyed getting rid of their corsets. Naked now except for her panties—she never wore a bra, had no reason to—she stood in front of the mirror and evaluated herself. Did she look as lousy as Victoria said? She moved closer to the mirror, pulling on the skin around her eyes. Yes, definitely crows'-feet. Thirty years old and looking forty. A face-lift might help. She'd always had a dim view of cosmetic surgery—she believed that a fine actor created his appearance from within—but now she gave the matter some thought. If she looked very, very closely she could also make out those awful lines around her lips, the lines that look like earth cracking during a drought. Try some moisturizer first. She stepped back to consider the rest of herself. Her bushy black hair fanned out like the headpiece of an Egyptian queen, and she liked that, but her body seemed so skinny and slight, almost as though the desert had dehydrated it. So . . . unfertile. She took one breast in each hand, lifted them to make a high bustline. If she had a baby, she thought, her body would fill up with milk and life, like a blossoming flower. Thirty years old. Time was running out. If she didn't get pregnant soon, it would be too late; and hadn't her mother always said that that was the *real* reason for living, the unique joy of having children, and that while a career was all very well, childless women understood only a fraction of what life was about?

Rebecca often thought about finding some man and getting herself knocked up, having the baby and raising it by herself, not out of spite for men, but simply because she had never met a man she loved enough to father her children—except for Leslie, and that was unlikely (although every now and then they discussed it, never quite seriously).

Rebecca lay down in the painfully hot bath-water and imagined it cleansing her of all the grit and dust of the desert, and of the abuse she had taken from Mack Gordon, Mack Gordon whom she loved and despised. Why was there always such conflict in her life? Why couldn't she ever have a moment's peace with herself? She touched her body the way she wished a man could love it, perfectly, reaching down into the coarse black hair between her legs, finding the ruby jewel buried in folds of skin and making it hard, making it transmit, like the ripples in a pond, waves of pleasure throughout her body, her being, her consciousness, finally carrying her to the very edge of the waterfall, where the pond of self joins that most cosmic ocean of experience, and sex becomes a link with eternity.

Afterward she felt annihilated, and lavished in the feeling until Victoria knocked on the door and entered, wearing a pink robe over her plum tights.

"Nice bath?"

"Wonderful," Rebecca sighed.

"What was he like?"

"Who?" Becky said.

"Mack Gordon, of course."

"How do you know?"

"There are no secrets in Tinsel Town."

"Seriously."

"You told me, silly. In the letter."

"Oh, that's right." Rebecca laughed at herself. "A beautiful sexy son of a bitch. I hope I never see him again."

"Another one of those?"

"Are there any other kind?"

Victoria pretended to ponder the question. "Let's see. The married . . . the queer and the kinky."

"And don't forget the Arabs. Know why L.A. men have such lousy character?"

"Tell me."

"Because they never have to dig their cars out of the snow."

"A unique new theory of human behavior."

"Vicky, I mean it. Snow builds character. Ever meet anybody from Chicago? Or New Hampshire? Or Buffalo, New York? They're loaded with character."

"I'll have to think about that one," Victoria said.

Rebecca climbed out of the bath, wrapped a towel around her head like a turban; then went to work on her body with a second towel.

"You're beginning to sag," Victoria said, watching her, frowning.

"Please, Victoria, I'm not in the mood for . . ."

"I can show you some wonderful exercises to pull your bust right up."

"Do me a favor? Bring me the mail?"

"Sure. You're not angry at me for saying that, are you? About sagging? I just want to help you stay beautiful."

"Of course not. But with my thirtieth birthday coming up . . ."

"I understand perfectly. It was stupid and insensitive of me. I'm sorry. I'll go get the mail before I do anything else stupid."

Rebecca put on a caftan and lay on the bed reading her mail. There were three autograph requests, two with little white cards to sign, one with an eight-by-ten glossy from *The Land of Lost Dreams* (was it true, she wondered, the rumor she had heard that four Rebecca Weisses could be traded for one Farrah Fawcett-Majors?) a letter from an old boyfriend back East, and another from an aunt whose daughter wanted to be an actress and was coming out to Los Angeles, and couldn't Rebecca please introduce her to a few important producers? And the usual junk mail from the Screen Actors Guild, and discount coupons, and an opportunity to win $25,000, and bills and more bills and more bills.

Rebecca threw the pile up in the air and let them drift to earth around her. The bills were a particular sore point: Victoria was supposed to pay utilities in return for her room and hadn't, not in ages.

The women had met years before, doing a television series called *Pearl Divers*, about three sisters who ran a scuba-diving operation out of St. Croix, and got involved in adventures that were mainly an excuse to show them running around in bikinis and wet T-shirts, pursued by sadistic murderers. It was the worst thing Rebecca had ever done, and although the series ran for only a year, it practically ruined her reputation as a serious actress. Leslie had warned her not to do it, even threatened to stop managing her, but at the time Rebecca was enduring a freezing February—this was before she had moved to California—and the lure of a couple of months in the islands with a fat per diem and a fatter salary was more than she could resist. She and Victoria played the sisters along with another woman, Stormy Simon, who later became a pop singer. It was after shooting had finished that Rebecca, faced with the prospect of returning to the ever-diminishing opportunities of the New York stage, had decided to move West. She took most of the money she had earned from the series and purchased the Benedict Canyon house, paying out the mortgage in full, against the advice of her accountant. He said that the mortgage interest was a valuable tax deduction and a hedge against inflation, but she felt as though she would never have that much money again in her life (she always felt that way when she made a good lump of money) and she wanted to convert it into the permanency of a home that was hers and hers entirely, pink flamingo and all.

She had been living in her new house for four months when, late one night, Victoria called, needing a place to stay. Her husband, a Cuban saxophone player, had gotten drunk and hit her in the side of the head with a chair, and she needed sanctuary. She was hysterical with fear that her face had been ruined and she would never act again. Rebecca drove to Victoria's house in the Hollywood Hills, packed her a suitcase—while her husband ranted and raved in the next room and finally threatened them both with a steak knife—and took her home to the new house. She told

Victoria that she could stay in the guest bedroom as long as she liked. No, no imposition, Rebecca insisted, she loved Victoria being there, loved her like a sister, felt safer, and so forth. As soon as she had enough money, Victoria promised, she would be moving into an apartment of her own. No hurry, Rebecca said. But the weeks dragged on and the women got along well enough, and eventually Rebecca proposed making the arrangement semi-permanent. One of them was sure to be married or at least living with a guy within the next year (her forecast would never be so optimistic today); until then they could share the burden of running the house. Victoria would "rent" the guest room, and the price of it would be the combined cost of the utilities, a bargain they both thought fair. For a few months Victoria paid the bills dutifully, but then she began to fall behind, claiming that she had run short of cash, an abortion for a friend, an expensive repair job on her nose (broken by the chair), and a loan for her now ex-husband, toward whom she felt great guilt.

Victoria always seemed to have such dire problems that Rebecca hesitated to add to them by asking for the rent; after all, Rebecca was working more, making a lot more money. If their roles had been reversed, Victoria would do the same for her, or so Rebecca liked to think. And Victoria did help with the groceries, and often lent her clothing, although the clothing rarely fit due to the disparity of their sizes.

A huge cat leaped into Rebecca's lap, pushed its head into the space under her chin, purring with the volume of a sewing machine.

"Charlemagne," Rebecca whispered. "Have you forgiven me for leaving you? Somebody's got to make some money to pay for those imported sardines, you know."

Charlemagne nodded understandingly.

"You could have written," Rebecca continued. "Even a post card would have been appreciated. A simple paw print would do."

"*Meow.*"

"This should cheer you up," Victoria said, entering the bedroom with two Margaritas.

"Bless you, Vicky—just what the doctor ordered." She took a sip. "Oooo, does that feel good!"

"Well, now that we're all comfortable, I guess I better tell you the news."

"What news?"

"Brace yourself."

"WHAT NEWS?"

"Leslie's missing."

"WHAT?"

"He's missing. He never came back from the desert. The police found his car broken down on the highway, but they never found his body."

"No," Rebecca said. "No, not Leslie. Not him, it's not fair."

The world became a puzzle missing its keystone, the center collapsing, the pieces separating, drifting off into space. She wanted to grab hold of something, so real was the vertigo she felt contemplating a universe without Leslie.

"Sheila's going to take over the business," Victoria said, reassuring her. "She's really very good. Meanwhile we're supposed to keep Leslie's disappearance secret in order not to jeopardize any negotiations."

If Victoria sounded less than totally concerned, it might have been because she didn't like Leslie. After *Pearl Divers* she had asked him to manage her career and he had politely refused, giving as his excuse that he had too many clients already. Victoria believed the real reason had to do with her not being Jewish—anti-Semitism was rife at the Navy bases where she had been raised, and her own paranoia about rejection didn't help—although she would never mention it to Rebecca.

"It's not just the business, it's *everything*. He's the only one I have, my only friend in the world."

"I'm your friend," Victoria said.

"I know you are."

"Come on now, stop crying. Let's have a hug."

Both women stood up and embraced each other, and for some reason the comfort of Victoria's arms set loose a deeper wail of misery, a further flood of tears.

"I can't survive without him. Victoria, I'm going to die, I'm going to die."

"Don't be silly, you'll be fine. Nobody said he was dead, just missing. Maybe when he broke down—maybe he hitched a ride with a queer."

Rebecca grabbed hold of the idea and clung to it.

"Sure! And they invited him to an orgy. And they've probably been fucking their brains out all weekend, sure, that's the only logical explanation. After all, it's Sunday, he's only been gone four days. He'll probably turn up tomorrow with the world's worst hangover, apologizing for worrying us so."

The reverse side of the thought popped into her mind: that he had been picked up by a carload of redneck ranchers who, realizing his homosexuality, had submitted him to some awful brutalization and left him lying in a ditch, the life draining out of him; the thought was so awful she didn't dare give it credence by mentioning it aloud, but rather changed the subject immediately.

"He brought me the most wonderful screenplay, *The Other Woman* it's called, and he was going to get me the lead. It's the most fantastic part. It would have turned my whole career around. Now I'll never do it."

"Sheila will get you the part. She's a great negotiator."

"No she won't. Leslie's gone, everything's ruined. I might as well kill myself."

"Don't talk like that! You're one of the best young actresses out here. You are so talented . . ."

The doorbell rang.

"Whoever it is," Rebecca said, "get rid of them. I can't stand seeing anybody now."

"Don't worry, I'll handle it."

Victoria went to the door; Rebecca buried her head in the pillows and wept. Then Victoria was calling for her: "Becky, I think you'd better come and see who's here."

Damn her, Rebecca thought. She ran into the bathroom, threw water on her face, pulled the brush through her hair, grimaced at her own red-eyed reflection—add a little tragedy and it was thirty going on fifty—and went to the front door.

Sylvie and Aaron Weiss were standing on the step, barely able to contain their joy; when they saw her they shouted "Surprise!"

"Daddy!" Rebecca squealed, running to her father, hugging him. "Hello, Mother," she said, kissing her mother on the cheek.

"We thought we'd surprise our little mouse on her birthday," Aaron said. Mouse was his pet name for her when she was a baby, and he called her that whenever he felt sentimental.

"But my birthday isn't until Thursday."

"Your father had to come in for a dinner. The Jewish Humanists of Los Angeles are giving him an award for his outstanding contributions to Jewish Art. The only other one who's gotten it is Chagall."

"No, no, no, Sylvie," Aaron said. "They give out dozens of them. Chagall was the *first* to receive it." He spoke slowly, as though educating a six-year-old.

"But it is a *very* important award," Sylvie said. She was a small, elegant woman of sixty, the same size as her daughter. At one time people had mistaken them for sisters, but now her tortoise-framed bifocals and short silver-streaked hair announced her decision to age gracefully as the Wife of the Great Artist.

"It's horseshit," Aaron said. "It's all horseshit. All that really matters is your work, Mouse. Remember that." He was short too, but big, barrel-chested, with bushy white eyebrows and a rosy complexion. His hands were covered with chisel cuts and calluses and were knuckly and exquisite. He looked out of place in slacks and a sport shirt; she always imagined him in the coveralls he wore while working.

"Are you going to invite us in?" Sylvie said.

"Of course—I'm sorry, Mother. I'm a little spacey. I just got back from location and I had some bad news."

Her mother entered the house, frowning. "Rebecca, dear, don't you have money for furniture?"

"This is furniture," Rebecca said.

"I mean *real* furniture."

"Now, now, Syl," Aaron interrupted. "I think it's very creative the way Mouse has fixed up the place. So you just shot a movie, eh? What's it called?"

"I'd rather not talk about it, Daddy."

"Mr. Weiss, Mrs. Weiss, can I get you a drink?" Victoria said.

"What time is it?" Aaron looked at his watch. "I guess it's late enough for a drink."

"We've been drinking Margaritas," Victoria said. Her robe was open and Aaron was staring, with little self-consciousness, at the outline of her breasts.

"I hate those mixed drinks," he said. "Bring me a Scotch on the rocks."

"I'll have the same," Sylvie said.

When Victoria had gone into the kitchen, where they kept the liquor, Sylvie whispered, "Are you still sharing your house with that . . . woman?"

"You mean Victoria? Why shouldn't I?"

"She's so," Sylvie hesitated, "so tacky. She looks like a show girl. I worry about her influence on you."

"Mother, she's my best friend. And I'm old enough so that other people don't influence me. I influence myself."

"Of course you do, dear. Let me look at you!" Sylvie took her daughter by the shoulders and stared at her, and their eyes were exactly level. "Dear, you do look tired. My, your skin is so dry. Don't you ever use any cold cream? And your eyes are all puffy. Doesn't that make it difficult for you to work? After all, it's an actress's job to look pretty."

"Mother," Rebecca said, straining to keep her voice level, "it is not an actress's job to look pretty. I know you don't have a great deal of respect for the way I earn my living, but you could at least . . ."

"No respect? Darling, what are you talking about? I have nothing but respect for you and your acting. Aaron and I have seen every one of your movies half a dozen times and we always watch the reruns of that dreadful TV series."

"If you came three thousand miles to disapprove of every little thing in my life, then I wish you'd just . . ."

"Why, Rebecca, of all the ungracious, uncalled for . . ."

"Syl," Aaron said, stepping between them, "why don't you go in the kitchen and help Vicky? I think she's trying to put together some cheese and crackers'"

"Aaron, we're not children," Sylvie said. "We don't need you to keep the peace."

"Who's keeping the peace?" he said, puzzled. "I'm worried about my cheese and crackers. See what's keeping her?"

Sylvia sighed and went into the kitchen. Rebecca smiled at

Aaron and hugged him again. "Oh, Daddy, I'm so glad to see you, I've been so unhappy."

"Poor Mouse," he said, grinning at her with love and sympathy. "Why don't you forget about all this and come back to New York with us? You know, we've been keeping your old room just the way you left it."

"That's sweet, Daddy, but I couldn't."

"It would be just like old times. I'd work in the morning, and in the afternoon we'd walk downtown together, and stop in at Doubleday's and buy a shopping bag full of books. And then we'd get a snack at the Russian Tea Room and maybe stop for a movie someplace . . ."

"Oh, Daddy, it's so tempting."

"So do it! What's stopping you?"

"Eight years of analysis."

They both laughed.

Victoria and Sylvie returned from the kitchen with drinks and cheese and crackers, and some smoked oysters and imported sardines, and just as the four of them were sitting down, the phone rang.

"You all stay put," Victoria said. "I'll get it," and she ran back to the kitchen.

Sylvie leaned over to Rebecca and said in a low ovice, "She's really a dear girl. And she's had such a hard life. Inside, just now, she was telling me about her ex-husband. Did you know that he broke her nose?"

"I'd like to sculpt her," Aaron said. "You think she'd mind sitting for me?"

"Oh, Daddy, you just want to see her tits."

"Cruel and untrue allegations," Aaron said, in his self-mocking voice. "I am only interested in art."

Meanwhile in the kitchen, Victoria was speaking to Sheila Gold, Leslie's partner, who was calling for Rebecca. Victoria explained that Rebecca was with her parents, that she was feeling miserable about Leslie's disappearance.

"Don't bother her, then," Sheila said. "I'll give you the message."

"Wait a sec." Victoria hunted frantically for the pen and pad they were constantly misplacing.

The pad had sprocket marks printed on both sides to resemble a frame of movie film, and on the top was a quote from Dorothy, in the *Wizard of Oz*, one of the immortal understatements of motion picture history: "Toto, I've a feeling we're not in Kansas anymore." It was a running joke between them; whenever they had drunk too much, or smoked too much marijuana, one of them would say to the other, "Toto, I've got a feeling we're not in Kansas anymore," and they would break down in helpless laughter.

"Shoot," Vicky said, returning to the phone.

"Tell Becky that Billy Rosenblatt will meet her for lunch tomorrow, one o'clock at La Scala, to discuss her part in *The Other Woman*. Nothing to be nervous about, he just wants to get to know her."

"*Tomorrow, one o'clock, La Scala, lunch with Rosenblatt, don't be nervous.*"

"Great. Bye-bye, honey."

"Who was that?" Rebecca called from the next room.

"That was . . ." Victoria hesitated as she tore the page off the pad, crumpled it and tossed it in the wastebasket, "one of those awful polls. They wanted to know," she continued, returning to the living room, "what kind of deodorant you used. I told them if they ever called here again, we'd sue them for invasion of privacy. The minute I said *sue* they got really apologetic and offered to send us a free case of . . . I don't know, Ban Roll-On or something."

Everybody laughed.

"I'm glad my daughter has friends like you," Sylvie said.

"And I'm glad to have a friend like her," Victoria agreed, squeezing her roommate's hand.

Victoria Dunbarr drove down "little" Santa Monica in her red Jensen Healy convertible, sitting on her hair—as she always did when she drove with the top down—for there was too much of it to bundle under a hat, and if she let it blow free, the length of it was such that she feared it would catch on a post or a passing car, snapping her neck Isadora Duncan style. (At times she felt that her own genius was not so much for acting as for discovering beauty secrets like these.) The Jensen had previously belonged to the male star of *Pearl Divers*, Matt Kern, who played the local police chief, and often helped the girls out when they were being pursued by psychotic murderers, which happened nearly every episode. While they were down in the Virgin Islands, Matt sought Victoria's aid in procuring for him women's dresses and underclothes (they were nearly the same size) which he wore in private, during his free time (the habit was harmless; it brought him pleasure, and didn't interfere with his love for his wife, or his two daughters). When they returned to L.A. Victoria informed him that a reporter from the *National Enquirer* had offered her five thousand dollars for any interesting gossip about what had transpired in the tropics. Naturally, the last thing she wanted to do was tell about Matt's strange hobby, or hand over that funny Polaroid she'd taken of him dressed like Marlene Dietrich, but, on the other hand, she really did need the money. Her husband had already lost most of her acting fee in a crooked real estate deal, and she was thinking of leaving him, but she didn't even have her own car, though she certainly did admire Matt's beautiful red Jensen Healy . . . No, no, she couldn't possibly accept it, not unless, oh well, if he insisted.

Victoria had read about people called sociopaths who could perform any sort of crime or scam without remorse, and sometimes when things were bad, she wished she were one of them. But she definitely did have a conscience because she felt so bad about "convincing" Matt to give her his car. She *knew* it was wrong (according to that book, the sociopath often didn't even know right from wrong), but sometimes she had to do the wrong thing because she was handicapped.

She never spoke about being handicapped—people wouldn't have understood—but she was, and her handicap was her extraordinary beauty, her incredible body. She first realized it when, at the age of twelve, she sprang, over the course of the summer, to her full height of five eleven. Her breasts began to swell and the boys in the class joked nervously about her while the girls grew envious. She had lived all over the world, a Navy brat following her father from one base to the next. Now he was a retired captain and they were permanently settled in La Jolla, a sleepy suburb of San Diego, only twenty minutes from the Mexican border.

When she was thirteen, high school seniors were asking her on dates. They were furious when she wouldn't make out, and the one time she did, word traveled so fast it might have been announced on the evening news, and every boy in town seemed to be whispering about her behind her back. La Jolla was a lot smaller than it is today, and everybody kept track of everybody else, since there was little else to do. Even though Victoria was not promiscuous, people decided she looked as if she was, or maybe they simply wanted her to be because the idea was so exciting; whatever the case, by the time she was sixteen a whole oral history had evolved regarding her largely mythical sexual exploits. Reacting against this, Victoria became even more prudish, which only served to make her dates angrier, and the lies about her more outrageous.

When she was sixteen she had one of those experiences that changes a person's life: the Miss Orange Blossom Beauty Pageant. One of the three judges was the admiral from the base. After Victoria won—and no subsequent achievement could ever match the thrill of that moment—the admiral invited her to a celebratory dinner at a chic French restaurant in San Diego. His driver picked her up that evening as arranged, but instead of delivering her to the appointed place, he dropped her off at the Ramada Inn on Interstate 5 just outside of town. Was it naïve of her to suspect nothing? The admiral had always been a figure of ultimate respectability removed, only once, from God. Yet that night she saw him drunk and obscene. When she pleaded her virginity, he told her not to pretend to be what she wasn't; he had a son in her class (a pimply boy with a frightened look) who had told him *all* about her, all about the nights on the beaches, and the back seats of the Buicks. She had promised him sex (with her eyes, with her body) and if she thought she could double-cross him now that she'd won, well, she had another think coming. He gave her one more chance to take off her strapless evening gown. She ran crying from the room. A day or two later, Vicky read in the papers that she had been disqualified for not adhering to the rules of the pageant. Although the transgression was not specified, rumors cropped up everywhere: that she had worn "falsies" in the bathing suit competition, that she had plagiarized her poem in the "talent" section, and worst of all, that she had been disqualified for trying to seduce the admiral. The more she tried to defend herself, the more they heckled her. It was then she decided to move to Los Angeles.

This episode of her life transformed her: it became clear that she was suffering because of her body, while denying herself any of the benefits it might bring her. Under *benefits* she did not include the sensual joy that defines sex at its best, for she was so disconnected from this that she didn't believe it really existed, thought it a fabrication of women's magazines and self-help books: no, by *benefits* she meant the manipulation of men in order to acquire power. After the beauty contest, she vowed to use what she had to get what she wanted, and to ignore the whisper of her conscience. She would have to bend the rules of society to overcome her personal handicap—but didn't they have special rules for the blind? the crippled?

Victoria parked the Jensen, shook out her long hair and strolled into La Scala, a favorite place for doing film business. The dining room was small, dark, elegant—old wooden tables and straw-covered Chianti bottles, banquettes sufficiently secluded so that a producer could not overhear the people plotting against him at the next table.

"Has Mr. Rosenblatt arrived yet?" she asked the maître d'.

He took her in at a glance, hiding his true feelings as carefully as a poker player, or anybody else who lies for a living, and led her to a corner banquette. The men at the tables—and they were mostly men during lunch—gaped at her, this six-foot slice of womankind clothed in a clingy plum-colored dress cut sleeveless and low in back, lips glossy and wet, eyes wide and innocent as a little girl playing grown-up.

Billy Rosenblatt was drinking a Perrier with a twist of lime, and reviewing notes he kept for himself on a small leather pad which bore the red and green Gucci stripes, an insignia as characteristic to Hollywood as the stars and bars is to the army. When Victoria stopped in front of his table, he stood up, puzzled but polite, and pleased with what he saw.

He was a compact man, darkly tanned, tightly muscled from daily tennis and fifty laps in an Olympic-sized pool. Although well into his sixties, he remained youthful and energetic, with clear, sparkling-blue eyes. There was a vanity about his appearance, the perfectly tonsured silver hair, the fingernails polished to a deep glaze, the blazer cut to his torso like a second skin and the diamond ring which blazed with fire, the vanity of a man who is sure of himself, and of his powers, both personally and professionally.

"You're not Rebecca Weiss . . . ?" he said.

He felt relieved, for he had been prepared for an intense and brilliant actress—a woman who, sources had informed him, was skittish as an overbred race horse—and instead here was this gorgeous thing.

"Victoria Dunbarr's my name. I'm Becky's roommate, and her best friend. She's had an awful emotional shock. The doctor wants her to stay in bed and rest. I came to apologize."

"Well, you didn't have to come down here. You could have called." He was still standing.

"To be perfectly honest," Victoria said, lowering her eyes shyly, "I've always wanted to meet you. I love your films, particularly *Chained Lightning* and *Tomorrow Will Never Know*. My favorite of all was *Barracuda*."

"*Barracuda*." Billy smiled nostalgically. "That's an old one. Gable, Bankhead. Sit down a minute and I'll tell you a story. Go ahead, sit down! There, that's better. I was twenty-seven years old when I produced *Barracuda*—the boy wonder of Hollywood— and I was desperately in love with Tallulah. She was an older woman, a very sophisticated woman, and she thought me, at best, amusing. I literally kneeled at her feet and said, 'Tallulah, let me buy you something, anything in the world, whatever your heart desires!' She thought about it for a moment and she said, 'Darling, if you *must*, buy me a Boy Scout knife.' So I bought her the most expensive Boy Scout knife I could find and I had it wrapped in a fancy box. She opened it and thanked me with a little kiss, and tossed it in the bottom drawer of her desk. Now, when she opened that drawer, I noticed five or six dozen other knives, Scout knives exactly like my own. 'Tallulah,' I said, 'what are all those knives for?' And she said, 'I won't always be young and beautiful, darling, but there's nothing a fifteen-year-old won't do for a Boy Scout knife.' "

Victoria clapped her hands and laughed with delight. Then she stood up, saying, "I have to go now. It was such a pleasure meeting you. And please excuse my friend Becky, don't hold it against her . . ."

"Not so fast! Why don't you stay for lunch?"

"I couldn't. I know how busy you are."

"I cleared the time and I made the reservations. Furthermore, the special today is poached salmon. *Marvelous.*"

"I'm sorry," Victoria said firmly, "but I have other plans."

"Well, in that case . . ."

"But I could cancel them."

"Why don't you make a call while I order you a drink?"

"A Margarita, please," she said, smiling, and made her way to the phone.

The poached salmon was entirely as good as Billy had promised, and the vintage wine he ordered with it enhanced the subtle flavors.

"You look troubled," Victoria said.

"Me? Troubled? No." He thought it over and changed his mind. "As a matter of fact, I am. See this?" He pulled a copy of the *Hollywood Reporter* out of his brief case, opened it and pointed to a column item underlined in red.

Victoria took the paper and read it out loud. " 'Angela Rosenblatt, ex-wife of producer Billy Rosenblatt, has just sold her first novel to Butterfield Press. Sources say it's a steamy *roman à clef* about a Hollywood producer who can't keep his hands off the women.' " Victoria handed the paper back to him. "Have you read it?" she asked.

"No, but I'm going to. And if there's one single libelous item in there, I'm going to sue the hell out of her."

"You mean *you're* the Hollywood producer who can't keep his hands off the women?" she asked innocently.

"Of course not," Billy snapped.

"Then you don't have anything to worry about, do you?"

"Haven't I seen you somewhere before?" Billy said, changing the subject.

"I did a TV series a couple of years ago."

He snapped his fingers. "*Pearl Divers*, am I right? I didn't recognize you with your clothes on."

Victoria laughed, although she had heard the joke before. "I'm amazed you remember."

"Like a friend of mine said, there were two reasons for watching that show and both of them were yours." Then he hesitated, looking uncomfortable. "That was vulgar of me."

"Not at all. I think it's funny. You're in pretty bad shape when you can't laugh at yourself now and then."

"Well, you know how it is. What with this fem-lib thing you have to be so careful about admiring a woman's body. You make a comment in jest and the next thing you know there's a bunch of them waving placards outside your window."

"I don't feel that way. I guess you could call me old-fashioned. I love to be admired."

"You must be very secure about yourself."

Victoria nodded without modesty. "That's because I know it's just a matter of time before people stop seeing me as a piece of meat and start seeing me as an actress. All I need is the right part, the kind of part where I'm not a whore or a mistress or an idiot or a man-hater."

"Think you could handle a part like that?" Billy said.

"I know I could. If only somebody had the guts to give me a chance."

"You're the sly one," Billy said, smiling. "I know what you're after."

"What?" Victoria looked at him, puzzled.

"You want to read for the lead in *The Other Woman*."

"*The Other Woman?*" Her brow creased in concentration, a gesture she tried to avoid for fear of leaving the footprints of thought on the clean snow of her forehead. "Oh! That script Becky's been reading. Oh no, I couldn't read for that, that's Becky's part. She's got her heart set on it. And she's perfect for it. Sort of down-and out-looking. A beaten woman. Somebody on the verge of suicide. I wish I could get that look. Then people would take me seriously. Tell you the truth, Mr. Rosenblatt, looking the way I do is more of a handicap than an asset."

"So you *don't* want to read for the part?" He seemed to be toying with her, but she couldn't tell.

"I—I don't know. This could be the most important opportunity of my life. Do you think I'd be betraying Rebecca if I did? She's my best friend in the world. I couldn't live with myself if I did anything to hurt her."

He considered the problem seriously. "Yup, you'd hurt her pretty badly. Better not read for it."

"On the other hand," Victoria continued quickly, "it might make our friendship stronger. Competition often increases mutual respect."

He felt a gentle pressure against his thigh, under the table, so gentle it might have been accidental.

"I'd better let you read for the part," he said. "I wouldn't want to be responsible for breaking up a friendship."

"Thank you." She gazed deeply into his eyes, and under the table he felt her big toe sliding up under his pants leg and tracing designs against the sensitive hairs of his calf. No sooner had it begun than it ceased.

"I really must be going," Victoria said.

Standing outside at the curb with her, waiting for the valet to bring their cars, he said, "I still have an hour before my next meeting. Why don't you come up to my place and we'll take a quick sauna and unwind. I'm only ten minutes from here on Mulholland."

The valet parked Victoria's Jensen at the curb, with the motor running, and held the door open for her. Instantly Billy crumpled a five-dollar bill in his hand. Out here, where the measure of a man was his money, the failure to pick up a check or put down a tip might mean a permanent loss of face: years of showdowns over restaurant checks had made Billy Rosenblatt one of the quickest draws in the West.

Victoria stood so close to Billy that the tips of her breasts, erect from rubbing unprotected against the front of her dress, just touched his shirt, and she whispered, "Not now—it's too soon. Let's get to know each other first, let's make it special."

Her lips touched his, just for an instant, the moist lip gloss sealing the junction like a gasket; then she was sitting behind the wheel, gunning the engine, grinning with triumph, and then she was driving away into the brilliant California sun, her hair flying behind her like an ebony pennant. When she was three blocks away, and certain that he could no longer see her, she pulled over to the curb, raised herself out of the bucket seat and, smoothing her hair down and under her, sat on it.

·3·

Cold and hungry and tired, the merchant came upon a great house in the midst of the forest. He thanked God for this happy discovery and hasted to the place, but was greatly surprised at not meeting with anyone in the outcourts. He entered the large hall of the house, and there he found a good fire and a table plentifully set out with but one cover laid. He sat by the fire, warming himself and resting his legs, hoping that the master of the house would excuse such liberties.

By the time the clock struck eleven he was so hungry he could wait no longer, but took a chicken and ate it in two mouthfuls, and a meat pie and sausage and several glasses of wine. And growing more courageous, he went out of the hall and crossed through several grand apartments with magnificent furniture, till he came into a chamber which had an exceeding good bed in it, and as he was very much fatigued and it was past midnight, he concluded it was best to shut the door and go to sleep.

It was ten the next morning before the merchant waked. He was surprised to see a good suit of clothes in place of his own, which were quite soiled; certainly, said he, this place belongs to some kind of magician who has seen and pitied my distress. He looked through a window and saw the most delightful arbors interwoven with the most beautiful flowers that were ever beheld. Returning to the great hall where he had supped the night before, he found some chocolate ready made on a little table. Thank you,

*kindly magician, he said aloud, for being so thoughtful as to pro-
vide breakfast; I am obliged to you for all your favors.*

*The good man drank his chocolate and went to look for his
horse, but passing through an arbor of roses he remembered
Beauty's request to him and plucked a most beautiful and perfect
flower from the bush; it was as darkly colored as blood and mar-
velously sweet to the smell. Immediately he heard a great noise
and saw such a frightful beast coming toward him that he was
ready to faint away. You are very ungrateful, said the Beast to
him in a terrible voice; I have saved your life by receiving you
into my castle and in return you steal my roses, which I value beyond anything in this world. Now you shall die for it! I give you
but a quarter of an hour to make your peace with God.*

*The merchant fell to his knees and lifted both his hands. My
Lord, said he, I beseech you to forgive me, for indeed I had no
intention to offend when I gathered this rose for my daughter
Beauty. Please, sir, I pray of you, I have two other daughters to
care for also, and debts aplenty. Spare my life and I shall do your
will however I am able.*

*Your servitude means nothing to me, the Beast grumbled, but
there is one condition under which I will let you go . . .*

Leslie awoke with a terrible, throbbing headache. He opened
his eyes and saw a blur of pink and blue and white which swam
in and out of focus, finally resolving itself into a circle of fat
cherubs playing in the clouds. He expected his lips to be cracked
and bleeding, but his tongue found them smooth, coated with Vase-
line. He was lying between linen sheets in an enormous canopy bed,
and the cherubs were painted on the inside of the canopy. Curiosity overcoming pain, he raised himself on one elbow and looked
around. The room had mahogany doors and wainscoting, all
trimmed with fine gold-leaf tracery, and gobs of gold-leaf ginger-
bread on the ceiling. In the middle of the ceiling there was a circular mural like the one in the bed canopy but more elaborate:
cherubs with little bows and arrows were being dispatched to
earth, and the theme was continued on the walls, where the cherubs invaded a sylvan glade, firing their arrows at some ancient
Greeks in togas. The carpet was an intricate floral design, the

chairs were upholstered in deep-green velvet, and a mahogany table had legs like a lion's claws.

Leslie sat at the edge of the bed and tried to make sense of it. He was used to waking up in strange places; it was part of his world. But this? For an instant he considered the idea of an afterlife, and promptly discarded it. If the soul was immortal, it would have to be to some higher end than experiencing this eighteenth-century glitz. Furthermore, the pain he felt was flamboyantly physical. What about time travel? He had gotten a script a couple of months ago, a science fiction adventure involving a time warp, people tumbling into prehistoric times, battling with dinosaurs, making friends with cavemen. Well, he hadn't believed it then and he didn't believe it now. Instinct—and that was the final arbiter in all his decisions—told him that he was neither dead nor involved in matters metaphysical. But then, what was the explanation?

The sound of running water diverted his attention. He stood up, overcame a rush of dizziness, and staggered toward the sound, which emanated from behind a half-open door. Only then did he notice that he was wearing pajamas, pearl-white silk pajamas, well-fitted and so light that he might have been naked. As he approached the door, the sound of the water became a roar, and he hesitated before pushing it open. The anticlimax was so unnerving it made him giggle: he was standing in a starkly modern bathroom, all bright chrome, black tile, and concealed lighting, with mirrored walls that reflected, back and forth in diminishing perspective, a haggard, unshaven, overweight figure in white pajamas; and the roaring sound came from a sunken whirlpool bath filled with steaming water. At the side of the sink, someone had laid out, as carefully as surgical instruments in an operating room, a safety razor, an expensive aerosol shaving cream, a toothbrush—still in the wrapper—toothpaste, a tortoise-shell comb, a hairbrush, a cake of soap and two hand towels. Closing the door, he noticed a black and white terry-cloth robe hanging by a hook on the back of it.

He thought about locking the bathroom door but decided it would be silly; his fate was obviously out of his own hands and whoever hands it was in, he had to assume, was benevolent. Still, he felt a terrible fear of removing his pajamas and lowering himself into the water. Even in the best of situations bathing scared him; he couldn't help thinking of the shower scene in *Psycho*, the spray of water, the flashing knife, the scream, the blood rinsing down the drain, a montage that had a permanent place in the repertory of his unconscious. To be naked and wet was a condition of ultimate vulnerability happily exploited by film makers throughout the decades.

On the other hand, he was also used to taking strangers, occasionally men he had known for no more than a minute, back to his apartment and lying down naked with them, a practice which filled Rebecca and his other straight friends with horror. All the times he had done it his trust had never once been betrayed. Oh, he had been robbed a few times, insulted a few times more, but never had he been assaulted or forced into anything against his will. And in the back of his mind was the thought that this might be the ultimate pick-up (who else but a fag would have all that gold leaf?) and that, if he were to lie in the water, at any moment fifteen beautiful golden-haired beach boys might descend upon him and scrub his back, not to mention the rest of him, until he was senseless with pleasure.

Unfortunately no such thing occurred—or perhaps it was fortunate, since Leslie's fatigue was such that he wouldn't have been good for much—but the rushing waters of the whirlpool did succeed in massaging away his aches and unknotting his stiff muscles, and finally sinking him into a sort of sensual stupor from which he woke only when his head slipped for an instant underwater. (In the dream he was a stuntman, the stand-in for one of his clients, going over Niagara Falls in a barrel.)

After the bath he performed his toilet, and finding his reflection acceptable, returned to the bedroom. The bed had been made, and his clothes cleaned and pressed and neatly folded on the bedspread. His white canvas loafers were together at the foot of the bed, but they would never be white again.

An old-fashioned serving cart was parked beside the lion-legged table; Leslie uncovered the plates and found an omelette aux fines herbes, sliced fresh fruit, warm croissants, in addition to a carafe of black coffee brewed to European strengths. He forced himself to eat slowly despite his ravenous hunger. In the middle of the omelette he remembered his brief case and panicked. What had become of it? He recalled dragging it across the plains, clutching it under his arm as he climbed the mountain, clinging to it right to the very end, for it contained two contracts he had to approve for one of his actors, and a big check for another actor, and his ancient tattered phone book, which was full of unlisted numbers and would take months to reconstruct. But just as he was persuading himself that those irreplaceable items could be replaced, he noticed the brief case in a corner, ran to it and found its contents intact. Whoever was taking care of him was benevolent indeed.

So far.

Having dressed and finished breakfast, he considered his next move. He dreaded leaving the room, which had become uterine in its security; on the other hand, comfortable as it was, he could not stay there forever. Billy Rosenblatt had mentioned making a lunch date with Rebecca on Monday to discuss her part in *The Other Woman*, and although Leslie trusted Sheila to arrange it, he was never completely satisfied unless overseeing everything personally.

He opened the door a crack and peeked into the hallway. There he saw nothing but more doors, all of them shut tight. Leaving the room, he crept along, senses alerted. The farther he strayed the more apprehensive he became; every few steps he would stop to listen, but all he could hear was the low-pitched hum of an air conditioner, like someone bowing a double bass. Coming to a bend in the hallway, he peeked around the corner and found himself confronted by a giant, dressed in livery, with a Neanderthal forehead and a jaw like the scoop of a steam shovel.

"Whoever you are," Leslie stammered, shaking with terror, "I didn't mean to mess up the bathroom . . . and I'm sorry I didn't make the bed."

Then he turned and ran all the way back to the bedroom, slammed the door and fell back against it, panting furiously.

"Stop it!" Leslie chided himself. "You're behaving like a child. There was something physically wrong with that man, which doesn't mean he was going to hurt you. On the contrary, he's been . . ."—Leslie stopped to pant—"he's been the perfect host so far. I probably scared him as much as he scared me. No, he didn't look scared at all. But who can tell? Please, relax!"

Moments passed. Leslie grew calmer. He ventured out a second time, retracing his path with a quickening heart, peering around the bend in the hallway and finding the giant standing there precisely as he had left him. This time Leslie forced himself to hold his ground despite liquid bowels and a pounding of the heart.

"Where am I?" he demanded, hiding his fear with indignation. "What's going on?"

The giant pointed to his mouth and shook his head. His movements were slow, lumbering.

"You're mute, is that it?"

The giant nodded, a hint of sadness in his eyes. The eyes were almost hidden in the shadow of his brow, and the rest of his face was bumpy and scarred. His coarse dark hair was trimmed in a sort of pageboy, in order, Leslie guessed, to deemphasize the malformation of the skull. He recalled learning about a pituitary malfunction in high school biology—one of the few things he recalled from high school biology—a disease called acromeglianism, where the hormones were thrown out of balance and a man grew to an enormous size, usually accompanied by a deformation of the skull and extremities. Leslie glanced at the giant's hands: they hung like sides of meat, outrageously long-fingered and thick. He felt sorry for him, for he too was a freak, his peculiarity just as profound but invisible, concealed within as though one man had been turned inside out to form the other, like some flexible topological model.

"Well, I've got to get back to L.A.," Leslie went on, brusquely. "I'm negotiating some very important deals for my clients, so if you'll tell me how much I owe, I'll give you a check. Sorry I don't have any cash on me."

His voice trailed off. His attention had been seized by the most exquisite music, so faint he feared he might be imagining it; but then he heard it more clearly, a solo violin playing measured phrases, simple in texture yet extraordinary in their logic, the logic that is closest kin to math, but finally comparable to nothing but itself. It reminded him of the unrelenting march of clouds across a clear spring sky, clouds ever-changing in form, now a lamb, now a rabbit, now a rocking chair; the mood shifted to the minor and it became the sun glittering off a slate-gray sea at dusk, not a hint of a breeze, everything unearthly still.

"What is it?" Leslie whispered.

The giant smiled, an expression that filled the ruin of his face with warmth. He motioned for Leslie to follow. They came to a door and as the giant opened it, the music was unmasked, as though layers of gauze had been torn away, and the sound became crisp, brilliant, almost unbearable in its intensity.

The room was wood-paneled, with a red velvet chaise, a writing desk, a music stand with gold scrollwork, and a harpsichord, like a prissily elegant little piano. On top of the harpsichord were twenty or so crystal paperweights, some brilliantly colored and opaque, some containing kaleidescope bursts of color, some containing actual flowers, perfectly preserved from the ravages of time. One paperweight in particular caught his eye, a rose, blood-colored, in a ball of crystal big as a fist.

The violinist stood with his back to Leslie, his body erect and motionless, as though his hands alone were playing the instrument. Occasionally, he would incline his head slightly to better hear a phrase, or so it seemed. He wore a wine-colored smoking jacket patched at the elbows, dark slacks, slippers, His hair was the color of chestnut streaked with gray, a long sweeping mane of it that fell over his ears and past his collar in back.

As Leslie listened he gradually lost awareness of his plight, of the strange house, the musty room, the rasping breath of the giant behind him. Even after the music reached its final cadence and the violinist lowered his bow, he remained thus, for the silence itself had become precious. Finally he cleared his throat.

"That was—*incredible*."

"Thank you," the violinist said, and turned around.

Leslie shrunk back when he saw the face; it was waxy, expressionless, smooth-skinned, only a stylized suggestion of humanity; because of the dimness of the light it took him a few seconds to see that it was a mask.

"Don't be afraid," the violinist said. "I shall explain everything in time. This is my house and you are my guest. You will not be hurt."

"I—I thank you. You've been very kind."

"I am Henry Wallace Beeze, the Third."

"Leslie Arnold Horowitz. The first and last."

Leslie offered his hand. Beeze hesitated, then grasped it, and Leslie felt a wave of revulsion; the hand was missing its last two fingers, and the skin had the layered texture of scar tissue. Immediately he tried to hide the feeling, shook the hand with added emphasis to cover it up, and perhaps Beeze didn't notice, though Leslie suspected he did.

"And this is Samson," Beeze continued, "my servant and companion."

Leslie nodded and smiled, but offered his hand no more.

"You probably have some questions," Beeze said.

"A few," Leslie agreed.

"I'll answer those that I can. Samson, will you excuse us?"

"Where am I?" Leslie asked, as soon as they were alone and comfortably seated in a pair of Morris chairs.

"In the desert," Beeze replied, "a few hundred miles southwest of Death Valley. I can be no more specific, since the location of my . . . *retreat* must remain secret. Let it suffice to say that you wandered a very great distance from your car, farther than I would have thought possible. The desert was kind to you—she rarely lets such carelessness go unpunished."

Leslie nodded. "I guess it was kind of stupid, but I saw a light."

"That was the beacon for the helicopter. We turn it on briefly when Samson is flying back at night, as he was the night before last."

"The night before last? Wait—today's Saturday!"

"Sunday."

"I don't understand."

"You slept a whole day. Samson spent Wednesday in Las Vegas buying provisions, and taking care of certain other business. Flying back to the mansion Thursday evening, he spotted your car, broken down on 127, and radioed the police."

"But I thought he was . . ."

"Mute? No, but he is proud. Because of the malformation of his

palate, his speech is almost incomprehensible. He prefers to remain silent, rather than suffer the humiliation of trying to be
understood."

"I know a lot of people who'd be wise to do that," Leslie said.

"Really?" Beeze looked intrigued. "I had always thought this
sort of giantism to be an extremely rare condition."

"No," Leslie said, "it was a joke. What I meant was . . . Forget
it. You were saying that he radioed the police."

"Yes, but by the time they arrived, you were gone. Samson
flew back and forth over the area several times looking for you
before he gave up and returned to the mansion. We wondered if
you had attempted to cross the mountains, and perhaps stumbled
upon our hidden valley, but it had never happened before and
seemed almost out of the question. Still, Samson was awake most
of the night, worrying. He monitored the police bands and sur-
veyed the mountains from the roof with high-powered binoculars.
He even took the helicopter up again but unfortunately it was a
moonless night. You would most certainly be dead if not for Samson's efforts. You see, he has an extraordinary sensitivity about
things. One might almost call it psychic if one had truck with the
occult. When the sun rose the next morning—I was still asleep—
he saw a few vultures circling and ran outside. There was your
body, unconscious, a mile away. Samson picked you up and carried you back to the house."

"Jesus," Leslie whispered. "A whole mile?"

"He dressed your bruises and fed you broth. You were half conscious, delusional. Muttering something about a television movie,
about how the vultures were too corny and you wanted jackals
instead."

Leslie smiled and nodded.

"Then Dr. Resnick gave you a tranquilizer—you have no need
to worry, she's one of the finest doctors in the country—and you
were put to bed in the guest room, where you slept for nearly
twenty hours. I'd like her to look at you again, if you don't mind."

"I don't know how to thank you enough. And your friend Samson—I'd like to give him some money."

"He would be deeply offended."

"What if I gave it to you?"

"Within these walls," Beeze said, "money has no meaning."

An odd thing to say, Leslie thought, considering the wealth which was everywhere displayed, but he made no comment; as he was fond of saying, where once there were three taboo topics in polite society—namely, money, sex and death—now, with your new libertarianism, only money remained forbidden.

"I don't mean to be rude," Leslie continued, "but if today is Sunday, I better be getting back to Los Angeles. I've got tons of business to take care of. Missed two days last week because of that stupid holiday."

"I was once like you," Beeze said softly. "My life was my work. I didn't discover what I was neglecting until it was too late."

"And what was that?" Leslie asked politely.

Beeze toyed with his violin, plucked the strings, tuning and re-tuning its perfect fifths.

The pause grew longer until finally Leslie said, "Anyway, I'd like to leave as soon as possible."

Beeze seemed to return from a dream. "What? Oh, of course. But would you, could you stay one more night? Then I would have Samson fly you back to Los Angeles first thing in the morning, and you would be home by nine or ten at the latest, I promise. You see, you're the first guest I've had in—I don't know how long, and I'd so enjoy talking to you."

"I guess I could manage," Leslie said. When had he ever turned down anyone who felt a sincere need? "But I can definitely return in the morning?"

"On one condition. You must agree never to say a word of what you've seen here, never a word about a mansion in the desert, or a mute giant or a mad violinist."

"I don't think you're mad. If you enjoy living like this . . ."

"Do you swear?"

"I—uh . . ."

"DO YOU?"

"Yes! Yes, I do. I swear I'll never tell anybody." Damn, he thought, and it's such a good story.

"It may seem fanatical," Beeze went on, evidently feeling the need to excuse himself for raising his voice, "but a man becomes fanatical when he . . . when he's been through what I've been through. Hopefully, your behavior will justify my trust in you."

"I've never gone back on my word," Leslie said. "If you do that in my business, you're through."

"I see. And what business is that?"

"I'm an actors' manager. That means I find talented actors and try to guide their careers, stop them from making stupid mistakes. And they ignore me. No, I'm kidding. But they do give me a rough time."

"Then you work in the movies?"

"And in television and the theater. When we were based in New York, Sheila and I—Sheila's my partner—we did more theater; now that we're in Los Angeles it's mainly television and movies, though occasionally we get involved in one of those vanity projects, you know, Charlton Heston in *Macbeth*. The truth is I miss the legitimate theater. On the other hand, we can get our clients ten times as much work out here." Leslie got defensive whenever he discussed his move from New York to Los Angeles; in his heart he had never come to terms with it, and still believed the cliché that he had been fed for so many years by the New York media, that their city was the center of all true and honest art and that Los Angeles, its evil twin, was the seat of all that was base and corrupt.

"How exciting it is for me to meet somebody from the movies!"

"Really?" Leslie said, taken aback.

"Oh yes. I admit to being an addict. I have a screening room and a collection of over a thousand prints, everything from Méliès' earliest fantasy to Hitchcock's latest thriller. My greatest pleasure in life is to sit in those deep velvet seats, to smell the ozone of the projector's lamp and finally to see those images, composed of nothing but light, the purest of mediums, glittering on the screen. You are familiar with Plato's cave allegory from the *Republic*?"

"Can't say I am."

"He compares us to men who have always lived in a cave, watching images of light being projected from a concealed balcony onto a far wall, and mistaking these images for life itself, while never imagining that outside a true sun shines a billion times more brightly. Extraordinary, don't you think? Predicting a movie theater centuries before the first nickelodeon. But of course the importance of the allegory is that we must constantly remind ourselves that we are in the darkness, that a higher order of reality exists and is ours if only we can escape the cave."

I'll be happy if I can just get back to Los Angeles, Leslie thought.

"I am not an artist," Beeze continued. "I could never make up a story or convert an idea to film; but if I could have my wish I would give anything to be involved in the making of movies."

How many millionaires had Leslie met who, after a lifetime of groveling for dollars on the stock exchange and in real estate and construction, had one supreme wish: to have some fun with their wealth, to surround themselves with glamour, to join the only nobility this democratic country has ever laid claim to, the nobility of Fame, by investing in a motion picture. For the last few years Leslie had been receiving offers to produce, offers he had never accepted because the terms had never been quite to his liking; but with an enthusiastic private backer like Beeze, a backer with apparently limitless funds (how much had it cost to build this immense mansion, flying materials from hundreds of miles away?), he could finally take the step. And think of the films he could make, starting with books he had always loved, casting his finest actors, Rebecca and Charles Grover and Ben Berman, hiring whatever director he wished without regard for whom the studio approved, without a thought for who was *bankable*.

"If you're interested in making movies," Leslie said, betraying none of the excitement of what he was thinking, "you should come out to L.A. I'll take you around to some of the studios and we'll watch them shoot something. It's easy to arrange and sometimes it's really fascinating. A couple of months ago I was over at MGM and Speilberg was shooting his new picture. They'd filled a sound stage with water and at one end built a perfect scale model of Pacific Ocean Park, you know, the old amusement park on the

Santa Monica pier? It was incredible! Little lights blinking on and off in the background to look like cars driving down the Coast Highway, men rocking boards to make waves."

"Wasn't it Orson Welles who said that making a movie was like having the biggest train set in the world?"

"Could have been," Leslie said. "Anyway, if you wanted to do it, I'd be more than happy to take you around, introduce you to some people."

"I can never be seen in public," Beeze said, his voice as hard and gray as iron.

Leslie felt he shouldn't pursue this line of questioning, but his curiosity got the best of him.

"Why not?"

"Isn't it obvious?" He tapped the mask with a fingernail, and it rang hollow, empty.

"Take off the mask." Leslie's pulse accelerated with the excitement of forbidden questions.

"Mr. Horowitz . . ." Beeze hesitated. "Mr. Horowitz, do you have any idea what a human face looks like after the skin has been charred through and the facial bones themselves crushed flat? Can you imagine damage so severe that the finest plastic surgeons in the country refused to operate on me, even when offered one million dollars? Can you imagine that, Mr. Horowitz?"

"No," Leslie said softly. "How did it happen?"

"I was the president of one of the largest chemical companies in America. For recreation I flew a small plane. One day, through my own carelessness, the plane crashed. I was pulled from the flaming wreckage and somehow I survived. The horror that I am now is the result of that accident. But every tragedy has commensurate rewards: that brush with death showed me the value of life. Business no longer held interest for me. I resigned and came to the desert. Here I watch movies, I play music, I practice Yoga and study philosophy. These are the things that still interest me. These are the things that matter."

Leslie suspected he was being told less than the entire truth, but didn't press, sensing that what had been omitted went to the very core of the millionaire's being.

"And now," Beeze said, "you must excuse me. I am not used to conversation, and I find it wearying. Before I go, however, I wonder if there is a particular movie you would like me to screen this evening. I have one of the largest and finest film collections in the world. And if the film you wish to see is not in my collection, then I can send Samson for a print. It's no trouble, he has to take the helicopter for supplies today anyway."

Leslie saw here an excellent opportunity to acquaint the millionaire with some of his clients' work, in case Beeze ever did decide to back a motion picture.

"I'd like to see *Land of Lost Dreams* again. A friend of mine is the star. Do you know it?"

"No. I remember when it was released. I read the reviews and it sounded like a love story. I cannot bear love stories."

"Okay, forget it," Leslie said amicably. "Let's watch something else."

"If you wish to see *Land of Lost Dreams*, then that will be our evening's entertainment. It is always of value, doing new things, breaking old habits. The experience will benefit me, I am sure."

Leslie was also weary, although how weary he did not fully realize until he returned to his room and lay down for what he thought would be a few minutes' nap. When Samson woke him it was time for dinner. Yet despite all this sleep, he felt groggier than before, more confused.

As Samson led him to the dining room, Leslie got his first look at the house, and found it to be fully as fabulous as he had imagined, a museum of fine paintings, furniture and sculpture, both antique and modern. Although he knew little about art, he knew enough to identify an El Greco hanging in the hallway, a ceramic bull by Picasso, a Chippendale cabinet in the Chinese style.

He had taken it for granted that he was alone in the house with Beeze and Samson; thus his surprise when he saw nine strangers seated around the long table in the dining room. Two additional places had been set, like the rest, with the finest crystal and linen and silver, for Beeze and himself he supposed. But his surprise was even greater when Samson, after showing him to the first empty seat, settled his massive frame in the second. Leslie nodded at everybody, smiling uncomfortably, and sat down.

"Welcome to our little family," said a birdlike woman of sixty-five or so. She wore her gray hair in a bun, and the kind of glasses Leslie associated with old women who played mah-jongg. Yet her speech revealed strength, severity and intellect. She introduced herself—Dr. Resnick—and the rest of them; and Leslie said, "Pleased to meet you," "It's a pleasure" and so forth, but hardly caught a name. His overall impression was of a mixture of races and classes, of beliefs and temperaments, that would not ordinarily dine together. A family of sophisticated Orientals, a Hindu gentleman, an older couple who might have been caretakers or servants of some sort, an aging Frenchman and a handsome young man named David. *That* name he remembered.

The first course, already set out in a tureen, was an icy gazpacho with garlic croutons. Leslie was reluctant to start.

"Isn't Beeze joining us?" he asked.

"He has no lips," Dr. Resnick said, "and what remains of his jaw does not properly align. Therefore he must take his nourishment in liquid form. For obvious reasons he prefers to eat alone."

Embarrassed, Leslie turned his attention to the soup. When they had all finished, the old couple cleared and brought the next course, a green salad. Then came a pilaf with flageolets in wine and summer squash in a tart golden sauce.

"This is delicious," Leslie said. "I've never tasted anything like it."

"Henri prepared it," David said, indicating the Frenchman at his side. It was obvious to Leslie that they were lovers. "He's one of the greatest chefs in the world."

"Really," Leslie said. He smiled at David and David smiled back. This small communication made Henri flush with anger. Leslie decided that he had better watch his step, for theirs appeared to be a relationship rife with distrust and jealousy.

"Who knows what Henri would be capable of," Dr. Resnick said, "if Beeze would allow him to cook with meat."

"So Beeze is a vegetarian?" Leslie asked.

"We can thank our mystical friend for that," Dr. Resnick said, glaring at the Hindu.

"You shall not provoke me this evening," the Hindu replied in a clipped Oxonian speech.

"It's a wonder we're not all anemic," she continued, to no one in particular. "So, Mr. Horowitz, you must tell us what's happening in the outside world. I rarely see a newspaper."

"Inflation's terrible. Property values in Los Angeles are up about thirty percent from last year."

"Really!"

"What's flation?" The question was posed by the little Oriental girl, to her mother.

"It's when things get expensive, Jasmine dear," her mother replied. "Now, eat your vegetables."

The Hindu nodded. "That is the karma of your country, for prices to go so high that even a rich man cannot afford a loaf of bread."

"I'd hardly call it karma," Dr. Resnick said, frowning. "It's simply a case of bad fiscal management. If our President had the nerve to impose certain restrictions on the oil companies, for example, then . . ."

"What's fiscal?" Jasmine said.

"It means having to do with finance, dear."

"And muscle building?" Jasmine asked.

"What?" her mother said, puzzled.

"And imposing wage and price controls which might be very unpopular with the American people."

"Muscle building. You know."

"I'm sorry, dear, I don't understand."

"You worship money instead of God," the Hindu said, "and God will take away your money."

Leslie interrupted, "I think she means *physical*. Physical culture. It's another expression for muscle building."

"Ah. Thank you." The Oriental woman smiled at him.

"That's the stupidest thing I've ever heard," Dr. Resnick said. "Really, Mr. Gnesha, I find your tendency to attribute *everything* to God and deny man any responsibility a bit tedious."

"I didn't mean to start anything," Leslie apologized.

"They do this every night," the Oriental man said quietly. "It's their favorite recreation."

"Are you into muscle building?" David called across the table.

"He seems to be into fat," Henri muttered, loud enough for everybody to hear.

"Someday, my good Dr. Resnick," the Hindu shouted, "you will learn that man *is* God—that the Brahmin and the Atman are one —and that he makes his own punishments, creates his own hells!"

"I go to a gym once in a while," Leslie said. "What about you?"

Dr. Resnick was keeping calm. "I find it remarkable that a person who claims to be a Hindu should have such an extraordinarily Calvinist attitude toward sin and punishment."

"Oh, I spend hours with the weights," David replied. "There's nothing else to do but cook and . . ."

Henri turned to him suddenly and snapped, "*Alors!* If you feel about it that way, then it is time you went somewhere else!"

"Mommy, what's Calvin?"

"Calvinist?" the Hindu roared. "I will tell you what is Calvinist! Your own simplistic, mechanistic, hubristic attitude toward the universe! You understand man's actions as poorly as you comprehend his physiology."

"Calvinism was . . ."

"I'll tell you about another interesting thing in the news . . ." Leslie said feebly.

"At least I don't believe that human health is benefited by swallowing six feet of gauze and yanking it out again."

"My good Dr. Resnick, the swallowing of silk clears the digestive tract of bile . . ."

"Bile! Bile! Well, welcome to the nineteenth century! Do you also practice bloodletting? What about phrenology?"

"As I was saying, the other interesting thing in the news is . . ."

And so it continued, not unlike Alice's mad tea party, through the final course of fruit and cheese, and all of it put Leslie at ease, for it was strangely like the dinner-table conversations of his childhood, his father and mother and uncles and aunts all speaking at once, all shouting to be heard.

While the old couple was clearing the table, Samson rose and signaled for Leslie to follow.

Beeze was sitting in one of twelve easy chairs in the rear of a small screening room. He motioned Leslie to the seat beside his own, while Samson exited silently.

As always, the quiet, the subdued lights, and stuffy atmosphere produced in Leslie an almost sexual sense of anticipation. His associations with movie theaters had been charged with eroticism from early youth. When he was just entering puberty, he would go, every Sunday, to the Oritani Theater in Hackensack, New Jersey, where he grew up, and spend the entire day in that dark and dusty temple of dreams, tasting the sacrament of Clark bars, watching cartoons and newsreels, coming attractions and travelogues, a horror movie, a Western. For a time they even raffled off prizes, Mr. Curtain, the theater manager, a tired, bald man with a cigar, up on stage, drawing ticket stubs from a fishbowl. Those were the hours of escape that allowed him to survive the intervening days, when he was subjected to the taunts and jeers of his fellow seventh-graders because he was fat and lacked grace in baseball, because he had such difficulty with reading and spelling and arithmetic.

There was an usher at the Oritani, a darkly handsome boy of eighteen who wore his hair greased back the way the hoods did. Leslie secretly worshiped him, because he was a teen-ager, because he wore a uniform with big silver buttons, because he was an acolyte in the temple of dreams. One Sunday, not long after his thirteenth birthday, he was sitting in the balcony when he saw the elliptical beam of the usher's flashlight approach his seat. The usher—Ricky was his name—sat down next to Leslie, simply sat for the next ten minutes before he looked over at him and said, "I brought you these," and handed him a half-dozen Clark bars. "I know you like 'em, I see you buy 'em all the time."

Leslie tried to say thank you but he could not form words. All inside was commotion. A few minutes later when Ricky put his hand on Leslie's thigh, Leslie made no objection. And when, sometime later, his hand found its way to the small, fleshy flower curled between Leslie's legs, the flower opened and hardened, producing, Leslie discovered later that night, while examining his underwear in the privacy of his bedroom, a sticky white residue. He destroyed the underpants rather than let his mother find them; he didn't understand what the residue was, but he knew it was evidence of such a high order of pleasure that his parents could not possibly approve.

Thus the erotic fantasies of the screen became endlessly intertwined with his own erotic life. Week after week he and his secret lover met in the darkness, and week after week their boldness grew. One Sunday Ricky whispered that Mr. Curtain was away, that he had the keys to his office, that they could go there and be alone. And so they crept like thieves to the small windowless room, and there amidst the musty ledgers, the roll-top pine desk, the ancient sofa of splitting leather, they consummated their longings.

Leslie bent over the desk, pants around his ankles, while Ricky bumped away from behind, the cold brass buttons of his jacket brushing occasionally against the younger boy's naked buttocks, sending chills along his flesh. He felt as though a fire had been ignited in his bowels, and when he feared he could bear it no longer, that his legs would crumple and his insides rip like tissue, the pumping of orgasm began, the unstoppable flow of jism and the jingle of keys; and there was the voice of Mr. Curtain saying, "What the Christ is going on here?"—old Mr. Curtain who had decided not to attend the exhibitors convention in Philly after all. Ricky was fired on the spot; Leslie's parents, informed of their son's crime, took him to the best child psychiatrist in New York, who said it was just a phase.

A pretty long phase, Leslie had been known to think in later years.

"Good evening, Mr. Horowitz," Beeze said. "I am happy to say that we had no difficulty obtaining a print of *Land of Lost Dreams*. As a matter of fact, I purchased it, unknowingly, along with a dozen other features, two years ago, and never even realized until today that it was in my possession. Mr. Munckle, my projectionist, located it for me. I'm embarrassed to admit that he knows my collection better than I know it myself. You said, Mr. Horowitz, that a friend of yours was the star?"

"A friend and a client. Rebecca Weiss is her name. She's one of the best actresses around."

"I have heard of her but never had the pleasure of seeing her work."

"Then you're in for a treat," Leslie said. "This is one of her best. She won the New York Film Critics' Award for it, and she should have won an Oscar, but you know how political those things are."

"You must have seen this film many times, then. Are you certain you don't mind seeing it again?"

"Are you kidding? I'll watch anything that moves across a screen. I'm an addict. Whenever I can't sleep, which is all the time, I watch crappy old movies all night."

"I too have difficulty sleeping," Beeze admitted. "Certain dreams trouble my peace. Then I come here and watch movies and wake with my head on my chest and a horrible ache in my neck."

"Nothing like a private screening room," Leslie agreed. "This is some setup you have here. I mean it. This place is fabulous."

"I have the pick of civilization's finest films, music, literature, and art. I have Yoga for the body and my violin for the spirit. I have the foremost chef of France and the learned company of Dr. Resnick and Yogi Gnesha, whose hostility toward each other produces an endless succession of thought-provoking dialogues. And then I have occasional fascinating visitors like yourself."

"Thank you," Leslie said, modestly.

"All my needs are satisfied."

"All of them?"

"I would say so. Why?"

"Well, it's none of my business, but . . ."

"Speak frankly, please."

"What about your emotional needs? A man can't live without love of one sort or another, can he?"

Beeze laughed, the sound of something rattling in a metal box. "A sentimental attitude, Mr. Horowitz. Love is a luxury, like cigarettes or liquor, another crutch to help one forget that death is walking in one's footsteps. I was forced to give up many luxuries after my accident, and love was one of them. Can you imagine a woman letting herself be caressed by this hand"—he held the three-fingered claw under Leslie's eyes and turned it slowly, like a lump of seared flesh on a barbecue spit—"or kissing a face that has no lips? Yes, Mr. Horowitz, I am the bogeyman of children's dreams made real, the ghoul who crawls half-rotted from an open grave. Love is not for my kind."

Leslie said nothing; he sat, looking down at his hands, wishing he had never broached the subject.

The telephone between their chairs buzzed. "Very well, Mr. Munckle," Beeze said into the receiver, "you may start now."

As the lights began to dim, he said to Leslie, "It would give me the greatest pleasure if you could explain technical details to me, or relate amusing anecdotes. Please don't hesitate to do so."

"Well, I don't know if you're aware of this, but *Land of Lost Dreams* was Rebecca's first big part in a movie—and she didn't want to do it!"

"How odd," Beeze said. "And why not?"

How to explain, Leslie wondered, the will to fail, the terror of success, to a man who obviously excelled in every task he attempted? He decided to simply describe the incident as it had occurred and let Beeze draw his own conclusions, always a good plan in storytelling. He remembered it all with great clarity; he had told Rebecca about the part on the phone and urged her to come West to test for it (she was still living in New York). He talked her into it, even sent her a ticket purchased at his own expense, and was waiting at L.A. International airport when she arrived. While he was driving her back to his apartment in West Hollywood, she announced that she had changed her mind and wouldn't test for the film. Leslie, who had been expecting something like this, tried to keep his temper.

"Why not?" he said.

"I don't like the screenplay," she said.

"It's a great screenplay," he said.

"Well, what I mean is, I don't want to be a movie actor."

"Last week you did."

"I know, but I've had second thoughts."

"Then why did you come out here with that three-hundred-dollar ticket I sent you?"

"I thought it would be fun to visit," Rebecca said.

"I'll kill you," Leslie screamed. "I'll kill you! I break my buns to find you this job and pay out three hundred dollars for a ticket and all you want to do is bury yourself in off-off-off-off-Broadway! You won't go out for a movie unless it has the commercial potential of *Ivan the Terrible, Part III*, and I honestly don't know why I keep wasting my time on you!"

"Well, if that's how you feel," Rebecca screamed back, "then I don't want your help or your shitty airplane tickets or your dumb advice about my career, my career, my career, I'm so sick of you criticizing every fucking thing I do just 'cause I want to maintain my integrity . . ."

"You don't want to maintain your integrity, you want to maintain your misery, you love being miserable, you enjoy punishing yourself every chance you possibly can!"

"Uh-oh!" Rebecca said, mocking him grotesquely. "Watch out, it's Leslie the Psychiatrist, shrinking without a license!"

"Make fun of me," Leslie cried, "but it's true."

"And what about you?" Rebecca screamed. "You're a great one to give advice. You've never slept with the same man twice. At least I have relationships with people. You just work and fuck, and work and fuck and work and . . ."

"Shut up!" Leslie shrieked. "You're a selfish cunt and I'm driving you right back to the airport!"

Blind with tears, he turned the car in a broad "U" on La Cienega Boulevard and smashed sidelong into a very fancy Excalibur sports car, backed into an ancient truck loaded with live poultry in slat boxes, and watched with horror as the boxes tumbled off the back, burying his car in screaming, squawking chickens, chickens who stared astounded at them, eyeball to eyeball through the windshield, while the driver, an enraged Chicano, jumped up and down and threatened them with physical violence. "Oh, Lord," Leslie whispered. Then he started to laugh. Rebecca threw her arms around him and said, "I'm sorry I called you those things, you're kind and you're wonderful and you're the best thing that ever happened to me, and I'll do anything you want including that dumb movie." And that was how she came to star in *Land of Lost Dreams*, her most successful film to date. Leslie's automobile insurance was raised so high he was forced to lease a car, but he was so pleased for Rebecca he didn't care.

Beeze seemed to be only half-listening. "Is that her?" he asked Leslie, of the figure on the screen.

"That's her," Leslie agreed. "Only now she's a little older and her hair's all frizzy."

"She's beautiful," Beeze whispered.

"If you like that kind of looks," Leslie agreed. "A lot of casting directors think she's too off-beat, and only let her do character parts. I'd like her to do more ingénue, just to show her versatility. The fact is, she can do anything. She's an incredible actress."

"I think she's the most beautiful woman I've ever seen."

"That's very nice. I'll tell her you said so. She'll be flattered."

"Are you and she," Beeze began tentatively, "lovers?"

"My tastes run along different lines."

"I suspected as much. Does she have many lovers?"

"A few," Leslie said. "They come and go. Sometimes I think there are certain people who are meant to live alone." (That was the decision he and Rebecca came to every time they discussed their disastrous relationships with men.)

"Perhaps she simply hasn't met the right man yet."

"The *right man*?" Leslie asked, amazed by the appearance of this sentimental cliché.

"Don't you believe that every man has a perfect mate somewhere on this earth, waiting to be found? And once that mate is found, happiness is assured him?"

"I think only people with perfect mates believe that one."

"It's an ancient idea, Mr. Horowitz. Are you familiar with Plato's extraordinary treatise on Love, the *Symposium*?"

"No."

"In it Aristophanes, the author of the comedies, speculates that man was once a 'two-backed beast' . . ."

"I've heard the expression."

"And that in his perversity God separated the beast into two beings, and forced them to wander the earth, forever trying to recover their missing half . . ."

"That's beautiful."

"Yogi Gnesha tells me that in Indian mythology famous lovers are said to be reincarnated time and again, joyfully reuniting in certain lives, vainly searching for one another in other lives; sometimes meeting only when they are very old and realizing that they have been cheated out of years of happiness, yet thankful all the same; sometimes meeting in their youth, only to have cruel death snatch one from the other's arms; sometimes, and this I think is saddest of all, being kept apart by nothing more than the obstacles they themselves have created."

"That's the worst," Leslie agreed.

"And perhaps this is the reason why man is born, life after life, on this earth: to find his perfect mate, his other half, and to perfect the love between them until it becomes a beautiful and holy thing that can lift them out of this endless cycle of misery and make them God-like. Well, Mr. Horowitz. What is your opinion?"

"My opinion? It's a pretty romantic notion for somebody who doesn't believe in love."

Beeze laughed his chilling laugh. "Very good, Mr. Horowitz, very good indeed! Now tell me about this scene." He was referring to the movie, nearly forgotten, flickering on the screen before them. "First it appears that the camera is on the ground, then in the air, yet I fail to see a break in the film. How is it possible?"

"He's carrying a hand-held camera," Leslie explained. "First he shoots on the ground, then he backs away, camera still running, and sits down on a seat that's attached to a helicopter. They strap him in—camera still running—the helicopter rises from the ground and *voilà*!"

"Fascinating," Beeze said, "fascinating!"

They talked until midnight on every imaginable subject. Finally Leslie pleaded exhaustion and made his way back to his bedroom, stopping by Beeze's library for a copy of Dickens' *A Tale of Two Cities* (somebody wanted to put one of his clients in a remake of it) to ward off the insomnia he always anticipated when sleeping alone.

He had just settled into bed when he heard a knock on the door and David entered, dressed in a blue silk bathrobe, carrying a tray upon which were all the fixings imaginable for ice-cream sundaes:

a big silver bowl full of ice cream balls of varied flavors, tureens of fudge sauce and caramel, strawberry sauce and marshmallow, plates of marron and chopped walnut and maraschino cherries, and fresh whipped cream in a spray canister; there was also a cup of hot chocolate with a marshmallow melting in it.

"I thought you might want a snack," David said, pulling over a table, resting the tray on it. "It's so hard to go to sleep in a strange bed."

"Particularly alone," Leslie agreed, putting down the book with vague regrets. The first sentence had captured his imagination; now he'd never get beyond it, he knew that for certain. On the other hand, David was awfully handsome, almost Arabian with his dark hair and mustache, his sparkling black eyes. His robe was open to the waist and Leslie could see a delta of chest hair and bulging pectoral muscles—he must have pumped iron within the hour to make them stand up like that.

"I'm a freak for ice cream," Leslie said.

"I knew you were. Now, tell me what you'd like and I'll prepare it."

"Start with vanilla."

"A purist, I like that."

David sat down at the edge of the bed, allowing his robe to fall open. His penis rose vertically, trembling from the restrained excitement, arching until it almost touched his stomach. Without changing position—the tray was right next to him—he took two scoops of vanilla and placed them on either side of his organ.

"Do you think it's excessive to have caramel *and* fudge sauce?" Leslie asked with concern.

"A trifle, perhaps. But excess is the essence of genius."

He carefully poured the hot fudge over one scoop, the caramel over the other.

"I can't wait to get at it," Leslie murmured. "Now, what about marshmallow and marron?"

"There I'd draw the line. One or the other. The marron is from Fauchon in Paris. The marshmallow is domestic. Still, some think that an ice-cream sundae shouldn't put on airs."

Leslie noticed that the other man's teeth were beginning to chatter and decided to hurry up for his sake, even though these leisurely gustatory decisions were the height of enjoyment.

"Marshmallow, chopped nuts, whipped cream, cherry."

While David was applying the first two, Leslie took the whipped cream canister and covered what small part of the penis remained exposed with white foam, which adhered sufficiently to allow him to place a maraschino cherry at the very top of this extraordinary culinary creation; then, without further ado, he began to eat. Later he made himself into a sundae and served himself up to David, and it was nearly three in the morning before they showered together and the assistant chef sneaked away, leaving Leslie exhausted and vowing to diet as soon as he returned to Los Angeles.

Leslie slept a sound and dreamless sleep. When he woke, the clock said nine A.M., and he hurried to dress, his mind teeming with details he would have to attend to at the office. Phone calls, contracts, meetings, screenings; he remembered more and more obligations until his head felt like a wastebasket jammed with memos. And Tommy would never forgive him for missing Thanksgiving dinner, and not even calling to apologize. His first "lasting" relationship in years (three weeks come Tuesday), with a man whose company he actually enjoyed, and who seemed to care for him, a man who might even stay with him into the homosexual wasteland of middle age. And now he'd wrecked it all. Tommy would never speak to him again. What if he came home sick? Leslie wondered. That would help. He could dwell on the hardships of his night alone in the desert and gloss over his day of luxury in the manor, and maybe Tommy would have pity enough to forgive him.

Leslie recalled his conversation about love and reincarnation from the previous night. Had Tommy and he been lovers in some previous life? He fantasized about the two of them in Medieval England, and Ancient Rome, and King Tut's Egypt. He wondered if they had been a heterosexual couple in past lives (was he the girl? was Tommy?) and if God had brought them both back in the same sex to see how much adversity they'd be willing to endure. Was their homosexuality punishment for something they'd done in ancient times, like worshiping a golden calf? Or was it the result of being born too many times in bodies of the same sex, so that the soul got sick of it? Or switching sexes so often that the soul got confused?

When he emerged from the bathroom the breakfast cart was waiting, but rather than the perfectly prepared fare of the previous day, he was dismayed to find black sulphurous-smelling eggs, two squares of charcoal that might have once been white bread, and an oily noxious kind of coffee. For a moment he was puzzled, then he realized what must have happened: Henri, suspecting David's infidelity the night before, had concocted the foulest insult he could devise. Leslie pushed the cart aside, gathered his brief case in preparation for departure, and went to find Beeze.

The door to the music room was open and Beeze was standing with his back to Leslie, playing as though nothing else in the world existed but the music. His bow drew quick arpeggiated figures from the strings, with such facility that it sounded as though several violins were playing at once. Leslie had been wondering how Beeze could play so beautifully with his deformed hand; he saw now that the bad hand was the one which held the bow, and that the other hand, the hand whose nimble fingers depressed the strings, had been spared from the flames. How much of the rest of him, he wondered, had retained mortal form?

When he finished the movement, Beeze turned and said, "Good morning, Mr. Horowitz. What a shame you are leaving, I'll miss your company."

"Well, me too," Leslie muttered. He couldn't wait to get away. He felt as though he were a laboratory animal, a white rat in a cage, well-fed, well cared for, but with no control over his destiny.

"I would like to send a gift to Miss Weiss," Beeze continued, "in appreciation of the hours of pleasure she brought me last night. Since you will tell no one about me, it follows that the donor of the gift must remain unnamed. You may say, simply, that a man you met in the desert wished for her to have it, only that and no more. Now, Mr. Horowitz, please pick the gift."

"What do you mean?"

"Pick a gift for her. Your choice of anything you have seen since your arrival."

"Really?"

"I say only what I mean, Mr. Horowitz."

Leslie looked around, at the treasures which lined the room, precious paintings and *objets d'art*. He recalled the ceramic bull by Picasso, the El Greco oil, and his head began to reel with the possibilities. Then he recalled that gifts incurred debts, regardless of the benevolence of the giver, and that it was a gift for Rebecca, who did not like the responsibility of expensive things. She was always nervous that if she owned something of value, it would be stolen from her house, or ruined by fire, or mud slide, or earthquake. She would be happiest with something that was not quite a museum piece, something whose value was more emotional, sentimental. A *tsatske*, as they were fond of saying when they went shopping together, a Yiddish word meaning a small piece of art, and encompassing anything from a Hummel figurine to a Snoopy music box.

Bring me a rose, Rebecca had said.

"This paperweight," Leslie said, picking up a crystal sphere from the twenty or so atop the harpsichord. Within it was frozen a perfect red rose. "She's got a thing for roses."

"Anything I own," said Beeze. "Anything but that. I can't explain why. It has certain significance."

Reluctantly Leslie returned it to the crystal garden atop the piano, and looked about for another object. Now he no longer cared; if he could not bring her the perfect present, he would bring any little thing. He simply wanted to get away from there, away from the madman who offered everything he owned but refused to part with one small paperweight.

He pointed to the most inconsequential thing in the room, a painting no bigger than a postcard, a scene of a windmill, a stream, some cows.

"That."

"A landscape by the nineteenth-century Dutch artist Van Hijn, generally considered the finest painter of miniatures who ever lived. A collector in Dallas offered me a hundred and thirty thousand dollars."

"Forget it, then." Leslie was growing bored and angry with this game. He felt that Beeze was playing with him, reducing him in stature. He wanted to get back to his office, back to his desk, where he and everyone else knew that he was a man of importance, a man to contend with.

"No," Beeze said, "I insist you take it. It means nothing to me—all of this means nothing. Samson, wrap the Van Hijn for Mr. Horowitz."

The giant, who had been standing behind Leslie, came forward, took the painting off the wall and left with it.

"You are ready to go?" Beeze said.

"The sooner the better."

"Wait here while I see that the helicopter is prepared."

When Beeze had gone, Leslie allowed himself to experience the depth of his anger. He felt that Beeze had humiliated him by giving him the Van Hijn after boasting about the expense of it; and, by claiming that the money meant nothing to him, had implied that it meant a great deal to Leslie. He had to remain cordial—his future was at the millionaire's mercy—but the anger was there nonetheless, and was the cause of what he did next. Looking all around, making sure that nobody was watching, he dropped the rose paperweight into his open brief case, closed the clasp and turned the combination lock. There were so many similar paperweights atop the harpsichord that Beeze would not notice its absence until long after he was gone. He felt precisely as he had felt, aged twelve, shoplifting in Woolworth's (all the kids did it, and he wanted to be one of the kids): a bloodrush of excitement, a chill of fear, a longing to panic and run, an urge to stay and confess.

"Mr. Horowitz?" Beeze said, standing at the door.

Leslie jerked around. He began to examine Beeze's face for any knowledge of his crime, before he remembered that it was only a mask.

He gathered up his brief case and followed Beeze down one of the twin stairways that embraced the vast entry hall, then across to the front door, their footsteps echoing from the polished marble floor to the high vaulted ceiling. He would have liked to say goodbye to David, but none of the staff was in sight.

Beeze opened the door and Leslie was blinded by the sun; he shut his eyes instantly and saw the outline of the door in a perfect purple afterimage. Shading his eyes and squinting, he perceived a helicopter, perched like a huge silver dragonfly a hundred yards from the house, and Samson sat in the clear plastic bubble, waiting for his passenger to join him.

"This is where we part," Beeze said. "I can go no further than these front steps."

"Thanks for everything. I hope you'll reconsider coming to Los Angeles. I really think you'd like it." Leslie tried to make his voice sincere, and struggled to quell the trembling that would betray his crime.

Neither man made a motion to shake hands.

"Goodbye," Beeze said.

"Goodbye."

Leslie started down the front steps, expecting, at any instant, a hand to grab his shoulder, to jerk him back roughly, to say, *Young man, what's that under your jacket? A plastic pencil case! Did you pay for this?*

Another step. He could feel Beeze's eyes on him, a cold spot on the back of his neck.

Young man, shoplifting is a very serious crime. I should call the police—but I'll get in touch with your parents first.

Another step, and another. The desert opened up around him, the parched plains dotted with bushes, the mountains like lizards lazing in the sun.

Horowitz? Not Nate Horowitz who runs Cedar Lane Hardware? Young man, I'm afraid your father's going to be very disappointed with you . . .

Another step and then he was walking on dirt, crossing the distance to the helicopter, trying to keep his pace leisurely.

He climbed into the seat next to Samson, holding the brief case in his lap, and said, "You know, this is really exciting. I've never been in a helicopter before."

Samson stared at him for a moment, the vast ruin of his face expressionless. Then he started the motor.

Ruck—a—ruck—a—ruck—a . . .

I can't believe it, Leslie thought, I'm actually getting out of here . . .

RUCKITA, RUCKITA, RUCKITA, RUCKITA . . .

And won't Rebecca be amazed when I tell her about this, and won't she be thrilled when I give her the rose . . .

Rhummmmmmmmmmmm . . .

The blades became a blur overhead. Leslie fastened his seatbelt and waited for the silver ship to grow light as a bubble and float off into the blue.

Something buzzed on the control panel, and Samson held the earphones to his head for a moment, listening attentively; then he glanced at his passenger and cut the engine. With a sinking sensation, Leslie watched the shadows of the rotors slow and stop. The ship seemed as heavy and immovable as a boulder.

"What are we waiting for?" Leslie said nervously.

Samson turned to him, raising one great slab of a hand in an unmistakable gesture. He wanted him to get out.

"No," Leslie said, his voice starting to crack, "take me back to Los Angeles."

Again the gesture.

"No," Leslie shrieked, "no, I won't!"

In one motion Samson unhitched the seatbelt and threw Leslie out of the 'copter with such force that he rolled ten feet after he struck the ground. He lay in the dirt, a terrible pain in his side, trying to clear his mind, to take in what was happening. The next thing he knew, Samson was standing over him, looking down from an extraordinary height, his face all the more distorted with anger. He gestured for him to stand, and Leslie, who was not brave when it came to physical pain, shook his head and whimpered. Samson reached down with one hand, grasped him by the collar, and yanked him to his feet as easily as another man might lift a kitten by the scruff. He twisted Leslie's arm behind his back so hard that a nerve pain danced from elbow to shoulder, and half pushed him, half carried him to the music room, where Beeze was waiting.

"Where is it?" Beeze demanded.

Leslie's voice was lost in tears. "That fucking baboon broke my arm."

"Where is it?"

"Why don't you leave me alone? You said I could go back to Los Angeles."

"WHERE IS IT?" Beeze exploded.

"I don't know, I don't know, I don't know!"

"Search him," Beeze said, controlled again.

Samson kneeled and frisked Leslie expertly. Then he stood and shook his head.

"The brief case," Beeze said. "Bring it to me."

Samson departed.

"So I'm to trust you, am I?" Beeze asked the figure curled on the floor in pain. "So I'm to let you return to the city, where you can tell your tales of the freak without a face who lives in the desert and spends his days watching movies and sawing on a fiddle . . ."

"I wouldn't have told, I *promised* . . ."

"What's the word of a thief worth?"

"Didn't steal it!"

For a time they both remained silent; then Leslie said, "That baboon broke my arm. I need medical attention."

Before Beeze could reply they heard the clump of Samson's feet on the stairs; the next moment he strode into the room and dropped the brief case into Leslie's hands.

Leslie played with the lock for a minute. "I—I'm so nervous I can't remember the combination."

Beeze nodded at Samson, who grabbed the brief case, took one side of it in each hand and tore it open as easily as a paper envelope.

"Wait," Leslie shouted, "don't break it, please!"

It had been a Christmas present from his clients, a beautiful thing of suede and gold, engraved with his initials.

Now Samson reached inside, took out the paperweight and gave it to Beeze, who cradled it as though it were a fragile egg.

"What a fool I was to trust you. But I hadn't seen a stranger in so long that I'd forgotten the extent of human duplicity."

He spoke about mankind as though they were a race apart from himself.

"If you could understand how much it would have meant," Leslie pleaded.

"Understand? I understand! I understand that you were dying, and that I fed you and restored you to health, and this is how you repay my hospitality. Now you'll never leave here, Mr. Horowitz, you'll stay until the day you die! Samson, lock him in the cellar."

Samson dragged Leslie down the stairs, and down another flight, this one carved from sandstone the color of dried blood, then through a series of man-made caves, their ceilings supported by timber frames where bats slept, where lamps with naked filaments burned their patterns into the eye. The caves housed groaning air-conditioning machinery and tanks to cool and purify the waters from the hot springs deep beneath the ground. They came to a door of oak braced with iron brackets, which Samson opened with an old-fashioned key. He hurled Leslie inside, slamming the door behind him, closing him into a darkness the likes of which is understood only by the blind.

Leslie lay there in terror, afraid to move, to utter a sound. Presently he slept. When he woke, the damp, chilly atmosphere of the room had only worsened the aching of his body, and his arm was swollen to the point of uselessness. The darkness was still complete, impenetrable. He felt a floor of slate squares, walls of crumbling sandstone (would the basement cave in, would he be buried here alive?) and iron racks cradling dusty wine bottles, all covered with a fine netting of spiderwebs. He giggled. Wine, wine, everywhere, and not a drop to drink. It would have eased the pain, passed the time. If only he had a bottle opener, even a Scout knife. Who was that actress he had heard the joke about, the one who was supposed to have a drawer full of Boy Scout knives?

A noise—the key in the lock! The door opened and the silhouette of a man in a mask appeared against the light.

"Please," Leslie said, "I've got to see a doctor. My arm."

"You'll see no one," Beeze said.

"You're sick! You're really sick! You're some kind of power-crazy paranoid maniac. Well, I'll tell you something—you can't go around locking people in your basement. There are laws. I'm very influential. I've got important friends who'll come looking for me. They'll find my car and then they'll find your house . . ."

"No," Beeze said, with such certainty that any hope perished immediately. "Nobody finds this house unless it is my will."

"I found it."

"That was God's will."

"You're really crazy, you know that? You should have yourself institutionalized. You need help."

"It's you who need help now."

"Yes, I do! Look at my arm, see how it's swollen? I'll get gangrene and lose it!"

"That's not what I meant. Your arm is merely sprained."

"But the pain . . ."

"Swallow the pain."

"If you let me go back to Los Angeles, I promise I won't tell anybody. I'll swear it on a Bible! Please, let me go. I'll do anything you say."

"Perhaps . . ."

"Yes?"

"Perhaps there is a way. You may go, Mr. Horowitz . . ."

"Yes?"

"On the condition that Rebecca Weiss comes to take your place."

Leslie was too stunned by the pronouncement to say anything.

"If she is in my keep," Beeze continued, "then I know you dare not go back on your word."

"I'd die before I let her come here."

"And so you shall," Beeze said, and slammed the door behind him.

· 4 ·

Billy Rosenblatt drove back to the office from La Scala, thinking about his lunch with Victoria Dunbarr. He had met his share of actresses, but never before had he encountered quite this mixture of slyness and sexuality in the service of ambition. Physically, he wanted her. Intellectually—and Billy's mind and body were rarely integrated in their desires—he knew he would give only a certain amount for the pleasure of having her. Specifically, there was no way he would give her the part of Jacqueline in *The Other Woman*, even if she offered to fulfill his most florid fantasies. At six feet, she would be physically ridiculous for the role. However, if she could act, she might possibly be right for the mistress. She had said that she didn't want to play mistresses anymore, but Billy wasn't worried. He would give her a screen test, as promised, and negotiate, as he always did when actors made unreasonable demands, and presently he would emerge sexually satisfied, and she, professionally content.

If something was bothering Billy it was not this pretty show girl, but the novel his ex-wife had written about him. Every time he thought about it, he cringed. Wasn't there a law against a wife revealing her husband's secrets? He reviewed the marriage ceremony in his head: *Love, honor and obey . . . death do us part . . .* No, nothing about keeping secrets. He knew that a wife was not allowed to testify against her husband, for that prop had supported many a sagging gangster movie in the old days. Perhaps one of his slyer lawyers could turn the law around and use it to get an injunction against publication. It was worth a try. Billy sighed. Had he known, twenty years ago, that a time would come when society approved of women tattling on their husbands, he would have been politer and a lot more secretive.

He drove into Burbank Studios, nodded at the guard, and parked in front of the Producers' Building, which, with the addition of a neon VACANCY sign, might have been mistaken for a motel. His suite of offices was on the third floor.

Florence McGee, his secretary, otherwise known as Flossy, greeted him gleefully. She had succeeded in tracking down a copy of Angela's manuscript! While reading the Barnard College alumni magazine, she had noticed that her classmate Harriet Oliver was working as an editorial assistant at the Butterfield Press, the same New York publishing house that had, incidentally, purchased Angela's novel. Flossy put through a long-distance call immediately and, after catching up on old gossip, asked if Harriet might send her a Xerox of Angela's novel. Rumors had gotten out about its fabulous film possibilities. Flossy's boss, a big-time producer who had to remain nameless, wanted first peek. If he decided to buy it for a major motion picture, Harriet could take the credit. Harriet, delighted by an opportunity to show her stuff, promised to get a copy in the mail that afternoon.

"That's worth a ten-dollar raise," Billy said, when he heard the news.

"Thanks!" Flossy said.

"After we get the manuscript."

"Awww," she said. She was a slight, bony girl with curly red hair and a redhead's fair complexion, skin that turned to a jumble of freckles whenever she stepped out in the sun. She had big blue eyes and crooked teeth and dimples. Billy had hired her, despite her labored typing and illegible handwriting, because she had more brains and ingenuity than he'd seen in ages. In fact, she was so useful that he'd never even made a pass at her, one of the few young women in his life to earn that distinction.

"How'd your lunch with Rebecca Weiss go?"

"She never showed," Billy said, looking through the log of phone calls that had to be returned. "I had lunch with an actress named Victoria Dunbarr instead." He proceeded to tell Flossy the details of their lunch, excluding those pertaining to matters sexual.

"I've got a suspicion," he said in conclusion, "that Rebecca never received my invitation in the first place. Let's try to unravel this. You spoke to Horowitz, correct?"

"I spoke to Sheila. You know, his partner."

"But I told you to speak to Horowitz."

"I tried. They kept giving me the run-around. Apparently he's out of town. Everything sounded crazy."

"It's a crazy office," Billy agreed. "I wouldn't do business with them, but they always have actors I want. Let me give you a piece of advice, Floss. Don't deal with fags if you can help it. They're erratic. Can't trust 'em. All they think about is getting laid."

"Unlike you."

"Your raise is cut to five dollars. So you spoke to Sheila, and for some reason she conveyed the message to Victoria. Could she have a gripe against Rebecca?"

"Or else she was thinking about something else and wrote the wrong name on the message. I've done that."

"Yes, but we're forgetting something. Victoria isn't their client."

"True." Flossy thought for a moment, then snapped her fingers. "They're roommates, right? Sheila calls. Rebecca's in the shower or something. So Victoria takes the message. But instead of passing it on like she promises . . ."

Billy nodded. "Exactly. Get me Rebecca Weiss on the phone and make damn sure it's her."

"Right, boss."

"And then get me Victoria's agent so I can arrange a screen test."

"You mean you're going to test her after what she did?"

"Floss, suppose this Dunbarr girl turns out to be another Garbo? Wouldn't it be stupid to waste her talent just because we suspect her of a little mischief? If I refused to work with anybody who ever betrayed a friend, I'd be a lonely man."

"But you've got to find out who's been lying!"

"Why?" Billy said. "All that would do is spread bad feelings. If it was Victoria, she'd be too humiliated to work for me. If it was Sheila Gold, she'd make it damn hard to use her clients. And what if Rebecca herself was behind this? I've seen stranger things in the way of self-sabotage. No, Floss, let me give you a piece of advice. I haven't gotten where I am today by exposing other people's intrigues." He laughed. "Lord knows I have enough of my own. The only thing that matters is—"

"Making the best damn movie I know how," Floss said, joining in on one of Billy's favorite maxims.

"You're learning," Billy said. "Now get me Rebecca Weiss on the phone."

Rebecca was so nervous she spent two minutes trying to start the car with the front-door key. It was the day of her screen test, the first one she had taken in years. She hated to test, probably because she did it so badly; knowing that it was not an actual performance, she could never give the entirety of herself that she could while onstage or shooting a movie. And she hated the idea of being judged; it reminded her of school and evoked all the anti-authoritarian feelings that had made her such a dismal student and disciplinary problem. These feelings were only aggravated by the surprise appearance of her parents, around whom she always became twelve years old again, helpless and dependent on Daddy, a feeling she despised. And if that weren't enough, she had gotten the strangest call from Billy Rosenblatt, inviting her to test and asking odd, oblique questions about a lunch date she knew nothing about; she couldn't figure out what he was getting at. (If only Leslie were around, he could have explained. He always understood the Machiavellian schemes behind the words. But by tomorrow he would be missing a whole week, and with every additional day the chances of his still being alive seemed more and more slim.) But the final blow was the news that Vicky was also reading for the part. Not that she wasn't happy for her roommate to have the opportunity. But they were such different physical types that the idea of their both being considered for the same part suggested capriciousness on the part of the producer, and she couldn't bear people playing games with her. As an actor it happened all too often: you were called up for a part and learned that the director simply wanted to date you, or was seeing you to satisfy some studio executive, when he'd cast somebody else for the part weeks ago. Without Leslie to protect her, she felt vulnerable to all the world, raw and exposed as a newly hatched chick.

She found five other actors waiting in the anteroom of Billy Rosenblatt's suite, reading paperbacks and knitting and studying scripts, and she knew every one of them. They all smiled at each other and said, "Not you too!" and "I guess the whole club's here" and "Oh God, it's old home week!" All in a friendly, good-natured way, thereby demonstrating what fine actors they really were. Rebecca gave her name to the receptionist, took a seat and tried to size up the competition. There was Ms. W., who, like Rebecca, had made one great film and whose three subsequent features had been disasters; Ms. X., who had appeared on the cover of *Time* magazine for her extraordinary performance as Susan B. Anthony and who hadn't worked since because she was so frightened by her success; Mrs. Y., a woman of breathtaking beauty who had done a lot of interesting work before her nervous breakdown, and was now, according to *Variety*, sufficiently recovered to attempt a comeback; Ms. Z., a superb comedienne, but really not much of a dramatic actress; and of course Victoria, who was not bad, damn her, and seductive enough to make most men do anything, including cast her in a part for which she was completely unsuited.

Taken as a group, the women in the room—Victoria excepted —were the brightest new names of the last five years; and today they were has-beens, having hardly "been" at all. And not because they were poor technical actresses, or lacking in charisma, but rather because of a curious disinterest in the audience. During the thirties and forties the number of male and female stars had been almost equal, yet today *Variety*'s list of the twenty most bankable actors included only two women. In the dark temple, America was no longer worshiping the fairer sex.

The receptionist called Victoria's name.

"Good luck," Rebecca said. "*Merde.*" She couldn't help noticing how young Victoria looked, how innocent in a simple cotton print dress that played down her sexuality. Rebecca instantly regretted not having worn a print dress instead of her French jeans and blousy silk shirt. She felt so sloppy. She was ready to go home that instant.

"I don't know why I'm bothering," Victoria whispered. "You've got the part, you're perfect for it. And you're a better actor than any of the rest of us. It's too bad about that skin thing."

"What skin thing?"

"That rash."

"What rash?" Rebecca fumbled with her purse, taking out her pocket mirror.

"Darling, don't worry about it," Vicky said, "break a Vitamin E capsule and rub it in. Love you."

Rebecca examined her reflection, but search as she would she couldn't find the rash.

Victoria was disappointed with the austerity of Billy Rosenblatt's office. She had expected the glamour of old Hollywood, and instead she found an ordinary room with corner windows overlooking a parking lot. A Formica-topped desk stood at one end, and the wall behind it was bare. There were no photographs of stars with their arms around Billy, no plaques from film societies and community groups, no Oscars artfully tucked out of the way so that they could be seen from any part of the room. Opposite the desk, a "set" had been improvised from a chair, a table, a champagne glass of ruby-tinted crystal. A portable TV camera, supported by a tripod, was connected to a video-cassette machine; Victoria found its silent Japanese efficiency menacing. Billy Rosenblatt introduced the three men who had risen when she entered, and the young woman who remained seated.

There was Harry Harris, the line producer, a bald man of sixty with a bulbous nose, watery eyes and a perpetual leer.

"Harry and I have worked together since the old days," Billy explained.

"That's right." Harris laughed. "He can't fire me because he owes me too much money."

(Polite laughter, but not much.)

And Joe Saltzberger, the director, forty-five, tall and rangy and boyish, curly hair and glasses, still the New York intellectual despite his years in California.

"Vicky, it's a pleasure," he said.

And Stanislaw Kovacik, who had generously offered to do the taping, a big bearlike man, with a thick black beard and a puckish smile.

"Stanislaw will be our director of photography," Billy said, "if he doesn't have too many other commitments when we start to shoot."

"Oh, Billy," he said, "I cancel them all for you."

"And this is Flossy McGee," Billy said, indicating the red-headed young woman with the clipboard, "my girl Friday. I'd be lost without her. Now, Vicky, why don't you tell us a little about yourself?"

They all sat down while Vicky moved to stage center. The camera was staring at her like a blind man.

"Well," she began, "I was born in Hawaii, but I lived all over the world because my father was in the Navy."

"'I joined the Navy,'" Harris sang, loudly and off-key, "'to see the world . . .'"

"That's right," Vicky said politely, "he was a real Navy man. When I was nine we settled in La Jolla. I was always very interested in theater and I used to put on plays in the garage, direct all the other kids in the neighborhood, you know. At college—that was Capistrano Junior College—I was head of the drama society and I did dinner theater during the summers. Usually the college kids had bit parts, but I got to play Stupefyin' Jones in *Li'l Abner*. I guess my big break came when I was sixteen and I won the California Orange Blossom Beauty Pageant. Some of the publicity people from the pageant helped me when I moved up to L.A. Still, it took a lot of pounding the pavement before I landed the part of Betty-Lou in *Pearl Divers*."

"The show about the three girl skin-divers," Billy said.

"That's right."

"Of the three of them," Harris said, "you filled out your part the best."

Nobody laughed except Victoria, who answered, good-naturedly, "Well, that was exactly the problem. Although I got a lot of exposure . . ."

"Any more exposure," Harris said, "and you would have gotten arrested."

"Harry, please," Saltzberger said.

"Sorry," Harris said. Chastised, he withdrew.

Victoria tried again. "Although I had a lot of exposure, people started thinking of me only as a body. Nobody would take me seriously. It was the same thing that drove Marilyn Monroe to suicide. I hope I'll be stronger."

"That's why we're giving you this opportunity," Billy said. "Joe, would you like to explain the scene to Vicky?"

"You're Jacqueline," Saltzberger said wearily (he'd explained it to fourteen other actresses in the last two days), "a thirty-five-year-old career woman. Your business is a fabulous success, but your personal life is a shambles. Now, in this scene your husband has just walked out on you and you're all alone in this enormous house you bought for him, thinking it would make him stay. You're bitter, you're furious—but you're not defeated. You're going to go ahead with your life and the hell with him. Any questions?"

"No," Victoria said.

"All right then, any time you're ready. Roll the tape."

"This is Test Number Fifteen," Flossy said loudly, for the microphone, "Victoria Dunbarr, Take One," and she noted it on her clipboard.

They all grew silent, waiting.

Victoria sat down on the chair and closed her eyes, preparing herself as she did in drama class, taking deep breaths to ease any tension that might inhibit the flow of emotions.

She had crept into Rebecca's room in the middle of the night, "borrowed" the script and locked herself in the toilet until the first light of dawn, memorizing the part. She needed every advantage, and not having to refer to the script would help her performance greatly. She let herself drift back in time, evoking the "sense memories" that would be useful in creating Jacqueline, one incident in particular when, following the junior prom, her date grew furious with her because she wouldn't sleep with him, a silly-sounding thing with a very real hurt to it. Presently she opened her eyes and whispered, "Damn him. *Damn him.* Damn them all, all the men with their frail egos and their overblown bravado!" She threw her head back to emphasize the statement, and her long hair flowed with the motion, just as she had practiced it so often before the mirror. "Show me one who's not an infant looking for a mommy to change his diapers, show me one who's not a tyrant searching for a daughter to tyrannize." She looked out, expectantly, as though someone might answer. When no one did, she shook her head in disgust. "Well, I'm not going to mourn his departure. No sir. I'll celebrate." She smiled, quite satisfied with her decision. "Where's the champagne?" She searched through an imaginary liquor closet, located an imaginary bottle of champagne, pantomimed pulling off the cork—being shocked by the pop, catching the overflow in the glass, sipping off the foam, laughing with delight. "To my freedom, to my freedom from men!" Her smile melted and she became cynical, rueful. "It's no good. Who am I kidding? I need them, I can't live without them." Now a touch of warmth. "For all the bullying and the crybabying, there are still the arms that hold off my nightmares and the sudden tenderness at the breakfast table." She sighed and delivered the final line to the champagne glass in her hand. "What a joker God must be to create two sexes and make one of them Man and the other Woman."

"That was very nice, Victoria," Billy said, and she could tell that he meant it.

"It really was," Joe Saltzberger agreed.

She detected the surprise in his voice and felt triumphant. She had shown them. Finally given the opportunity, she had shown them, just as she had known she would. She felt with certainty that the part was hers, despite her physical inappropriateness. After all, wasn't casting against type one of the most potentially dramatic devices?

Billy Rosenblatt stood up. "Thank you very much, Vicky. We should have a decision within the next few days."

"Thank you," she said, "thank you all for giving me the opportunity." She smiled at them, particularly at Harris, and started for the door slowly, reluctant to leave without some last action to insure her success.

Billy turned to Flossy. "Who's next?"

Flossy consulted her clipboard. "Rebecca Weiss."

"Send her in. And put some more water in the champagne glass."

"Oh, I'll do it!" Victoria said, and before anyone could protest, she had the champagne glass in her hand, and was entering the bathroom that adjoined the office. "I need to freshen up anyway," she added, closing the door behind her.

She locked the door, ran to the sink and threw open the medicine chest, the vague outline of a plan forming in her mind. Put something in the water. Colorless, it would have to be colorless. Hydrogen peroxide? No, that was poisonous. She didn't want to kill Becky, just break her concentration. Listerine might do the trick. In the bottle, the liquid had an amber tint, but the small quantity she poured into the glass appeared colorless, the more so since the glass was ruby crystal, a perfect long-stemmed rose, a red, red rose for Rebecca. She added a few drops more. What the hell, she thought, and filled the glass the rest of the way with Listerine. Then she flushed the toilet—oh, and she could put down the seat, that would be a nice touch—and then she ran the tap. When she emerged from the bathroom, Rebecca was standing onstage, telling them about her experience in the theater. Victoria ran, on cat's feet, to the table, put down the glass, flashed a smile at her old friend, and started for the door, indicating by her speed and stealth that she had had her time and now it was Rebecca's turn. She didn't wish to detract from it in the least.

Rebecca felt more comfortable now that she was actually here, in front of them, ready to do her scene. As with a dentist appointment, the expectation was far worse than the reality. Having a camera aimed at her made her feel wonderful, as though the machine were irradiating her, destroying the cancer of her self-doubt.

"Any questions?" Joe Saltzberger asked, after setting the scene for her.

"No," she said.

"All right, then, anytime you're ready. Roll the tape."

"This is Test Number Sixteen," Flossy said loudly, "Rebecca Weiss, Take One," and she noted it on her clipboard.

They all grew silent, waiting.

Despite her protestations, despite her plans to return to New York and do Off-Broadway, her thoughts had been with *The Other Woman* ever since Leslie had left the screenplay with her and she had stayed up until 3 A.M. reading it. That night in Death Valley, Jacqueline Hollis had come alive, and since then every time Rebecca sat down for a meal, Jacqueline was there with her at the table, and when she went to bed Jacqueline lay with her in the dark. They were more intimate than twins, because they were nearly the same person, bright, masochistic, ambitious, talented, rebellious, self-sabotaging, unable to sustain a relationship with a man. The part fit her soul as naturally as a Bach suite did a violinist's left hand. Rebecca Weiss sat down in the chair, but when she raised her head, Jacqueline Hollis sat in her place.

"Damn him," she said, her voice seething with rage, "DAMN HIM! Damn them all, all the fine men with their frail egos and overblown bravado! Show me one who's not an infant looking for a mommy to change his diapers, one who's not a tyrant searching for a daughter to tyrannize." She shook her head. "I'm not going to mourn his departure—no, I'll celebrate! Where's the champagne?" Her rage turned to determination, she forced happiness upon herself as though it were Juliet's poison. She found an imaginary bottle of champagne in an imaginary liquor cabinet, uncorked it after several tries—cutting her finger in the process—and filled the glass—the only real object in the pantomime—to overflowing. "To my freedom!" she shouted, raising the glass at arm's length. "To my freedom from men!" And she swallowed the contents of the glass in one gulp. She hesitated for perhaps a fraction of a second and continued the monologue, the flame of her anger dying suddenly, leaving only blackened embers of resignation. "What's the use? I need them, I can't live without them." Her voice became soft, almost melodic. "For all the bullying and the crybabying, there are still the arms that hold off my nightmares and the sudden tenderness at the breakfast table." She resumed her place at the table, her head propped philosophically on one arm. "What a joker God must be," she said lightly, "to create two sexes, and make one of them Man and the other Woman." Then she started to cry and lowered her head into her hands, returning to the position in which she had begun.

After several moments of silence, Joe Saltzberger began to applaud and then the others joined him.

Rebecca stood up suddenly and said, "Where is the bathroom?"

"The door on the left," Flossy said, and being a little more perceptive than the rest, added, "Are you all right?"

"Fine, thank you."

Rebecca hurried to the bathroom, slammed the door behind her, kneeled in front of the toilet and began to gag. Someone had put mouthwash in the champagne glass, and only her extraordinary concentration had prevented her from vomiting in the middle of her test. When it was over, she lay down on the floor, resting her cheek against the cool tile, and cried and cried until Flossy came to the door to see if she needed any help.

Billy Rosenblatt drove along Mulholland Drive, admiring the lights of the valley far below, neat grids twinkling in the smog. He came to a turnoff, a smaller road of cracked blacktop, and continued along it, circling ever higher, until he reached a wooden gate topped with barbed wire; it opened at the touch of a device clipped to the sun visor of his car, and he drove on into a partially fenced courtyard that seemed to have been placed at the very top of the world. To his right, a swimming pool reflected the moon in its still waters; to his left, a four-car garage and a guest house were connected, by a breezeway, with the main house. All three were one-story, white clapboard buildings with enormous picture windows to take in the view on every side, and brilliant sprays of red and pink bougainvillaea climbing the walls and clogging the drain gutters. To many people it would have seemed like a palace; to Billy it had the feel of a guest cottage on somebody else's estate. Five years ago home had been a twenty-six-room Bel Air mansion with two gardeners to keep up the grounds and a domestic staff of four; today he was reduced to this, six rooms and one servant, his Japanese houseboy Edo. Billy Rosenblatt, whose every picture, nearly, had made a profit! Such were the vicissitudes of community property. If he ever married again, he would do so in Nevada.

Edo opened the door just as he was searching for his key, bowed to him and took his jacket and brief case. He was a small man of fifty, with a round face, a flat nose, eyes almost hidden beneath epicanthic folds, as if his features had conspired to be as inconspicuous as possible, in order not to disturb Billy Rosenblatt's concentration. He was so quiet, so perfect in his attentions, that Billy sometimes wondered if the man were real, or some extraordinary contrivance of the Sony Corporation.

"Before you go inside, Mr. Rosenblatt," Edo said—he was a Nisei and spoke impeccable English—"I should warn you that there is a young lady waiting. She arrived an hour ago and told me that she was a very dear friend of yours."

"And I assume, Edo, that she is a very attractive young lady—or else you would have told her that I was not coming home this evening?"

Edo nodded, and perhaps the slightest smile crossed his lips. "A man should always be surrounded by beauty, I believe."

"What would I do without you?" Billy said.

He strolled into the living room and found Victoria Dunbarr stretched out, like a cat, on one of the black velvet sofas, reading a fat paperback. She was wearing a beige dress of some shiny silk-thin synthetic, which was cut like a slip, with spaghetti straps and inserts of lace, and her hair was spread across her back like a shawl. A spot overhead provided barely enough light to see the print—somebody had turned the dimmer to its lowest setting—and the only additional light came from a compressed paper log on the fireplace, the reflection of which made the twelve Oscars placed about the room glow a sensuous red. The valley could be seen in the picture window behind her, like a quilt outlined in light.

"Hi," she said, her voice a silky sound against the crackling of the log.

"Hello, Victoria. What a nice surprise."

"I thought I'd take you up on that offer."

"Which one?"

"The sauna."

He sat down on the couch opposite her.

"Good book?" he said.

She shrugged. "It's a Hollywood novel. But it's not like any Hollywood I've ever been to."

"What do you suppose it would be like if somebody wrote a novel about Hollywood as it really is?"

Victoria thought it over carefully. "Well, I don't know if an average reader would be interested in a bunch of narcissistic children taking advantage of each other. On the other hand, it's the only place left where there's any magic, and everybody's interested in magic, don't you think?"

When Billy didn't answer, she went on. "It sounds like you're still worried about that book your wife wrote."

"Worried? I'm mortified. It could make me the laughingstock of the business. Why, Vicky, do you know I can't sleep anymore? I lie in bed at night, thinking about all the embarrassing things that happened during my marriage, wondering which ones she wrote about. It's hell, it's sheer hell."

"I wouldn't worry. If it's an honest book, it will say you're handsome and distinguished and charming, and probably the greatest movie producer of all time."

Edo came in with a plate of crudités and set it on the glass table between the sofas along with a dry martini for Billy, another Margarita for Victoria.

"What's for supper?" Billy said.

"Onion soup, capon stuffed with wild rice, a green salad and fresh strawberries for dessert."

"How does that sound to you?" he asked Victoria.

"Wonderful."

"Set another place. Miss Dunbarr will be joining me."

"The place has already been set," Edo said softly, allowing himself a fleeting smile.

During dinner they talked about which artists had made deals with which producers, how much they were getting, how good was their last film and what was the potential of their next; and when this grew dull, they turned to who was sleeping with whom and how long they would continue to do so; for it was between these two branches that the emaciated sparrow of Hollywood conversation fluttered for sustenance.

When they had finished their coffee, Billy said, "Still feel like a sauna?"

Victoria smiled and nodded.

Billy told Edo to prepare the sauna, and Edo replied that the sauna had already been prepared, and if there was no further use for him, he would be retiring.

Billy showed Victoria to a dressing room supplied with an assortment of towels and robes; she thanked him primly and shut the door behind her while she changed. Billy slipped out of his clothes and moved, naked, toward the sauna—it opened off the bedroom—pausing as he caught a glimpse of himself in the mirror.

He was pleased to see how he had maintained the slim, tightly muscled form of his youth; this was the payoff for all the tedious hours swimming laps in the pool, all the painful tennis elbows, all the desserts he had denied himself. But then he looked again and he saw that the skin was bagging at his belly; and his cock, which in his youth would have curved heavenward in expectation, pointed down, only half-hard with desire. Suddenly he thought he could see the outline of his bones beneath his flesh, the organs in their cage of brittle white sticks, ever deteriorating, the red ball of a heart muscle growing weary, the miles of veins and arteries worn thin by the never-ending flow of blood. The thought flashed in his mind that, despite all the movies he had made and the women he had screwed, the machinery was wearing out, he was going to die and he was going to die soon. In the material faith he lived by, death meant annihilation, a cessation of consciousness so complete and total that it chilled him even to contemplate it. But no sooner had this thought of Death crept in than it was expelled by the sentries that guarded his peace of mind, and in its place they erected dreams of new movies, bigger grosses, and the marvelous woman he would soon experience; in less than a minute, order had been restored, and Billy Rosenblatt was feeling his old self again, cocky and confident, ready for anything.

The sauna was no bigger than a walk-in closet, a room paneled in raw redwood with a metal bucket containing stones which, heated electrically, raised the temperature of the air to a dry one hundred and sixty degrees. Billy sat on a redwood bench, the towel across his lap. Within minutes rivulets of sweat ran from under his arms, and his hair hung in wet tendrils down his forehead. Now the door swung open and Victoria entered wearing only a towel. She had plaited her hair, and coiled the braid on top of her head, leaving her neck and shoulders bare, so that he could admire their perfect shape. Her legs were smooth and straight, her feet remarkably delicate. She sat down beside him, rearranging the towel modestly to cover the space between her legs, and smiled at him.

"This is divine," she said.

"It helps me unwind," he agreed.

"You work under such pressure, poor baby."

She looked down at his lap, where a tent had been erected on the terry-cloth plain, and her smile grew wider.

"You know," Billy said, "you look good in a towel."

"I look better without one," Victoria said, and let it fall.

She sat up straight and tall, arching her back, pulling back her shoulders so that her breasts rose at an impossible angle.

Billy felt his pulse accelerate, and the tent in his lap grow into a circus big-top.

"I know what you're wondering," Victoria said. "Nobody can believe they're real. Know how silicone implants feel like rocks sort of?"

Billy nodded. He had made love to women with siliconed breasts, and always felt vaguely cheated; though huge, the glands were, as a rule, inhumanly rigid and refused to sway to gravity.

"Well, feel mine," she said. "Go ahead, it's all right."

Invited thus, he felt like a bashful teen again. He reached out and caressed the surface, the remarkable softness.

"Go ahead," she purred, "don't be shy."

He placed his hand around it, squeezing ever so gently, and it gave like a pillow of the finest goose down, yet returned to shape with extraordinary resiliency.

"Ohhh," she moaned. "Do it again."

He reached out, found the outline of the nipple perfectly recessed into the aureola and, taking it between his thumb and first finger, pulled gently upon it.

"Oh, God," she gasped.

He rolled it back and forth as though it were a little ball of clay he was kneading into shape, and it grew and stiffened until finally the entire aureola had swelled up red and ridged as a cinnamon cookie.

Until this moment she had sat apart from him, her hands at her sides, her eyes closed, swaying slightly and making soft, inarticulate sounds. Now she opened her eyes and, smiling slyly, moved him into a reclining position on the bench, as a mother would a baby.

"Just relax," she said, kneeling on the floor beside him, "forget about everything. Go on, close your eyes. That's right."

Billy felt the sweat-soaked towel being pulled away, and he heard the sigh of admiration. Soft, moist lips closed around the head of his cock, while a gentle hand cupped his balls.

"Before you go any further," he said, his sense of humor triumphing over his lust, "you better ask me about the part."

The lips were gone. He opened his eyes and saw Victoria standing as far from him as the small room allowed, staring at him with hurt and anger.

"Is that all you think this is?" she said. "Some dumb, busty starlet bedding down the producer so she'll get the part?"

"I'd never call you dumb," Billy said.

Victoria grabbed the towel from the bench, wrapped it around her and marched out of the sauna, slamming the door behind her —or at least she would have slammed it if not for the pneumatic device that closed it slowly.

Billy grabbed his own towel and followed her into the bedroom, calling, "Wait a second!"

She turned, and spit out the words: "If that's all you think of me, then I don't want the damn part! Who the hell needs it? I am an actress and a damn good one! And I've got my integrity and self-respect—despite people like you!"

Her voice was trembling, her eyes were clouding with tears; she looked like a little girl caught in a lie, strangely touching. Any anger Billy might have had dissolved at that moment.

"Take it easy," he said. "Before you go steaming off, let me say my piece. The fact is, I thought you were very good today. So did Saltzberger. And Harris is helplessly in love with you."

"He is?"

"We were all very impressed."

"Then I've got the part?"

"You've got the part—of Lydia, the mistress. It's a great part, with all kinds of depth to it. It's the kind of part that could get you *best supporting actress*."

"But I don't want Lydia. I want Jacqueline."

"You're completely wrong for it. You're too tall . . ."

"My leading man could stand on a box like Alan Ladd used to do."

"And you're too beautiful . . ."

"I don't have to be, I can look ugly."

"And Rebecca Weiss is so perfect we never even considered another actress."

"Let me test again!" As she implored, she moved ever closer, and now she was standing in front of him. "I can do better, I swear I can."

"Victoria, no! I have made up my mind and there is no more discussion about it. Rebecca Weiss is Jacqueline. And we would all be delighted if you would take the part of Lydia."

Victoria looked at her feet and shook her head.

"Let me tell you a story about my family," he said, sitting down on the bed and motioning for her to sit beside him. "I have four sisters, two of them older then I am, two younger. The youngest one's named Ruth, and being the baby of the family, she was always my parents' favorite. Amy, who was a year older than Ruthie, couldn't stand her being the center of attention. She'd always try to get Ruthie into trouble. When Ruthie had a boyfriend, Amy would try to steal him away; when Ruthie made mischief Amy would make sure Mom found out. Then, when Ruthie was sixteen, she came down with tuberculosis."

"Oh, I'm sorry," Victoria said.

"Don't worry. She recovered and today she's living in Palm Springs, and she's got a fat stock portfolio and twelve grandchildren who adore her. But when she got sick it was the height of the Depression and Mom and Pop didn't have a dime. I remember like it was yesterday. I came home late from work—I was pushing a cart in the garment district . . ."

"You did that?" Victoria said, incredulous.

"I did worse things than that," Billy said, laughing. "Anyway, I came home late from work and Amy was sitting in the kitchen with all the lights out, crying and crying. I asked her what was wrong and she said, *I want to have tuberculosis too*. I think that's what this is all about. Rebecca's *your* baby sister and you want tuberculosis too."

She smiled at Billy and took his hand. "You're very nice. I'm sorry that I acted like a lunatic. Sometimes I just go crazy. It's so hard being an actress and getting rejected all the time, and being helpless to do anything about it. Billy? One more thing and then I won't mention it again."

"All right."

"If Rebecca doesn't want it—or if something happens to her—then will you reconsider me for the part?"

Billy sighed but kept smiling.

"I'm afraid that if I say yes, you'll kill her."

Victoria laughed. "I'm not that bad, am I?"

"All right. If she doesn't want it, or if something happens to her, then we will reconsider. All I'm saying is *reconsider;* I'm not making any promises."

"You're very nice," she said again, and brought her mouth to his. Towels fell away, and soon they were rolling on the bed, tight in each other's embrace. Victoria, enflamed beyond endurance by the possibility of Rebecca's part, begged for Billy to penetrate her; when he didn't, she investigated and found that his cock, exhausted by the excitement of the sauna earlier that evening, could not stay sufficiently rigid, despite all efforts of her mouth and her fingertips. Always the gentleman, Billy made her lie back on the bed, and concentrated on bringing her to orgasm by nibbling at the rosebud between her legs. She asked for him to insert a finger and he complied; she asked for another, and soon he had inserted his whole fist and still she was not satisfied.

She murmured a man's name and Billy thought that, in her passion, she was confusing him with another lover; then he realized whom she had in mind, the most powerful man in Hollywood, short of stature, cold to the touch, almost featureless, with a skin like burnished gold. He ran to the living room, grabbed an Oscar off the mantelpiece (incidentally it was for *Barracuda*, Best Movie, 1946) and, returning to the bedroom, inserted it slowly, head first, into the moist mouth between her legs. Deeper and deeper he thrust it, reluctant to harm her yet urged on by her hysterical pleading, until the statue was buried nearly to its base, at which moment she came, screaming and shuddering with pleasure, and then, exhausted, satisfied, spent, went limp.

·5·

Your servitude means nothing to me, the Beast grumbled, but there is one condition under which I shall let you go: that is if your loveliest daughter, the one named Beauty, comes to suffer in your stead. If she refuses, you will return in three months' time to meet your death. Do not even consider trying to deceive me, for my power is such that I will find you, even in faraway lands, and bring you hence.

The merchant had no mind to sacrifice his favorite daughter to the ugly monster, but he thought that, since he must die in either case, he would obtain the respite that he should have the satisfaction of seeing her once more.

Then the Beast told him he might go, and the merchant took his horse from the stable, leaving the miraculous place with grief equal to the joy he had first felt upon entering it. The horse, of his own accord, took one of the roads of the forest and in a few hours the merchant was home. His children came around him, but instead of receiving their embraces with pleasure, he looked on them, and holding high the thorny rose he had plucked from the Beast's garden, burst into tears. Here, Beauty, said he, take this rose, but reflect not on how dear it is like to cost your unhappy father. Then he related the fatal adventure. Immediately the other daughters set up lamentable outcries and said all manner of ill-natured things to Beauty, blaming her for the terrible fate that had been decreed their father. But Beauty shed not a tear.

*Look, her sisters cried, she weeps not though she herself is the
cause of his death!*

*There is no need to weep, Beauty said calmly, for our father
will not die. Rather will I deliver myself to the monster's fury,
and be peaceful in knowing that my death will save my father's
life and be proof of my love for him.*

*Although I am charmed by Beauty's kind and generous offer,
said the merchant, I cannot yield to it; being old I have but a few
years to lose, which I regret only for your sake, dear children.*

*Beauty smiled at his words and said nothing more; that night
while the rest of the family was fast asleep, she set out for the
enchanted place from which her father had so recently returned,
prepared for whatever terrible fate lay in wait for her there.*

Leslie slept and woke and slept and woke and always the darkness was absolute, unchanged. He never wore a wrist watch because knowing the time made him anxious, and he was usually
anxious enough without it; but now he would have given anything
for the comforting blue iridescence of the dial, as much to vary
the darkness as to know the time. By his best estimate, he had
been there two days, possibly three. Three days without food,
without drink, without conversation or the sight of another human being, without any solace whatsoever except the thought that
he might be losing some weight. He would have never believed
he had it in him, the ability to endure such torture, and yet he
would endure more. Yes, he would endure death before he agreed
to turn Rebecca over to the hands of this monster, this madman.

Footsteps.

A key in the lock.

Leslie's heart raced with fear. He braced himself for another
confrontation with Beeze, but to his surprise, another voice spoke
to him from the darkness.

"Leslie? Don't be scared—it's me, David."

"How'd you get in?" Leslie said, struggling to his feet. The
pressure on his arm made him want to scream.

"I'm the wine steward. I'm in charge of the key."

He held up one finger and the key dangled from it by a chain,
glinting golden in the dim light from the outer caves.

"What day is it? How long have I been locked up here?"

"Ten, twelve hours. It's two o'clock, Wednesday morning, November twenty-eighth."

"That's all?" He sounded disappointed. "Isn't that funny. I was sure . . ."

"Listen," David interrupted, "there's no time for talk. Beeze is asleep—he hardly ever sleeps—and he'll be up in an hour, two at the most. By then you'd better be miles from here. Can you walk?"

"Not twenty miles I can't."

"A couple of hundred yards?"

"Sure."

"Then follow me."

Something clicked in David's hand and a flashlight beam illuminated their path. Leslie followed him out of the wine cellar, through a labyrinth of caves made all the eerier by the dim yellow light the other man carried. It cast monstrous shadows of them against the walls, shadows that seemed to pursue them from chamber to chamber, as though they were the spirits of Beeze and his butler, vigilant even in sleep.

"That Beeze is a lunatic," Leslie whispered angrily, and his whisper reverberated from every wall and sent a hundred bats racing from their homes in the timbers.

"He's not like us," David said, guardedly, "but he's not crazy. He's sort of a different species, the way a wolf is different from a dog. Henri's known him for years and says he was always like that, even before his accident."

"Where are we going?"

"There's a jeep in one of these caves. Beeze keeps it for emergencies, in case anything happens to the helicopter. That's another example of how he's different. Anybody else would have built a garage onto the house. But Beeze didn't want to disturb the symmetry, so he brought in a construction crew—blindfolded!—and had them dig another cave under the house, with a tunnel leading to the surface, and a trick door, like something out of a James Bond movie. It's a good thing for us. I don't think we'd ever get out if we had to go upstairs. He has ears like a cat."

They came to a fork, a tunnel opening on either side, and David hesitated with indecision.

"Shit. I don't know. I think it's the one to the right."

Just when Leslie had decided that his friend had made the wrong choice, and that they were hopelessly lost in the labyrinth, doomed to wander about until found by Beeze, who would mock them and torture them and put them to death, just then the tunnel opened onto a cave, and a sweep of David's flashlight revealed a jeep and a pick-up truck, in addition to a five-hundred-gallon fuel tank and the various jacks, air pumps, ignition timers and other equipment that are the standard fixtures of a garage.

"Do you know how to drive one of these?" David said, helping Leslie into the jeep.

"All the boys in Los Angeles have CJs and Land Rovers."

"Really?" David said, with interest.

"It's sort of gay-macho-chic. You know, crew cuts and lumberjack shirts, jeans and pick-up trucks."

"Really!" He sighed. "I'd love to see it."

"You're coming with me, aren't you?"

"No."

"What do you mean? You can't stay here. When Beeze finds out you helped me escape, he'll kill you."

"No he won't. We're toys to him. Sometimes he punishes us terribly for inconsequential things, and sometimes he forgives us when we disobey him completely. The only unforgivable crime is telling the world about Beeze."

"I wish you'd come with me," Leslie said, putting a hand on his shoulder. "I could help you find work in L.A. I owe you my life."

"Not unless you get out of here this instant."

"Why won't you come?" Leslie demanded. "I won't go until you tell me why."

"Because of Henri. I couldn't leave him here. We've been through too much together."

"When I get back to L.A., I'll call the police. I won't rest until I know that you and Henri are both safe."

"It's no use," David said. "No one can touch Beeze. You'll see."

"Don't be so sure. I may not have his money, but I have some pretty important friends."

David ignored the boast.

"You'd better go, you haven't much time. You'll see one bright star near the horizon. That's Venus. If you drive toward it you'll come to a pass over the mountains, a dirt road the prospectors used to travel. From the top of the pass you'll see the lights on 127. Hide the jeep at the foot of the mountains and hitch-hike. Otherwise Samson may go after you in the helicopter and spot it. It won't be long before a trucker picks you up."

"I won't feel safe till I'm home in Los Angeles." Leslie noticed the expression on David's face. "What's the matter?"

"I guess it's better I tell you, so you'll be prepared for whatever happens. When I first came to work here, Beeze had a gardener, a man named Simon Hall. The two of them didn't get along and week after week it got worse. Finally, after a fight about some silly thing, Simon packed up a knapsack with food and water and marched out the front door, raving about how he'd get Beeze, how he'd expose him to the newspapers and TV and radio. Beeze didn't do a thing to stop him; he watched as calmly as if it happened every day. But I had a portable radio at the time that I kept hidden in my valise. (It's since disappeared. Beeze has gotten stricter about contact with the outside world.) A few days later I was listening to one of the Vegas stations—that's all you get out here—and I heard a news report about a man who was found in his hotel room, still conscious but losing blood quickly. His tongue had been torn out. The man's name was Simon Hall."

"Oh my God," Leslie whispered.

"You may be perfectly safe when you get back to Los Angeles. But it can't hurt to remember that every big city has a criminal underground that will murder for a fee. Beeze has agents all over the country, unlimited funds, and a morality that's as different from ours as that of a Martian. Now, please, you must go! We've spent far too long talking."

"Thank you," Leslie said, and leaning down from his seat, took David's face in his hands and kissed him. "I'll see you again."

David said nothing. He went to a gray box mounted on the wall, opened it and pressed a switch. A slot appeared, lengthwise across the darkness, and the slot expanded, revealing sage-spotted landscape and starry sky. Venus burned like a beacon on the horizon.

Leslie left the headlights off—after so many hours of total darkness, his eyes had become extraordinarily sensitive—and turned the ignition. The engine sputtered and caught. He engaged the four-wheel drive "low range" in preparation for the tortuous terrain to come and, with a last wave to David, started up the ramp to the outside world.

A banging on the door woke Tommy Troy. He had been having the most marvelous dream: he was an ice-skater again, gliding across an endless, mirror-smooth surface that seemed to be suspended in the clouds, performing a dance of his own invention to the fifth Brandenburg Concerto. His jetés were perfect, his spins dervish-like, and when he leaped, the earth grew small beneath him. Then suddenly the music was interrupted by thunder; it began to rain, and the ice melted, catching his blades, tripping him up, and then he opened his eyes and the thunder was somebody banging on the door. He climbed out of Leslie's bed, pulled on his robe, and ran downstairs shouting, "All right, all right, I'm coming, give me a chance for Christ's sake."

Passing through the living room, he noticed that the mantelpiece clock said ten and his anger was deflated. He had imagined that the hour was closer to seven or six, because of the dryness of his eyes, the bleariness of his perceptions. In fact, he himself was at fault for having gone to sleep so late. He had been out most of the night practicing his secret profession, the profession he dared not let Leslie learn about for fear he would not understand. When Leslie was around, he confined his "work" to Thursday nights, when he was supposed to be at acting class. But now that Leslie was gone, he was working every night with the hope that by the time Leslie returned—and Tommy was certain he would return, the idea of Leslie's loss was simply too terrible to contemplate—he would have had his fill of it, would be prepared to retire forever and devote all his efforts to acting, a profession of which Leslie approved wholeheartedly.

Now looking through the peephole, he saw a hideous old man—made all the more hideous by the swollen perspective of the fisheye lens—his hair combed yet horribly oily, his face covered with a thick gray stubble, his cheek gashed under the eye, the kind of cut one gets from barroom brawling. His suit, a Salvation Army special, was ornate with oily dark spots and crusts of dried vomit.

"Go away," Tommy said, "I don't have any money."

"Are you Billy Boy?" the old man shouted.

"Go away, or I'll call the police."

"I got a note for Billy Boy," the old man said, and it occurred to Tommy that he might actually be saying "Billy Troy" and meaning "Tommy Troy," because, clearly, liquor had eroded the man's faculties.

Tommy put the door on the chain and opened it a few inches.

"What kind of note?"

The old man pulled a piece of paper out of his pocket and unfolded it and squinted at the signature.

"It's from Les-ter . . ."

Tommy caught a glimpse of the handwriting, the indecipherable scrawl which could only be Leslie's, and grabbed for it, heart racing with excitement.

The old man pulled it away, smiling craftily.

"I'm a poor old fellow. Once was a stuntman at Republic till my back gave out. Used to double for Bill Elliott, doubled for Sunset Carson, doubled for Rocky Lane, even doubled for the Duke. Ever see *Night Riders*? That was me, fell eighty feet from a cliff. That's what fixed my back. Hurts awful and that's why I got to take my bourbon. You'd help out a poor old fellow if you had a couple of dollars for a pint of Jim Beam. I don't mean to bother you with my troubles, but I got a daughter who's married to . . ."

"All right, all right."

Tommy shut the door, ran up to the bedroom, got his wallet out of his pants, ran back downstairs and slipped a ten-dollar bill through the door.

"Thank you kindly," the old man said, sticking the money in his sock (Tommy caught a glimpse of purple skin stretched like paper over the bone). But instead of handing him the letter, he continued, "Now, if I had me another ten dollars, I could buy a ticket to Long Beach. Know a woman there who'll wind my clock for ten dollars! That's the only thing that stops the pain, a bottle of Beam and a woman to wind my clock. Ain't had my clock wound in . . ."

Tommy lost control, threw open the door, grabbed the note from the old man and unfolded it, barely able to read it for the trembling of his own hands.

Tommy,
I am hiding in the old Laurel Canyon house. Somebody is after me and I'll explain it all when I see you. Meet me at two o'clock tonight and bring Rebecca Weiss with you. Make sure you're not being followed and don't tell anybody where I am or even that you know I'm alive. Bring food.

Love,

Leslie

The old man smiled at him and said, "Now, that's worth a pint o' Beam, ain't it?"

Late that night Tommy drove Rebecca up to the old Laurel Canyon house. It was a three-story wood frame house of thirties vintage, with front porch and curlicue trim, and gables on the roof, and in its heyday it must have been a pretty little place. But now, after years of being abandoned, it looked like nothing so much as a haunted house in a movie, the porch collapsed, the shutters hanging at angles, windows broken by kids, paint peeling like a leper's skin. It was one of the places where gay men went for the ritual that was exclusively theirs, the sprees of compulsive, anonymous sexual couplings. It was, in their parlance, a meat rack; little known, scarcely as popular as the dark cave beneath the Santa Monica pier, the glades of Greenstone Park, the back alleys of Bierce Place, but a meat rack nonetheless. On certain nights men would pass through it in a shadowy ballet, finding each other, enjoying a moment of ecstasy, and moving on with never so much as a word exchanged.

The old house was one of the first places Tommy had visited after defecting from the Ice Follies. Defecting was the word he liked to use because it reminded him of his hero, Baryshnikov, defecting from the Kirov. Tommy had been trained, from the age of eight, to be a ballet dancer (his mother, who taught ballet at the Omaha "Y," had once almost danced with the New York City Center), but a car crash following a bacchanalian high school graduation party permanently impaired the flexibility of his left hip. Knowing that he would never be a great dancer, he turned to his second love, figure skating, where standards were noticeably lower and, while visiting New York, auditioned for the Ice Follies. He toured with them for two years before a destructive affair with another dancer led to his defection. When the troupe arrived in Los Angeles, a town he had always wanted to see, he quietly returned his costumes and disappeared into the streets.

He didn't know where he was going, or what he was going to do, and for the first time in his life he felt so free of guilt that he did a little *pas seul* right there on the sidewalk. A car slowed down at the curb and the driver, a handsome older man with pipe and graying sideburns, offered him a ride.

Don't do it, said a conscience with a pronounced Nebraskan twang, *you know what happens to boys who take lifts from strangers. They'll find you in a ditch with your arms and legs chopped off.*

"The hell with you," Tommy murmured. "I want to go home with him."

"What?" said the driver.

"I was just trying to get rid of somebody I thought I'd left in Omaha."

The driver looked around. "I don't see anybody."

"Well, I think he's finally gone," Tommy said, climbing in beside him.

"What's your name?" the older man said, as they pulled away from the curb.

Tommy hesitated; now that he was a defector, he would need a new name to go with his new life.

"Tommy," he said, after Tom Sawyer, who had been one of his childhood heroes (were Tom and Huck really just good friends?), a symbol of all the adventures he could never have as a boy because he had been so busy practicing ballet. And "Troy," after

Troy Donahue, with whom he had fallen hopelessly in love after seeing *Parrish*.

The older man smiled at the fabrication. "You may think this is a strange request," he said, "but I'd like to watch you make love to other men. Lots of them."

He's a pervert, a Nebraskan voice said, a voice strangely like Tommy's father's. *He'll get you into trouble with the police. Your family will find out and you'll be the scandal of the neighborhood.*

"Sure," Tommy murmured. "I'm game."

"We'll go to the old Laurel Canyon house. Not too many people know about it. And only the best-looking young men go there. You'll be right at home."

Such was Tommy's introduction to gay life in Los Angeles. While the older man stood outside, watching, Tommy strode bravely through the door. At first the place seemed to be empty, but then as his eyes adjusted to the darkness, shadows appeared in the corners and the doorways, men kissing and caressing other men, bringing each other to climax with mouths and fingers and rectums, until it appeared to him as a Greek frieze come to life. He steered one of them in front of the window so the older man could watch. That added to the excitement, and soon there were a dozen of them tangled together in front of the window, exhibiting themselves to the voyeur who stood outside, masturbating. Afterward, the older man dropped Tommy off where he had picked him up, and leaning over to kiss him, slipped his hand into the front of the skater's jeans. Tommy felt paper pressing against his cock; he reached in and took out a fifty-dollar bill.

"Hey . . ." he said, but the older man just smiled and drove away.

All that day Tommy thought about the fifty-dollar bill, guilty and confused about the pleasure he derived from it. Finally he came to the conclusion that he who had felt worthless throughout his childhood, a third-rate ballet dancer, a second-rate figure skater, appeared to be a first-rate hustler, even without trying. He had sold himself in a highly competitive market, and gotten a good price for it. The whole experience made him euphoric. By the time night came, he was determined to try it again. He located a section of Santa Monica Boulevard, directed by a man he met in a bar, yet feeling all the while that he could have found it without help, could have located it solely by an inner radar, so close was the affinity he felt toward it. There he joined an army of young men like himself, and within an hour, what he had suspected was confirmed: that he was special. Whether it was because of his training in the dance, or his looks, or simply because he wasn't particularly interested in the money, he didn't know, but by dawn word had gotten around, and men were seeking him out, offering him more than they offered the others. It was a glorious experience, better than the applause at the end of the third act finale, because it was for him and for him alone. He was finally a featured performer. Yet at the same time he knew that they were buying his youth, and in a few years he would stand on this same corner, his shirt off to exhibit his thin muscular chest, and they would drive by without slowing down. Yes, it was a heady addiction, but one from which he would have to break himself before it broke him.

He parked a hundred yards up the road from the old house and sat there with Rebecca, waiting to see if they were being followed. It sounded like paranoia to him—who would want to harm Leslie?— but he was determined to do precisely as he had been instructed in the letter. When no other cars appeared, he got out, balancing a bag of groceries, helped Rebecca out the other door, and together they walked back to the weedy lot, wrapping sweaters and jackets tight to ward off the chill of a California night. This was the first time they had met, although Leslie had already told each one so much about the other that they felt like childhood friends. All evening they had talked about Leslie, about who was after him and why, and now, suddenly talked out, they were as silent as strangers on a blind date. Far away someone gunned a motorcycle; a dog barked furiously and then the only sound was their own footsteps in the gravel. When they came to the house, Tommy forced the gate of the picket fence, and the hinges cried like animals in pain.

"Spoo-ky," Rebecca whispered, and Tommy laughed, letting off nervous energy. He wondered what children had once played with the wagon that now lay rusting in the tall brown grass.

The front steps were warped, the part of the porch still standing sagged dangerously under their weight. Inside, veils of spiderwebs fell across their faces, refusing to be brushed away. The rooms were empty of furniture, drapes or pictures, but the walls had been covered with spray-painted graffiti and the floor was littered with beer bottles, porn magazines, food wrappers and other trash. A circle of rocks had been arranged in the fireplace for cooking, and the floor was charred where the fire had escaped its confines. The air smelled of urine and amylnitrite and, curiously, the jasmine blooming in the yard across the way. He was relieved to see that there were no other men present, relieved for Rebecca's sake (although she probably would have been amused by it), relieved because of his own possessive feelings toward Leslie. Whether this absence was due to the place's having passed out of fashion or because of the late hour, or possibly a recent police bust, he didn't know.

"Leslie?" Rebecca called, in a cautious whisper.

Something thumped in the next room. Tommy moved in front of her, protectively, and advanced on the door, saying, "Who's there?"

"It's me and Mr. Beam. We're having a party and everybody's invited."

The old man who had delivered the note to Tommy earlier that day staggered through the door, holding a bottle of bourbon and displaying a grotesque crescent of crooked yellow teeth.

"Don't worry," Tommy said to Rebecca, "he's harmless." And to the vagrant he said, "All right. Where's Leslie? If anything happened to him, I swear to God, I'll kill you."

"It won't be necessary," said a voice behind them. They turned around at once, and there was Leslie, grinning at them. His face and his clothes were covered with grit, and his left arm hung in a sling torn from his pants leg.

They ran over to him and embraced him carefully, because of his arm, and all three laughed with joy and relief, and told one another all the things they wanted to hear at such a time. Leslie gave the old man a dollar to make him go away, and led his friends to a small room in the rear of the house, a room that had once been servants quarters. Unlike the other rooms, it had one piece of furniture, a bed with a frame of tubular steel and a mattress on which Leslie had spread newspaper to insulate himself from whatever vermin dwelt within.

Tommy looked around in amazement and disgust. "God, Leslie, how long have you been here?"

"I got back this morning."

"From where?" Rebecca said. "What's this about people following you?"

Leslie smiled. "Well, it's quite a story. Sit down and make yourselves comfortable. I'd offer you something to drink . . ." He looked around and shrugged; it was particularly funny because he had a reputation for being a wonderful host.

"I brought some orange juice," Tommy said, digging into the shopping bag, "and roast beef sandwiches and oranges and apples and cheese cake."

"So you forgive me for missing Thanksgiving?" Leslie asked.

"I knew it was something terrible when you didn't show up."

"I was hoping you'd figure that out. I swear, we'll have a real bash for Christmas. Give me some orange juice. I haven't had anything to drink all day except a little bourbon. That old guy's been selling it to me for a dollar a shot and I'm too tired to negotiate."

"I never thought I'd see the day," Rebecca said, smiling.

"Well, don't worry. I'll be back to my old self in no time. Just get me a telephone and a producer to haggle with."

"It's a good thing you didn't break your dialing arm," Tommy said.

"Which reminds me," Leslie went on, his mouth full of sandwich. "Did you test for *The Other Woman?*"

Rebecca nodded.

Leslie sighed. "That's a weight off my mind. I was worried you wouldn't get there."

"Me?" she said in mock amazement. "Not get there? What could ever give you that idea?"

"Just a crazy thought."

"Not only did I get there," she went on, casually, "but I got the part."

"Naturally," Leslie said, as though he had known it all along.

"I signed the deal memo yesterday," she continued, when congratulations had been completed.

"Without letting me look at it?"

"I didn't know when you'd be back—or if you'd ever be back. But Sheila went over it a hundred times."

"Sheila," Leslie harrumphed.

"You're always saying Sheila's as good as you are."

"Sheila's good. But Billy Rosenblatt's better. Behind that kindly old I-am-a-legend-of-Hollywood exterior lurks Hitler."

"You told me he was a nice man," Rebecca protested.

"He is—until something goes wrong. Look, that's what making a deal is all about, not what's probably going to happen, but what might happen, the best and the worst possible situations. If the picture does okay, nobody complains. But if the picture makes a hundred million dollars, suddenly everybody's suing everybody else and the precise definition of three points of gross after recoupment means the difference between an ocean-going yacht and a rubber duck for the bathtub. Oh well, it's probably okay. Sheila's good. I just can't stand the idea of anybody making a deal without me."

Leslie ate another sandwich, finished the quart of orange juice and half the cheese cake. Then he leaned back against the graffiti-covered wall, cleared his throat and told them, in all the detail he could recall, what had happened from the time the Lincoln had broken down to his return to Los Angeles (excluding only the ice-cream sundaes he had shared with David, and the amorous clean-up session that followed).

They listened, fascinated, interrupting only to express sympathy for the discomfort Leslie had endured, to assure him that in his place they would have done the same, and simply to exclaim on the extraordinariness of his adventure.

When he finished, Rebecca was irate. "I know a lawyer who will put this Beeze maniac behind bars for the rest of his life. We'll go see him first thing in the morning . . ."

"I'm not going anywhere," Leslie said. "This place may be disgusting, but it's safe."

"You can't stay here forever," Tommy said.

"Why not? You can bring me food. Sheila can come here with the phone messages."

"Leslie," Rebecca said, "be serious. We have to go to a lawyer and you have to go with us, to tell him the story and answer questions. Beeze is hundreds of miles away from here—what harm can he possibly do?"

"I don't intend to find out."

"Look," Tommy said reasonably, "if he's really so shy about making himself known, he'll probably want to forget it ever happened."

"You don't know Beeze. He's not the kind who forgets anything."

"You're being paranoid," Rebecca said. "I think you should come home now, and have a good night's sleep in your own bed. In the morning, after we see a lawyer, you can go to the office. Wouldn't you like to go to the office?"

"Would I ever," Leslie said, smiling at the thought of it.

"Then let's go!" Rebecca said, rising to her feet.

"I'm not moving."

Argue as they would, he was adamant. Finally they struck on a bargain: they would bring him food and messages from the office and whatever else he needed for one week and if, at the end of that time, no one had seen or heard from Beeze, then Leslie would come out of hiding.

As they were leaving, Leslie asked if he could speak with Tommy privately for a moment. Rebecca, understanding perfectly, said she'd wait in the car.

"I missed you so much," Tommy whispered, when they were alone.

Leslie took him in his arms and kissed him. Afterward he said, "Nothing's changed, has it?"

"Nothing."

"We're still a couple?"

"A couple of lunatics."

"Seriously."

"For as long as you want me," Tommy said, "I'm yours."

"If I ask you a question, will you tell me the truth?"

Tommy stiffened, anticipating what would come next.

"Since I disappeared," Leslie went on, "have you been with other men?"

"Damn it," Tommy said, turning away from him, "what's the difference? Why do you always have to be cross-examining me like I was some kind of criminal? Can't you just trust me? Can't you, please?"

"I'm sorry," Leslie said. "That was stupid of me. I'll never ask you again. Forgive me?"

Tommy sighed, nodded. "Forgiven."

"Could I stay at your house tonight?" Rebecca asked. She was staring out the window at her reflection, pierced by the lights of passing cars, as Tommy drove them back to town. "I'm scared—I don't want to be alone."

"You know you can, you don't even have to ask." He thought for a moment. "Didn't Leslie say you had a roommate?"

"Victoria. The kind of girl who always manages to be somewhere else when you need her. Tonight she's at a pajama party with her new love."

"Sounds like there's a little friction."

"I'm just kidding. She's my best friend in the world. I'll tell you what happened last week. During my test for *The Other Woman* I was supposed to gulp down a glass of champagne, only somebody filled it with mouthwash! Can you imagine? I thought I'd vomit my guts out right on camera."

"Why would anybody do that?"

"Let's just say there are a lot of people who'd like to see me fail. Victoria had the audition before me and she noticed Billy Rosenblatt's assistant, this skinny red-headed girl who's always so ass-kissing sweet, filling the glass. You see, you have to know who your real friends are. That's the way this business is."

"I guess so," Tommy agreed.

Tommy and Leslie lived in a white stucco apartment complex on Fountain Avenue, grandly named El Palacio and referred to, by certain wags, as El Fellatio, in reference to its large gay population. It was Moorish in style, horseshoe-shaped, with a garden in the middle, and a fountain where a little plaster cherub had peed continuously until the drought of '77, at which time he had been disconnected. Their apartment was an elegantly appointed corner duplex. Tommy and Rebecca reached it, after parking in the subterranean garage, by staircase and corridor.

"It's open," Rebecca said, trying the door.

"That's impossible." Tommy was searching for his keys. "I always lock it when I go out. You know what kind of crazies live in West Hollywood."

"See for yourself."

Tommy tried the door and it swung open. The doorframe around the lock, he noticed, was hacked to splinters.

"Oh my God," Rebecca said.

The velvet sofas had been stabbed, so that they disgorged stuffing, like pus from various wounds, and Leslie's precious antique film projector had been smashed against the floor, reduced to a pile of gears, frayed wires, cracked lenses. In the dining room a table Leslie had ordered specially made, because he could not find one long enough to seat all his clients and friends at once, had obscenities gouged deep in its surface. On the Oriental rug beyond it, a pile of human feces, still fresh, steamed in the cool night air.

"Now I know how it feels to be raped," Tommy said.

Rebecca was too angry to comment.

Then Tommy remembered something. "The Marilyn autograph," he said, running for the stairs. He was referring to Leslie's prized possession, a picture of Marilyn Monroe which she had autographed to him personally, shortly before her death. Rebecca followed Tommy up the stairs and stood at the bedroom door while he knelt, picking through the shredded papers on the floor until he found a corner of the picture, an eight-by-ten glossy, and another corner, and another. Trying to reassemble this impossible jigsaw, he began to cry. Rebecca hugged him and Tommy murmured, "This will break his heart, it really will."

Two men from the sheriff's office arrived in fifteen minutes. Tommy took one look at them and knew it was all a waste of time; he saw the homophobia in their eyes, the hatred and contempt, the envy of the luxurious apartment. He could hear them thinking, *We risk our lives for pennies while these faggots live like kings. They deserve everything that's coming to them.* They frightened him almost as much as the anonymous criminals who had ravaged the apartment. Yet they went about their jobs in a professional way, asking questions, making notes, searching for evidence, fingerprinting.

All the time Rebecca remained silent; but as they were preparing to leave, she could no longer contain herself and began to tell Leslie's story to them in a wild, disconnected way. When she came to the part about his meeting Beeze, Beeze who wore a mask and played the violin, the first deputy interrupted her.

"Are you under the influence of drugs?" he asked. "Marijuana, hashish, LSD?"

"No," she said, "I am not, damn it! What I am saying is the truth! People are trying to kill my friend Leslie and you've got to help him!"

"Is it true that people are trying to kill you?" he said to Tommy.

"No, they're trying to kill Leslie. I'm Tommy."

"And this is your apartment?"

"It's Leslie's apartment. I live here with him."

"Where's Leslie?" the first deputy said.

Tommy glanced at Rebecca; neither of them said a word.

"Do you want to press charges against this Beeze?"

"No," Tommy said, after a minute.

"Then I guess we'll be going," the first deputy said.

"Hey, aren't you an actress?" the second deputy said. "Weren't you on that TV show about the skin-divers?"

"Yes," Rebecca said, tight-lipped with anger.

"Could I have your autograph for my kid? I try and get him an autograph every time I meet a celebrity."

Rebecca gripped the pen and pressed it against the paper—a parking summons—so hard her hand shook.

"Thanks," the second deputy said. "Get in touch with us if there's any more trouble."

"I should have known that would happen," Tommy said, after they had left. "If there's one thing an L.A. cop hates more than a murderer or a rapist or a child molester, it's a well-to-do fag."

"I got him a little," Rebecca said. "I signed it Veronica Lake."

"He probably thinks you *are* Veronica Lake. Well, what do we do now?"

"My daddy's staying at the Beverly Wilshire. When it gets to be a reasonable hour, we'll go see him. He'll fix everything, you'll see. He'll know exactly what to do. In the meantime you come and sleep at my house."

Aaron Weiss was sitting at the little writing desk, toiling over a piece of paper, when he heard a knock on the door. He got up to answer it, delighted at being interrupted. If he had been sketching on that piece of paper, he might have ignored the door altogether, but he wasn't sketching, he was writing, a skill for which he had little talent and less patience, and any excuse to stop was welcome. He had been up for a few hours, but he still wore his pajamas and a striped terry-cloth bathrobe. A room service tray with a carafe of cold coffee, a cantaloupe rind, and a half-eaten bran muffin sat on top of the television. He opened the door and was delighted to see Rebecca, in jeans and a frilly blouse. She looked as if she hadn't slept in days, but he decided to make no mention of it, knowing how sensitive she was to criticism about her looks.

"How's my little mouse?" he said, wrapping her in his burly arms.

"Oh, Daddy, I'm so glad to see you. I've been so scared."

"Scared, Mouse?" He stood back and looked at her, eyebrows raised in disbelief. "Come on in and tell me all about it."

"Where's Mom?"

"Down on Rodeo, shopping for a beige slip. She tried on her gown this morning and discovered that the black slip showed through. Panic and hysteria. I hope you have something picked out. It doesn't have to be an evening gown, but it should be something nice. No jeans. Is it all right for a father to ask his daughter not to wear jeans?"

"It's fine, Daddy, but what are you talking about?"

"Tonight. The Jewish Humanist Award. You didn't forget, did you?"

"Oh, that," Rebecca lied. "No, I didn't forget. I thought I'd wear my forties black silk suit. That's pretty formal."

"Will your mother like it? She's nervous enough already and I don't want anything to upset her. As for me, I couldn't care less. I think this whole award business is horseshit. It's the work that counts, never forget that, Mouse. Hey, have you had breakfast? I'll send down for room service."

"No, Daddy, I'm not hungry."

"You sure? Are you getting enough to eat? You look skinny."

"I weigh what I always weigh."

"Well, that's good."

"Daddy? I need your help. I'm really scared."

"Sit down here and tell me everything." His voice was filled with concern. He seated her on the couch and sat down beside her.

"It's Leslie," she said.

"I don't like to say I told you so, but *fagalas* will always cause you grief."

"Daddy," she cried in frustration, "please, listen! He's in trouble and we can't go to the police, and we can't go to a lawyer, and you're the only person I can turn to."

"Don't worry, Mouse," he said, taking her hand, squeezing it. "I'll make it better—don't I always?"

"You do, Daddy."

"Remember when you were a little thing, and you'd scrape your knee roller-skating, and you'd come into the studio crying for me? You never went to your mother. You'd come to me and I'd give you a little kiss on the knee—like that—and then I'd tell you the story about the roller-skating bears in the Russian circus . . ."

"Daddy, not now, there's not time."

"Of course there isn't. So, what kind of trouble is Leslie in? Tell me the whole story from beginning to end."

So Rebecca did. At first Aaron listened intently, brow furrowed in concentration. Then he took out his pipe, scraped it, reamed it, filled it and tamped it, puffed up a head of smoke and relaxed back into his listening pose. As Rebecca continued with her narrative, he rose and strolled around the living room, pausing to gaze out the window at the pool below and murmur "Beautiful day." Then he wandered over to the small writing desk in the corner and leaned over it, gazing at a piece of paper. Suddenly decisive, he picked up the paper and turned to face his daughter.

"Mouse," he said, interrupting her, "can I read you something? I'd love your opinion."

"But, Daddy, I was in the middle of . . ."

"I know, I know. This will just take a minute. It's my acceptance speech. I'm having trouble with the tone. Now, the problem is I'd like to talk about my pacifist beliefs, but I want them to know that I hang tough on the Middle East. Or maybe I should keep the whole thing simple and nonpolitical? Tell me what you think. I start like this . . ."

He put his bifocals on his nose and, squinting at the paper, read:

"Fellow Jews, how can I express the honor I feel at having been chosen as a recipient of this award? Today the traditional view of the Artist as a self-centered egotist is no longer viable . . . Rebecca?"

He heard the door slam and looked up. The room was empty; she had left. By the time he had put on his slippers and got out into the hall, the elevator door was closing. "Wait!" he called, but he was too late. He sighed and shuffled back inside, depressed. Why did she always behave thus, with such disrespect, such lack of concern? To walk out in the middle of his speech! Surely he had always done everything he could for her, given her every advantage. Perhaps that was the problem: perhaps he had given her too much. Another sigh, a sigh so deep, so ancient that certainly the Jews who worked in the shadows of the great pyramids, hauling those big blocks of stone, must have sighed just so over their own daughters. He returned to the writing desk, thinking that surely there was no clay as difficult to shape as that of a growing child.

Victoria came home from shopping at six that evening, eager to try on the outfit she had just bought, a snappy yellow T-shirt with "Joe's garage" embroidered on the back, a pair of red shorts with yellow trim, and bright-red roller skates that laced all the way up the ankle. Her new boyfriend, a TV producer named Freddy Dilucci, had invited her to a "roller-disco" party where celebrities would skate to disco music until the wee hours of the morning, and she was determined to be the center of attention.

When she called "Anybody home?" there was no answer, but the light was on in the living room and the television was speaking in tinny tones. Puzzled, she walked inside and found Rebecca sitting in the easy chair, drinking a Margarita and ignoring the news. Apparently she also had plans for the evening, for she was wearing one of her best outfits, a black silk moiré pattern suit cut in forties style, shoulder pads and all, with nothing underneath but a lacy-topped camisole. She had stuck rhinestone clips in her bushy hair and she wore black stockings with clocks, and spike heels that made her almost as tall as a normal person (she liked to quip).

"Wait till you see what I bought at Fred Segal's," Vicky said, bounding into the living room.

Rebecca turned to the look at her and Victoria took in the eyes, red from weeping, the heavy mascara running like clown's make-up, the almost empty blender jar which indicated that the present Margarita was not the first.

Her initial reaction was an inner groan: *Oh, no, not this again, not another jag of misery, of weeping, of suicide threats; what a bore*. For an instant Vicky even felt that Rebecca was doing it on purpose, to spoil her own gay mood. But then some subtle motion, a futile gesture of the hands, gave her sudden awareness of the intensity of Rebecca's pain. She knelt beside the easy chair, stroking Rebecca's hair, and said, "Baby, what's wrong?"

"Everything," Rebecca said, and started to cry.

"That's right," Victoria said, taking Becky's head on her shoulder, "have a good cry, get it out of your system."

Rebecca raised her head. "I got mascara all over your blouse."

"It's dirty anyway. Now tell me what's the matter."

"Nobody will listen, nobody cares. I told the police and they thought I was stoned, and I told my father but he was too busy, and now Leslie's life is in danger and I've got to spend the evening at this stupid award ceremony."

"Is that why the limousine's out front?"

"Limousine?" Eyes wide with terror, she ran to the window, pulled back the curtains and looked out. Then she crumpled, almost as if she had been struck a blow.

"It's him," she whimpered. "It's the servant. He looks just the way Leslie said, like some kind of horrid ape."

"What are you talking about?"

"Don't you see? Leslie escaped and Beeze wants *me* in return. The way they wrecked his apartment was just a warning—next time they'll kill him unless I go—but I can't go, I won't! Oh God, Vicky, help me, help me please . . ."

Victoria took her by the shoulders. "Stop that. You're hysterical. Calm down. Get ahold of yourself and tell me what is going on."

Her voice quivering, she told Victoria all about Leslie's adventures in the desert, and unlike the others, Victoria listened sympathetically, at times urging her on, at times having her backtrack to clarify a point.

"I don't know what to do," Rebecca finished, weeping. "I don't know what to do."

"The way I see it there's only one thing you can do."

"What?"

"Get in the limousine and go. Otherwise he'll kill Leslie. That's what he said and it looks like he means business."

"Well, yes, but you can't really expect me to . . ."

"If you love Leslie as much as you say, it would be a small sacrifice."

"Of course I love Leslie."

"Who knows? It might not be so bad, living in a fabulous mansion with servants and your own screening room. A woman might come to enjoy that kind of life." Her voice was musical, persuasive, almost hypnotic.

"But, Vicky"—she searched for words—"I've got commitments. I've got this award dinner tonight, and *The Other Woman* starts shooting in six weeks."

"It's up to you. You have to decide what's more important. The trouble with being young and single and an actor is that everything you do is for yourself. You become so self-involved. But suppose that once in your life you get a chance to perform some incredible gesture, a gesture that's entirely for the benefit of somebody else, somebody you love. It's a chance to make up for all the selfishness that came before. I'll tell you something, Becky, if it were me, I'd do it in a second."

"I can't," Rebecca said.

"I wish you didn't have to. But think about this: if you don't go, they'll kill Leslie, sure as sure can be. And you'll have to live out your life knowing that you could have saved him and you chose not to."

Rebecca nodded mutely. She seemed to be in a kind of trance.

"I'll get your coat," Victoria said.

"Let us show," Aaron Weiss said in conclusion, "that six thousand years of pacifism won't stop us from fighting for what is rightfully ours. We must be steadfast in our beliefs, valiant in our defense and dauntless in our courage!"

He watched with delight as the audience rose to their feet, cheering. He smiled down at Sylvie, who sat at the table closest the stage, glittering in all her best jewelry, eyes watery with admiration. But then he glanced at the empty seat alongside her, Rebecca's seat, and felt both sad and angry. It was so like her to miss this, his finest moment. Where was she? Probably with a boy.

He remembered the first time he had come to Los Angeles, in 1963, to supervise the mounting of a show of his work at the Los Angeles Art Museum. He had come out alone in April, leaving Sylvie to take care of Rebecca, planning for them both to join him as soon as school recessed. At first the tropical freedom of the place overwhelmed him; he bought modish clothes, rented a convertible, and started an affair with an assistant director at the museum; by the time his family arrived, he was so guilt-ridden that he was delighted to see them.

Sylvie said that Rebecca had been impossible all the time he was away. She was reaching that age when all she could think about was boys, and clearly many of the boys she knew could think of no one but her. Determined to keep his daughter out of trouble, he and Sylvie planned an elaborate activity schedule, swimming in the morning, then shopping and lunch, sightseeing and dinner at a fancy restaurant, a movie and bed. Two weeks of this would be capped off with a three-day trip down the coast to Disneyland, an uncle in San Diego, and the entertaining tackiness of Tijuana. But that final evening in Los Angeles Rebecca was nowhere to be found. They looked all around the hotel and, at twelve-thirty, called the police, who returned her within forty-five minutes, thereby convincing Aaron that they were the greatest police force in the world—the N.Y.P.D. had never recovered anything for him —a fact that he brought up frequently at dinner parties over the years to come, and on the truth of which he often staked his reputation.

Actually the police had unraveled the mystery with a minimum of deductive technique. They asked the man at the front desk, who told them that Rebecca had gone for a ride with a handsome pool attendant, in his red Corvette, and that they were probably parked on the corner of Mulholland and Coldwater, since that was where he usually went (he bragged of his exploits endlessly); and indeed, that was where they found them. What the kids had actually done there Rebecca refused to say, but Sylvie noticed that her daughter's slip was on inside out and informed her husband. Outraged by such goings-on, Aaron flew them all back to New York the next morning, even though it meant their missing the opening of his show, the biggest event of his career.

Maturity, Aaron always used to think, would change her; yet once again she had disappeared, scrapped responsibility to spend an evening with some fellow she probably hadn't known for more than an hour or two, one of these slick L.A. good-for-nothings with the chains around his neck. Well. Clearly he and Sylvie had made some serious mistakes raising their daughter (he knew that Spock was wrong, why hadn't he trusted his instincts?) but the damage was done, and remorse was a parasite that consumed the soul. Having thus put it all behind him, he smiled at the audience and stepped forward to receive his award.

The roller-disco party was being held at a skating rink in Reseda, in the valley. Hundreds of beautiful people (attendance by invitation only) circled the rink, bathed in psychedelic lights and pounding disco music, their nylon wheels hollowly humming, scuffing the high sheen of the oak floor. The most proficient skated in couples while performing elaborate disco steps; the less skilled simply skated; the well-meaning novices, the lion's share of the guests, struggled to keep their feet from slipping out from under them, and eventually thudded to the floor nonetheless.

Victoria belonged to the first group. She had spent a large part of her childhood cruising around various naval bases on roller skates; furthermore, she had taken jazz classes ever since her junior year in high school, when it occurred to her that dancing might be a useful skill for her career. The last few Sundays she had gone down to Venice Beach dressed in nothing but a bikini and her high red skates, to practice steps before the appreciative eyes of the bikers and muscle builders and other inhabitants. Now as she danced and skated, she sensed that she was the center of attention; people were pointing her out, and a photographer from *Newsweek* had shot two rolls of film of her. Her date, Freddy Dilucci, only a fair skater—and not much of a lover either—was having trouble keeping up with her. Since the moment, earlier that evening, when he had announced that he could not use her in his new TV series, she had found him more and more of a burden. She felt as if she could do anything on those skates, and that he was a weight around her ankles, keeping her earthbound when she wanted to fly.

So it was only natural that, spotting a familiar face at the other side of the floor, she took off like a roller-derby queen, leaving the poor fellow in her dust. She came up fast behind her friend and tapped him on the shoulder as she sped past; then she spun around in front of him and grinned.

"Hello, Billy," she said.

"Hello, Victoria. You look sensational. What an outfit."

"Really? It's just some old things I had lying around. Want to dance?"

"Remember, I'm an old man."

"Don't be silly!"

At just that moment the D.J. put a Johnny Mathis song on the phonograph; Billy took Victoria in his arms and began to skate her in graceful circles.

"You're great," she said. "Where'd you learn to skate like that?"

"Delancey Street. If you were eight years old, living on Delancey Street, and you couldn't skate, you were really out of it." (He said "out of it" as if it was something he had read in a screenplay.) "Here I am, sixty years later, discovering that if you live in Beverly Hills and you can't skate, you're really out of it. Guess I've come a long way."

"Oh, Billy."

She put her head on his shoulder and let him guide her around the dance floor. She felt so secure in his arms. There was nothing, she decided, as romantic as an older man who really knew how to dance.

"Billy," she said, "I've got some bad news. Bad news and good news, like they say in the joke."

"Bad news?" He frowned.

"It's Rebecca. She's disappeared."

Billy stopped dancing and held Victoria at arm's length, so he could watch her face.

"What did you say?"

"She's disappeared. I think she went to Europe with her boy-friend or something."

"*The Other Woman* starts shooting in six weeks."

"Well, it's not my fault if she's a little irresponsible."

"Jesus H. Christ," Billy whispered.

"Want to hear the good news?"

"Yeah."

"Well, *I* think you could call it good news."

"Go ahead . . ."

"The good news is—I'd still be willing to play the part of Jacqueline."

A vein, crooked as a worm, was throbbing on Billy's right temple.

"You killed her," he said.

"I don't think that's a very funny joke."

"I'm not joking. You killed her so you could have the part."

Victoria stood up straight and raised her chin. "That's the most insulting thing anybody's ever said to me. Becky's my closest friend in the world. I'd sooner kill myself than see her come to any harm."

"If you're such good friends," Billy said, with remarkably well-controlled rage, "you tell her that I've got a deal memo with her signature on it, and if she's not here bright and early first day of shooting, I'm going to sue her for the entire cost of this film, eight million dollars. Furthermore, I will win the suit—I will *not* settle —and she will be paying off the damages for the rest of her life. You'll tell her that for me, won't you?"

"I—"

But before Victoria could reply, Billy turned his back on her and skated away.

A minute later Freddy Dilucci came straggling along.

"Who were you talking to?" he said.

"Nobody." Vicky smiled at him. He was actually kind of cute, and premature ejaculation was often simply anxiety, or so she had read, and vanished with love and patience. Furthermore, he had two other series in development and they both had perfect parts for her, as far as she was concerned.

"Come on," Vicky said, taking him by the arm. "I'll teach you how to dance on skates."

At Leslie's request, Tommy dropped by the office that evening to pick up the phone messages that had accumulated during Leslie's absence, the scripts, the mail, and most important, a copy of Rebecca's deal memo from Sheila. She was thrilled to learn that her partner was still alive, and furious that Tommy would tell her nothing more. He loaded the trunk with this material—several cartons full—and started for the old house, stopping first at their apartment for a change of clothes for Leslie, then at the Pioneer Fried Chicken stand on Sunset for a family-sized bucket. Even when all these tasks were done, he was still an hour early for their meeting, so he decided to pay a call on Rebecca. Tommy knew she was busy that evening—she had to attend some kind of award ceremony for her father—but she might want to send along a message. It was just getting dark as he drove up Benedict Canyon, the early darkness of late fall. As he turned on to West Wanda, a long black limousine passed him, and even though he saw the driver and the passenger for only a second, their faces remained fixed in his mind as clearly, as permanently, as a snapshot: in front, a giant whose grotesque features conformed perfectly with Leslie's description of Samson, Beeze's servant; and in back, shrinking fearfully into a corner of the seat, Rebecca.

Before he could shout to her or honk, or blink his lights, the limousine had passed. He swerved into the first driveway, made a U-turn and, jamming his foot to the floor so that the tires squealed and let off smoke, he raced back to the corner, where a police car stopped him and ticketed him for a variety of offenses. When, finally, the cop let him go, he drove up and down Benedict Canyon, pressing the speed limit, looking everywhere for the limousine.

An hour later he parked in front of the old house in Laurel Canyon.

"Boy, am I glad to see you," Leslie said. "But where's the stuff you promised to bring?"

"Out in the car."

"Why didn't you bring it in?" Leslie was a little irritated; he longed for those scripts and phone messages like a junkie, his dope.

"No need to," Tommy said grimly. "You can come home now, you're safe."

"What do you mean? Have the police got Beeze?"

"No." Tommy hesitated. "Beeze has Rebecca."

·6·

Beauty was astounded by the splendor of the Beast's magnificent palace, yet at the same time greatly frightened, for she believed that the monster would strip the flesh from her bones that night, and drink her blood for soup; but as she was a mistress of extraordinary resolve, she recommended herself to God and swore not to be uneasy about the little time she had left to live. She thought she might as well walk about till then, viewing this fine castle, which she could not help but admire. She was greatly surprised to see a door over which had been writ "Beauty's Chambers." She was dazzled by its furnishings, which boasted, among other luxuries, a large library, a harpsichord and several music books.

Well, she said to herself, I see they will not let time hang heavy on my hands for want of amusement. Then she reflected, Were I but to stay here a day, there would not have been all these preparations, and this consideration inspired her with fresh courage.

At noon she found dinner ready and while at table was entertained with an excellent concert of music, though no musicians could be seen; but that night as she was sitting down to supper she heard the noise the Beast made and was so frightened she feared she would swoon.

Beauty, said the monster, will you give me leave to watch you sup?

That is as you please, answered Beauty, trembling.

No, replied the Beast, you alone are mistress here; you need

only bid me gone if my presence is troublesome and I will im-
mediately withdraw; for you must find me ugly indeed.

That is true, Beauty answered, for I cannot tell a lie, but I
believe you are very good-natured and I do not find your com-
panionship dreadful in the least.

Eat then, Beauty, said the monster, and endeavor to amuse your-
self in this palace, for everything here is yours, and all that happens
does so to serve your pleasure.

You are very obliging, answered Beauty. I own I am pleased
with your kindness and when I consider it, your deformity scarce
appears.

Yes, yes, said the Beast, my heart is good, but still I am a monster.

Among mankind, said Beauty, there are many who deserve the
name more than you.

Beauty ate a hearty supper and had almost conquered her dread
of her host; but she had like to have fainted away when he said to
her, Beauty, will you be my wife?

She was some time before she durst answer, for she was afraid
of making him angry if she refused. At last, however, she said in
a trembling voice, No.

The poor monster hissed and sighed so frightfully that the whole
palace echoed with it, and she was sure that he would set about
devouring her then and there, and she prayed for her immortal
soul . . .

The limousine stopped at a gas station beyond the last lights of
the sprawling city. It appeared to be perpetually closed, unat-
tended, existing merely to facilitate the transfer between limousine, which Samson parked inside, and helicopter, waiting out
back. Rebecca boarded the aircraft with trepidation, knowing
that the distance between herself and her old life was no longer
bounded by the freeways.

The noise of the rotors was painful, the lurch as they left the
ground, nauseating. Airplanes frightened her enough; this device
which flew without wings was terrifying. Nothing protected her
from the outside but a clear plastic bubble, a soap bubble, she
thought, like children blow, which might pop at any instant. The

machine reminded her, as perhaps helicopters would always remind a generation of Americans, of Vietnam. She remembered Jason Pine, who was tall and slim and soft-spoken, handsome in a hippie sort of way, with shoulder-length hair, and possessed of a gently self-mocking sense of humor. Although he had only just graduated from Wesleyan, he had published a piece in *The New Yorker*. She met him during a Sunday afternoon cookout the spring of her sophomore year, when the trees were weighted down with blossoms. He walked up to her unintroduced and slipped a ring of golden paper around her finger, the ring from the cigar he was smoking. Rebecca, who had a weakness for theatrical gestures, was charmed. All day she strolled the campus with him, relishing the feeling of being reunited with an old friend. They smoked three joints and went to a fancy restaurant in Bronxville, from which they were expelled for giggling and spilling things. Back in her dorm room they made love, but she was so comfortable with him that the sense of sin which made sex so exciting with others was lost. Afterward they went to the dorm lounge and he played old Gershwin songs on the piano (he had paid his tuition playing cocktail piano) while she sang along in her hoarse, sexy cabaret voice. Soon they had attracted a crowd of students. They were so good, they decided, that they would put together an act and tour South America, particularly Argentina, where they would play for Nazis in hiding. And all the time Rebecca was thinking, He's the only lover I've ever had with whom I'd care to be friends. It was all making her a little nervous.

She invited Jason to stay the night, but he declined.

"Do you remember," he said, "the old World War II movie about the boy who's going overseas? His last night in town he meets Judy Garland and realizes she's the one he's been looking for all his life, but he dare not get too involved with her because he doesn't know when or if he'll ever be coming back?"

"That's a pretty corny movie," Rebecca said, grinning.

"It's not a movie."

"Are you going to Vietnam?" she asked, shocked. Nobody she knew had ever gone to war. They went to graduate school or got married and had a baby; they pretended to be crazy or gay or, as a last resort, took off for Canada. This was, for rich New York girls like herself, a television war, a war to watch, to protest, but never to be actually touched by.

"Why?" she demanded.

"Curiosity."

"That's not a real reason."

"All right, a real reason. Let me see. All my life I've been part of the elite. I lived in the wealthiest ghettos, went to the best private schools, the most expensive summer camps. *Sheltered* is too mild a word for it. And I always wondered how it would feel to be—I hate to use such a snotty expression—one of the less fortunate."

"In other words, you're going because you're guilty."

"I'd like to ascribe it to a higher motive, but you may be right. Every time I see those news clips, and all the soldiers are black . . ."

"It's not your fault! We need you. You could do more good writing about the war than you could ever do fighting it."

"That's an argument intellectuals have been using for years."

"I've got a car. We'll start driving tonight and by tomorrow we can be in Canada. I'll wire my father for money. That'll give us time to get on our feet. I'll find a job and you can stay home and write . . ." Rebecca blushed; it was the first time she had ever proposed.

Jason laughed and shook his head. "This is a bargain I've made with myself, and those are the bargains one has to keep. But two years isn't a long time if you stay busy."

"Two years is an eternity if you're in love."

"I've got to go, Rebecca." He put on his jacket. "Will you write me?"

She shook her head. "If you leave tonight, I never want to see you again." Having ruined it all with this impossible ultimatum, she felt comfortable again. "You can come to Canada with me, or you can get out of my life forever."

"Goodbye," he said, and bent forward to kiss her.

She turned her head away.

He left without another word.

She cried half the night, a pleasurable misery, for she was even more masochistic in those days than she was now.

Weeks passed and months, and one night the following year, when she was feeling particularly nostalgic, she picked up the phone, dialed the alumni office at Wesleyan, and asked for Jason Pine's army address. She had decided it might be fun to write him after all. She would send him a picture of herself in a sexy bathing suit, a pinup just like Betty Grable, for him to tape above his bed.

The alumni office put her on hold and returned a moment later. "Deceased," they said.

She asked for his parents' phone number; she had to know more about it. She hung up and called them, identifying herself as an old girl friend. Jason's mother told her matter-of-factly that her son had piloted a helicopter, that the helicopter had been shot down only a few weeks after his arrival in Vietnam, that he was believed to be dead although the body had not been recovered. Then the mother invited Rebecca for dinner—Old Greenwich was only a half-hour away—pleaded, in fact, for her to join them and spend an evening sharing her reminiscences of their son. Rebecca quickly responded that she was too busy, papers, examinations and so forth, but would call them as soon as the work load lightened up. She never spoke to her again.

Now she herself was aloft in one of those screaming carriages of death, but she did not despair. Beeze had made one serious mistake, and that was daring to kidnap her while her father was in town. For her father was the most resourceful, clever, daring man she knew. He would organize an expedition, he would find Beeze's desert estate and rescue her and bring her home in his arms.

The trick was to be brave until help could come. She would allow herself no show of fear, none whatsoever.

"You don't scare me, you ugly son of a bitch," she said to Samson, who was sitting beside her, working the controls with single-minded intensity.

He turned his enormous head, gazed at her for a moment and returned to his instruments. The hurt she saw in his eyes was such that she remained silent the rest of the flight.

A beacon flashed from the darkness and then they were landing before a structure that resembled, outlined against the stars, a massive mausoleum. Samson helped her down from the helicopter and together they crossed the hundred yards of desert separating them from the house, and climbed the stone steps. As if in a dream, she entered the great hall, taking in the precious carpets underfoot, the Grecian busts—some on plinths, some recessed into depressions in the walls—the sweeping staircases on either side of her, their banisters carved in intricate wreaths and floral patterns, the pastoral scenes painted on the ceiling so high overhead. Immediately facing her was a second double door and now, as she stood there, immobile with fear, her heart like a captive bird fluttering against the cage of her chest, the doors opened and a figure strode forward, a tall man in evening clothes with a waxy, frozen face.

"Welcome to my home," he said. "I am Henry Wallace Beeze the Third, and I am deeply honored by your presence. I will do everything within my means to make your stay here as pleasant as possible."

Rebecca stared in disbelief. Was this the terrible Beeze, this man who delivered welcoming addresses like the social director of some snooty British cruise ship?

"You must be hungry after your trip," he continued. "If you like I will have my chef prepare a light supper. Unfortunately I cannot join you because of my—*condition*, but I would be honored to sit with you while you eat. There are so many questions I've wanted to ask you."

He stopped again, waiting for Rebecca's reply, and again she was silent. His mask fascinated her, each eye deep behind its slit, glittering like the water at the bottom of a well. The mouth that remained closed even when he spoke reminded her of the masks the Japanese used in their Noh plays.

"If you don't want to eat right now," he went on, becoming a trifle self-conscious, "Samson will show you to your room and you can familiarize yourself with the accommodations. I'm sure you will find them adequate. You could spend the evening by yourself, if that is what you would like. I have a library with numerous volumes. Or if you would prefer to see a movie, I have a screening room with prints of all the great classics, not to mention many contemporary films."

He finished and the silence grew longer and longer. Finally Rebecca spoke.

"Mr. Beeze," she said in measured tones, "you can steal me away from my home and my friends and my career, and you can keep me prisoner here until I am old and ugly and feeble, but I am not going to eat with you, or read your books, or watch your movies, or be your buddy, because I find you despicable. You tortured my friend Leslie . . ."

"I found him starving in the desert and I gave him food and shelter."

"And you beat him and locked him in the cellar!"

"He stole from me."

"That's no reason to . . ."

"I make my own reason!" Beeze exclaimed, with such a powerful voice that Rebecca involuntarily moved backward. "This is my world and I am the Lord of it, and within these walls all live according to my rules."

"You're crazy," Rebecca whispered, backing away.

"And how would *you* be if fate had turned your face into every child's nightmare?"

"I don't want to talk to you." She was edging toward the staircase.

"You don't want to think about it, because if you do, you'll start to understand me. You want to hate me . . ."

"Yes," she said, "I do, I do!"

"Because hate and fear make you comfortable."

"You're screwing up my chances for the most important role of my life! And I'm going to be thirty tomorrow and then my career will be finished."

"Stop hating for a moment and you'll understand that I brought you here because I'm so lonely that I . . ."

"Shut up!"

She put her hands over her ears, and ran up the staircase nearest her, although she had no idea where it led, simply to get away from him. At the top of the stairs she turned left and ran down the hall. A door opened to her tug; she ran inside, shut it behind her and leaned against it, panting for breath, knees trembling. As the pounding of blood in her ears subsided, she became aware of another sound, a woman singing a lullaby in a lovely voice.

Rebecca was standing in the entrance of a small apartment. Ahead of her was a living room with a dining alcove and a kitchenette, and a hall leading, she assumed, to the bedrooms, for it was from there the singing came. The furniture was modern and expensive, and interspersed with Chinese antiques of even greater value, a vase glazed a brilliant yellow, a wooden writing desk inlaid with intricate ivory designs, a scroll depicting a peasant in a bull cart. She followed the singing and came to a little girl's room, a room full of stuffed animals and pink gingham, dark except for a night light. Standing just outside the door, Rebecca could distinguish the outline of the child beneath the covers, thumb plugged into mouth, hair fanned across the pillows, and a slight woman sitting on the edge of the bed, stroking her back and singing.

The woman glanced up at Rebecca and smiled. She was Oriental, pale-skinned, a classical beauty as fragile as a lotus. Yet there was a boldness, a cleverness in her eyes that seemed at odds with the rest of her. She signaled silence with a finger across her lips, rose from the bedside and left the room, closing the door all but a crack behind her.

They faced each other in the half-light of the hall.

"Please help me," Rebecca said, close to tears.

Although they were strangers, there was an instant rapport. The Chinese woman put her arms around her, saying, "I understand perfectly, you are the new one and of course you are lonely and frightened. I remember how I felt my first day. Come, we'll have some tea." As she spoke, she led Rebecca into the kitchen, where she put on a kettle of water and prepared a lacquered brass pot of exquisite detail. "My name is Ann Chin. My husband Larry is an endocrinologist. He and Dr. Resnick are doing research on organ transplants. I would tell you more, but it's much too complicated for a simple woman like me. Would you care for green tea, Miss Weiss?"

"How do you know my name?"

Ann smiled. "The rumors have been spreading for days. Beeze spends all his time in the screening room watching your movie, *Land of Lost Dreams*, over and over again."

"It must get awfully boring."

"Not for him. He's not like the rest of us."

They sat at the dining-room table and drank from beautiful little cups of lacquered brass. When Rebecca admired them, Ann said, "This is a tea service my father brought with him from the Mainland. He came to America to study medicine at Harvard. He was supposed to return to help the people's revolution, but he fell in love with my mother and she convinced him to stay. She was a waitress at a Chinese restaurant in Cambridge. Isn't that too much? My father spoke beautiful English, but whenever people came to the house selling encyclopedias, or proselytizing for Jehovah's Witnesses, he would pretend to be the cook and he'd say, 'Me so solly, nobody home now, so solly.' "

Both women laughed.

"My husband," Ann continued, "was one of my father's students. After we married, I left college so that I could work and help him finish medical school."

"Why'd you do that?" Rebecca asked, the feminist in her railing.

"Because I wanted to. Don't get the wrong idea. I'm very much in favor of equal rights. But for those of us who do it by choice and not through obligation, child-rearing can be a most wonderful occupation. Attraction becomes greater too, for the husband and wife are polarized like Yin and Yang and, although each may be less by themselves, together they create a more profound unity."

"You don't really believe that?" Rebecca asked with all possible politeness.

"Yes. Although it may be simply an elaborate rationalization. My father and husband both criticize me for having too Byzantine a mind."

"Sometimes I've thought it might be nice," Rebecca admitted, "to say fuck it to the whole stupid thing, the agents and critics and producers, and get knocked up. I'd love to have a little girl like yours."

"That would be impossible," Ann said gravely, "—unless you were Chinese." And she cracked a grin.

Rebecca laughed. "You know what I mean. She's so adorable."

"More adorable when she is asleep."

Rebecca yawned, covering her mouth with the back of her hand.

"And you had better go to sleep too," Ann said. "It's nearly midnight and you must be exhausted. Come, I'll show you to your room. We'll have plenty of time to talk tomorrow, I promise."

Rebecca hesitated. "I don't want to leave here. I'm scared."

"There's nothing to fear—as long as you do what Beeze says. And even if you don't he wouldn't harm you. From what I hear, he's infatuated, like a schoolboy."

"How can you stand it, living like a prisoner?"

"We are not prisoners. Larry needed a great deal of money to carry on his research and Beeze offered to supply it. In addition he gives us all this." She spread her hands, which were tiny and perfect, to take in the suite of rooms, the elegant furnishings. "He is a very generous man."

"But aren't you lonely?"

"Larry is happy because he can do his research. And if my husband is happy, I am happy. There, for once I have made a simple statement. Now let me take you to your room before my husband returns."

"Where is he?" Rebecca asked, as Ann led her down the hallway, padding on slippered feet so small that even Rebecca felt clumsy behind her.

"He and Dr. Resnick are working late in the laboratory. He probably won't be home until one. I am waiting up to prepare him dinner. Jasmine wanted to wait for him too, but she couldn't last. Here we are."

Ann opened the door to the room where Leslie had stayed—Rebecca was awed by the furnishings—and made her promise to come to her suite at any hour if she was frightened, or had trouble sleeping. If, on the other hand, she wanted something to drink, or a hot water bottle, she was to yank the bell pull for Samson, who, Ann assured her, was as gentle as a spaniel. As it turned out, neither alternative was necessary; Rebecca fell asleep moments after her head touched the pillow and slept the night through.

In the morning, when she crawled out of bed, she found six boxes on the floor, the largest of which was four feet in length, the smallest seven inches. Puzzled, she removed an envelope from the smallest box. The card within was of fine vellum with a calligraphic message:

> For Rebecca on her birthday,
>   "Who well lives, long lives; for this age of ours
>   Should not be numbered by years, days and hours."
>   Your humble servant,
>   H. W. Beeze, III

Of course. Today was her thirtieth birthday; in the chaos of recent events she had forgotten entirely. But Beeze hadn't. Somehow, somewhere he had found her presents. Perhaps they were old things that had been lying about the attic, or possibly he had sent Samson to Vegas on a late-night shopping spree.

Or had he known she was coming all along?

She tore the wrapping off the box, opened it and removed, from the velvet cushion within, a choker of several hundred small perfect diamonds. When she held it to the light, the jewels launched a thousand rainbows into her sleep-blurred eyes. She wanted to put it back in the box immediately, for she felt that every moment she held it she became more contaminated by Beeze's wealth, as if it were a disease; still, she couldn't resist seeing it on herself, if just for an instant. She approached the mirror and reached behind her neck to fasten the ribbon of gems, her small breasts rising as she did; then she stood back and posed, and streaks of age in the silvering slivered her reflection like an antique pornographic postcard. Nothing like being naked, she thought, with a million dollars' worth of diamonds around your neck. If Vicky could see this, she'd die. She opened another box and found a dress of red velour, low-cut, with an empire waist and lots of embroidery in gold thread, a princess costume from a fairy tale. Another box contained golden slippers, another box, pearl combs for her hair. She dared not open any of the rest, and those she had opened she repacked quickly, although her fingers hesitated over the fiery stones of the necklace. It was all too tempting. She was frightened by the voice in herself which said, What the hell, this isn't so bad, why break your back acting when you could have a nice little life here? She had to get away immediately, she realized in panic, because every minute she stayed, the voice swayed her more. She remembered stories about P.O.W.'s being isolated from all things familiar, from newspapers and magazines and every memory of home, and subtly indoctrinated until something snapped and their minds were no longer their own. She would have to take drastic measures; otherwise her soul would be stolen, she would die, she would become somebody else and never even know it.

She tugged the bell pull, and by the time Samson knocked she had put on the clothes she was wearing the previous day, the black silk suit. She opened the door and faced him fearlessly.

"Hi. Do me a favor? Take these boxes away."

Samson stared at the boxes and then at her, making no move to comply.

"You heard me," Rebecca insisted. "Take them away. I don't want the stuff."

Reluctantly he gathered up the boxes and moved them outside the door.

"And tell your master I want to see him as soon as he's got a minute free, okay?"

Samson nodded, bowed and left, closing the door behind him.

Rebecca sat on the bed, waiting. A few minutes later there was another knock and Beeze entered. He was wearing gray flannel slacks and a long-sleeved white shirt open a few inches at the collar. Between the collar and the lower edge of the mask, Rebecca could see a triangle of flesh and she watched with perverse fascination the folds of smooth red scar tissue that appeared there and disappeared as he moved; she didn't want to embarrass him by staring, yet she couldn't take her eyes away.

"I hope you slept well, Miss Weiss." The social director again.

"Pretty well, thanks. What do you want from me?"

"Want? Nothing."

"Come on. You went to a lot of trouble to get me here."

"Yes, I suppose I did want something. To see your face in person after watching it on a movie screen. To hear you say words that weren't written for you by a host of writers. I suppose that is what I wanted."

"And what were the words you wanted to hear me say?"

"I'm sorry, I don't understand . . ."

"Sure you do." Now she was the aggressor, moving in on him while he shied away, protecting himself as though her words were stings. "All those presents. It's commerce, right? You're paying me for a service. Well, you've got yourself a bargain. I'll do it for free—I'll do anything to get out of here."

"Really, I don't understand what you're talking about."

"Would once be enough? Twice? I'll really pretend I'm enjoying it."

Savagely she tugged the zipper at the side of her skirt, let the skirt fall to her ankles, and stepping out of it, faced him in camisole and slip. She was a slight figure to begin with and the lacy satin made her all the more frail. Yet she was big with anger, swollen with it, and nobody in his right mind would have crossed her then.

"No," Beeze said, "don't do that, please don't."

"I always said nothing would ever make me sell it, but I was wrong. I'll do anything to get away from you and this grotesque crypt you call home, *anything*—anything your weird little heart desires."

She stepped out of her slip and pulled her camisole over her head.

"No, no," Beeze said, "I don't want that. Please stop—put your clothes back on."

She faced him, her arms folded across her chest, wearing only her panties, the chill of the air conditioning goose-pimpling her flesh, drawing the skin of her nipples tight.

"It's all wrong," he said. "It's not the way I planned. I wanted to be friends, I wanted you to admire me and . . ." His voice choked and he could say no more. He stumbled backward, averted his eyes, fled the room.

"Welcome to our little family," Henri the chef said at dinner that night. Rebecca was relieved to see that Leslie's sins were not being held against her. "Here you will find," he continued, "the finest intellectual achievements of mankind. The best music and literature and painting."

"And cooking," David said.

"Ah, *oui*," Henri nodded. "But modesty prevents me."

"Henri is a superb cook," Dr. Resnick agreed. "There's no telling what he could do if Beeze would allow a piece of beef into the house."

"Dr. Resnick," Yogi Gnesha said, "I fear you do not give Beeze sufficient credit for his wisdom."

"I give Beeze great credit for wisdom. But like anybody, he's subject to influence, and somehow or other you've sold him a bill of goods about eating vegetables. It's a shame when the finest beef in the country is grown within a few hundred miles of here."

"The killing of a cow is an atrocity!" Yogi Gnesha said.

"Nonsense," Dr. Resnick said. "You must know, from the history of your own country, that the edict against harming cattle was created by the Aryans, who were herdsmen, in order to stop the tribes they conquered from killing livestock."

"This may be the origin of the sacred cow," Yogi Gnesha condescended, "but not of *Ahimsa*, the code of nonviolence, nor of the Yogic *Niyama*, which prohibited the taking of life long before your Judeo-Christian 'commandments.' Quite simply, man was not meant to eat flesh."

Dr. Resnick groaned. "Isn't it a little early in the meal to discuss teleology?"

"It is not teleology," Yogi Gnesha insisted, "and you cannot dismiss an argument merely by labeling it with a Latin word."

"Greek," Dr. Resnick said.

"Latin, Greek, Sanskrit. What difference? I refer not to what God wants for man, but to the purpose for which his digestive tract was designed."

"I ate meat for years," Dr. Resnick said, "and digested it a lot better than I ever digested beans."

Everybody laughed—fart jokes being ever popular—everybody but Yogi Gnesha, who was stammering with anger.

"Look at the carnivores," he said, "look at them! Claws and teeth for tearing. Skin without pores. Acidic saliva and urine. Simple stomach, smooth intestinal canal. We see them in the zoo and they are pacing nervously, ridden with anxiety, discontent, pent-up violence. Now look at the herbivores: no claws, skin with pores. Alkaline saliva and urine. Complex stomach and long convuluted intestines. In the zoo they are calm, content. Often they smile, like the giraffe."

"I never seen a giraffe smile," the old man who was helping serve dinner muttered. His name was Mr. Munckle and he seemed to be disgusted with the whole conversation.

"I have," Rebecca said, defending Gnesha. There was an arbitrariness to his intellect that she found charming.

"It's been a long time since I studied comparative anatomy," Dr. Resnick said, "but if I remember correctly, the difference between herbivores and carnivores is just as great as the difference between herbivores and anthropoids. Herbivores have hooves and flat teeth for grinding. Occasionally, as with the pachyderm, the skin is nonporous as with any carnivore. As for the digestive system, the stomach is in three parts—four, in the case of the ruminants—unlike the single stomach of man. As for whether or not giraffes are smiling, I feel only another giraffe should be the judge of that."

Everybody laughed again.

Larry Chin, Ann's husband, spoke for the first time. "I think science and religion both make a mistake by trying to determine the 'natural' behavior of man through animal analogy. Every animal seems to have evolved for a certain purpose, in the sense of beavers having teeth for gnawing wood, birds having hollow bones to make them light enough to fly, giraffes having long necks to reach the upper branches of trees. Man, on the other hand, seems to be naturally suited to nothing. He does not run well, he has no fins or gills for swimming, no claws or tail for climbing, no wings for flying, no 'purpose' for which his physiology especially suits him. Likewise, he has no 'natural' diet. If he wishes to avoid eating animals because he dislikes the cruelty of slaughter, that's something else—and something highly at odds with nature, who rarely acts from kindness." Larry paused to take a bite of food and continued. "I often think that this lack of biological purpose is what gave rise to human consciousness. Man said to himself, If I am fit for nothing, then what am I doing here? And that was the beginning of consciousness."

"The first existential dilemma," Rebecca said.

Dr. Chin nodded, and having put things right, returned to his dinner.

"Well, I got a purpose," Mrs. Munckle said, "and that's keeping this big old house clean!"

"Speaking of eating meat," Mr. Munckle said, "anybody here interested in a little rabbit stew? Just happens I found me a rabbit this morning."

"How interesting," Dr. Resnick said.

"Like to see it?"

"I want to see the rabbit," Jasmine said. "I want to see it."

"Here's the rabbit!" Mr. Munckle said. He had cleverly folded his napkin and slipped it over his hand so that he could manipulate it like a puppet. "Seen any carrots around?" he squeaked, wiggling the napkin at Jasmine, who began to laugh uncontrollably.

Dr. Resnick watched with tolerance grown weary over the years. But Rebecca, who loved cheesy jokes, couldn't help smiling.

"We all have fortune," Henri said, "to serve the master as kind and generous as Beeze."

"He is unquestionably one of the great patrons of science," Dr. Resnick agreed. "Through Beeze's generosity we have accomplished work that would have taken us years if we had had to go through the usual channels of applying for grants, skimping on equipment, and teaching to support our families."

"He is a truly remarkable man," Yogi Gnesha agreed. "He was a cripple when I met him and today he is adept at one hundred and nineteen *asanas* and ten *pranayamas*. Spiritually, he has also made great progress, although in that realm his handicap is even more severe."

"Handicap?" Henri said, as though the idea of Beeze being handicapped was simply unbelievable.

"What does the Old Testament say?" Gnesha mused. "That it is harder for a rich man to enter heaven than for an elephant to pass through the eye of a needle."

"A camel," Dr. Resnick said.

"No, no." Gnesha shook his head fiercely. "An elephant."

"I believe it is a camel," Dr. Chin said. "They didn't have elephants in the Mideast."

Henri interrupted. "But Beeze, he is the exception. For him the money is of no importance . . ."

Rebecca slammed down her glass, and everyone fell silent and turned to stare at her.

"I'm sick of this!" She spat out the words. "All of you worshiping this degenerate just because he showers you with gifts. Do you know what he did? Sent a bunch of thugs to Los Angeles to kill my friend Leslie. That's right. But they couldn't find him, so instead they wrecked his apartment, and destroyed all the beautiful things he spent a lifetime collecting. This is Leslie, who's one of the gentlest souls on earth. That's what your wonderful Beeze did. Now if you'll excuse me, I'll get out of here before you make me sick."

Back in her room, she picked up one of the gilded chairs and flung it at the wall so it broke in several pieces, exposing joints of raw wood and dowel. "That's for breaking the Marilyn Monroe autograph," she said, gasping. Then she grabbed the velvet curtains that hung from the bed canopy and yanked them down, tearing a great rent in them. "And that's for cutting the sofa . . ." Now she took a lipstick out of her purse and, on the broad strip of white plaster between the murals, scrawled a crude calendar, marking the date with a slash of red. "And that's for shitting on the carpet!" Spent, as after sex, she fell to the bed and tried to catch her breath.

Lying in bed that night, unable to sleep, Rebecca heard a violin, very distant, very faint. She listened for a time, overcome by the sorrow, the beauty of it; then she got out of bed, put on a bathrobe she found hanging in the closet, and went to search for the musician.

She found Beeze all alone in the music room, and settled herself on the chaise to listen, discovering that it was almost impossible to remain angry at a man who played so beautifully, a fact which has protected the marriages of great artists for centuries.

As she sat there, entranced by his music, her gaze wandered to the paperweights arranged on top of the harpsichord. In the forefront, she noticed a rose encased in crystal, which seemed to her the perfect embodiment of the music: the redness of it, as vibrant as the petticoat of an eighteenth-century whore, the petals as perfectly proportioned as a Greek temple; watching it while she listened gave her an extraordinarily sensual pleasure.

"I've never heard anything so beautiful," she said, when Beeze finally lowered the violin from his chin.

"I've never played so beautifully. Physicists have shown that the desires of the observer can influence the motion of certain sub-atomic particles. Perhaps in a similar way, the listener influences the beauty of the music."

She rose from the chaise, walked to the harpsichord, lifted the paperweight she had been gazing at.

"Where did you get this? I'd love to have one."

"How odd," Beeze said. "Of all the objects in this house, you have seized upon the single thing of any value to me."

Of course, she thought, this is the famous paperweight that almost cost Leslie his life.

"Was it a gift from someone you loved?" she asked.

"Yes."

"A woman?"

"My son."

Curiously she felt disappointed, let down. "I didn't know you were married."

"I haven't seen or heard from her in twenty years."

Her spirits rose again. "Where's your son now?"

"Dead."

"I'm sorry. Does it hurt you to talk about it?"

"Can there be more pain when everything is pain?"

"How did he die?" Rebecca asked.

"I killed him."

"No. I don't believe you."

"I was the greatest killer this country ever made."

"I don't understand."

"I was head of a chemical company. We produced, among other things, a compound of naphthenic and aliphatic carboxylic acids. Combined with gasoline, it created a sticky thixotropic gel, a substance ideal for fire bombs and flame throwers."

"Napalm," Rebecca whispered.

"From 1962 to 1969 we manufactured in excess of *seventy mil lion gallons* of it, all with my knowledge—no, with my eager co-operation. Those were years of record profit, of record growth. My grandfather had started the company seventy years ago by inventing a type of dry-fueled fire extinguisher. He worked out of the garage of a little house in Pennsylvania, while my grandmother did the bookkeeping. And seventy years later we were the third largest chemical company in the world, with an excess of eight billion dollars in sales. I wanted my son to take over the business from me, as I had taken it from my father, and he from his, but the boy had a will of his own. He wanted to be a concert violinist—and perhaps he could have been; he was quite talented. He seemed to have inherited my musicianship, my sensitivity and intellect, while being spared the qualities that make me a monster, the need to control, to acquire, to conquer at the expense of anything and everything. Of course in those days I didn't yet know I was a monster—no, I was still handsome then, a perfect chairman of the board, silver-templed and distinguished. I considered myself a gentleman, a philanthropist and a patriot. My son considered me the greatest killer since Hitler. I told him that this was the finest country on earth and that a few thousand lives were not too great a cost to preserve its safety. And do you know what he said? He said, 'If you represent this country, it's not worth saving.'"

"Sometimes people say things they don't mean," Rebecca said.

"In 1968 he was drafted. General Pierce was a very close friend of mine. I'd lunch with him whenever I went to Washington, and try to squeeze in a few sets of tennis. He said he'd pull strings. All my son had to do was complain of a trick knee and he'd be classified 4F, no questions asked. But he never complained of that knee. He went through the physical without a word and a few months later he was inducted. When I asked him why, he said 'To pay for your sins,' and he gave me this paperweight. 'A peculiar present,' I said. 'The only flower you could appreciate,' he replied, 'a flower trapped in glass, that will never wilt or lose its petals.' I still don't know what he meant by that. He came home a few weeks before Christmas with an honorable discharge. His left arm had been blown away by a grenade. For three months he languished in the house, rarely gathering enough energy to get himself out of bed. Then one morning he seemed completely recovered, cheerful in fact. He shaved and dressed and went for a long walk. When he came home he shot himself in the head with one of my pistols.

"After his funeral, I took out my private plane, a Cessna I flew for my own enjoyment. Do you know how, sometimes, on very cold days, the air is as clear as crystal? The patchwork quilt of farmlands spread as far as I could see. At eight thousand feet I cut the motor and the silence was absolute, as though all motion in the universe had ceased. I put the plane into a nose dive and in a few moments I blacked out, feeling a strange sense of happiness and release to know that I would never wake again. I didn't suspect at the time, what Yogi Gnesha has since taught me, that death is no escape, that suicide is simply a prolongation of our agony, that we must live again and again to repeat our mistakes until we have learned better, until wisdom and compassion can guide us along the proper path. When I awoke I was burning and the pain was so great I howled like an animal. God was denying me even the small mercy of death, for there were lessons I had yet to learn in this life. They rushed me from the accident in an ambulance, then they flew me to Brook Army Medical Center at Fort Sam Houston, Texas, the country's foremost center for burn treatment. It was also, incidentally, where they sent the boys returning from Vietnam, the boys who had been showered with napalm.

"I spent months there, getting transplants and skin grafts and plastic surgery. I pleaded with them to kill me, but doctors don't know the meaning of compassion. They are simply, doggedly determined to keep every man alive as long as possible, regardless of circumstances. Every day new boys were arriving, boys whimpering in pain or blessedly unconscious. What I remember most vividly was the smell, a smell like roasting pork. Yet their wounds must have cooled hours, days before they arrived at the hospital. Perhaps it was only my imagination. I was delirious most of the time.

"During my stay at Brook, I resigned as chairman of the board, sold my stocks, divested myself of all holdings in the company. I began to plan my desert retreat, sketching the house on paper, making lists of the people I would need to run it—the fewer the better—calling realtors to look for land. Here in the desert, I decided, I would try to understand my life, to make amends for my crimes, to learn the lesson for which God had spared me."

He plucked casually at the strings of the violin, tuning and re-tuning. Presently he said, "And yourself, Miss Weiss? Have you any children?"

"I wish. A couple of abortions." She laughed, bitterly. "That's as close as I've come. Someday I'll do it."

"Why wait?"

"Because I've never met a man I want to marry."

"Come now! A woman as talented and attractive as yourself? I find that difficult to believe."

Rebecca laughed. "You see, all the men in Los Angeles are either married or queer or kinky. It's because they never have to dig their cars out of the snow . . ." Her voice trailed off. Here in the desert, her brittle explanation had a falseness that made her cringe. She forced herself to think about the question seriously and started again.

"If I am attractive, as some men seem to think, it only serves to scare them away. Somebody once told me that he never asked me for a date because he thought I was *unattainable*. I had to laugh when he said that, I really had to laugh. As for being talented, that's even more dangerous. No man wants a woman who's going to eclipse him, make more money, be more famous. It's hard enough competing with his enemies, he shouldn't have to compete with his wife."

"But there must be exceptions," Beeze said. "Men who are secure enough that they don't mind the competition. Men who aren't threatened by a woman who is beautiful and smart and spirited."

"You're right, there must be. Maybe I just haven't met them. I went to an analyst for eight years, and he told me that I was so involved with my daddy that I wouldn't give another man a chance. But I think there's more to it than that."

"I often imagine," Beeze said, "that if I had a wife like yourself my life would be complete."

"Complete for you. She'd go insane."

"Oh? Do you think so?"

"A normal person needs contact with the outside world. News-papers, magazines. You don't even have a television, do you?"

"I could get one easily enough," Beeze said.

"She'd need people, excitement. Parties."

"Parties?" He spoke the word as though it were of a foreign tongue.

"Yeah, parties. Dancing and music and getting dressed up."

"And if she had all those things, would she still go insane?"

"Maybe not if she had her career."

"Yes, I would permit her to have a career if she agreed to remain in the mansion."

"What would she do, count cactuses?"

"If she were, let us say, an actress, I might build a film studio for her, right here in the desert. I could hire the finest writers and directors and technicians . . ."

"Now there you've got a very appealing fantasy."

"I could do all that for you."

"Oh, no, not for me," she said quickly, feeling her will start to buckle. "But you wouldn't have trouble finding somebody else. Put an ad in the *Hollywood Reporter*. Beautiful girls will line up for miles."

"I don't want them. I want you."

"Oh, Beeze," she said, playfully, "what am I going to do with you?"

"Learn to love me."

"You can't love a man who keeps you captive. You can't love a jailer."

"I don't want to be a jailer. I don't have to be."

"Then you'll let me go?" she asked, hardly daring to hope.

"No. Not yet."

"But soon? Someday soon? I'd come back and visit, I promise. I'd stay with you for weeks."

"I—I don't know. Give me time to think."

·7·

"Aaron," Sylvie called, "where are the Baggies we used to wrap your shoes?"

"What?" Aaron shouted from the bathroom, where he was shaving. The running water masked the sound of her voice.

She left the suitcase she was packing, stomped into the bathroom, turned off the water and repeated herself far louder than necessary.

Still Aaron had difficulty with the question; his mind was already back in New York, back in his studio, doing preliminary sketches for a commission he had received. A real estate tycoon who had attended the award ceremony was building a two-hundred-unit condominium in Marina Del Rey. He had asked if Aaron would be interested in constructing a sculpture for the courtyard of the complex, something commemorating the struggle for a national homeland. He had been that moved by Aaron's speech. Aaron, who didn't particularly feel like taking on the job, had asked a ridiculous sum and the Humanist had agreed on the spot, making Aaron wonder if he shouldn't have asked for even more. Enflamed by the subject matter—and by the money—he and Sylvie had booked an early flight and were hurrying to pack.

"If you want me to pack your shoes," Sylvie said, hands on her hips, "you'll have to tell me where you put the Baggies."

"Maid probably threw them out," Aaron mumbled. "Use the hotel towels."

"We'll get arrested."

"Don't be ridiculous," Aaron chided her. "Say, did I ever tell you that joke where the Smiths come back from their trip and the Joneses ask them how they liked it. And the Smiths say, 'Oh, the hotel was wonderful! The towels were so thick we couldn't close the suitcases.' " He laughed deeply, from his belly.

"I'll use the towels," Sylvie said, frowning, "but I won't be responsible if we're arrested."

"Sylvie, darling, there is no hotel in the world where they give half a damn about stealing towels. They expect you to steal them! They add them to the hotel bill. That's why the rates are so high. We should take a couple of ashtrays too."

Sighing over her husband's moral laxity, she pulled two towels off the rack and went back inside to wrap his shoes.

Someone was knocking on the door.

"Jesus," Aaron yelled, "that must be the limousine. Tell him to wait while I put on some clothes."

Aaron finished dressing and returned to the bedroom to find Leslie waiting awkwardly while Sylvie scurried about, ostentatiously ignoring him. Sylvie and Aaron had met Leslie at least a hundred times since he began managing their daughter's career so many years ago; still Aaron could never remember his name, probably because he refused to refer to him as anything but "the *fagala*"—a Yiddishism for homosexual, literally the diminutive of "bird." Sylvie made no pretense of liking him, but Aaron always tried to be cordial—that was his manner with everybody. Why they disliked him so was hard to say: superficially, they believed that he was, in some way never precisely clear in their minds, responsible for Rebecca's never getting married, never having children, and that was a grievous responsibility to bear. But a deeper reason had to do with his criminal sexuality, with the aura of revolution that is intrinsic to every homosexual life. Divested of their own revolutionary strength, the presence of it in anybody else seemed an unbearable critique of themselves.

When Leslie saw Aaron, he stepped forward, offering his hand. "Leslie Horowitz," he said, knowing that Aaron never remembered.

"Of course," Aaron said. "You think I don't remember the name of my daughter's best friend? How are you? We meant to get in touch with you while we were in Los Angeles, but so little time, so much to do. Now we're leaving. Maybe next time. You be sure to call us when you're in New York."

"Mr. Weiss," Leslie said. "Rebecca's in trouble."

"So what else is new?" Sylvie said wearily, acknowledging him at last.

"This is really serious," Leslie said.

"If it's another abortion . . ."

"It's much more serious than that. She's been kidnapped."

"Oh my God," Sylvie said, dropping to the bed. She held a hand over her heart as if to stop it leaping from her chest.

"Kidnapped? How much do they want? It's a good thing I'm well connected. I can get on that phone and have a million dollars cash in one hour."

"Nobody wants a ransom," Leslie explained, patiently. "Let me tell it from the beginning. Here, sit down. A couple of weeks ago I was driving back from Death Valley when my car broke down . . ."

They listened for a minute or two; then Aaron said, "Wait a minute, I've heard this before. But where? I know—Becky told me—but then *you* were the one who was kidnapped and *she* was trying to save *you*. You're not trying to play some kind of trick on us, are you?"

"Frankly," Sylvie said, "it all sounds highly suspicious to me."

"I was being held prisoner. Then I escaped, but Beeze wrecked my apartment. Rebecca went to his mansion because she knew that if she didn't, he'd probably have me killed."

"Wait a second," Aaron said. "Who's this Beeze?"

"The crazy millionaire who lives in the desert."

"And he's the one who kidnapped Rebecca?"

"He didn't really kidnap her. She went willingly."

"She went willingly," Sylvie said, nodding her head as if she'd known all along. "That's our daughter."

"I wouldn't worry if I were you," Aaron told Leslie. "She'll spend a few weeks in Palm Springs with this guy and get bored and come back to town. That's what always happens with Rebecca. That's the story of her life."

"No, you don't understand! It's not Palm Springs, and it's not some kind of romance. This man Beeze is sick. He's dangerous . . ."

"Rebecca can handle him," Sylvie said.

"For God's sake," Leslie said, "this is your daughter! Don't you care what happens to her?"

This implication that Rebecca was not the single most precious thing in his life—a statement that Aaron was fond of making—sent him into a rage he could barely contain.

"Now you listen to me, young man. This may be difficult to believe but I care about Rebecca as much as you do—and probably a lot more. I nursed her through the chicken pox, and I cheered her up when her prom date never showed. I went to the openings of every one of her motion pictures. But when you love a daughter the way I do, you have to protect yourself. Rebecca is a trifle self-involved, a bit oblivious to others."

Sylvie sniffed as if to indicate that this was an understatement.

"It's my own fault," he continued, "for loving her too much, for being too kind, too indulgent. When she was a teen-ager she would stay out all night, never a word about where she was going. I can't tell you how often we called the police, thinking she was in terrible trouble, only to have her appear next morning and make fun of us for our worrying. Sylvie and I made a decision years ago. We would continue to give Rebecca money and love and whatever else she required, give and give and give, asking nothing in return—as it should be with parents—but we would no longer allow ourselves to worry over her."

"That's right," Sylvie agreed. "As far as I'm concerned, I don't give a damn if she ever gets married and has children. Let her spend ten years with this millionaire in Palm Springs. If that's what she wants, God bless her."

"And now," Aaron said, "if you'll excuse us, we've got to finish packing. We have a plane to catch."

It soon became clear to Victoria that Rebecca was not coming back to their little house on West Wanda. Like most changes in routine there would be advantages and disadvantages, perhaps more of the former. For example, Victoria could move out of the small guest bedroom, which she had never particularly liked, and into Rebecca's bedroom, with its walk-in closet and large bath and view of the city. She could sleep on Rebecca's antique brass bed, under the beautiful quilt Rebecca's grandmother had sewn for her, and she might be able to get away with it for some time. The mortgage was paid up and Rebecca's accountant wouldn't come snooping around until April. As for Rebecca's friends and parents, Victoria would simply tell them that her roommate had run off to Italy with some man. Rebecca had a reputation for acting on impulse, and people were always eager to think the worst of her, a common attitude toward celebrities in general, actresses in particular. As for the disadvantages, there were people to pay: Manuella, the cleaning lady; Pepe, her brother, who did the gardening; and of course, telephone and utilities. Victoria was literally down to her last dollar. Her checking account was empty, her credit cards had all been canceled. She had taken the emergency-reserve-don't-dare-touch-it-unless-you-absolutely-have-to fifty-dollar bill from the bottom of the cookie jar in order to buy a pair of silver spike heels that were on sale at Pleasure Dome (if that wasn't an emergency, what was?). Yesterday she had been reduced to shoplifting groceries, which she hadn't done since her teens. Fortunately, Freddy Dilucci, the TV producer she had been dating, was taking her to dinner that night. Even if he couldn't get her a job, perhaps he'd be willing to lend her a few dollars. And if he refused, maybe she could blackmail him about his premature ejaculating—but who would she threaten to tell? Well, if worst came to worst, at least she'd get a free meal out of it.

He picked her up at eight in his Honda, giving her the same story he'd been giving her since they met, about how the Rolls was still in the shop and they were sending for parts to England. He took her to Ma Maison, a restaurant so exclusive that the phone number was unlisted. They waited an eternity to be seated.

"Hey, Patrick," Freddy called to the owner, "think you could find a table for an old pal?"

Patrick stared at him, puzzled, then turned his back to talk to some guests.

Oh, brother, Victoria thought. This is the pits. We're going to wind up at McDonald's if I don't do something fast.

She looked around the small indoor dining area reserved for the very famous—the less illustrious sat beneath a tent on the front lawn—and recognized Mack Gordon, the director. Sitting beside him was a graying, stoop-shouldered man in his early sixties, battered yet kindly in appearance.

"Excuse me," she said to Freddy, "I see someone I know."

Before he could reply, she had strolled over to the table, with a tread that she knew from experience would grab the attention of everybody in the restaurant, making the women despise her, the men wish they were taking her home that night.

She smiled at Mack Gordon and said, "Hi. You'll excuse me for coming over to say hello? You see, I'm a friend of Rebecca Weiss's. She's talked about you so much that I feel like we're old friends."

Mack smiled back and nodded, but it was the older man who stood up and offered her the chair, and gazed at her with the cow eyes which she knew meant that anything she wanted was hers.

"Please join us," he said.

"Well—just for a minute."

She glanced at the door and saw Freddy watching her, perplexed.

The older man introduced himself as Roy Gleason, and Victoria, running a lucky streak, remembered that he was a screenwriter—a first-rate screenwriter whose income probably exceeded half a million a year—and gushed about how much she liked his work. She couldn't remember just what he had written, but she thought that if she played along, he would sooner or later mention a title and she would be on safe footing. He, in turn, remembered her from *Pearl Divers*, and gallantly praised her performance.

Mack Gordon listened, polite but bored. His gaze wandered about the dining room, searching for celebrities equal in importance to himself; when he did glance at Victoria and Roy, his lackluster eyes seemed to be focused just beyond them.

"You'll have a bite with us, won't you?" Roy Gleason said.

The waiter overheard, flew over and hovered like a moth.

"I really can't."

"The shrimp scampi is very special," the waiter said.

Victoria sighed in despair over her own weak will. "Oh, all right, if you insist."

"We do," Roy Gleason said.

When she was through ordering, she turned to Roy and asked him, eyes glittering with fascination, what he was working on at present.

"The truth is, I'm doing some rewrites on *Web!*"

"Rebecca's film? But I thought it was all finished."

"It is," Mack said. "The film is sensational but the story stinks. So Roy and I are working up a new story. Once we're finished writing we'll get the actors in to dub it."

"But the words won't match the lip movements. It will look like a Sergio Leone film."

"What's wrong with Sergio Leone?" Mack said. "He's the greatest director who ever lived. *Once Upon a Time in the West* is the greatest American movie ever made."

"Wasn't it Italian?" Victoria asked, puzzled.

"It was made by Italians," Mack said slowly, as though trying to explain Shakespeare to a moron, "but in spirit it was quintessentially American. I met Leone once. We talked for seven hours straight in Rome one night. He said I was the greatest living American director under thirty. This was a couple of years ago, naturally."

"Who are you going to get to do Rebecca's voice?" Victoria asked innocently.

"Rebecca will do her own voice," Mack said.

"I don't think so. You see, she's disappeared. Nobody knows just what's happened to her. I heard a rumor that she just ran off to Europe."

"I'll kill that bitch," Mack said through clenched teeth. "She's just doing this to screw me up."

"I'm sure that's not true. She has such admiration for you. I'll bet she's back in time to do it!"

"She goddamn better be," Mack muttered.

"And if she's not, you'll just have to get someone else, someone who sounds a lot like Rebecca. Someone who can say, *Oh, God, I'm so depressed I don't think I can get out of bed this morning.*"

Both men looked at her with amazement, for she had spoken the last sentence in a remarkable parody of Rebecca's voice.

"That's very good," Roy said. "Very good!"

Victoria shrugged modestly. "I used to do impressions."

"What do you think, Mack? Do you think she could dub for Rebecca?"

Mack looked coolly from one to the other and raised an eyebrow. "Let's try to get aged cheddar before we settle for the Velveeta."

"Well!" Victoria said. "I don't know how to take *that*."

"Don't be offended," Roy said. "Mack's sense of humor is a little rough sometimes."

"Victoria?" Freddy was standing next to the table, trying to hold his temper. "Could I talk to you alone?"

"I'm sorry, but I'm busy."

"*Victoria* . . ." Freddy said, and now his anger was getting the best of him.

Mack Gordon stood up and positioned himself so that their noses were only inches apart.

"She said she was busy," Mack said. "Now why don't you leave her alone?"

"Listen, pal," Freddy said, "this is none of your fucking business."

"Before you start talking tough," Mack said—he was speaking very quietly—"take a look at what I've got in my hand."

Freddy glanced down and saw, hidden from general view by the lapel of Mack's jacket, a snub-nosed .38-caliber revolver of the type known as a "detective's special," nickel-chrome plated and sincere in its promise of violence. He looked at Mack's eyes again and this time he recognized the cold craziness of a man who just might pull the trigger on a whim, ruining two lives, destroying two careers. Victoria was extraordinary, but no piece of ass was worth this. Being a wise and temperate man, he turned and left the restaurant without another word.

"Who was that?" Roy Gleason asked.

"Oh, nobody. Tell me more about rewriting *Web!* You must be so clever to make the new lines fit the situations."

"It's not as hard as it sounds," Roy said modestly, "once you get the hang of it." Under the table he felt a stockinged toe lift his trouser cuff and trace designs on his calf, and he began to make up excuses to tell his wife about why he would be so late getting home that night.

And Victoria calculated precisely how much money she'd need to borrow from this nice man to keep her household running.

For two hours now, Leslie and the helicopter pilot had been cruising low over the desert, trying to find Beeze's mansion. They were handicapped by Leslie's confusion over where precisely his car had broken down, and also by his refusal to open his eyes, which he had kept squeezed shut in terror since takeoff. Furthermore, the meter, like a device from a nightmarish taxi, was clocking $295 an hour, the going rate for chartering this particular kind of helicopter, a flying limousine known as a Bell "Jet Ranger." Cheaper helicopters were available, but the charter agent insisted this was the safest. The pilot was a craggy-faced, iron-haired man named Jed who wore mirrored sunglasses, like a motorcycle cop. Discovering that Leslie worked in the movies, he asked if it would be possible to get an autographed picture of Leonard Nimoy for his son, who was a *Star Trek* fan; Leslie thought he could and from that moment on they were friends. Still, Jed was dubious about this mansion in the desert.

"Even if it is there," he said, "you're never going to find it unless you open your eyes."

Leslie opened his eyes, glanced down, shut them and covered them with his hands. "That's not the place."

Jed sighed, "Tell me about it again, everything you can remember."

"I was driving on 127 and the fan belt popped and I pulled over to the side . . ."

"Right, I've got that part."

"And there was a big field of little bushes and a mountain range and—wait, I remember! The mountains were blue."

"What time was it?"

"I don't know. Five, six."

"All the mountains look blue about then."

"Oh," Leslie said, disappointed. "But there can't be *that* many mountains . . ."

"Listen," Jed said, wearily, "There's the Avawatz Mountains, the Soda Mountains, the Owlshed Mountains, the Shadow Mountains, the Cady Mountains. I'll tell you what else. There's Fort Irwin

Military Reservation fifteen miles over that way, and if that's where the place is, well, you're out of luck because if we fly anywhere near there, they'll send a batch of F-14s after us."

"Shit," Leslie said.

"Let me make a suggestion. The closest town from here is Silurian. The police chief's bound to know if somebody's built a mansion in the vicinity. Let's go talk to him."

Leslie agreed, mainly because it would be an excuse to land. Silurian would have a bar where he could get a drink. That was the only way he survived his frequent flights to New York, by getting as drunk as possible, as quickly as possible. Rebecca was also phobic about flying and once, discovering that they both had to be in New York at about the same time, they decided to fly together, thinking that each could give strength to the other, a practice proven successful by organizations such as Weight Watchers and Alcoholics Anonymous. Unfortunately, just the opposite happened; minutes after the plane left the runway, Rebecca became convinced that something was wrong with the outside left engine and the stewardess' calm only confirmed it ("They're trained to pretend nothing's wrong," Rebecca whispered, "that way they have time to run up front and take all the parachutes for themselves"). Meanwhile, Leslie decided that the dark Latin man sitting in the next aisle was a hijacker, the brown paper package clutched in his arms a bomb. By the time they reached Kennedy, they were about to have nervous breakdowns. After that, they made a point of flying separately.

From the air, Silurian reminded Leslie of the exoskeleton of a cricket he had found when he was a child, cellophane-thin and amber, its juicy insides dried away entirely. They landed on the "lawn" in front of the town hall, raising a mountain of dust, rousing a yellow dog from his cool spot of shade beneath the steps.

The town hall was an air-conditioned, one-story structure of cinder block with a roof of corrugated metal. A framed print of a forty-mule team dragging a Borax wagon across the desert hung by the entrance.

Wandering down the hall they found a door marked "Police," but the officer who was stationed there, monitoring a CB radio, said that Chief Robertson was having lunch at the Desert Vu

Diner, and shouldn't be bothered while he was eating unless it was an emergency. He stared at Leslie and Jed as though they were nude or deformed.

The Desert Vu Diner was a shabby little adobe next to the Desert Vu Garage (two pumps). Flies scattered as Leslie flung open the screen door. Chief Robertson was the only customer; he sat at the counter, joking with a pretty waitress in a yellow uniform. He was perhaps sixty, with tiny eyes that seemed to squint against the sun, even here in the air-conditioned shade. A khaki uniform stretched tight across his belly, but the cowboy hat and the boots and the revolver at his waist all fit perfectly. His stool squeaked as he turned around to look at them. Judging them by whatever standards he judged men, he apparently found them wanting, for he turned away in disgust.

"Excuse me," Leslie said, "are you Chief Robertson?"

"That's how Momma christened me."

"I'd like to ask you some questions."

"Ask away. It's a free country. Everybody's got the right to talk their fool heads off. Don't they, Daisy?"

The girl behind the counter giggled and wiped away an imagined stain with a dishrag.

"Well, we've been riding around all morning in a helicopter . . ."

"That the helicopter you landed behind City Hall?"

"Yes," Leslie said.

"Well, I'd best inform you that it's parked there in violation of city ordinance one-ought-four-four-three, encumbering or obstructing government property, fifty-dollar fine or five days in jail."

"We're going just as soon as . . ."

"Sorry, son, the law's the law. You got fifty dollars?"

Leslie, finally comprehending, took out his wallet and gave the police chief fifty dollars. The waitress was laughing so hard she had to go back to the kitchen in order to retain control of herself, and even Chief Robertson allowed himself the smallest smile.

"You from around here?" he asked.

"No," Leslie said.

"Didn't think so. You come up from Los Angeles, from Beverly Hills?"

"More or less."

"That's what I figured. Hey, Daisy," he shouted, not wanting her to miss his next gambit, "bring me some more coffee." And he waited until she came back from the kitchen, before he continued.

"Guess how I knew you was from Los Angeles?"

"How?" Leslie said.

"Because that's the closest place where to find men of an effeminate temperament."

Leslie turned white. Jed's eyes narrowed. The waitress laughed out loud.

"We're looking for . . ."

"Guess how I know you're of an effeminate temperament?"

Leslie said nothing.

" 'Cause of the way you got your sleeves rolled. My daddy used to say you could tell a fruit by the way he rolls his sleeves. A man who does real work rolls them to the shoulder, and a man who does desk work keeps them buttoned to the cuff. But the fruit— who's no man at all, really, just a poor unfortunate freak of nature —he rolls them exactly twice, and he's always real neat about it."

Leslie pulled back and swung at the police chief, but Jed, who must have sensed it coming, grabbed him from behind and held him back.

"Now, friend," Chief Robertson said, "I suggest you get back in your fancy helicopter and fly away, 'cause whatever you're looking for, I don't suspect you'll find it here. If you're looking for gold, well, it's all been dug up years ago, and if you're looking for borax, well, chemical companies got a monopoly on that. If you're looking to shoot animals—though I can't recall ever hearing of a fruit who liked to hunt—I'll advise you that anything that's big and pretty enough to hang on the wall is probably an endangered species. And," he hesitated, "and if you're looking for a certain person, you'd best remember that people come to the desert to get away from the likes of you. Understand my meaning? So, friend, while you still have the use of your legs, I suggest you be on your way."

·8·

---

*B*eauty ate a hearty supper and had almost conquered her dread of the monster; but she had like to have fainted away when he said to her, Beauty, will you be my wife?

She was some time before she durst answer, for she was afraid of making him angry if she refused. At last, however, she said in a trembling voice, No.

The poor monster hissed and sighed so frightfully that the whole place echoed with it, and she was sure that he would set about devouring her then and there, and she prayed for her immortal soul. But to her heartfelt relief, he simply said, Farewell, in a mournful voice and left the room.

When Beauty was alone, she felt a great compassion for poor Beast. Alas, said she, 'tis a thousand pities anything so good-natured should be so ugly.

Beauty spent three months very contentedly in the palace. Every evening Beast paid her a visit and talked to her during supper, conversing with fine logic and sense, but never with what the world calls wit; and Beauty daily discovered some valuable qualification in the monster; and seeing him often had so accustomed her to his deformity that, far from dreading the time of his visit, she would look to the hall clock to when the hour of nine would strike, for he never failed to visit her at that time. There was but one thing that gave Beauty any concern, which was that every

*night before she went to bed the monster would ask if she would
be his wife.*

*One day she said to him, Beast, you make me uneasy. I wish
I could promise that someday we would marry, but I would not
think to thus insult you with lies. I shall always esteem you as a
friend, and would that you were satisfied with this. Love cannot
grow within stone walls such as these; it will wither and die like a
plant in need of sun; set Love free if you would see it flourish.*

*Alas, I cannot, Beast said, for if I were to do so you would flee
and never return.*

As you would have it, Beauty said sadly.

One evening after dinner, Samson led Rebecca to the library.
Beeze was waiting there, dressed in a smoking jacket and flannel
slacks and slippers, arranging magnificent ivory and obsidian chess
pieces on a board.

"Do you play?" he said, hopefully.

Rebecca shook her head. "I know how, but I hate it. It always
seemed like too much brain work for a silly game." Seeing Beeze's
disappointment, she added, "But I'll tell you what I do like:
Checkers."

Beeze opened a cupboard and took out a box of checkers, and
set them out on the board. By the time Samson returned with a
glass of brandy, Rebecca and Beeze were engrossed in their game,
both concentrating so deeply that they hardly spoke. They played
for hours, one game after another, skill sharpening with practice,
determination increasing with defeat.

Beeze won the first few games but then Rebecca beat him once
and beat him a second time. He was surprised at her cunning,
her ability to outthink him. His pleasure was such that he would
reset the board after every game, demanding another match, until
finally, warmed by the brandy and excited by the intimacy of
competition, she had to comment:

"You're the strangest man. All you want to do is play checkers."

"What more can I do?"

"Do you mean"—despite her boldness she had difficulty phras-
ing the question—"that's *all* you can do?"

"I can compose music and play the violin. I can speak Greek and Latin and . . ."

"No, what I meant was . . ."

"What you meant was—am I physically capable of sex? Or did the accident rob me of that too?"

"Thank you."

"The answer is yes, I am. Although I haven't been with a woman for ten years."

"Holy shit," Rebecca said. Then, embarrassed, she added, "Excuse me, that was pretty crude."

"Not at all. I am charmed by people who say what they feel. It is a long time to be celibate. Yet one has little appetite of any sort in the depths of depression."

"That's the truth," she agreed. "Are you still depressed?"

"Not for the past few days."

For a time Rebecca sat silently, toying with the checkers. The idea of a man who had been celibate for ten years fascinated her; it seemed an irresistible challenge.

Finally she spoke: "Do you find me attractive?"

"I think you are the most beautiful woman in the world."

Rebecca laughed. "I think I look like a rodent. See my rat teeth?" She bared her lower teeth and growled playfully.

"Your teeth are perfect. Everything about you is perfect."

"So?" Rebecca said. "If we're going to be stuck here together, we might as well have some fun."

"No," said Beeze.

"Look, if you're angry about yesterday morning . . ."

Beeze shook his head.

"Or about me breaking the chair in my room?"

"The chair is worthless."

"Then what's the problem?" she demanded.

"You don't love me."

"If you had to love somebody to have sex," she said, gently, "the human race would have died out a million years ago."

Beeze raised his right hand and held it in front of her, a pear-shaped lump of flesh layered with scar tissue, a flap of loose skin vaguely thumblike coming off the side.

"Would you care to feel the touch of this?" he said.

"Yes," she replied, without a moment's hesitation, "I think I would."

Rebecca reached for his hand, but Beeze withdrew it.

"I can't," he said.

"Come on, it's not such a big deal." She reached out and took his hand and held it between both of hers, squeezing it, stroking it softly. She smiled at him and said, "There, that's not so bad, is it?"

"You don't find it horrible?"

"No," she said quite honestly, "it's a little weird, but it's not horrible. Now take off your mask."

"What?"

"Take off your mask. It's the only way I'll ever get to know you."

"I can't. Aside from a few doctors, no one has ever seen my face."

"Then I'll be the first."

She reached for the mask and Beeze brushed her hand away, almost violently.

"I'm a monster."

"Will you stop this self-pity! I worked in a hospital when I was a kid. I've seen burn victims."

"You've never seen the likes of this."

"If you let me see who you really are, I might be able to love you."

"If you saw who I really was, you would loathe me. You would never be able to speak to me again, and the very thought of my face would make you physically sick."

"I think you're wrong, Beeze."

"I don't intend to find out," he said, rising abruptly, signaling that the evening had come to an end.

During the following days in the mansion, she fell into a routine. She would sleep late, have breakfast in bed, choose a book from the library and, stripping down to her panties, lathering herself with coconut oil she had borrowed from David, stretch out on a marble bench in the garden to read; when she was so hot she could no longer bear it, she would jump in the pool, a huge round marble fountain with dolphins spitting water. The rest of them thought she was crazy—they'd never venture out until four or five in the afternoon—but Rebecca loved the sun, despite what it did to her skin, drying her out, aging her. Beeze, in the best style of ancient potentates, let it be known that anybody caught watching Rebecca while she was nude sunbathing would have their eyes put out, a threat she found flattering though hardly to be taken seriously. It made even less sense considering that nearly everybody in the mansion had, by now, seen her nude scene in *Land of Lost Dreams*. But Beeze seemed to think one experience qualitatively different from the other, and nobody offered to argue it.

Around noon she would dress for lunch—she was still wearing the clothes she had arrived in, washing out her underwear in the sink every night while doggedly refusing the dresses which appeared in her closet every day or two—and after lunch she would usually pass a few hours with Ann Chin while Jasmine was taking her nap.

Around four o'clock she would join Yogi Gnesha for an hour of private instruction, or else she would go to the kitchen and watch Henri prepare dinner. The avuncular Frenchman, delighted to have an audience, would lecture her as he went along, and occasionally let her assist with some menial task, such as whipping egg whites. After dinner, and the inevitable debate between Dr. Resnick and Yogi Gnesha, she would spend the evening alone with Beeze, either reading or playing checkers, or talking together over brandy.

Her Yoga instruction came about as a result of her expressing interest in that most difficult discipline over dinner the third night of her stay. She mentioned that Will Roach, her drama teacher in college, had recommended Yoga as a means of gaining grace and self-assurance onstage, and she had always intended to study it but had never found time. Yogi Gnesha had immediately volunteered his services.

She arrived for her first class wearing a black leotard she had borrowed from Ann Chin. The "Yoga room" was unfurnished but for a beautiful Bokhara rug and a small table which displayed a vase of flowers, an incense burner and a framed photograph of an emaciated Indian with beatific eyes (it was the nineteenth-century Hindu saint Ramakrishna, she learned later). Yogi Gnesha sat in front of the altar, cross-legged, wearing nothing but a loincloth. To her surprise he looked a little flabby, although radiantly healthy, his dark skin as fine as silk. He rose to meet her, smiled, shook hands firmly. She had expected some kind of orientation lecture, but instead he simply said, "Let us begin."

Then, resuming his cross-legged position, he began to drone instructions. For an hour he directed her through positions of increasing difficulty, balancing on one foot, stretching her hamstrings in a split, arching her back until she was scared she'd slip a disk, bending forward for minutes at a time; then inverted postures, standing on her shoulders, standing on her head—she used to do that when she was a little girl—and finally lying on her back, exhausted, in what was called *Savasana*, the dead-man's pose. Every muscle in her body ached and her mind raced with insults for Yogi Gnesha, who was sitting peacefully nearby with not a trace of sympathy for the pain she was suffering. He seemed to take a sadistic pleasure in making her hold the most difficult postures longest, until her whole body started to shake from fatigue, and then scolding her for overexerting herself. Yoga, he said, was tension within relaxation. Not once had he complimented her or encouraged her. He simply sat as he had been sitting, eyelids drooping, voice droning on hypnotically. She wanted to wring his neck.

Then, suddenly resuming normal speaking tones, he said, "Do you know Ava Gardner?"

"No," Rebecca said, still lying on her back. The question was so nonsensical and nonspiritual and irritating that she wanted to get up and leave at that moment, yet she was too tired to move.

"Do you know Lana Turner?" he continued.

"No."

"Hedy Lamarr?"

"No!"

He sounded precisely like Rebecca's aunt Sophie, who would whenever she had her on the phone, quiz her remorselessly about movie stars of the forties.

"I thought you might have met them in Hollywood. They were

the women I had seen in the cinema in Delhi. When my guru asked me to go to America to spread the Master's teachings, I said, 'Please, not me. How will I ever remain celibate around American women?' You see, the joke was I thought they would all look like Ava Gardner. Ha! Was I mistaken!" Yogi Gnesha laughed and laughed and laughed. He was one of those who laugh hardest at his own jokes.

"But what shocked me most," Gnesha continued, "was their behavior. You see, a wealthy patron in Great Neck, Long Island, passed away, leaving us his house as a Yoga Center, and I was to be in charge. Well, let me tell you, I was not optimistic. No, indeed. I did not expect more than four or five people at my first class. After all, Great Neck, Long Island, is not Mount Kailas, or Benares—that is to say, it is not a great center of spiritual study. Then imagine my surprise when thirty-eight women arrived. Thirty-eight! They told me they were housewives and their fondest ambition was to learn all about Yoga. Well, I was really too pleased with myself! I thought I was another Jesus Christ. I could not wait to write a letter to my guru telling him of my marvelous success. The joke was on me!" He laughed again, a roaring laugh straight out of his belly. "The next day, of the thirty-eight women, only twelve returned. The day after that there were four and the next day, one. Then nobody. Thus I learned an important lesson about Americans.

"They all want to change. The fat ones want to be skinny and the skinny ones want to be fat. The brunettes think that platinum hair will fetch more men and the blondes think the same of brunettes. The bachelors yearn for marriage, yet those who have married want nothing more than to be single again. But if you offer them the possibility of true change, of the change which is possible through Yoga, they will run like scared rabbits. Ramakrishna had a saying, 'Man is willing to part with anything but his own misery.' Once you understand that statement, you understand half of what stops man from the final evolutionary step."

"What evolutionary step?" she asked.

"The raising of the Kundalini."

"What's that?"

"Literally in Sanskrit it is the serpent. You recall the serpent that dwelt in Eden, the serpent that tricked Eve into eating the apple of knowledge? That serpent is Kundalini. But he is as maligned as Eve. He is the bringer of bliss, of cosmic consciousness. He is the one who came to Jesus, after he had fasted forty days in the wilderness, and he is the one who visited Buddha after forty days beneath the bodhi tree. He is the one who blessed Blake with visions of billowing light as he stood on the seashore, and he is the one who gave my beloved Ramakrishna sainthood. In legend he lies asleep at the base of the spine, waiting to be awakened by the *asanas*—the physical postures—so that he may pass up the tree of the body, activating each of the vital centers, the *chakras,* until finally he reaches the lotus with a thousand petals, the *chakra* atop the skull, where cosmic wisdom resides. Yes, that is what it says in legend, but I myself think it is both too literal and too metaphorical, and that Kundalini is simply the force that permeates the universe, the force that knows itself. To some it is a serpent, to some a blue light of blinding brilliance, to others an overwhelming feeling of love, like suckling at the breast of Kali. Five thousand years ago the composers of the Upanishads, foreshadowing the work of modern physicists, wrote that energy existed in three forms: as matter at its lowest frequency, as light at a higher frequency, and, at its highest frequency, as pure consciousness. How wise they were to believe that man evolved according to the form of consciousness, rather than thinking, as modern scientists do, that the opposite was the case, that consciousness was simply an evolutionary accident. How could there be such an accident? Could one *accidentally* build a jumbo jet? No, Miss Weiss, consciousness predates all, consciousness is Kundalini and consciousness is God. Consciousness is a process, but at the same time it is an energy, dual-natured like light, to which it is closely akin. Consciousness is bliss and understanding and love in its purest form."

"But love is misery," Rebecca said. "Nothing makes people unhappier than love."

"What I speak of is love at its highest level, like that which a mother feels for a helpless infant, love so totally involving that it dissolves the ego, so pure and rich that it fills the heart with bliss. This is the love of Bhakti Yoga, that brings enlightenment through devotion. This is the love one must finally feel for God if one is to transcend this vale of tears we call life."

"And how can I learn to love like that?" Rebecca asked, her whole insides starting to quake. "Will it come from doing the Yoga postures? Or should I meditate?"

"They are only a small help," Yogi Gnesha said. "If you truly want to learn to love, God will instruct you. But you must be an attentive student and watch for His lessons."

It has been said that Boredom is Anger's favorite mask. Despite the way she crowded her days, Rebecca soon found herself wearying of every diversion. The one movie she felt like watching was inevitably the one missing from Beeze's catalogue; of the remaining five hundred films, she couldn't find one that interested her. A wrenched muscle in her shoulder made Yoga impossible. While tasting one of Henri's creations, she had grimaced in jest, and he had banished her forever from the kitchen, ending her cooking lessons. Even the sunbathing had to stop when her skin broke out in red blotches.

One of the few activities she could still enjoy was her chats with Ann Chin.

"I don't know how you've lasted so many years without going bonkers," she told her, one afternoon. "A couple of more days and I think I'll blow my brains out."

"It's not much more boring than the life I lived outside," Ann replied. She was embroidering, industriously, an old-fashioned sampler which read "God Bless Our Home," the letters festooned with flowers and ribbons. "You'll get used to it."

"*You'll get used to it. You'll get used to it.* That's what everybody keeps telling me. I feel like a hostage. Doesn't anything special ever happen? Like holidays or festivals? Veterans' Day parades?"

"We have wonderful Christmas celebrations. Henri cooks a feast and Beeze gives us marvelous presents. Last year he gave me enough Bal à Versaille to take a bath in. And he gave Jasmine one of those enormous stuffed tigers from Germany."

"Well, I don't intend to wait around here for Christmas."

"It's only three weeks away."

"My God," Rebecca said, "is that possible?"

"And then we have a big New Year's party with champagne punch and noisemakers."

"I need a party right now. I want to get high and dance and hear people laughing. That's something I haven't heard since I got here—people laughing. Except for Yogi Gnesha laughing at his own jokes."

"Have you asked Beeze? It seems to me there's nothing he wouldn't do to make you happy."

"If I asked him for anything, and he gave it to me, then I'd be indebted to him—I'd feel like his mistress. And I couldn't bear that."

"But you mustn't! Nobody thinks of you that way. You're a woman with a career, a famous actress."

"Am I? I sure don't feel like it. I feel like a helpless little girl who doesn't know how to tie her own shoes."

"And when Beeze gives, he never expects anything in return. Money has no value to him."

"Is that possible?" Rebecca said. "I mean, doesn't money have value for everybody? Maybe money means less to him because he has so much, but it still means something. And as long as money means anything at all, taking it involves some kind of obligation."

"What if *I* were to ask Beeze to give a party? Certainly you would incur no obligation then."

"I think we'd better just drop the whole idea," Rebecca said.

Despite Ann Chin's company, Rebecca felt lonelier and more depressed as the day wore on. She summoned Mr. Munckle to screen *Petrified Forest*, a motion picture which had never failed to raise her spirits with its unbridled romanticism. But the sight of Leslie Howard made her homesick for Leslie Horowitz, and the gradual realization that this was a tale of a girl living alone in the middle of the Mojave Desert, and going out of her mind from boredom and loneliness, pushed her to the point of tears.

The film stopped, the houselights went up. Mr. Munckle emerged from his little projection room and hurried to Rebecca's aisle. He was seventy, tall and skinny and solemn, dry as a strip of jerky that had been hung out in the sun to cure. You could see the skin between the strands of thin gray hair slicked back over his skull. He had hound-dog eyes and a growth the size of a grape on the side of his nose.

"You hurt?" he said. "You sick?"

"Yes. No. I don't know. Please leave me alone. I'll be all right in a minute."

"What's that in your ear?" he said.

"What?"

She looked up, and at that moment he removed a quarter from the pink shell of her ear. He held the coin in the air, waved it back and forth a few times, then clapped his hands. It vanished.

"Where'd it go?" Rebecca said.

"To Uncle Sam. That's where it all goes. But sometimes you get a refund."

He snapped his fingers and the quarter reappeared between thumb and index.

"Tried to stop smoking once," he said, lighting a cigarette. He took a few puffs, then crushed it into the ashtray beside Rebecca's seat. "Trouble was, I always managed to find another one." He opened his mouth, rolled down his tongue, and a new cigarette appeared, already lighted. He kept on crushing out the cigarettes and replacing them from the seemingly endless source within his mouth until Rebecca couldn't help laughing.

"There," he said, "that's what I like to see. Can't let the clouds cover up the sun. Got to keep smiling even when things look lousy. That's something I learned in vaudeville. I was a child star, you know. Munckle, the Minute Magician, Presenting Spectacular Sleight of Hand and Fabulous Feats of Prestidigitation. I played the big time, the Keith Orpheum Circuit, when I was only ten years old." He smiled to remember it. "During the finale, I materialized one hundred red, white and blue doves, which landed on my shapely assistant so as to suggest an American flag, while the orchestra played 'The Stars and Stripes Forever.' That was some effect, yes sir."

"Why did you stop?"

"Motion pictures. I couldn't believe it at first, folks preferring them to real life, but that's how it was. One by one the vaudeville palaces all turned into movie theaters—except for the ones that turned into burlesque halls. After a time I saw the handwriting on the wall. I said to myself, Munckle, your days as a magician's finished. Oh, you may work now and then but you'll never play the Palace, you'll never hear 'em cheer like they used to. Movies, I decided, was the way of the future, so I learned me to run a projector and I been working steady since. That kind of work don't give you no big highs—nothing like the sound of a crowd applauding—but it don't leave you broke and lying in the gutter, neither. Truth is, I needed the security. Don't regret it one bit. You feeling better now?"

Rebecca sniffed and smiled and nodded.

"I don't want to see no more clouds covering the sun," Mr. Munckle said, "you hear?" He pulled a quarter out of her ear, tossed it back and forth between his hands, then hid it in one fist.

"Which one?" he said, holding both fists in front of her.

She stared at one and then the other, as though if she stared hard enough she would see through the flesh, and finally pointed to his right hand. He opened it and it was empty. She pointed to his left hand, but that was empty too.

"Uncle Sam?" she said.

He shook his head. "This time I got wise and put it in a savings bank. You got to learn to stretch your money."

A rectangle of green rubber appeared—it had been printed to resemble a dollar bill, but the effect was none too convincing—and he stretched it between both hands until it was as long and narrow as a rope.

Rebecca, who had a weakness for dumb jokes, laughed and laughed.

That night, while playing checkers with Beeze, she said casually, "I know you never intend to leave here, but have you ever thought of inviting people from the outside? What I mean is, Samson could pick up a carload of my friends and bring them back here. Just for a day. We'd get high and listen to music and dance a little. Make them swear not to mention a word about what they saw. Even if they did talk about it, nobody would believe them. Leslie's already been here—what harm could there be if he came back?

And he'd bring Tommy, his, well, you know, his *inamorato*. And Victoria. You'd love her, I never met a man who didn't. She's six feet tall with a sensational body, and so nice. And a few others, only people we knew really well and trusted, mostly actors, clients of Leslie's. For all the bad things you can say about actors, they really know how to party. Oh, Beeze, could we do it, could we please? It would be such fun."

Beeze was so intent on the checker game that she thought he hadn't heard her. But later, as she was leaving, he said, "Ring Samson before you go to sleep tonight. Have him bring you pen and paper. List your friends, their phone numbers and addresses."

For a moment she stared at him, astonished. Then she threw her arms around him, pressing her face to his cold mask, and said, "Oh, Beeze, I love you."

Next morning Samson arrived at her door with an envelope on a silver tray. Rebecca opened it and found an invitation done in calligraphy on the finest vellum.

> *Henry Wallace Beeze III*
> *takes pleasure in inviting you to a ball*
> *in honor of*
> *Rebecca Weiss*
> *Black Tie*
> *8:00 P.M. this evening*

"My God," she murmured, "this thing's for real, old Beeze has decided to let down his hair. Well, hallelujah. I can't wait. We'll get stoned and drunk and boogie till three A.M. But what will I wear? This suit is really starting to stink."

Samson opened the closet, and the velvet dress that Beeze had given her for her birthday was hanging there along with five other evening gowns of varied style and color, each a designer's original. How Beeze had gotten them made so fast—and cut to such a perfect fit, as she would soon discover—was almost a miracle, but Rebecca was beginning to realize that the miraculous became more and more ordinary as one's wealth became more and more miraculous. Fifteen pairs of shoes were arranged on a rack. Samson opened the dresser, and there was the black box containing the diamond choker. Rebecca held the necklace to her throat and regarded herself in the mirror backing the closet door.

"When Victoria sees this," she murmured, entranced by her own reflection, "she'll croak."

Although she dared not admit it to herself, this was a turning point, this decision to accept Beeze's gifts and throw away the silk suit. The garment seemed to be growing day by day stiffer and more rank, as though it were a layer of herself, to be disposed of as a snake sheds his skin, in order that the next phase of her life could begin. She stuffed it, vengefully, in the wastebasket along with her old underwear, which was threadbare from being washed every night, and lay down in the black-tiled bathtub for a long soak. Then she washed her hair and brushed it out, shook it loose and let it dry, thankful that she had changed to a style that required neither curlers nor dryer.

Yesterday the medicine cabinet had been bare. She checked it again today, for she was beginning to understand Beeze well enough to anticipate his more obvious moves, and found, as she had expected, a fabulous selection of perfumes and cosmetics. The present had to be shared; she threw on her robe and ran down the hall to Ann Chin's room. Ann was sitting on the floor, teaching Jasmine a lesson in American history.

"Aren't you going to the ball?" Rebecca asked.

"I received an invitation."

"Then we've got to get dressed!"

"But it's not for another nine hours."

"Barely enough time. Beeze has stocked my medicine cabinet with every cosmetic ever made. We've got to start making up immediately if we're going to use them all."

"Will you make my eyelids purple?" Jasmine asked.

"I'll make your eyelids purple and your nose green," Rebecca said.

"I don't know," Ann said. "You haven't finished your history lesson."

"I'll do twice as much tomorrow, Mommy, I promise."

"Let's go," Rebecca said.

"But it's only eleven A.M.," Ann pointed out.

"We'll design our make-up now and put it on again tonight. I'll show you how to make cheekbones and hide bumps. All the secrets of the Hollywood experts, fifty cents."

"Please, Mommy?"

"I know when I'm beaten," Ann said.

The three of them sat before the long mirror in Rebecca's bathroom, making up themselves and each other, then washing their faces and starting again. They compared perfumes by spraying them on their fingers until the air was such a confusion of scents that nobody could determine which perfume was which. Ann, though taller, was also a size four and Rebecca's wardrobe fit her nearly as well. Jasmine insisted that she try on everything too, and the older women could barely contain their laughter, watching her traipse around the room, dresses dragging behind her, shoes wobbling under uncertain ankles. All the while Rebecca described her friends to them, those whose names she had listed the night before, those whom they would meet in the evening to come. Leslie, Victoria, Tommy, and others both gay and straight, actors and civilians, famous and unemployed, a waiter who was also a playwright, and a songwriter who also parked cars, an exotic dancer and a tennis pro, a florist and a masseur.

The women were happy as children at play and a sound rarely heard in the mansion rang through the corridors and echoed in the great halls; it made Mrs. Munckle hesitate in her vacuuming, and Samson, who happened to be passing by, cock his head, puzzled. It was, of course, the sound of laughter.

Rebecca had been wondering what Beeze would do about music, whether he would hire a first-rate band from L.A., blindfolding them to keep their destination secret, or a disk jockey with a trunk full of records. When she arrived at the ballroom—only forty-five minutes late, so eager was she to see her old friends—she found to her disappointment that records were the order of the evening, and not the kind of music she had been hoping for, but instead Frank Sinatra, Nat King Cole, Patti Page, Doris Day—Mrs. Munckle's private collection of 78s. A further disappointment was that her entrance was wasted since, despite her tardiness, none of her friends had yet arrived. Only the regulars were there, waiting awkwardly in black tie and evening gown, not dancing and barely talking. Ann Chin was holding up Jasmine so that the little girl could see the whole of the banquet table, presided over by Henri and David; Larry Chin and Dr. Resnick were huddled in conversation; Mrs. Munckle, enormous in organdy, was standing by herself, gulping down canapés as though, at midnight, a law against eating was scheduled to take effect, while Mr. Munckle ran back and forth, attending to the phonograph, checking the air conditioning, and pouring himself a glass of Scotch when he thought nobody was watching.

Samson and Beeze were nowhere in sight. Rebecca assumed that the giant was piloting the helicopter back from Los Angeles and would arrive, along with the guests, momentarily. They would come flooding through the door, like some crazy carnival in their brightly colored, sequin-studded clothes, shouting "Surprise!," bringing the party to life like a sudden shot of adrenaline. She had a terrible thought: the helicopter only seated two passengers! But then she realized that Beeze would have hired a bigger helicopter for an occasion like this, perhaps even a troop carrier. As for Beeze, perhaps he was still dressing, or had gone to play the violin or read. Rebecca would not have been surprised to learn that he had no intention of appearing at all that night. Yet she hoped he would, simply to see her among her own kind. She felt that she appeared cleverer and more attractive when surrounded by her friends, just as a precious jewel glitters more brightly from a setting of lesser gems.

Rebecca strolled by the banquet table, sampling the caviar, the smoked salmon. David, who was tending bar, poured her a champagne cocktail, and the grenadine colored the glass like a rose. He remarked that she was the very image of a princess just stepped from the pages of a fairy tale. This was a perfect description. Imagine her in the red velvet gown, empire-waisted, embroidered in golden thread; with golden slippers, high-heeled, curled and delicate as wood shavings; her lovely long neck emphasized by the diamond choker; her bushy hair tamed by mother-of-pearl combs. She carried her glass to a corner and sat, waiting for her friends to arrive.

"You are a vision of loveliness," Yogi Gnesha said, approaching her chair.

"Thanks," she said. "You're looking pretty good yourself." Actually, his tuxedo seemed to be ancient, closeted for decades, and several sizes too large, as though inherited from an older brother.

"And how is your shoulder?"

"My shoulder?" Then she remembered that only the day before a wrenched shoulder had prevented her from practicing Yoga. "Oh right, my shoulder." She wriggled it experimentally, and smiled. "Seems to be fine. It stopped hurting this morning, when I got my invitation to the party."

"Laughter can cure more ills than penicillin," Yogi Gnesha agreed.

"And you know what else? That terrible sunburn rash I had— all the little red spots? They went away about the same time." She laughed.

"Now that you are in such fine health, perhaps you would do me the honor of this dance?"

On the phonograph, Tony Bennett crooned a scratchy "Blue Velvet."

"Thanks," Rebecca said diplomatically, "but I just want to sit for a while."

"You need not be embarrassed. I am an excellent dancer."

"It's not that. I want to wait until my friends get here. I'd feel funny being the only one on the floor."

"I attended the Fred Astaire School of Dancing in New York City," the Hindu said proudly. "The instructor said I was the finest pupil he had taught in years."

"No kidding. I always wondered who went to those places."

"I learned the mambo, the cha-cha, the waltz, the fox trot and the lindy."

"This must have been some time ago."

"Nineteen fifty-nine. I had just arrived from India and wished to steep myself in American culture. I was also depressed about my first efforts, the housewives from Great Neck."

"And did the dance lessons help?"

"They certainly made me feel better."

"Aren't you bored just teaching Beeze?" she asked.

"To have one true, dedicated pupil is all a teacher could ask for. And . . ." He hesitated, debating whether to go on. "It is only temporary"

"What do you mean?"

"All this," Yogi Gnesha said, taking in the sumptuous setting with a gesture, "will not last long. This morning in meditation I saw a vision of Kali, she who purifies through destruction, surrounded by a halo of fire. She told me that by New Year's Day Beeze's mansion would be no more than a memory and I would be back in New York with my students."

Rebecca felt a chill on her shoulders, a light perspiration break out under her arms. "Why? What's going to happen?"

"Do not worry," he said. "Whatever it is, it will be for the best. Trust to the divinity to supply us with the lessons we need and remove us from this incarnation when we have learned all we can."

As David was refilling her glass for the fifth time, everything grew silent. She glanced toward the door and there was Beeze's tall, powerful form; she stood motionless, cheeks burning, blood rushing in her ears, as he advanced upon her. Then he was standing directly in front of her, looking down at her, eyes gleaming from deep within the holes of the mask.

"You are so beautiful you don't seem quite real." He spoke softly, for her ears alone.

Rebecca made a mock curtsy. "Thanks. I love this dress. It makes me feel like the princess in a storybook."

"I am delighted that you have accepted my gifts."

"Well, I haven't accepted them. Let's just say I'm borrowing them."

"They are yours. Everything I have is yours."

"I might keep the dress. But this necklace makes me too nervous. I feel like Liz Taylor."

"May I have this dance?" Beeze asked, offering his hand.

"To tell you the truth, I feel a little funny dancing all alone Let's wait till the others get here."

"Others?"

"You know, Leslie, and Victoria, and . . ." Her voice trailed of as the truth occurred to her. "There aren't going to be any others, are there? That list you had me make up—it was another one of your sadistic tricks. You never had any intention of inviting guests."

Beeze hesitated. "There are guests. There are Yogi Gnesha, and Dr. Resnick and Dr. Chin . . ."

"Those aren't guests, those are employees."

The others seemed to be holding their breath, so still was the silence, so tense the atmosphere.

"Guests are friends," she went on. "Employees are people you pay. But you wouldn't understand that because all you've ever had are employees. They may pretend they like you, they may smile and listen to your stories, but don't let it fool you. They'll never tell you the truth because they're too damned scared of losing their jobs—and their lives. But I'm not scared, I've got nothing to lose. So I'll tell you what they're thinking, what they're all afraid to say: *It's grotesque! This ball is grotesque! And so are you, and so is this overdecorated crypt you live in! And I don't care if you kill me for saying so, I'd rather be dead than live here another day!*"

She tore the diamond choker from her neck, flung it at Beeze and ran from the room.

She lay on the great canopy bed, weeping, first for herself, but later, as the hours wore on, for Beeze, for the terrible things she had said to him. She had begun to understand and respect, and even admire him—although none of this diminished her anger toward him—and the memory of shouting insults at him, of humiliating him in front of the people who worked for him, was simply too awful to bear.

And so she was relieved when, late that night, Beeze knocked at her door—though she gave no sign of it when she let him in.

"I'm sorry," he said. "I only wanted to please you."

"Forget it," she said curtly.

"You said a woman would need a party once in a while. An opportunity to go dancing."

"This wasn't a party, this was a farce."

"I did what I could."

She turned on him suddenly and snapped, "Then why didn't you invite my friends?"

"I couldn't! They don't understand me out there. They would have talked about me behind my back and called me a freak."

"For God's sake, how do you know? It's been so long since you've given anybody a chance. You've holed up here since your accident like some kind of ground hog or prairie squirrel, or whatever they're called."

"I know. I know what people are like."

"Do you? You don't seem to know very much about me."

"I've tried everything I can to please you."

"Then set me free!"

"Perhaps," he muttered, "sometime soon."

"You're always saying that."

"Rebecca, I need you."

"That's the first time you haven't called me *Miss Weiss*," she said, in a different tone of voice. "It's funny, but every time you say Miss Weiss I think you're talking about my maiden aunt."

"You do what medicine and Yoga and music cannot do. You make me feel alive."

"And you can't have me unless you let me go. Can't you understand that?"

"I'm trying," Beeze said, "I'm trying harder than I've ever tried anything in my life."

Rebecca stared at him for a long time. "Yes, you are," she said finally, "I can see that."

"Do you know why I was so late? I was sick. I had a nervous stomach over whether you would be pleased with my preparations."

"Poor Beeze."

"I wanted so much to make you happy tonight."

"Yes, I know."

"I wanted to have my arms around you. I wanted to dance with you."

"Did you really?" She smiled.

"Yes."

She stood right in front of him, arranging his right hand so it circled her waist, his left so it clasped her right.

She began to hum, a tune she had heard somewhere, a waltz she could not name, and the two of them circled the room with exquisite grace, dancing, dancing with no one else but each other.

Roy Gleason, having been given an office at the Burbank Studios to use while rewriting *Web!*, had invited Victoria to meet him there at lunchtime, thinking it would be an exciting place to have sex, and relatively safe, since he worked there all alone and his wife had never yet dropped in unannounced. Sex in unusual locations was something Roy Gleason loved to fantasize about, since at home his coital adventures were limited to the bedroom by the presence of various children, maids, nannies and grandchildren (their son-in-law had walked out on their daughter last year and now daughter and grandson were threatening to become permanent residents), and to hours either very late at night or early in the morning, when likelihood would be least of somebody barging in with the news that little Julius had swallowed a safety pin, or that the cocker spaniel had fallen into the swimming pool again. Unfortunately, either Roy or his wife, or both of them, were often asleep at these times. When Roy suggested, at the urging of his analyst, that they check into a motel for a few hours' amusement, his wife refused to take the proposal seriously.

"I'll pretend to be a businessman," Roy had suggested, "and you can be a hooker. I'll pick you up in the bar, buy you a few drinks, invite you to my room. You're a good girl and very smart. You went to Radcliffe on scholarship and wanted to be a doctor. But your father and mother died in a plane crash and you turned to hooking to support your five brothers and sisters."

Thirty years of screenwriting had left their mark.

His wife had simply smiled, and shook her head and said, "Oh Roy."

He had spent the morning imagining the office as an erotic locale for sex with Victoria—cunnilingus under the desk, fellatio over the file cabinet—and the thought of it excited him so that he found it impossible to concentrate on the screenplay he was supposed to be rewriting. He simply stared at the same paragraph for hours, while his mind performed the entire *Kamasutra*.

When she finally arrived at one, an hour late, he could scarcely keep the tremble from his voice.

"I thought it might be fun to send out for Chinese and have lunch here in the office," he said, a gambit he had been rehearsing all morning. As soon as it was said, however, he realized his mistake.

Victoria looked at him with hurt in her eyes. "Are you embarrassed that someone will see us? Because if you are, I can go home. I don't need this. I've taken enough abuse in my life."

"I'm sorry," Roy said, "that's not at all what I meant. I could never be ashamed to be seen with you. You're the most marvelous woman I've ever met. If you want, I'll call up my wife right now and tell her all about you."

Victoria hesitated and for one horrible moment, Roy thought she would take him up on it. Then, to his immense relief, she said, "No, of course not. I'm just oversensitive. If you'd been through what I have, you'd understand."

"I do understand," Roy insisted. "I do. At least I think I do. What exactly do you mean?"

"Men. The way they treat me. It's the curse of looking the way I do. Of course it hurts me most professionally. I'm constantly being cast as whores and mistresses and dumb bunnies. But I'm not worried because I know that someday I'll get my chance. And then they'll eat their words."

"Maybe you'll get that chance sooner than you think," Roy said. "I'll tell you about it while we walk to the commissary."

They strolled down a street of thirties-vintage brownstones, past a grand old movie palace and a burlesque hall, all plywood and plaster fronts with nothing behind them but two-by-four framing.

"I don't think we'll be able to make all our story changes," Roy said, "by dubbing, as we'd planned. It's too confining. We're going to have to reshoot certain scenes. Since we can't seem to get in touch with Rebecca Weiss, I've suggested to Mack that we reshoot her entire part with somebody else."

"Anybody I know?" Victoria said, slyly, taking his arm, pressing it to the side of her breast.

"I think you might," Roy said. "She's tall and long-limbed,

graceful and full of talent. Her name is Victoria. And a gray old writer named Roy is determined to see that she gets a chance."

"A gray old writer?" Victoria said, puzzled. "I don't know any gray old writers. I know a writer with lovely silver hair, but he's not old. Not when he's with me."

"What would you say if I told you that I'll be sixty-five in January?"

Victoria dropped his arm, put her hands on her hips and stared at him incredulously. "I thought you were fifty."

"Sixty-five," Roy said, nodding his head. "I kid you not. A gray old writer who's seen it all and lived to tell the tale."

She took his arm again, more tightly than before, and they continued their walk.

Roy told her an anecdote about a horse he had bought his teenage daughter a few months ago. They had built a corral for it on one corner of their Malibu Canyon property, but the rascally horse had an insatiable appetite and, having thoroughly grazed the area in his corral, leapt the fence in search of food. Just about that time, Roy was working in his office at home, pounding on his typewriter, which was placed just beneath an open window so that he could catch the breezes, the smell of fresh-mowed grass. Reaching a rough spot in the narrative, he got up and went to the kitchen for a Tab. And when he got back the horse had stuck his head in the window and was eating the page right out of the typewriter!

Victoria laughed, but in truth didn't believe it, just as she didn't believe most of Roy's stories. As a skilled deceiver, she found them embarrassing in their phoniness and sentimentality and hoped his screenwriting was of a higher caliber.

They turned a corner and a man in a light-blue leisure suit greeted them. Apparently he and Roy were old friends, for Roy dropped her arm that instant and put a few feet of space between them. He was also a writer, she learned, upon being introduced, and he was working on a project for another independent producer on the lot. The two writers chatted for a few minutes, exchanging stories about the atrocities committed upon them by directors they had worked with in the past, and how pleasant, in comparison, were the directors with whom they were now employed. Meanwhile the blue leisure suit was looking back and forth between Roy and Victoria, trying to assess the degree of involvement, the potential for gossip. As blue leisure suit was leaving, he told Roy to look in on Sound Stage 8 if he wanted to take a real stroll down memory lane.

Since Sound Stage 8 was only a few hundred yards out of their way, Roy led Victoria to it, being careful now to avoid any physical contact with her lest he run into someone else he knew. The red light at the sound stage entrance was off, indicating that shooting was not in progress, and people could enter. Roy pushed back the heavy sound-proofed door, and a few paces led them into a South Pacific jungle, where tanks, foxholes and camouflage nets indicated that World War II was still in progress.

Cameras, lighting and sound equipment stood ready, but the technicians had gone for lunch, so they were entirely alone on the set.

Roy, who remembered his own adventures in the Pacific theater with a nostalgia that would baffle a younger generation, was enchanted, particularly by the enormous Patton tank at one end of the stage.

"I used to drive one of those honeys," he told Victoria. "Let's go have a look."

He started to climb up the rungs to the turret.

"Are you sure it's all right?" Victoria asked. "I wouldn't want to disturb the set."

"The camera's pointing in the other direction. Nothing to worry about."

He reached down and helped pull her up. She had difficulty negotiating the rungs in her high heels, but went along gamely, seeing how much Roy was enjoying the experience. The hatch on the turret was open and Roy slid down inside. Victoria followed, avoiding landing on his head only with some difficulty. Inside, the tank was claustrophobic in the extreme, hot and fetid, and smelling of steel and oil. She squeezed into the seat beside him, so that only a transmission hump, bristling with levers, separated them.

"Boy, does this bring back memories," Roy said, letting his fingers caress the controls. He began telling her which lever initiated which function, and within minutes he had started in on his war stories, something he almost never did without three drinks or an old war buddy to inspire him. Victoria, who had spent her childhood listening to accounts of her father's exploits in that same war and ocean, was instantly overcome with boredom, a crushing, deadening kind of boredom, and kissed him on the lips just to shut him up.

"I think we need a little privacy," he said, reaching up, shutting the hatch above his head.

Thrilled at the prospect of finally having sex in a peculiar location, or any sex at all for that matter, he grabbed her and kissed her back, dragging her, in his passion, across the transmission hump and onto his lap. Fortunately, she was something of a contortionist. In her new seat, she could feel Roy's own little transmission lever growing hard beneath her. Panting, he began to fumble with the buttons on her blouse, and somehow managed to pull it down from her shoulders. She helpfully arched her back so that he could reach under her and unhook her bra, an act he performed with the finesse of a fifteen-year-old. Her breasts came out of confinement so quickly that they too seemed to be longing for air. Roy bent down to kiss her nipples, but found that an overhanging panel of meters blocked his head. Victoria wriggled onto her side so she could get at Roy's lever, the angle flattening her breasts like two thickish pancakes. She tried to open his fly, but the dashboard inhibited her movement.

"Try this," Roy panted. "Put one foot on this side of me and the other foot over there. Then stand up and I'll pull down your jeans. Then you can sit on my lap."

Victoria wedged herself into the position as described, bending over so as not to bang her head on the cabin's low roof. Roy opened his own pants, took out his penis, held it ready. She unfastened her jeans, lowered them to her ankles along with her panties, and tried to sit on Roy's lap. Alas, the clothing bunched around her ankles made it impossible to move.

"I'm stuck," she said, with a trace of panic.

"Don't worry," Roy advised her. "Just relax."

Looking up, he saw the fresh fig of her cunt only inches above his face and by rising out of his seat, and straining his tongue, he found that he could just reach her clitoris.

"Not now," she snapped. "I'm stuck. I've got to get out of here."

"Just relax and . . ."

"Stop it! Let me out! I've got to get out!"

Desperate in her claustrophobic terror, she threw open the hatch directly above her head, and stood up straight, stretching her cramped back, neck and shoulders, taking a deep breath of air.

"Shit!" she cried.

During the time they were squirming around in the tank, the crew had returned from lunch and were now busy setting up for the afternoon's first shot. They watched her pretty head pop out, her broad shoulders, her open blouse and bobbling breasts, and they burst into applause, one and all.

When Roy Gleason answered his telephone and heard Victoria's voice, he said, "Hi, Mack. Trouble with the script? Well, in that case I'd better take it in my office. Can you hold on a sec?"

Victoria waited, feeling once again that sense of embarrassment for a lie badly told. If she were Roy's wife, she would have seen through it in an instant. But maybe the woman was blind and deaf, or maybe she simply didn't want to know.

"Victoria?" Roy was whispering. "I thought I told you not to call me at home unless it was an emergency."

"It is," she replied. "Remember last week, in the tank?"

"My God, how could I forget. But you said nobody recognized us. I pulled my shirt up over my face and everybody was laughing so hard . . ."

"That's what I thought. But this morning a man stopped by my house. He's the still photographer on the film. When he saw me coming out of the tank, he started snapping pictures and then he took some pictures of you, too."

"Oh my God. Oh my God."

"Roy, dear, it's not so bad. There are ten pictures in all, and he's agreed to sell them to me, with the negatives, for a hundred dollars apiece."

"Buy them. Right away."

"I will. The problem is I don't have any cash on hand, and it's too late to go to the bank."

"Meet me at the studio in an hour."

"Roy, I love you."

"Yeah," he said, and hung up.

When Victoria arrived at Roy's office, he gave her an envelope with ten crisp hundred-dollar bills in it. He looked pale and anxious and even declined her offer of oral sex, his favorite. He was so worried, and she was so concerned about him, that she almost told him the truth, but she knew that this way would be the best. If she had simply asked him for a thousand dollars for herself, he might have felt that she didn't really love him, that she merely wanted him for a sugar daddy. He was so sensitive, after all. Yes, she had certainly done him a favor with her little fabrication.

She went directly from his office to the offices of *Daily Variety*, where she handed them a cover letter typed on letterhead stationery she had snitched from Roy's office; a full-page ad drawn up by an old beau of hers who worked in an advertising agency; and seven hundred and fifty dollars, the going rate for full-page space. The ad read:

Arachnid Pictures

Is proud to announce the reshooting of portions of

WEB!

Introducing

VICTORIA DUNBARR

An extraordinary young screen presence

And at the bottom was a sexy, yet tasteful, glossy of her sitting on the rocks at Malibu, at sunset.

Of course Mack Gordon wasn't absolutely positive that he wanted to reshoot Rebecca's role, at least not yet. But perhaps the ad would help sway him. And if he decided not to reshoot, well, the ad was already in print, nothing could be done about it. The ad was the important thing, even more important than the spider movie, for Billy Rosenblatt was sure to see it, and every day his start date for *The Other Woman* grew closer, he would be more and more willing to consider her for Jacqueline.

The part that would make her a star.

To celebrate, she took the two hundred and fifty dollars left over and went to her favorite boutique, where she bought a gloriously slinky black evening gown with sequins.

One afternoon Rebecca went down to the kitchen to watch Henri prepare dinner—he'd long since forgiven her the nasty face she'd made over one of his dishes—and to chat with David, whose gay sensibilities were a pleasant reminder of Leslie.

As she walked through the kitchen door, a cast-iron frying pan missed her by inches. She took in the scene at a glance: Henri, his face purple with rage, his silver hair seemingly charged with electricity, was grabbing culinary armaments from the pot rack on the wall. David hid behind a counter, pleading for an armistice, a chance to talk peace. Every time he raised his head, Henri would launch another missile.

"Bastard!" Henri screamed, his voice cracking into the falsetto. "You are infidel, you torture me, you make me miserable! Be gone, be out of my life forever!"

"You were the only one who ever mattered," David called back. "I swear to God!"

He stuck his head out from the side of the counter, so Henri could see his expression of sincerity, but no sooner had he done so than a copper saucepan grazed his ear.

"Liar!" Henri shouted. "Cheat! Deceiver!" His face seemed to be growing darker and darker, his hair lighter, as though he were the developing negative of a photograph.

"For Christ's sake," David shouted, "take it easy, remember your heart!"

As though in response to these words, Henri suddenly gasped, grabbed his shoulder, grew rigid with pain.

David dashed out from behind the counter, caught Henri as he was crumpling to the floor and lowered him gently. Going through the older man's pockets, he found a vial of pills and inserted one under Henri's tongue.

"Get Dr. Resnick!" David barked, and Rebecca ran from the kitchen to comply.

The laboratory was next-door to the kitchen. It was the one

room in the house, aside from Beeze's private suite, where she had never ventured, for she knew they were engaged in some sort of experimentation involving live animals, and Rebecca was an animal lover. She regularly sent money to protect baby seals from trappers, and to prevent the Japanese from killing dolphins while tuna fishing. Whenever she passed the heavy swinging door of the laboratory, with its secretive pane of frosted glass, she thought of her beloved cat Charlemagne enduring unspeakable tortures under the knives of crazed Nazi doctors. Now, however, a life was at stake, and there was no time to indulge the fears of the imagination. She barged into the laboratory without knocking, took a few steps and stopped, dumbfounded by what she saw:

Tiled floors, white walls, zinc counters, dazzling under fluorescent light. Along the far wall a refrigerator and other machines more difficult to identify, one with a spinning chamber within it, one which agitated a rack of test tubes, one which must have been some kind of oven. Racks of bottles, carefully labeled, filled with colored liquids, and networks of glassware where chemicals commuted between beakers via corkscrew tubes. Through the door of an adjacent room, cages filled with pigs, gently snorting, rooting through the shredded newspaper floors of their homes. But what drew her attention—and made her knees want to buckle—was the operating table directly before her, a brilliant spotlight burning above it, a pig lashed belly up to its cold steel surface, a pig as pink and naked and helpless as a baby, its eyes staring stupidly at the ceiling, its stomach slit open, its entrails spilling over onto the antiseptic floor.

Dr. Resnick was bending over, holding on to the side of the table—the blood was running onto her hands but she didn't seem to notice—while Dr. Chin stood behind her grinding his pelvis against her buttocks. For an instant Rebecca couldn't figure out what they were doing (could it have been some new scientific procedure?); then she noticed that Dr. Resnick's dress was pulled up and Dr. Chin's pants were around his ankles, and what they were doing was nothing but a variation of an old, old theme. Dr. Chin stopped his bumping and Dr. Resnick her moaning, and they both raised their heads and stared at Rebecca with amazement.

Rebecca whispered, "Excuse me"—she was finding it difficult to talk—"but there's a man with a heart attack . . ." Then the room spun around and the tiled floor came up to meet her head with a crack.

She woke in her canopied bed in the guest suite, head aching and throat dry, cherubs floating overhead as though depicting concussion in an animated cartoon. Dr. Resnick was sitting on a gilded chair beside the bed, reading. She put down her book when Rebecca spoke.

"Is Henri all right?"

"He's fine, dear. The question is, how are you?"

Dr. Resnick began to interrogate her to determine whether damage had been done to the brain, but Rebecca interrupted.

"What were you doing? It was some kind of devil worship, wasn't it? Some kind of black magic . . ."

Dr. Resnick laughed. "These days, dear, we call it science."

"But I saw you and Dr. Chin . . ."

"Sometimes the sight of blood can be disturbing if we are not used to it. The shock and ensuing hysteria may cause hallucinations. It's not unusual in cases of concussion."

"The dead pig . . ."

"Now, if you'll just give me a chance, I'll explain. As you may know, the only lasting injury from Beeze's accident was the loss of his pancreas. During the airplane crash an aluminum spar penetrated his abdomen, tearing the omentum, filling the area with blood. The liver was torn also, but with new surgical techniques, it was successfully repaired. The spleen was ruptured, but one can survive without a spleen. Much more serious was the loss of the pancreas. The pancreas performs two vital functions: discharging digestive enzymes into the duodenum and secreting insulin and glucagon into the bloodstream, to break down carbohydrates. Fortunately, both these functions can be duplicated by ingested and injected chemicals. By taking four pills of synthetic pancreatic enzyme with each meal, food is satisfactorily digested. By injecting forty units of insulin a day, keto acidosis is prevented. In keto acidosis, because of the absence of insulin, the blood cannot burn carbohydrates and must burn fat instead. As a result the blood becomes more and more highly concentrated with keto acids. The potassium level rises until the heart stops, causing death.

"So, even without a pancreas, Beeze could lead a relatively normal life. The problem is, Beeze is not a normal man. The thought that he was dependent on certain chemicals was intolerable to him. Beeze detests weakness and dependence of any kind, as I'm sure you've noticed. And so he hired Dr. Chin and myself—the leading transplant specialists in the country—to develop a successful pancreas transplant. I'm not sure how much you know about organ transplants. Quite simply, the problem is that the transplanted organ is a foreign object, and the body tends to reject foreign objects. For all its marvels, it cannot distinguish between a deadly microorganism and a lifesaving organ graft. The factors that control graft rejection are called histocompatibility antigens. There are several approaches to overcoming them, and these are the real subject of our research. Obviously, if the organ donor and recipient have identical antigens, there will be no chance of rejection. Usually this is only the case with identical twins, but it is still not to be ignored as a path of research. More fruitful is the use of drugs with immuno-suppressant qualities, for example, the anticancer drugs azathioprine and adrenocorticosteroids. But most of our research centers on the development of an effective antilymphocyte serum, one without damaging side effects.

"We use pigs to test these drugs because, in many ways, they are physiologically most similar to man. They are large enough to facilitate a pancreatic transplant (in the last eight years I believe we have performed more than three hundred transplants), they are cheap and easily obtained. It is important that they be easily obtained because obviously until we perfect our procedure every pig we operate on dies. Beeze can't bear it. In the beginning he didn't want us to use experimental animals. That damn savage Gnesha convinced him that he would suffer *bad karma* for every pig that was killed in his name. It's remarkable what pagan idiocy an intelligent man like Beeze will tolerate! But I suppose it's understandable considering what he's been through. Personal tragedy will often turn a man to religion and superstition. Still, I do wish we could have a slice of steak once in a while. And so, my dear, what you saw was simply another biopsy on another poor pig with an unsuccessful pancreas transplant."

"What I saw," Rebecca replied, "was you and Dr. Chin fucking."

"Now, my dear, don't you think it would be better if you . . ."

"Don't give me any of that *now my dear* crap, I know what I saw! You two were fucking. And I think that dead pig was turning you on." She shivered from the thought of it.

"All right," Dr. Resnick said, suddenly changing tone. "I'll level with you. After all, we're both single, we're both professional women, highly regarded in our fields. We're both rather more intelligent than the others, and we know how to take what we want. If there is one difference between us, it's age. You are young and attractive, and I—well, I've seen better days. But inside, dear, inside I'm still a girl and I need to be admired, I need to be loved. And who is to admire me here in this odd little world that Beeze has created? Only a man who loves science and medicine, only a man whom I can dazzle with my brilliance. Yes, you have your looks, dear, but all I have is my brains. And if that particular man happens to be turned on by the spurt of blood, by the choking breath and the death rattle of a poor animal, then I must take advantage of the opportunity. Men fall into bed with you, dear, but with me, well, they need a little encouragement."

"It's so sick," Rebecca said.

"The scientist tries not to make a fetish out of death. We consider life an accident, a flash of lightning in a sea of primordial methane, and consciousness a coincidence. Death is another meaningless event, another machine breaking down, nothing more. If a man finds it sexually stimulating, well then, all the better for me."

"I'm going to tell Ann all about this," Rebecca said.

"You can if you wish. Have you ever been to Japan, my dear? I ask because the houses there are very small and crowded, and the older ones have walls of paper. Everybody can hear what everybody else is saying, but because crowding is the prevalent condition of their society, they *pretend* not to hear. This mansion is a little bit like Japan. We are all stuck in very close quarters. Nobody is leaving despite what Beeze may tell you. So we can tell each other the truth about everything, and see how much we enjoy living with that, or else we can be like the Japanese. And now I think you'd better rest."

Dr. Resnick gave Rebecca an injection and when she woke it was night. The headache and feelings of nausea were gone, and in their place was a ravenous hunger. She yanked the bell pull and ordered Samson to bring her food. Minutes later David arrived with a tray of tea and dry toast and a bowl of clear soup.

"How is Henri?" she asked him.

David gestured with his right hand. "He'll be fine, they say. Fortunately they've got a ton of hospital equipment from the pig experiments, so they could improvise an intensive-care room for him. They really know their stuff. I was very impressed watching them work."

"Fine folks," Rebecca said, barely suppressing her irony.

David sat down on the edge of the bed and started feeding her the soup, much the way her mother had done years ago.

"If he'd just listen to me," David said. "I told him to exercise. The doctors say it's the only thing for a heart attack. And I've got all that equipment in my room—loose barbells and a bench, 'lat' pulleys and a leg-press machine. But he refuses to do anything more strenuous than lifting the fork to his mouth. And the food he prepares! It may be vegetarian, but it sure isn't low cholesterol. Do you know that, cooking for the twelve of us, he uses almost five pounds of butter a day? And upwards of two dozen eggs, and at least a half a quart of heavy cream. Every time I mention it, he says, 'Ah, my dear boy, first I give up ze *boeuf*, zen you ask me to give up ze milk and ze eggs! What is left to cook? Shall we eat only rice, like ze Chinese?' "

The imitation was so accurate that Rebecca couldn't help laughing.

"I'm so angry at him," David said. "I don't know what I'll do if he dies . . ." And he started to cry.

Rebecca smoothed his hair. "Hey, it's all right," she said. "He'll be okay, I know he will."

"It used to be so good between us. We never fought. It was like an endless honeymoon. Oh, I got restless—on the bad days I felt like a caged animal—but I was the only fag in the house. Then your friend Leslie came and everything changed. Henri was just like he used to be in Paris, nervous and irritable, consumed with jealousy. I told him that Leslie meant nothing to me—which wasn't entirely true—that it was all just a meaningless fling, but he wouldn't listen. Things got worse and worse and then this . . ."

Again David's narrative dissolved in tears.

Rebecca felt responsible. She and Leslie had invaded this sterile community like some kind of virus, and the community was too frail to endure their onslaught. What had Dr. Resnick said?

The body tends to reject foreign objects. For all its marvels, it cannot distinguish between a deadly microorganism and a lifesaving organ graft.

As David was tidying up to leave, they heard another knock, and Ann and Jasmine entered.

"Is the patient taking visitors?" Ann asked.

"She sure is," Rebecca said.

"Here's a card I made for you," Jasmine said, presenting Rebecca with a folded piece of purple construction paper. Inside was a drawing, in bold crayon strokes, of Rebecca, recognizable by bales of bushy black hair, kissing a man in front of a movie camera.

Underneath it said: "Get well kwick! Love, Jasmine." The "J" was backward.

"Why, it's lovely," Rebecca said. "Who is the man?"

"Just a man," Jasmine replied.

"But he's wearing a mask."

"That's not a mask," Jasmine said, irritated at the public for mis-understanding her work, "it's the edge of his face."

"Well, it's beautiful anyway, just beautiful." Rebecca leaned over the side of the bed and kissed Jasmine on the cheek. "Ann," she continued, her voice growing more serious, "I've got to talk to you alone."

"Can Uncle David put me to bed?" Jasmine asked. "Can he tell me another story about being down and out in Paris?"

"You'll have to ask him," Ann said.

"My pleasure," David said, bowing deeply. He picked Jasmine

up in one arm, balanced the tray in the other and started for the door.

"Not too down and out, please," Ann called after him. "Remember this is an eight-year-old child."

"Have no worry, madam. My bedtime stories are all rated 'G.' Unless you'd like me to stop by later and tell you one . . ."

"Please!" Ann said. "I'm a married woman." But her whole face lit up with appreciation.

When the two women were alone, Rebecca said, "She is the most adorable little girl. I want to giggle every time I see her." (She would start gently and work up to the ugly revelation of Dr. Chin's affair with Death and Dr. Resnick.)

"I worry that she doesn't spend enough time with her father. He's working late again tonight."

"As long as somebody's there for her, that's the important thing. And you're a great mother. If I thought I could be half as good, I'd go out and get knocked up and have a baby all by myself."

"Out of wedlock?"

"Better one happy parent than two grouchy ones, don't you think? If I have to wait for a man I can get along with, I may be waiting the rest of my life."

"But the child would be a bastard!"

"Everybody else is."

"Rebecca, a child's life is no joking matter. I have read that the divorce rate among children of divorced parents is over twice the rate for those whose parents remain married."

"For God's sake, Ann, I was just kidding. I probably won't ever have a child in or out of wedlock, so let's drop it."

"I'm sorry, I didn't mean to upset you. But I'm very sensitive on the subject of divorce. Keeping my marriage together hasn't always been the easiest thing in the world. But how ungrateful of me to complain about a husband who works so hard and treats his wife with such respect! Now, what was it you wanted to tell me?"

"I have to tell you about"—Rebecca hesitated—"how nice it is having you for a friend."

"And I am happy to have you for a friend," Ann said. She laughed. "I'm so relieved—I thought you had bad news."

"No." Rebecca shook her head. "Only good news in Never-Never Land."

Perhaps the most miraculous aspect of Beeze's mansion was the formal garden which backed it—four acres of fountains, topiary hedges, flowerbeds and avenues, shade trees and benches, all laid out with the symmetry and correctness of the seventeenth-century parterre garden, and surrounded by a twelve-foot-high stone wall. There was even a maze at the far end of the garden, a twisting, turning path past high hedges, complete with false turns and culs-de-sac. Late one afternoon Jasmine led Rebecca through the maze and they wandered for what seemed like half an hour, before arriving in an exquisite miniature garden with a brass sundial.

The entire garden would have turned brown after a few hours if not for the careful selection of the plants, the subterranean water table—which was close to the surface, as is the case in every oasis—and the sprinkler system which drenched everything every hour, except between eleven and two, when the intensity of the sun would have caused scorching. A bell would ring first, warning anyone who might be strolling past the flowerbeds to return to the main avenues or risk a soaking. But when Rebecca was nude sunbathing, which she tried to do every morning once her rash had cleared up, she would, at the sound of the bell, intentionally remain motionless on her towel, a few feet away from the sprinkler head, waiting for the spray of cold water on her oven-hot skin, a sensation both pleasurable and masochistic in the extreme. Or if she had missed the sprinkler, she would jump into the enormous bowl of the marble fountain and shower beneath a stream from the mouth of a marble dolphin.

Nobody but Rebecca was allowed in the garden before 2 P.M. because of Beeze's Peeping Tom edict, which was still in effect; but after that time Mr. Munckle and Mrs. Munckle and occasionally Samson, and even Beeze himself, if he felt like it, were outside, fertilizing, weeding, pruning and trimming, planting flats of flowers flown all the way from Los Angeles. By five o'clock the work would be done; that was the time when the air began to grow cool with the promise of evening, and the garden was at its loveliest. Then the people who lived in the mansion would stroll down the avenues, talking quietly, or enjoying the air, and peace and perfection on earth seemed indeed a possibility.

One afternoon Rebecca found Beeze in the garden, sitting on a bench in the shade of an umbrella, working with a pad and several huge books, writing, then crossing out and rewriting. She skipped over to him, feeling very seductive in a new sundress she had found in her closet that morning. (She had no more than to mention a certain item of clothing in the evening and it would appear in her closet next morning, as if by magic.)

"What's that?" she said, glancing at one of the open books. "Chinese?" She kneeled in front of him, grinning, waiting for a reply.

Beeze shook his head. He was so intent on his work he barely seemed to notice her, the new dress notwithstanding. He was often like that when engrossed in a problem or playing the violin, concentrating to such an extraordinary degree that the rest of the world seemed to vanish. It reminded her of the way her father used to behave when he was working on a piece of sculpture, single-minded and deaf to her demands.

"Bee-eeze," she taunted softly, "this is Rebecca communicating to you from the Planet Earth; do you read me? Come in, please."

"Moment," he muttered, scribbling on the pad.

He put down his pencil and raised his head.

"It's classical Greek," he said. "I've taught myself the language in order to translate Plato, particularly the *Symposium*, which seems to me one of the seminal works of Western thought. You see, none of the existing translations really made sense to me, so I decided to translate it myself."

"Boy, Beeze, you're so smart. When I was in school, I used to hate kids like you."

"I'm sorry," Beeze said. "From now on I'll work only in the privacy of my room."

"For Christ's sake, I'm kidding. To tell you the truth I love watching you work. It's like watching Einstein discover $E = mc^2$."

"Hardly," Beeze said, although she could tell he enjoyed the comparison. "Would you like to hear a little?"

"I'd love to." Rebecca made herself comfortable in a cross-legged position and waited.

"I don't know if you're familiar with the *Symposium*. I suppose you could say it's philosophy expounded in the form of drama. The setting is a dinner party given by a Greek named Agathon, a great tragic poet, and attended by a host of the most learned, brilliant men of the time: Eryximachus, the doctor; Aristophanes, the comic poet; Alcibiades, who was a very powerful general. And, of course, Socrates, the greatest of the Greek philosophers, Plato's teacher and the central character in his Dialogues. During the course of the dinner party, all the guests decide to discourse, in turn, on the subject of Love. Now, the fascinating thing about Love is that it exists on so many levels, from lust and obsession to a means of attaining the very highest realm of experience, a term we might freely translate from the Greek as supreme knowledge. Each of the guests speaks of a different sort of love until finally Socrates puts them all into perspective with his own all-encompassing discourse. The climax of this discourse—both dramatically and philosophically—is the section where Socrates relates his own education in Love at the feet of a great wise woman, Diotima of Mantinea. This is the part I'm just completing."

He cleared his throat and began to read from the pad, pausing occasionally to correct a word with his pencil.

" 'And Diotima, the woman of Mantinea, the great teacher of Love, said to her student Socrates, "When a man desires to leave this shadow world we dwell in, and ascend to the higher realms of consciousness, and glimpse the Absolute Beauty which is Supreme Knowledge, he must use Love to guide his way. First he must learn to love an example of earthly beauty, a work of art or a beautiful boy; then he must generalize from one object to two, learning that Love is not the province of any single thing; then he must generalize from physical beauty to moral beauty, learning that Love does not dwell only in the physical; then from moral beauty to the beauty of knowledge, growing ever more abstract until finally he arrives at the Supreme Knowledge, which is itself Absolute Beauty. Having arrived there, he should spend his life contemplating it, for the briefest glimpse will convince him that it is valuable beyond gold or fine clothing or pretty boys. Imagine the bliss of he who has seen it in its essence, pure and unalloyed, that beauty which is eternal, unlike the fleeting beauty of flesh; immutable, unlike the rubble time makes of art. Will he live a poor life, he who keeps his gaze fixed upon It, who contemplates It with a calm mind, who dwells in unity with It? Isn't this the moment when he will perceive reality itself and not merely the image of it reflected in his imperfect mind? And having thus perceived reality, he will have the privilege of being beloved of God and obtaining, if ever a man can, immortality . . ." ' "

Beeze looked up from the page for her response.

"It's beautiful," Rebecca said. "But I'm not sure I understand what he's talking about."

"If you did, you would be one of the wisest men alive."

"*Women*," Rebecca corrected him, amused, "or hadn't you noticed?"

She wanted a compliment on her sundress, but Beeze was too involved with his work to oblige.

"The extraordinary thing about this passage," he continued, "is how closely it parallels the technique Patanjali described in his Yoga Sutras, an ancient Sanskrit work I have been studying with Yogi Gnesha. Patanjali says that in order to obtain Supreme Knowledge, the mind must first focus on concrete objects—*Savitarka samadhi*, in the Sanskrit; then on abstract forms—*Savichara samadhi*; then on mind itself—*Sa—sananda samadhi*; and finally on Nothingness—*Sa-asmita samadhi*. I have no doubt that the similarity is more than coincidental. Plato has too many images in common with the classic Sanskrit texts. For example, his metaphor of the mind and the senses as chariot and horses appears, slightly modified, in the Katha Upanishad—the famous dialogue between Nichikitas and Yama—and so does the discourse concerning the distinction between the 'pleasant' and the 'good.' Then, as always, Brahmans wandered all over Europe and the East, and I have little doubt that Socrates was one of their students. All the vagaries of Plato make perfect sense when interpreted in the context of the Indian mystical tradition."

"Want to play checkers?" Rebecca said.

The whispering waters of the fountain were vying with Beeze's voice, and she found it more and more difficult to concentrate. She felt beautiful and sexual and earthly, and matters metaphysical seemed of no more reality to her than the life she had left behind in Los Angeles. Furthermore, this sort of pontificating was precisely what her father used to do at the dinner table, lecturing in such a way that all were forced to listen and none could answer back, and it made her extremely antsy.

"Not now," Beeze said, beginning to rework one of the phrases in pencil.

"How about a walk?"

"Later."

Rebecca stood in front of him, hands clasped behind her back, going up and down on her toes like a little girl, and waiting for him to notice her. When it became apparent that he would not, she looked elsewhere for a means to distract him.

Mr. Munckle, as skinny as a cactus, was standing a few hundred feet from them with a hose, watering a new planting, a border of crimson coleus leaves, and humming to himself. All during the preceding conversation between Beeze and Rebecca, he had not so much as glanced in their direction, out of respect for their privacy; now that she was approaching him, he smiled and tipped his straw farmer's hat.

"Glad to see the sun finally come out from behind them clouds," he said.

Rebecca looked at the sky, puzzled, for she couldn't remember a day when it had been overcast.

"No, no, no." Munckle grinned. "What I mean is, glad to see you smiling again!"

"I'm feeling much better, thank you. Listen, I'm so hot. Think you could get me a little iced tea?"

"Be delighted. Just let me turn off the water."

"Don't bother," she said. "I'll water the plants."

"You don't want to . . ."

"I do!"

So he gave her the hose and went inside to get her some iced tea.

As an experiment, she held her thumb over the nozzle, forcing the water into a narrow, pressurized stream. Then she turned the hose toward Beeze, estimated the proper trajectory, and directed the slightest stream, no more than a drop or two really, at his head. He didn't even look up, simply brushed his ear as though a bug had been bothering him. Rebecca held her hand over her mouth to keep from laughing. She pointed the hose again, angled it like an antiaircraft gun, and fired off a few more drops. Again Beeze merely brushed at his ear. His concentration was quite incredible, as though perhaps he was already practicing the mysterious Yogic technique of *Sa-asmita samadhi*. Finally growing bored with his indifference, Rebecca turned the hose on him full stream.

Beeze screamed and leapt to his feet, agile as a cat; he was looking every which way, hands poised, ready for anything.

"Sorry," Rebecca said.

"There's water all over my papers! And you did it on purpose, didn't you?"

"I said I was sorry"—but now she was giggling uncontrollably.

"I'll beat the daylights out of you!" he said, coming toward her.

"You'll have to catch me first," she said, and turned the hose on him. The spray of water against his mask sounded like rain on a tin roof.

He turned away from her and retreated to the bench. There he remembered the umbrella that had shaded him during his work, pulled it out of its stand, and holding it in front of him like a shield, advanced on Rebecca.

"Uh-oh!" she said.

Even the hardest hose spray drummed uselessly against the taut red cloth of the umbrella. When Beeze was a few feet away, she dropped the hose and ran. He abandoned the umbrella and chased her down one avenue and up the next, shouting threats of what he would do when he caught her, and laughing. His laughter had an unused sound, like machinery being cranked back to life after years of neglect, and when, before recognizing it for what it was, she stopped, in concern for his health, he almost caught her. But then, at the last instant, she skipped away. She was light and quick on her feet, and she teased him as she ran, a teasing that promised she would soon let herself be caught. And the heat made their bodies slick with sweat and left their lungs heaving for air. Finally, in a deserted glen, she contrived to fall, and Beeze fell to his knees beside her.

"Now you'll pay," he gasped, grabbing her arms. His smell was musky, animal-like, overwhelming.

"Oh, I hope so!" she gasped. "But did you know that highly

intelligent people are more susceptible to tickling?" And she began to tickle him.

"Two can play," he said, retaliating.

She squealed with pleasure and tried to squirm out of his grasp. His hands moved lightly, yet authoritatively over the stretches of skin the sundress left naked, the particularly sensitive areas beneath her arms and down to her waist. As though by accident, they brushed against her breasts and touched her thighs. Her cheeks grew as hot as the sands beyond the garden. She felt his cock, like a ridge of bone, straining against the front of his pants.

"Oh, yes, Beeze," she whispered, "yes, yes . . ."

She moved on top of him, straddling him, wondering if he could feel her wetness, like an invitation. His smooth round mask hovered inches from her face like an unknown planet; the eyeholes were excavations to the soul. She wanted to kiss his mouth, she wanted it more than anything in the world.

"This is ridiculous," she said, and reaching up, pulled the mask from his face.

How many times had she prepared herself for this moment? *Is that all?* she would say, caressing his scarred face. *Is that what all the fuss was about?*

But all her preparation hadn't prepared her for this.

The shock of what she saw blew away all resolve, emptied her mind of admiration and respect and desire as a grenade might empty a foxhole. Yet she couldn't take her eyes away. A strange strangling sound came from deep within her, from the cave where primordial animal fear survives in even the most civilized of souls. She crawled to her feet and backed away from him, eyes widening, breath quickening. Helplessly she shook her head, trying to deny what she saw. Then she turned and ran for the house.

"Your iced tea . . ." Mr. Munckle said, passing her at the doorstep with a pitcher and glass on a tray, looking after her with confusion.

She ran up to her room, slammed the door and locked it, climbed into bed with all her clothes on and pulled the covers over her head as she had done in childhood when awakening from nightmares. And despite her time in the sun, despite the covers and the clothes, she found herself shivering.

After that Beeze disappeared. She thought he would keep to himself for a day or two and then gradually return to the life they had lived up to that point, allowing her to apologize, to restore his honor. But the "X's" marched relentlessly along the ranks of the lipstick calendar she had scrawled across the wall in her early captivity, and still there was no sign of him.

Each afternoon she walked in the garden, past all the shaded benches where Beeze might be working on his translations, but she never saw any sign of him. Each evening she went to the library and set up the checkerboard and waited, but Beeze never came. Sometimes, late at night, she heard the haunting sound of his violin, a new tragedy to the notes, a cadence that tore at her heart, and then she hurried from her bed and, wrapped in a robe, ran down the hallway to the music room; but she always found it empty. None of the other residents of the mansion had seen him either. Samson, who personally brought Beeze his food, refused to nod or shake his head in response to Rebecca's questions, and stared at her so reproachfully that she left him alone after that. But David informed her that the purées which were Beeze's breakfast and lunch and dinner were being returned to the kitchen barely eaten, and Dr. Resnick had expressed concern over whether Beeze was keeping up his medication.

She had to confront him. She went to the foot of the circular staircase that led to his room, the eight-sided cupola atop the mansion, and steeled her nerve to climb the lonely distance, where none but Samson and Beeze had gone before her. Dozens of times she had stood there, contemplating the climb and its ramifications. Beeze's private chambers seemed to be the heart of the mansion, its most intimate and lofty aspiration. To invade this space would be the ultimate irreversible commitment. She began the ascent, and with every step a wire wound tighter around her heart. She had never been so afraid in her life. A million years later she reached the landing outside his room and knocked at the door.

"Come in," he said. His voice was flat, lifeless.

Rebecca opened the door. Eight plaster walls, three of them hidden by bookcases. A simple bed, a desk, a rocker with a wicker seat. A rag rug and a music stand, and his beloved violin on a cushion nearby. There was no luxury, no ornamentation besides the framed photographs on the night table, a boy playing the violin—his son, she assumed—and another that she recognized as a publicity still of herself from *Land of Lost Dreams*. The realization that she alone shared the space with his son, she, whom he had known only for a matter of weeks, was sad and moving.

"Put it on the table, Samson," he said, without bothering to turn around, "and leave me alone." He was sitting in the rocker, his back to her, reading, the mask on the floor beside him. He must have thought the servant was bringing him lunch.

"It's not Samson," Rebecca said.

Beeze grabbed the mask from the floor and, holding it tight against his face, rose from his seat and turned to her.

"Get out of here!"

"No. We've got to confront this thing."

"Please go away." His voice was filled with anguish.

"Not until you show me your face."

"Impossible. Out of the question."

"Take off your mask."

"Leave me alone."

She reached up gently, put her hand on his wrist and lowered the arm that held the mask. This time she knew what to expect and, although she couldn't repress the shiver that passed through her, she kept smiling. They stood like that, staring at each other, motionless for minutes. At first his face grew more frightening, but then, as she studied the peculiar texture of the skin, the odd geometry of the facial planes, it began to be familiar. Although it was incapable of human expression, she thought she saw signs of such pain and fear and suffering that her whole being swelled with compassion for him. She rose on her tiptoes to kiss the mouth that had no lips, but he turned away, murmuring "No."

"Yes," she insisted, and holding his face in her hands, kissed him and kissed him again.

They undressed and lay together on the bed, simply looking at each other. Most of the burns, she noticed, were confined to the upper right side of his torso, and the rest of the body was not unattractive: slim-waisted and broad-shouldered, with powerful arms and a cruciform pattern of hair across his chest. The scar where the aluminum spar had penetrated his stomach was a ridge of white tissue, hard as a callus when she traced it with her finger. Her hand strayed lower, to his fierce cock, and he reciprocated, caressing the soft lips of her cunt until they grew thick and wet and warm.

"We must be quick," he whispered. "I can't wait."

She straddled him and had no sooner lowered her buttocks over his organ than he came, in spasms so violent they seemed to rend her very bowels, spasms which drained off the tension of years of sexual abstinence. Then he rolled over on top of her and began again, cautiously at first, as though afraid that her slight, brittle frame would break under his enormous bulk, then harder as he grew assured of her durability, restraining himself while she came again and again, then finally allowing himself to join in the frenzy of release.

For hours they dozed and made love, the waking time becoming more and more sleepily sensual, the sleep becoming increasingly, erotically dreamy, until it became difficult to discern one from the other. Her body, wrung out with orgasm, ached deliciously, and her mind seemed devoid of any thought except Beeze. In the dim light of his chambers, her sleep-blurred eyes made a Rorschach of his face—for it was little more than a field of shadows and scars—and she saw there all the important men of her life, her father and Leslie, Will Roach and Jason Pine and Mack Gordon. And then she imagined that she could see, through some supernatural intervention, his face as it had been before the accident, the finely drawn features, the high intelligent brow, the penetrating eyes, the cool smile which could, at rare moments, and only if he wished, betray his secretive inner moods.

She imagined how he must have looked playing the violin in those days, his eyes half shut, his face serene, contemplative. That was how she would remember him, always and forever.

Some days later Rebecca learned that Mrs. Munckle wanted to speak to her. She made her way to their suite of rooms in the basement, near the closets that held the cleaning supplies, close enough to the air-conditioning compressors that the sound of those enormous machines underscored all conversation. Mrs. Munckle opened the door, her small eyes red from crying. A blue terry-cloth bathrobe, faded from washing, hung over her like a tent, and her hair was gathered under a cheap orange scarf. Tiny hands massaged each other in worry. The room behind her was dark and cluttered with bric-a-brac, porcelain figurines, tourist mementos, plaques with religious mottoes and commemorative plates. The smell of pine disinfectant made Rebecca's head reel. The furniture seemed to have been scavenged from some northern hunting lodge; everywhere the walls were covered with wildlife prints, some apparently torn from magazines and framed—everywhere, that is, except the space over the mantel, which was occupied by a life-sized oil painting of Mr. and Mrs. Munckle dressed in their best attire and posed as stiffly as the farmer and his wife in Grant Wood's "American Gothic."

When Mrs. Munckle saw who her caller was, she grimaced with revulsion.

"Well, look who's here. Miss Hollywood Whore, paying a charity call."

"What?" Rebecca said, astonished. "You asked to see me."

"That's right. I want to ask you a question. I want to know why don't you just kill me and get it over with. Why don't you just take a knife and stab me *here*?" She pulled open the top of her robe, exposing her enormous cleavage.

"What are you talking about?"

"Go ahead. Pretend you don't know. That act may fool the others—it may even fool Beeze—but it don't fool me."

"What *are* you talking about?"

"After all, you're an actress, and in my book the difference between an actress and a whore is that the whore works harder and the actress gets better pay."

"I came here because you wanted to talk to me," Rebecca said, her patience wearing thin, "but the next time you call me a whore, I'm leaving."

"Then leave! We had a good life before you came, me and Munckle. We was getting more money than we ever seen, money to live real good, with enough left over to buy us a condo in Miami when we retire. Then you come along and all the trouble started. Beeze mooning around like a lovesick cow, Henry and

David fighting all hours of the night, and now poor Munckle . . ." Exhausted by her anger, she broke down in tears.

"What about him, damn it?"

Mrs. Munckle was crying so hard she couldn't answer. Rebecca tried to comfort her, but the big woman shied away from her touch. She blew her nose into a handkerchief, rubbed her eyes with her palms and, staring straight at Rebecca, said in a voice trembling with hatred, "Mr. Munckle's been watching you get naked in the garden. Beeze found out and now he's going to put out his eyes. Hope you're happy with what you done."

Rebecca felt sick to her stomach. She remembered the night before when, lying in bed with Beeze, she had mentioned, simply to amuse him, that she had noticed Mr. Munckle staring at her through an opening in the hedge during her sunbathing, and for fun had put on a show for him, oiling herself with excessive languor, striking pinup poses on her marble bench, pretending to find a pimple just below her right nipple. Wasn't a thread of exhibitionism woven into the cloth of every actor? How incredibly stupid of her. Now that it was too late, she recalled Beeze's threat to blind any voyeur—and still she couldn't believe it.

She shook her head at Mrs. Munckle. "He must have been . . ." She was going to say *joking*, but then she thought about those other stories of Beeze's justice, the unhappy gardener whose tongue had been cut out, the men sent to ravage Leslie's apartment, and left the sentence unfinished.

"I'll talk to Beeze," Rebecca promised. "I'll make him change his mind."

"Make the wind stop blowing," Mrs. Munckle said, "make the world stop turning."

Learning that Beeze and Munckle were in the music room, Rebecca sat on the chair outside, waiting for their audience to end. Soon Mr. Munckle appeared, drawn and spiritless as a beaten dog. He stopped when he saw Rebecca, who was on the verge of tears herself now, and from somewhere managed to find a smile.

"Don't let those clouds cover up the sun," he murmured, pulling a nickel out of her ear, dropping it in her palm.

"I'll make him change his mind," Rebecca whispered.

"Beeze knows about justice," Mr. Munckle said. "He'll do what's right and I'll get what's coming to me." He smiled weakly and, turning his back on her, shuffled down the hall.

Beeze was resining his bow when Rebecca entered, moving the wooden applicator along the horsehair with long even strokes.

She laughed and said, "There's a big misunderstanding. Remember that story I told you about Mr. Munckle watching me sunbathe? Well, I just made it up. I thought it would turn you on."

"Munckle has confessed," Beeze said, impassively. "He must be punished."

"You're not serious? You're not actually going to . . ."

"I said that anyone watching you would be blinded. He has disobeyed and must suffer the consequences."

"Beeze!" She held out open hands. "You said you wanted to learn how to love. Well, here's your chance, damn it! If you love me—if you've ever loved anybody—please, *please* don't hurt Mr. Munckle. He's a harmless old man and he didn't mean anything. It's my fault for provoking him."

"I made a law and now I must live by it. If the law sets me back ten thousand lifetimes on my path to enlightenment, then that is my punishment for making the law in the first place."

"You can't do it," she cried. "I won't let you."

"I must," he said, simply.

"Harm one hair on his head and it's all done between us. I can't love a man who acts with this kind of cruelty."

"It's not cruelty. I made a law and . . ."

"It's *cruelty*, it's horrible cruelty. You're no different from when you were working for the war machine. All this mysticism and philosophy and vegetarianism, it's all just a pose. You're still the monster you were and I hate you, I hate you, I hate you!"

·9·

One day Beast found Beauty sitting in the garden by herself, and weeping, with none to console her but the animals of the forest, who drew near in sympathy and nuzzled her and licked her hands.

Pray tell me, Beauty, said he, why do you weep so? I have given you all that I have; my palace and everything within it are yours for the keeping.

You are a very kind Beast, to be sure, she said, and I do not weep for want of beautiful things; no, I weep for my poor dear father, whose face I fear I shall never see again.

Go to the mirror in the hall, the Beast said, and look upon it; for it is a magic mirror and within it you will see whatever place or person your heart desires.

Learning this, Beauty hastened to the mirror in the hall and wished with all her might that she might see her dear father once more.

The mirror grew hazy, as though the mist of early evening had settled across it, and when it cleared she saw her father; but oh, the sight filled her with misery, for he was lying abed, and looked sick and pale unto death, and Beauty's two sisters were gathered around the bedside, as was the doctor, and a priest who had been called to read the last rites. And Beauty heard the doctor tell the priest, Be quick, for he is dying of a broken heart for his daughter Beauty, the person who is, in all the world, most precious to him.

Beauty ran at once to the Beast and said to him, You must let me return home, for my father is grievously ill and dying for want of me, and I believe that the sight of me may restore him to health. If you wish me to be your wife, grant me this boon; in seven days I shall return and from that day on I shall never again leave your side; I shall plight my troth to you and we shall be man and wife as long as we both may live.

Go then, said the Beast, but know this: every day you are away my grief grows like a cancer; and if you do not return after seven days and seven nights, I will surely die of unhappiness.

Oh, Beast, Beauty cried, I should never allow that! I shall return in seven days, be there no doubt in your mind on that account.

Take this golden ring, Beast said, handing it to her, and place it on your finger. When you remove it again, you will find yourself at your father's bedside. Then you need only replace it upon your finger to return to my palace.

You are indeed a kindly Beast, she said, taking the ring from him and placing it upon her finger. I swear before God that I shall return to you in seven days and serve you forever after as wife.

And saying this, she removed the ring from her finger . . .

"And this is the bedroom," Mopsy said, switching on a lamp from Ambiente.

"A single bed?" Samantha asked, raising an eyebrow that had been carefully tweezed at Georgette Klinger's skin salon.

"My husband, Charley Goldenblatt, the famous international film producer, works long hours. We decided it would be simpler if we had separate bedrooms."

"Poor Mopsy," Samantha said, sitting sensuously on the bed. "No one has given you pleasure in a long time, have they?" She ran her tongue over her lips, which were outlined in Payot lipstick and gave her a glance made more smoldering by her Estée Lauder eye shadow.

"I . . . I don't know what you're talking about," Mopsy stammered.

"Come, sit beside me." Samantha patted the stylish Laura Ashley bedspread.

Mopsy sat down beside her.

In an instant Samantha unbuttoned the top of Mopsy's Missoni knit suit, pushed aside her Bulgari gold necklace, inlaid with small diamonds and one large ruby, unhooked her silk bra from

Bendel's, and began to kiss Mopsy's magnificent soft round breasts. "Don't be afraid . . . Let me be good to you . . . I know how to give you pleasure . . . You must simply lie there without moving a muscle . . . Let me do all the work . . ."

"I never dreamed it could be like this," Mopsy breathed, intoxicated by the scent of Bal à Versailles.

"When will your husband be home?" Samantha asked, burying her face in the other woman's Venus mound of tangled chestnut hair.

"Who knows? He said he was going to the studio. But most of the time I think he goes to see his mistress. I wonder that he ever finds time to make a film."

Billy Rosenblatt slammed the manuscript down on his desk, muttering, "Flopsy, Mopsy, Cottontail," and punched the intercom: "Flossy, come in here."

"Yes, boss." She was trying not to grin.

"What's your opinion of this?"

"Well." She phrased it in her head before answering. "The story is compelling. It's a real page-turner. And the theme of a single woman finding herself is pretty popular in publishing today. Look at *Princess Daisy*."

"Tell me this, Flossy." He thought he was containing his temper admirably. "Do you think the book's going to sell?"

"Well, from what I understand about publishing, it's too early to say. My friend Harriet at Butterfield Press says that so far the book clubs aren't interested and the paperback houses want to wait and see how the first printing goes."

"In other words," Billy Rosenblatt said, slightly relieved, "it may sink without a trace?"

"Maybe. But I'd better tell you—there's film interest. Your ex-wife's had feelers from Fox and three independents. They want to make a big movie out of it, all-star cast, like *Valley of the Dolls* or *The Other Side of Midnight*."

"God help me."

"Universal's interested too."

"Flossy, does this seem right to you? That a man who is practically a legend in the movie business should be subjected to this kind of humiliation?"

Flossy looked at her feet. "No, boss."

"Does it seem fair that such a man's wife should turn on him and write a book revealing all the most intimate secrets of their marriage? Does that seem fair? And reducing it to tawdry comedy and pornography?"

Flossy shook her head.

He rose from his desk and began to pace the office.

"Flossy, I'll tell you why there's movie interest. It's not because this piece of illiterate cow shit will make a good movie. No, that's not the reason." He was talking to himself now, and suddenly he seemed very old and tired. "It's because over the years, I've made my share of enemies. Let me pass on an important bit of advice. If your work is good, you'll make enemies. Oh, I know who they are. They've been out there for a long time, waiting for an opportunity like this. Know what they'll do, Flossy? Find somebody who looks just like me to play the part of myself. Put him in sexually humiliating situations. Make him out to be a second-rate producer. A phony. A crook. Bah."

"I don't think they'd do that, Billy."

"They'll do it, all right, and I've got to figure out a way to stop them."

"How about a libel suit?"

"Then I'd have to prove that I was actually that loathsome character in the book. The publicity would help sales. I'd be tying my own noose."

Flossy thought some more. "Why don't you buy it yourself and put it on the shelf? Write it off and take the deduction."

"She'd never sell it to me. She knows me better than that." He beat the palm of his left hand with the fist of his right. "There must be a way."

The phone rang and Flossy picked it up.

"Billy Rosenblatt's office. Who's calling? I'm sorry, I think he's in a meeting. Can you hold on a minute?"

She pressed "Hold" and said, "Leslie Horowitz returning your call. Do you want to call back when you're not so angry?"

"Angry? I'm not angry." Billy Rosenblatt sat down at his desk, took the phone and punched the blinking light.

"Horowitz," he said, "where's Rebecca Weiss? I've been trying to get in touch with her for weeks. I want her, you hear? I've got her signature on a piece of paper. Shooting begins in eighteen days and if she's not here I'm going to slap her with the biggest damn lawsuit she's ever seen. She'll be paying damages for the rest of her life! I'll see to it that she never works in this town again! And that goes for you too! And all your clients!"

Billy slammed down the phone, breathing heavily. His face was red and his hands were trembling.

"I'd hate to see you when you're angry," Flossy said.

Billy jumped to his feet, pointed to the door and screamed, "GET OUT OF HERE!"

"Yes, boss," she said, and quickly retreated.

Billy sat down at his desk, cradled his head in his hands and groaned. Why did everything insist on going wrong at once? It was preposterous to be this close to shooting and have no star. Insane! Throughout a difficult career, he had always been able to relax, but recently certain stomach pains had suggested the beginnings of an ulcer.

He picked up *Daily Variety*, leafed through it absently, stopped when he came to a full-page ad announcing that Mack Gordon was planning to reshoot *Web!* with Victoria Dunbarr in the leading role. What unnatural acts had she performed, Billy wondered, to make that reptilian director decide to undertake such a drastic last-minute measure? And yet, at the same time he was impressed. If Mack Gordon thought Victoria could carry *Web!*, well then, perhaps Billy had underestimated her. Perhaps she could play Jacqueline. She would certainly be less difficult than Rebecca Weiss, and other, more personal benefits would be worth considering too —such as a reprise of the delightful time they'd shared in the sauna. Yes, the more Billy thought about it, the more sensible it seemed. Sometimes the young unknowns, offered that choice part, gave the performances of their lives, for example Brando in *Streetcar*, James Dean in *Rebel Without a Cause*.

He stabbed the intercom and asked Flossy to set up the videotape machine so he could view Victoria's screen test one more time.

Eighteen more days. He had to do something.

Leslie put down the phone and stared mournfully across the office at Sheila Gold.

"What did he say?" Sheila asked.

"He said," Leslie replied, "that he would slap her with the biggest damn lawsuit she had ever seen."

They kept their desks at either end of the long narrow room, and alternately spoke on the phone and shouted at each other—shouted to be heard over the noise from the recording studio downstairs, where, it seemed, L.A.'s loudest rock musicians laid down tracks from early morning till well into the night. Leslie refused to move because the location, a two-story beige brick building on Sunset, was close to his apartment and the film studios in the Valley, and because the rock musicians who strayed upstairs had with them the very finest of drugs. That was, in fact, how Leslie had obtained the paper of cocaine he was now spreading into rows on top of a glass paperweight with the aid of a letter opener.

"It could be worse," Sheila said.

"How?"

"You could have cancer."

"At least I'd be dead. I could stop worrying about everything." He gestured at the cocaine. "Want some?"

"I'm cutting down," she said.

She was a short, plump Jewish girl from the west side of Greenwich Village, with a round face, pleasant features, and straight black hair which she kept short. She liked to wear black leotards with wraparound skirts, a style she clung to because it made her feel as though she was still only visiting from New York. Why were New Yorkers so reluctant to admit to themselves that they had moved to Los Angeles? She had actor clients who had come here years ago, and still kept their New York apartments for the day they would be moving back—a day that would never come.

"And you should too," she added.

She hated to remark on it, but in the weeks since Rebecca's disappearance he had been drinking so heavily and taking so many drugs that it was beginning to interfere with his work. He arrived late at the office, hung over and sallow-complexioned, and sometimes he couldn't recall whom he had just spoken to on the phone.

Although Leslie refused to talk about it, she suspected that he held himself responsible for Rebecca's disappearance, and she was afraid that the guilt was more than he could handle.

"*I'm cutting down, I'm cutting down,*" he said, mimicking her New York accent. "Everybody's cutting down."

"Everybody but you. You're cutting *up.*"

"That's right. I'm a notorious cut-up."

He raised the glass paperweight to his nose and began to suck the rows of powder into his nostrils, using a rolled-up fifty-dollar bill for a funnel.

Then he lay back in his chair, feeling the white powder permeate the delicate membranes of his nose and rush to his brain, numbing the folds of gray matter, providing him temporary respite from his anguish over Rebecca. He stared at the ceiling, a pleasingly uninteresting grid of acoustical tile, studded with fire sprinklers like little metal mushrooms.

"Leslie," Sheila said, gently, "we've got to call Mack Gordon about that ad in *Daily Variety*. If he's really cutting Rebecca out of the movie— I don't know. We should take some kind of action."

"It's a bluff," Leslie said. "I don't know why he's doing it, but it's a bluff."

"How can you be sure?"

" 'Cause who ever heard of reshooting a movie that's already in the can? A couple of scenes, maybe. But Rebecca's in more than half of it."

"Well, I'm going to call him up and find out what's going on."

"Be my guest," Leslie said.

As soon as she was through dialing, he lifted the receiver, with exceeding care, and held the earpiece to his ear, the mouthpiece level with his forehead lest his breathing be heard.

"Yeah?" Mack Gordon said, on the phone.

"This is Sheila from the Horowitz-Gold office. Someone just brought to my attention an ad in *Daily Variety* expressing your intentions to . . ."

"Yeah, well, I don't know who the fuck bought that ad, but when I find out I'll bust their ass. I'm not reshooting anything. The picture is visually perfect. It's a fucking masterpiece. Emilio Pugliosi watched the rough cut with me and said he thought it was the finest piece of American film-making since *Nashville*. But what I am going to do is redub the whole goddamn thing. Now, everybody's telling me that Rebecca Weiss went to India with her guru, or she's back in New York, or else she's in Timbuktu. The truth is, I don't give a shit where she is as long as she's in the dubbing studio Monday morning, got it? And I want her for two weeks."

"Excuse me, Mr. Gordon, but I believe Rebecca's contract only stipulates two days of dubbing."

"And I stipulate that she's caused me a hell of a lot of trouble already and if she causes me any more I'm going to sue her for ten million dollars' damages and make sure that she never works again in this town. And the same goes for all your other clients."

"Thank you, Mr. Gordon," Sheila said. "Mr. Horowitz and I will discuss your offer with our client."

"Fucking better," he grumbled, and hung up.

"Delightful fellow," Sheila said to Leslie, putting down the phone.

"A charmer," Leslie agreed.

"There's one thing I don't understand."

"What's that?"

"Who's Emilio Pugliosi?"

"Somebody with very strange taste," Leslie said.

Leslie didn't finish work until nearly seven-thirty that night and hurried home, hoping to see Tommy before he went off to his acting class. But when he arrived, the apartment was empty. He desperately needed someone to talk to about all the things that were troubling him, but Rebecca and Tommy were the only one he could confide in, and neither of them was available. Loneliness and depression overwhelmed him. The homosexual life seemed some kind of insane joke. He took a shower and a hefty snort of cocaine and went down to the garage. He would drive along that section of Santa Monica where the street was lined with boys, and buy a friend for the evening. His long white Lincoln Continental had been recovered by the Highway Patrol a month ago, but due to bureaucratic stupidity and the difficulty of finding a bonded driver to bring it back to Los Angeles, he was still driving a rental. The leasing agency had, with some difficulty, located another huge white Continental, almost identical to his own car, the only model Leslie would drive.

He climbed inside and turned the key. When it was evident that the engine would not be starting that evening, he ran around to the front of the car and kicked it so hard that the fender crumpled like a beer can in a strong man's fist. Back in his apartment he called the agency which had rented to him, and screamed at them over the phone, accusing them of every chicanery. When they realized that it was Leslie Horowitz (they did lots of business with him, renting cars to his New York clients when they came to work on the Coast), they apologized and promised to send another car immediately. It had to be a white '79 Lincoln Continental, Leslie insisted, angrily irrational, he would accept nothing else. They assured him they could supply something serviceable until his leased Lincoln was repaired, which work they would begin first thing in the morning.

He waited downstairs and was horrified when a red Toyota sedan pulled up in front of the building. It was the kind of car he imagined seeing in the circus, an impossible number of clowns and dwarfs and trained dogs spilling out of the front door. Still, he signed the receipt and took the wheel, and soon he was cruising down Santa Monica, shopping for young flesh.

Up ahead he saw a lean, blond young man in jeans so tight that they outlined his buttocks, and a Western shirt. This was his favorite type, not overly muscled, but sinewy, lithe, a dancer like Tommy. He slowed and cranked down the passenger window, nervously preparing a line, something like *You look good enough to eat,* which usually made them smile. Without his long white Lincoln Continental, he felt naked and afraid, as though all his accomplishments had been stripped from him.

To his dismay, the black Porsche in front of him pulled to a stop beside the blond young man, and Leslie could see the driver leaning across the seat, flirting, negotiating. The blond young man crouched beside the car, turning his profile to Leslie.

It was Tommy.

No question about it.

They talked for a few moments and then the driver pushed open the door and Tommy climbed in beside him; they drove away together in a roar of supercharged pistons and a cloud of squid-ink smoke. Leslie sat where he was, too shocked to drive. The car behind him honked, but he didn't seem to hear. It honked again and again, and only then did he realize that he had parked his car in the middle of the street. He put the engine in gear and drove away, deaf to a hustler propositioning him from the sidewalk.

Tommy came home at 2 A.M. He found Leslie sitting in the easy chair in the bedroom, finishing a bottle of bourbon. The television was on, the volume turned up high, but whatever station he was watching had already signed off the air, and all that remained were climbing bars of static and a mind-deadening *hiss* of random noise.

"Good Lord," Tommy said.

He went to the television and began to turn it off.

"Stop," Leslie said. "That's my favorite movie."

"There's nothing on. The station's signed off."

"Are you sure?" Leslie squinted at the screen.

"I think you need a cold shower and some hot coffee."

Tommy tried to help Leslie out of the chair.

"Don't touch me," Leslie said.

"What's this all about?"

"Your acting class. You never told me it was on Santa Monica."

Tommy opened his mouth, started to speak, tried again, could find nothing to say. For need of a release, he made a sound like the air being let out of a tire. He went to the sideboard where they kept the liquor, bending with marvelous grace for a bottle of Scotch, poured himself a shot, which he downed, shivering, in a gulp, and another. Better. He nodded and began:

"I'm guilty, I admit it. I should have told you but I was scared it would ruin everything. And what we have is so precious, I didn't want to take any chances. You see, I love you, Leslie. I really do. I've never felt this way about anybody before and I doubt if I ever will again. But I have to hustle!" It was a plea from the bottom of his soul, filled with anguish. "That's my dope. Know how you feel when you're on the phone and you're cooking up a deal for one of your clients? And something in your blood starts to sing? And you're surfing and you've caught a hundred-foot wave that's never going to let you down? Well, that's how

I feel when I have a good night on the street. Leslie, that's the feeling that makes it worthwhile being alive! If it was anything less than that, I'd cut it out, I swear I would."

Tommy waited.

Leslie stared at the TV set, now silent, cold. After a minute he said, "Get out."

"Leslie, don't do this to me. You were on the street tonight too. You were buying. I was selling. There's not that much difference."

"If you'd been *here*, I wouldn't have had to go *there*."

"Oh yes you would. You like to cruise. That's nothing to be ashamed of. I can sell and you can buy, and we can still be lovers."

"I can't live like that."

"It's the only way we *can* live, Leslie."

"Why don't you just admit it? The only reason you moved in with me was because you thought I could help your career as an actor."

"That does it," Tommy said. He left the room and returned with a suitcase which he laid open on the bed. Then he went to the closet and came back with an armful of clothes.

Leslie stumbled to his feet. "What are you doing?"

Tommy ignored him, returned from the bathroom with a load of toiletries, dumped them in the suitcase on top of the clothes. He had to sit on it to close it and even then corners of shirts and ends of ties stuck out from between the clasps.

"Stop!" Leslie screamed. Dramatically, he threw open the double doors that led to the balcony overlooking Fountain Avenue. A cool breeze blew the gossamer curtains into the room and street sounds filtered up from below. "Take one more step and I'll jump."

Tommy sighed. "We're only on the second floor. At worst you'll sprain an ankle."

"I'll fall on my head. A car will hit me."

"Goodbye," Tommy said, and walked out the door.

"I'LL JUMP!" Leslie screamed after him.

He was halfway down the stairs, muttering to himself, "Of all the silly, infantile threats . . ." when he heard the *thunk*, like a sack of potatoes thrown from a truck, and a screaming of brakes, and a crunching of metal. He dropped the suitcase, turned and dashed back to the bedroom. Hanging over the wrought-iron rail of the balcony, he could see how the two cars had collided, swerving to avoid the object which had fallen from above. And he could see the object itself, Leslie's body, face down on the pavement, motionless.

Rebecca slept alone in the guest suite, rather than sharing Beeze's bed in the eight-sided room atop the mansion, as had been her habit. She could no longer bear his presence since he had decided to blind Munckle. At night she lay twisting and turning between the sheets, trying to imagine how the deed would be done. Would they drag him, screaming, to the sterile white basement laboratory, where slaughtered pigs left the floor slick with blood, or would they seize him suddenly in the hallway, without warning? Would he be anesthetized, or made to feel the pain of his eyes being punctured like shirred eggs beneath the fork? And what would become of him now that he could no longer work as a projectionist? Rebecca vowed to take care of him. She would house the Munckles in her guest room (after all, she was sponsoring Victoria, who had no handicaps at all) and find him a job both absorbing and useful to society. Only after having made these vows could she find peace to sleep.

In the morning, on her way to breakfast, she passed Samson in the hall. He was carrying a silver tray with a white linen napkin on it. Laid out on the napkin was some kind of surgical instrument smooth, sparkling silver with a point like an ice pick. Next to i was a box of cotton, a bottle of alcohol and several sterile dressings. Rebecca felt her stomach turn.

"Where are you going?" she demanded.

Samson ignored her.

She stood in front of him and he pushed her away, as though she were furniture. Then she chased after him, pulling at his coat hitting with her fists, growing ever more frantic as he came eve closer to the Munckles' apartment. He was invincible, like som kind of demonic machine, oblivious to her except when her his trionics threatened to overturn the tray, and then he shoved he gently and firmly away. When he reached the basement, and Re becca could no longer entertain the slightest doubt about his de tination, she ran ahead of him to the Munckles' apartment and banged on the door.

Mrs. Munckle opened it, grim, calm. Beyond her, Rebecca could see Mr. Munckle sitting stiffly in one of the overstuffed armchairs, with a gaze so blank that the blinding might have already taken place.

"He's coming," Rebecca gasped. "Mr. Munckle's got to hide . . ."

Mrs. Munckle stared at her, saying nothing.

"Please," Rebecca went on, "you haven't much time!"

"Beeze been good to us," Mrs. Munckle said, her voice flat with resignation. "We benefited from him, now we got to bide by his laws."

"You can't just stand by while your husband gets . . ."

"Don't tell me what I can or can't do, girlie! I take my orders from Munckle. This is what he wants."

"Mr. Munckle," Rebecca called to him, "won't you please hide!"

Munckle shook his head, but kept his eyes fixed on the wall. He was obviously terrified, and doing everything he could to contain his fear.

At that moment Samson pushed past her.

"No," she cried, "NO!"

She fell to her knees and buried her face in her hands, unwilling to watch the horror. The scream never came; instead she heard a ripping noise, like cloth being torn. She looked up and saw Samson jab the surgical tool into the painting above the mantelpiece, and tear out eyes of canvas and oil. Finished, he turned and started for the door, betraying as little emotion as when he had entered.

Mrs. Munckle burst into tears. She grabbed her husband by the arm, shouting, "It's all right, it's all right!" But Munckle wouldn't look up. She had to stoop down in front of him, inserting her massive form into his line of sight and explain over and over that Beeze had granted him a reprieve; and even then he was not convinced.

Rebecca left the room without a word.

That evening when she went to the library, Beeze was waiting for her, sitting at the checkerboard, arranging the pieces. He wore the mask, as he always did, except when they were actually making love. (Although she was used to his real face by now, and undisturbed by it, he had grown so accustomed to the mask that he simply was not comfortable without it.)

"Red or black?" he said, casually.

"Thank you," she said.

"For what?"

"For—changing." Sensing his embarrassment, she continued quickly, "Let's play some checkers. I'm feeling lucky tonight."

"There's something I'd like to show you first. Call it an early Christmas present."

He led her to where two easy chairs had been rearranged to face a wall of bookcases. A cabinet had been built into the middle of the wall—whether it had been there before, Rebecca couldn't recall—and now, as she made herself comfortable in one of the chairs, Beeze unlocked the cabinet and opened it, and stood proudly to one side.

"Far. Out." That was all she could say.

A small color television faced her, wired, Beeze explained, to a powerful amplifier and a sixty-foot antenna near the house. He had installed it expressly, he explained, so that Rebecca could watch the Los Angeles news and learn what was happening in her hometown.

After weeks of abstinence, television was a great treat. Rebecca felt as though she were peering through a window, into another world; her time in the mansion had made her that much of a foreigner, and as with a foreigner, details that would have otherwise gone unnoticed in their ordinariness now made an enormous impression on her. A story about the Vietnamese boat people, for example, whose frail vessel, refused harbor by neighboring countries, sank finally, drowning them like so many unwanted kittens, brought tears to her eyes. A human-interest piece concerning a dog from the pound that had won the title of Ugliest Mutt, and the fame and honors accompanying it, had her rocking with laughter. But it was the story following that which brought her to the edge of the seat, made her catch her breath and clench her fists till the knuckles turned white:

"Traffic on Fountain Avenue was interrupted early this morn

ing when a man jumped from a second-story window after a heated domestic quarrel. The man, Leslie Horowitz . . ."

"Oh no," Rebecca said.

". . . a theatrical manager whose clients include several well-known actors, was taken to UCLA Medical Center, where he is now reported to be in critical condition. Gang violence broke out again in . . ."

"Beeze, it's Leslie," Rebecca cried, pulling at his arm. "He's hurt and he needs me. Let me go to him for a week, and I'll come back to you, I swear I will. I'll never ask anything of you again. I'll be your wife and I'll live with you and be faithful to you as long as you like, here in the desert, or in Los Angeles—or wherever it is you want to live—but please, let me go to him!"

"You may go," Beeze said, simply as that.

Rebecca sniffed back tears, looked up at him, trying to see into the eye-holes of the mask, those deep tunnels to Beeze's soul, but the distance was too far, the light too dim. She had been so prepared for his refusal that she didn't know what to say.

"I may?"

"Yes."

"Oh, Beeze!"

Now she was crying again, crying with happiness. She covered his hands with kisses.

"I'll be back in a week," she murmured. "I swear I will. And after that we'll never be apart again."

Beeze didn't reply. He let her go on for a minute or more, then he pushed her gently away.

"Excuse me, please," he said. "There are many things I must attend to."

And with that he left her, alone except for the gay patter of voices on the television.

During the night she dreamed she was struggling through a rain forest, searching for civilization.

I've got to get back in time to start shooting, she kept saying.

Beeze appeared beside her, dressed like a railroad conductor, holding a withered rose. *You will,* he promised, *I've seen to everything. It's all taken care of.*

Yet at every turn tendrils wrapped about her ankles, impeding her progress, and the shifting soil seemed to swallow up her steps. Then the mosquitoes came, thousands of them, some as big as sparrows, buzzing louder and louder. Sitting up in bed, she realized it was the sound of helicopters that had woken her, helicopters flying over the mansion. She lay awake for hours wondering what it portended.

In the morning the mansion was deserted. She rang for breakfast, but no one came. She ran to Ann's room and banged on the door, but the door was open and the suite of rooms was empty, stripped of the fine antiques, the scrolls which had adorned the walls, the furniture and carpets. The other rooms were empty too, and as she ran down the hall, the rap-tap of her heels echoing like the drum roll before an execution, she was seized with a panic she had not felt so vividly since childhood, the terror of being abandoned.

She strained her ears for the familiar sounds of pans clattering in the kitchen, of Mrs. Munckle berating her husband, of movies being screened and gardens being watered and sutras being chanted; all were gone and nothing remained, not even the groan of the air conditioner, the heartbeat of the house.

Fear of abandonment, fear of desertion. A fear worse even than death. Rebecca ran wildly down the great staircase, almost stumbling on the smooth marble steps, and across the high-ceilinged entryway—and then she stopped short. Beeze was waiting for her, standing where he had stood when they first met, weeks ago, weeks that seemed like lifetimes in retrospect.

"Hello, Rebecca," he said. "Are you ready to go?"

"Where is everybody?"

"Gone."

"Gone? Where?"

"Back to their old lives. Dr. Resnick and Dr. Chin have research fellowships at prominent American universities, Henri and David have bought—with some help from myself—a three-star restaurant in Burgundy. Yogi Gnesha has returned to his students in New York—now their need is greater than mine—and the Munckles have been given a condominium in Miami. Mr. Munckle will entertain children at a local hospital with his magic."

"All that overnight?"

"Contingency plans were made years ago. It was simply a question of putting them in motion."

"And Samson?"

"Samson remains. He is outside now, warming up the helicopter."

The words made Rebecca's blood sing. He really was letting her go; she hadn't dared to believe it until that moment.

"What does it all mean?" she said.

"Come with me."

He led her downstairs to the basement laboratory where she had seen Dr. Resnick and Dr. Chin copulating in the presence of Death. They were gone now, as were the pigs and the cages and the glassware and the strange machines, everything in fact except for the enormous refrigerator with its twin steel doors. Beeze unlocked it, and removed, from its spotless interior, a tray of hypodermic vials filled with a clear liquid.

"Insulin," he said, holding it in front of Rebecca. "Without it I die."

He took one of the vials from the tray and dropped it, and it shattered on the floor. He held up a second vial and dropped that, and then a third. One by one they broke against the stone tile. Rebecca took a moment to gather her wits; then she cried "Stop!" and tried to wrest the tray from his hand. He pushed her away, and she found herself forced to watch as the vials struck the floor like tiny bombs, spattering the precious fluid so it seeped between the tiles.

"Please stop," she cried. "*Please.*"

And finally he did, when only two vials were left. He held them up, one in each hand, so the liquid glinted in the light.

"Each vial contains three c.c.'s of insulin," he said. "That is all that remains. I require forty units a day to survive." He returned one vial to the refrigerator. "This being a U-100 solution, it will last me seven and a half days. Twelve hours more than a week." He handed the second vial to Rebecca, who accepted it as though it were the most precious of relics. "Take this to Los Angeles with you," he continued. "If you wish to return in seven days, you will bring me the gift of life. Then perhaps I will go to the city with you and try to live like a normal man. But if you do not return in seven days, then I will die. It is no sacrifice for me, for I have no desire to live without you."

"Beeze, I can't . . ."

"Your bags are packed and loaded in the helicopter. Goodbye, Rebecca."

·10·

---

*S*he removed the magic ring the Beast had given her and in an instant appeared on the doorstep of her father's house. Her heart filled with joy, she ran inside and found her father in his bed surrounded by the physician and the priest and Beauty's two sisters, precisely as she had seen them in the reflection of the enchanted mirror. One look at Beauty revived him and he left his bed at once, dispatching the physician and the priest, but not without thanking them for their attentions, and paying them handsomely.

Beauty's sisters were less pleased, however, particularly when they discovered a chest of fabulous dresses and jewels which the Beast had also sent by means of his magic; for they had both married men who were lazy good-for-nothings, although handsome and clever and blest with a sense for the latest fashion. Beauty thanked good Beast for the wonderful chest, and taking only the plainest of the dresses, presented all the rest to her sisters, saying that she had no need of them. Now that she was to take Beast for her husband, she was possessed of the greatest riches of all: the happiness of a union founded in love and respect.

But this fine act of generosity only served to fan the fires of their envy. They went down to the courtyard so none could see their bitter tears; and said one to the other, In what is this little creature better than we that she should be so much happier?

Sister, said the eldest, a thought just strikes my mind; let us endeavor to detain her above a week and perhaps her silly monster

*will grow so enraged at her for breaking her word that he will
not have her back.*

*Right, sister, answered the other. And therefore we must show
her as much kindness as possible, lest our deception be detected.*

*Having taken this resolution, they went up to their father's room
and behaved with such kindness and affection toward their sister
that poor Beauty wept with joy. When the week had expired, they
cried and tore their hair and seemed so sorry to part with her that
she promised to stay a week longer.*

*In the meantime sensitive Beauty could not help reflecting on
the uneasiness she was likely to cause poor Beast, whom she sin-
cerely loved and longed to see again. The tenth night she spent at
her father's, she dreamed she was in the palace garden, and that
she saw the Beast, lying still upon the green, and that he implored
her, in a dying voice, to come kneel by his side and hold his hand
while he depart this earthly vale.*

*Beauty awoke at once, filled with remorse for having been so
easily swayed from the solemn oath she had made to the Beast.
Immediately she placed the golden ring, which she kept safe on
a string around her neck, on her index finger and, being a magic
ring, it instantly transported her back to the Beast's palace. She
ran thither and hence, looking for him, and finally she came to
the place in the garden of which she had dreamed; and there she
found poor Beast stretched out quite senseless and, she feared in
her deepest heart, dead . . .*

Leslie couldn't do anything but watch the tiny television suspended a few feet above his face. Reading required a certain motion of head and arms which inevitably caused his fractured pelvis
to tilt ever so slightly, sending a pain like the probe of a dentist's
tool throughout his body. Thinking had become circuitous, an
infinite regression starting with his inability to live with Tommy,
ending with the inevitable conclusion of suicide. As for talking,
there was no one with whom he desired to converse. Sheila had
come by that morning bearing chicken soup (no self-parody now;
the making of it seemed almost an atavism in the face of crisis)
and candy and books. She stood by his bed for half an hour and

he finally had to ask her to leave. Quite simply, he had nothing to say to her. He had nothing to say to anybody except Tommy and Rebecca, and they were both unavailable to him.

Which was not precisely true. During Sheila's visit she had told him that Tommy was waiting in the little lounge at the end of the hall, that he had been there all night, that he was beside himself with worry and had asked her to ask him if he could come visit, if just for a minute.

"No," Leslie said, and that was that.

Our worst prisons, our worst hells are of our own construction.

So all he could do, really, was watch television. It might not be so bad, he had thought at first. He rarely had the opportunity —except for a late, late movie, when he was in the thralls of insomnia—and he was curious. He remembered when, as a child, he had stayed home from school with a heaving, croupy cough in his chest, and his mother had made a bed for him on the living-room sofa and let the old Philco run for hours. How marvelous to spend a day in the homes of "normal" sit-com families, where the greatest problem was whether Beaver would get his new baseball mitt in time for the game, whether Sis would get a date with the captain of the football team. He would dream himself into these "normal" lives, and for the first and last time feel that he belonged, that he was part of a group, a community, a family. What wonderful memories those were.

But he had changed, or television had changed, or some of both, for he now found it irritating in the extreme.

When, at noon, one of the local networks ran *Barracuda*, a superb old Marlene Dietrich film, it was like a reprieve from the tortures of Torquemada. But even that had its hidden sting; the producer was Billy Rosenblatt, as the credits reminded him in giant script, backed by blaring music, the same Billy Rosenblatt who was preparing to sue Rebecca for everything she owned. However, he soon forgot about the lawsuit as the movie worked its magic. He forgot about Tommy and Mack Gordon, and the monster in the desert who was holding Rebecca prisoner; he even forgot about the network of shining wires and pulleys and weights which, like the rigging of some diabolic ship, held his mastlike legs aloft in order that the break in his pelvis might heal. When someone knocked at the door and opened it a crack, he barked, without raising his eyes from the set, "Go away."

"Grou-chy," a familiar voice remarked.

Leslie craned around so fast that the wires and pulleys and weights yanked him back into place, and he groaned from the pain.

"Don't get up," Rebecca said, coming into the room, weighed down with flowers and fresh fruit and the movie-star magazines which she knew to be his favorite junk reading.

"I'm so glad to see you I could cry."

"Me too." She kissed him on the forehead.

"How did you escape?" Tears were running down his cheeks.

Before responding, Rebecca rang for the nurse, who put the flowers in water and joked with Leslie about getting her a part in a movie. When she had left, Rebecca pulled a chair over to the bed.

"First tell me how you're feeling," she said, taking his hand. "What happened? It said on TV you jumped out the window."

He recounted for her how his guilt and depression had been building for days, and how finally the fight with Tommy had driven him to the conclusion that he no longer wished to live.

"You goddamned better wish to live," Rebecca said. "How am I supposed to survive without you?"

"Do you really mean that?" he said.

"You know I do."

"If I really believed that my life was of some benefit to somebody . . ."

"Yeah, well it's of benefit to me, so let's not have any more talk about suicide, all right? Now, Tommy's waiting in the lounge."

"He's still there?"

"Yeah, and it looks like he hasn't slept all night. He asked me to ask you—"

"No," Leslie said.

"You mean you won't see him?"

"No."

"You're really being a stubborn idiot, you know that?"

"I said *no*."

"He loves you and you love him. You make each other happy. That doesn't happen so often that you can toss it away like an old Tampax."

"I don't want to discuss it," Leslie said. "Tell me how you escaped."

"I didn't. He let me go."

Rebecca told how her relationship with Beeze had metamorphosed from the hatred of a prisoner for her jailer to a powerful sexual love between peers, and how she wanted nothing more now than to marry him and bear his children. She insisted that he had changed, citing the incident with Mr. Munckle as an example, and the dismissal of the staff, and of course, his letting her leave with the last precious vial of insulin. But Leslie wasn't convinced.

"As your friend," Leslie said, "I suggest you stay in Los Angeles and let the guy drop dead."

"Leslie!"

"And as your manager, I want you to promise me you'll spend the next two weeks looping Mack Gordon's masterpiece."

"Two weeks? Two days, that's all the contract calls for, and I think the son of a bitch should be happy to get that."

"The point is not what the contract calls for. The point is you're getting a reputation for being difficult, and you're not big enough to survive that, at least not yet. Billy Rosenblatt's ready to sue you for disappearing right before shooting, and somebody took out an ad in *Variety* announcing that Mack Gordon's going to reshoot *Web!* with Victoria Dunbarr in your part."

"No!"

"He says he doesn't know anything about it, and that may be. But I don't want to give him any excuse to cut you out of this film. It may not be the greatest movie ever made, but it will give you the visibility and credibility and that's what you need right now."

"I am not going to waste two more weeks of my life with that bastard. I wouldn't even spend two minutes with him. You tell him he can just go ahead and reshoot it with Victoria. I don't give a shit."

"Well, in that case you can just find yourself another manager," Leslie shouted. "I'm sick and tired of trying to save your career. You are the single most masochistic, self-destructive—"

"I could get better representation," Rebecca shouted back, "from the man who works the Danish cart at the Morris Agency. If you think you're going to threaten me and bully me into doing . . ."

She stopped suddenly, gazed at him with tears in her eyes, and wailed, "Oh, I'm sorry, Leslie, I'll do it. I'll do whatever you say." And she knelt beside his bed and held his hand to her cheek. "But I promised Beeze I'd be back in a week."

"Suppose I can get Gordon to finish looping in a week?"

"But you can't negotiate from a hospital bed."

"My dear, as long as there is a breath of life left in this magnificent body of mine, I can negotiate. Get me Mack Gordon on the phone. Pretend you're my secretary. You can play a secretary, can't you?"

"I kin type six hundred words a minute, Mr. Hur-witz," she said, in her best New York-ese. "But I don't fix no coffee."

"Easy on the dialect. And don't let him know I'm in the hospital."

Rebecca called the studio and soon Mack Gordon's secretary was on the line.

"I'm sorry," she said, "but he's in post-production and it's very hard to get ahold of him. If you'll leave your number . . ."

"It's Mr. Leslie Horowitz calling," Rebecca said in her secretarial voice, "in reference to Rebecca Weiss's looping session next week."

"One moment." Then: "He just stepped in the office."

"Hello?" It was the gruff voice of Mack Gordon, and despite everything it made her heart race. She took a deep breath to compose herself and said, "Just a minute, please."

Leslie gestured for her to hold the phone beside his head. "Hello?" he said. "Yes, I just wanted you to know that Rebecca is back in town and she'll be at the studio bright and early Monday morning . . . Where was she? In New York. You know how things are. She was at a party and she met Arthur Howard, the movie critic for the *Times* . . . What? . . . No, no, Rebecca has only good things to say about your movie. I guess they got along pretty well; he invited her to spend next week skiing with him in Vermont. He was pretty upset that she had to fly back to L.A. on such short notice . . . Yeah, I guess you could even say angry. Probably felt rejected. It's a shame, all right. Too bad you can't finish looping in a week; then she could catch a plane for New York, spend the week with him, patch up the hurt feelings . . . Gee, do you think you could? Oh, Rebecca would be very grateful, I'm sure . . . Yes, she has only good things to say about your movie. Thanks very much, Mack. Bye-bye."

Rebecca hung up the phone and gazed at Leslie for several moments with undisguised admiration.

"How do you do that without giggling?" she said.

"Years of practice lying to my parents, lying to my teachers, lying to my friends. Lying to myself."

"Who's there?" Victoria said, worrying about burglars and rapists. Then she realized it was the middle of the afternoon—one-fifteen according to the clock on the night table—and relaxed. Probably Manuella, the cleaning girl, letting herself in with her key (but why was Charlemagne mewing at the door like that?). Victoria climbed out of bed wearing the oversized Princeton T-shirt she used for a nightgown, and did a few stretches holding on to the brass headboard. Then she jogged into the bathroom and splashed cold water on her face. She had a lunch appointment at one and it really wouldn't do to keep poor Roy waiting any longer than she absolutely had to. When she came out, Rebecca was standing at the door to the bedroom, looking puzzled.

"Becky!" Victoria cried, running to her, embracing her. "I'm so glad you're all right!"

"What are you doing in my room?"

"I missed you so much I couldn't stand it, so I started sleeping in your bed. I know it sounds silly, but it made me feel better. Please say you don't mind."

"I don't mind—I guess. You look a little disappointed to see me."

"I'm delighted to see you! Well, I guess there's no use lying to somebody who knows me as well as you do. Mack Gordon was going to reshoot *Web!* with me playing your role. Now that you're back, he'll drop the whole idea. But I'm so happy to see you, I don't care. Anyway, it's such a shallow part. When I get a lead I want it to be something I can sink my teeth into."

"It never fails to amaze me what a son of a bitch that guy can be. He probably offered it to you just to break up our friendship. And because you're such a good actor," she added hastily. "Is everything all right? Has Charlemagne been eating?"

"You're not going to believe this but Charlemagne caught a mouse."

"No!"

Rebecca picked up the cat, who hung from her grasp like a length of heavy elastic, and stared into its amber eyes.

"Is this true?" she asked. "Did you eat a mouse?"

"Meow," the cat replied.

"You *animal*," she said, disparagingly. She kissed it on the forehead and tossed it on the bed.

"Don't keep me in suspense," Victoria gushed. "How did you escape?"

"He let me go. He's not at all the way Leslie described him. I mean, maybe he was, but he isn't anymore. He's brilliant—he translates Plato from the original Greek—and the way he plays the violin just makes me weak in the knees. And he's got a fabulous body."

"Rebecca, you didn't!"

"I did."

"But isn't he—deformed?"

"It's not so bad when you get to know him."

"Leslie said he wears a mask."

"His face is pretty bad, but I'll bet we can find a plastic surgeon to fix him up. I mean, if not in Beverly Hills, then where?"

"Dr. Martin who did my nose is fabulous. I'll bet he could help."

"Give me a hand with my bag?" Rebecca said.

The enormous suitcase was standing just beyond the pink flamingo where Samson had left it after taking Rebecca home from the hospital. As the two women maneuvered it over the doorstep, the limousine glided past the front of the house, like the sweep hand of a stopwatch counting off the seconds.

"What's *in* here?" Victoria said.

"Stuff Beeze gave me."

They pulled it up onto the bed in Rebecca's room and opened t and began to unpack. Victoria found the diamond choker and gasped. She tried it on in front of the mirror, examining her reflection from every angle.

"Can I wear it?" Victoria pleaded. "Just once?"

"You can have it," Rebecca said.

"Can I really?"

Rebecca nodded. "All these expensive presents make me feel like a hooker. Take everything—except this." And from between he piles of dresses she removed the crystal sphere with the perfect ose preserved within.

Victoria didn't notice, she was so blinded by the light from the diamonds.

"He must be very rich," she said.

"Loaded," Rebecca agreed. "He's thinking about moving to L.A. nd becoming an independent producer. He'd finance anything I vanted to make into a movie." She couldn't resist sparking a little nvy in her friend.

"*God.*"

"But I'm not sure it's such a good idea for a husband and wife ɔ work together."

"Whoa! You're going too fast for me. Husband and wife? You ɪean, you're getting married?"

"He asked me, but I haven't accepted yet. I'll tell him when I go ack Friday night."

"Can I be the maid of honor?"

"As far as I'm concerned, Vicky, you can be the rabbi."

"I'll wear my white lace dress with the bows."

"Well, don't look too good. I don't want him changing his ind."

"Oh, I'm so excited! Weddings make me cry!"

Victoria followed her into the kitchen.

Standing by the refrigerator, Rebecca removed a tiny vial of ear liquid from her purse.

"What's that?" Victoria asked.

"Insulin. He needs it to survive."

"You mean he's diabetic?"

"No, it's got to do with his pancreas. It was destroyed in an airplane accident and his body can't make insulin. I never was very good in biology. This is all the insulin he's got left. He gave it to me to hold for him, and if I don't get it back to him by Friday night, he'll die."

"You mean he set it up like that? Sounds like some pretty neurotic game-playing if you ask me."

"Well, he's not like other people. Under his superman exterior he's very sensitive and insecure. He needs me to prove my love to him, and I understand why he does, and I'm willing to do it."

"You really sound like a changed person," Victoria said.

"Maybe I am. Maybe I'm tired of one-night stands and men who treat me like some kind of garbage off the street."

She opened the refrigerator and placed the vial of insulin inside the white plastic butter dish.

"It makes me feel so good to hear you talk like that," Victoria said. "Let's go out to lunch and celebrate! My treat—if you'll lend me a couple of dollars to get through the week?"

"I don't think I have any cash," Rebecca said. "Just a couple of million in diamonds."

Suddenly Victoria's eyes opened wide in horror. "Oh God, my lunch date with Roy! What time is it?"

"One thirty-five."

"He'll kill me. He'll absolutely kill me. Meet you for dinner okay?"

And before Rebecca could reply, Victoria was out the door.

Rebecca picked up Charlemagne and stared into his amber eyes.

"Teach you a lesson, cat. Nothing changes up here in Benedict Canyon. Nothing."

"Meow," said Charlemagne and licked her nose.

Rebecca was so busy that week she barely had time to think. Every morning at seven o'clock she would shower and dress and drive to the studio in Burbank. There, in a special recording studio, dark and cavernous as an aircraft hangar, they would view a minute or two of the film, which had been made into a "loop" so it could be played again and again. The first three times they would watch themselves on screen and practice fitting the new dialogue to the lip motions. Sometimes, when the character was far from the camera, or facing away from it, the job would be simple; at other times, particularly during close-ups, it was extraordinarily difficult, and sometimes the actors would be forced to make up new dialogue themselves, subject to the approval of Mack Gordon. After viewing the film loop three times, they were given three opportunities (or more if necessary) to "lay in" the new dialogue. The film loop would begin, and just before the time came for their dialogue, they would hear three *bleeps* on their headphones so that they would know precisely when to speak. After eight or nine hours of this, the three *bleeps* became as irritating as Chinese water torture.

At seven each evening she would leave the studio exhausted, pick up supper at a deli or a Chinese restaurant, and bring it to Leslie's hospital room. While they ate she told him anecdotes about work and read him the personal column from the *L.A. Free Press* (the surest thing for a laugh, they both agreed), and flying saucer stories from the *National Enquirer* and tidbits about his clients from the fan magazines. And every day he seemed a little less depressed, a little more interested in staying alive.

Every evening at ten when the nurse shooed her out of the hospital room, she would find Tommy waiting in the lounge at the end of the hall. He would look to her pathetically for an answer and she would shake her head no. It made Rebecca just as sad as it made him, for she knew that until her two friends could reconcile their relationship, neither would find peace of mind.

And finally home to bed, too exhausted to read or even to watch television; but awake enough to notice Beeze's long black limousine cruising slowly past the house like a spaceship orbiting a planet. Did it pass thus all day while she was at work, she wondered, lying in bed; did poor Samson take time for meals and sleep, for gas and toilet, or did he simply drive around and around her house, night and day, in order to be there in case she decided to return early, and more important—knowing Beeze—to be there as a reminder of her other life, of the desert, of the pure air and blinding sun? And if something happened to her—if she died suddenly of a vessel bursting in her brain, or a freakish strike of lightning—

then would the car continue to circle her house forever, and become a myth, like the Flying Dutchman, who waited an eternity for the reprieve of a true woman's love, or the mysterious veiled lady who wept at Valentino's grave?

Flossy McGee sat in the rear of a 747, toying with her meal. Had the food been prepared by the finest chef in France, she still would not have eaten it, for her lack of appetite was due to an attack of conscience rather than to the nausea-evoking quality of the meal. She was on her way to New York to buy the film rights for Angela Rosenblatt's sensational novel. She would be acting as a "front" for Billy, a tactic not unknown in Hollywood, and would pass herself off as a young, independent producer with limited funds. Although she could pay, as the story had been concocted, only a trifle for the rights, she would offer, in compensation, the enthusiasm of youth, a feminist consciousness and a viewpoint as yet untainted by the mercantilism of Hollywood. Plus all sorts of creative control, including sole authorship of the screenplay. Billy was counting on his assistant's charm and verve and charisma to clinch the deal. He knew that his ex-wife was a sucker for industrious kids about to mount the ladder of success—after all, wasn't that why she had married him long ago? Once Angela had agreed to Flossy's proposal, Flossy would turn around and sell the property to Billy for a dollar, and he would shelve it, thereby consigning it forever to oblivion and assuring that his private life would be spared public exhibition, at least on the wide screen. The novel would still be published. But since few of Billy's Hollywood friends, as he was fond of pointing out, could read, that didn't bother him unduly.

The food grew cold in her tray, the sauce congealed into paste as she contemplated the ignominy of her mission. Feminism was one of the few contemporary ideals she was willing to fight for, and the notion of exploiting it in order to trick another woman— one she'd never met—simply to save Billy Rosenblatt a little embarrassment, seemed reprehensible. Despite the awkward writing, despite the flurry of brand names on every page, and the predictability of the pornographic scenes (man-woman, man-woman-

woman, woman-dog), Flossy liked the book. The narrator's voice had energy and a cynicism to it that somehow managed to be charming. And the book had a real story, and lots of suspense, and scenes that would be visually thrilling. Flossy let herself imagine how it would feel if she really were producing the movie, casting the principals, finding a decent director, helping the scriptwriter trim the story to a workable size. The fantasy was so engrossing that it seemed as though only minutes had passed when, an hour later, the captain announced their arrival over Kennedy.

That evening Angela Rosenblatt came to her suite at the Sherry Netherland. The woman Flossy had heard described so often as "the wicked witch of the East," "the ball breaker," or simply "the psycho," the woman who, according to Billy, had no aim in life but to "make a pauper out of him," "give him an ulcer" and "stay single all her life," was, in fact, delightful. Fast-talking, witty, brittle, still vibrant at fifty-eight, a frosted blond beauty whose taut skin and faintly Oriental eyes suggested a face-lift or two under the best knives of America. She wore a suit of coarse tweed, a silk shirt and a contrasting scarf, and she carried a brief case with a gold clasp and corners. She sat on the sofa, legs crossed, puffing on a cigarette, while Flossy made her proposal.

Halfway through, Angela interrupted her. "Say no more, dearest, the book is yours."

Flossy gazed at her in shock.

"There's no point in going on," Angela continued, "because I don't believe a word you say. It's nothing personal, dearest. I don't believe anything any producer says. It's the result of living with Billy Rosenblatt for half my life. Before this meeting I decided to rate you on my own criteria, and if you scored well, I'd give you the book. For example, if I came into your suite and noticed a matched set of Vuitton luggage, that would be minus two points. If you kept me waiting while you took a phone call to the Coast —a call from 'Laddie' or 'Swifty' or 'Ray'—minus four points. And if you had called my book a 'property,' or said you'd read a 'coverage,' or offered me a 'rolling gross,' or a 'walking gross,' or even a 'crawling gross,' well, I would have been out the door in a second. But the fact is, you're a young woman who has obviously got a brain and a heart and that's plus a hundred points right there. So consider the book yours. After I leave here I'll phone my agent and tell him of my decision. And he will call me a fool and a softy and tell me how much more we could have gotten and finally do what I say. You see, dearest, for him losing money is like losing blood. For me—well, I don't care. I have all I need. The children are grown and out on their own; I have my investments and a bit of alimony I insist on just to make sure Billy isn't *too* comfortable. Dear Billy, he does miss his millions. Ever met him?"

Flossy admitted she had.

"Isn't he the perfect old Billy Goat? Kiss the girls and make them cry—at his age! You'd think he'd realize how silly it looks. But don't get the idea I don't respect him. I do. I think he's the finest of the old breed. And you, dearest, my instinct, my *infallible* instinct, tells me, are the finest of the new. Do you know that for a time I actually thought Billy would try to bid on my book!"

"That *is* a crazy idea," Flossy said, nervously.

"Well then, we're in agreement," Angela said, crushing out her cigarette, standing up. "Let's go out and celebrate."

"I think I'll stay home and kill myself," Flossy muttered.

"Pardon me?"

"I said I think I'll stay home and drill myself—on some of the details of the deal. Points and stuff. You know."

"That's the difference between the old and the new," Angela said. "Somebody like Billy would arrive in New York and spend the evening wining and dining a dozen mistresses. But you stay in your room working. Serious, devoted. You'll accomplish great things, dearest. Great things."

The next day, lunching at the Four Seasons with Angela Rosenblatt and her agent, Flossy clinched the deal. Later that afternoon she flew back to California, wondering how many points one lost for impersonating a human being.

"I think we'll finish looping by tomorrow," Rebecca told Leslie, sitting at his bedside.

"You mean it's only Thursday? God, I feel like I've been here for months. This must be what prison's like. Except convicts don't have itchy casts that can't be scratched."

"Want me to try?"

"No, I'm getting to enjoy it. I pretend I'm a heretic during the Inquisition and this gorgeous priest is trying to make me confess to dirty things."

"You know, you're a very strange person."

"Thank you."

Rebecca hesitated, reluctant to broach a certain subject, yet feeling she had to.

"Leslie, there's something I've got to say. You've been here a week now and every night Tommy's been . . ."

"Don't start this again."

"*Leslie, listen to me!* Every night Tommy's been waiting out in the lounge, and every night he asks me if you'll see him."

"I won't."

"You're so fucking stubborn!"

"He lied to me! He told me he was in acting class when he was out on the street turning tricks. And you expect me to talk to him?"

"Leslie, hustling is no big deal."

"I don't see you on a street corner, in a minidress and a fright wig, saying, *Hello, big boy, want to have a good time?*"

"It's different when you're gay, and you know it. It's not a case of men exploiting women."

"It's a case of men exploiting men."

"No it isn't. Remember that time you explained hustling to me? And you said that the money wasn't really important, it was just more make-believe, more playacting? You made it sound pretty harmless."

"All right, it's not the hustling I mind, it's the lying."

"You never lied to Tommy?" Rebecca said.

"We were going to be faithful."

"Leslie, you're a jack rabbit, you've got round heels."

"It was going to be beautiful and precious and perfect, like Gable and Colbert in *It Happened One Night*."

"This isn't a movie, Leslie," she said, gently, "and you're not Gable."

"Don't remind me!"

"Give Tommy a chance?"

"I'll think about it," he said, stubbornly.

"Leslie, it's ten to ten. That master sergeant of a nurse is going to be in here in a few minutes to kick me out. Please see him now. Please. For me? To make me happy?"

Leslie sighed. "All right."

She started for the door.

"Wait," Leslie cried. "How do I look? Oh God, I wish I could get up and comb my hair. And this nightshirt makes me look like a tub."

"You're beautiful. Now relax, everything's going to be fine."

Rebecca left the room and walked down the hall.

The lounge was empty.

"I don't understand it," she said, returning to the room. "He's not there."

"Of course not," Leslie said. "It's Thursday night. He's out on the street, peddling his flesh." He sounded as if he was going to cry. "Well, I don't give a shit. Let him fuck every boy in L.A. More power to him."

There was a knock on the door and the nurse entered. "You'll have to go now," she said. "It's ten P.M."

Rebecca said good night, but Leslie wouldn't answer. He stared at the ceiling, eyes wet, lip trembling. She walked down the hall to the elevator. The elevator door opened and Tommy stepped out, holding a Coke.

"Where were you?" Rebecca demanded.

"Downstairs at the vending machines. I got thirsty."

She grabbed his hand and dragged him in the direction of Leslie's room, explaining how she had been unable to find him, how life was on the verge of irreparable ruin. Just as they reached Leslie's room, the nurse emerged—Attila the Cunt, as Leslie called her—scowling at them.

"Just a moment! It's ten o'clock. Visiting hours are over."

"Oh, please," Rebecca said. "We've got to see Leslie, just for a minute."

"*Visiting hours are over.*"

"You can't believe how important this is. I swear, we'll just be in there a minute."

"Young lady, the hospital has its rules and they were not made to be ignored. It is now ten o'clock and . . ."

Rebecca gasped, grabbed her side and sunk slowly to the floor. Her face was rigid, her breathing labored.

"What is it?" the nurse demanded. "What's wrong?"

"Pain . . ." Rebecca could hardly speak.

"Just lie there," the nurse said. "Don't move. I'll be back in a second." She ran for the desk, shouting, "Dr. Greenstone! Dr. Greenstone, we have a coronary!"

Tommy knelt beside her. "Is it very bad?"

"Just when I cha-cha." Rebecca winked.

"You're some actress." He was really surprised.

"I better be. Now, go inside and make up with Leslie before that old witch gets back."

Tommy did as directed. Leslie was lying on his back, tears streaming down his cheeks.

"Hi," Tommy said. "I was just downstairs getting a Coke. I haven't been on the street since you left. And I'll never go again if you don't want me to."

"You have to hustle," Leslie said, sniffing, "and I have to live with it."

Tommy sat beside him on the bed, took Leslie's hand and held it tenderly in his own; in that position they remained, not saying a word, simply gazing at each other dewy-eyed, until a ruckus in the hall made him think that Rebecca might need his help.

Outside he found a doctor and two orderlies—in addition to Leslie's nurse—trying to force Rebecca to lie down on a gurney.

"I'm not having a heart attack," she insisted. "It was just a joke."

"You must cooperate," the doctor said. "The sooner we get you into I.C., the better your chances for survival."

She saw Tommy and shouted to him, "Help me."

He yanked her from the clutching hands, raced her down the hall, pushed her into the elevator just as the doors were closing, then squeezed through himself. As they started to descend, they both fell back against the wall, laughing so hard they gasped for breath, to the mystification of the other passengers.

"They wouldn't believe it was a trick," Rebecca said.

"You're wonderful," Tommy said.

He hugged her and they laughed some more.

John Guilford filled the screen, bruised and ragged and dripping sweat, kneeling at the window with a twelve-gauge shotgun, picking off a giant spider whenever one approached. The camera pulled back to include Rebecca Weiss in her tight jeans and tailored shirt (carefully torn by the wardrobe mistress) crouching on the floor, filling old bottles with sand and gasoline, and stuffing their necks with gasoline-soaked cloths to make Molotov cocktails.

Having fired both barrels, John tossed the shotgun to her for reloading, and she in turn passed him a tray of the incendiary bombs, which he immediately began to light and throw at the spiders.

"Quick," he said, "they're gaining on us."

"I'm working as fast as I can," Rebecca replied.

"Listen. There's something I've got to tell you."

"Yes?"

"There was never anything between Janice and me."

"No time for that now," Rebecca said, breathlessly, "we need more bottles." But despite her words, she seemed relieved by the news.

"Under the sink," he said.

The camera followed her to the kitchen, where she knelt beside the cabinet and began to pull out bottles. She was so intent on her task that she did not notice the long, hairy arm of a spider appearing at the window above the sink until quite suddenly it smashed the pane and, wrapping itself around her waist, began to pull her toward the window, as easily as a child would pull a rag doll from a toy chest. Then she screamed. She struggled. She grabbed a butcher's cleaver that happened to be lying on the counter and, with one mean sweep, chopped the tentacle in two so it twitched and spurted blood like a fire hose gone out of control. Then she gathered the armful of bottles and returned to John Guilford's side.

"Now there's something *I've* got to tell you," she said, stuffing bottles with sand.

Opposite the screen, Rebecca and John Guilford stood around

a microphone, holding their scripts, watching the silent movie and reading their lines to fit.

"Oh?" John said.

"I'm pregnant."

"If we ever get out of this alive, I'm going to marry you."

"Just say you love me."

"I love you."

The actors remained standing where they were and seconds later the film was replaced by leader. The projector went dark, the houselights went up. Inside the recording booth Mack Gordon rose, brushed off his hands and said, "That does it for me. It's a wrap. Five o'clock Friday, just like I promised."

Everybody sighed, almost in unison, and applauded, and began to pack up scripts and notes and needlepoint and head home. Mack personally thanked John and Rebecca for working so hard and well for him, and apologized for any trouble he might have once caused them, provoked by the hot desert sun and the faulty machinery of the spiders. Indeed, his behavior that week had been exemplary. He seemed like a different person, patient, polite, encouraging—even warm. Now he blocked Rebecca's way as she made for the door.

"I'm having a little celebration tonight," he said softly. "My place in Malibu. It would be great if you could come."

"I don't think so," she said. "I'm pretty exhausted."

"I've been thinking about you ever since we left the desert." His voice was low now, almost a whisper, and he stood so close she could smell his tobacco breath. "That afternoon we rode away on horseback and found that rock formation, and made love under the burning sun—that was one of the greatest moments in my life."

"What about that time you called me a weepy cow and said I could take acting lessons from Sandra Dee?"

"You didn't think I meant that, did you? Jesus! That's how I direct, that's how I get a little extra out of my actors."

"Really?"

"That affair we had in the desert was one of the wildest, most beautiful things that's ever happened to me."

"That's how I felt," Rebecca admitted.

"I was sorry you were in such a hurry to leave. I was going to ask you to take a trial run playing house with me in Malibu. If it worked, we could make it a permanent arrangement."

"You knew my number in L.A." She lowered her voice. "And I'm in love with somebody else now."

"I guess that's why I'm so unhappy. I let all the magic slip through my fingers. It's nobody's fault but my own. I hope you and this mysterious millionaire are . . ."

"What millionaire?" Rebecca said, recalling the lie Leslie had told him on the telephone. "It's Arthur Howard, the film critic. I'm flying to New York tomorrow to spend the week with him, skiing."

"Like hell you are," Mack said, smiling. "You're going to the Mojave to meet this recluse millionaire with the burned-out face."

Rebecca stared at him for a moment, trying to decide whether to bluff it out or to admit the truth. What was the difference, she thought, now that the looping was completed?

"Who told you?" she said.

"No secrets in Tinseltown." He grinned, teasing her like a big brother.

"*Who told you?*"

"All right. Your roommate, Victoria. She's been hanging out with a writer I know."

"Damn her!"

"It's okay. You could have told me the truth to begin with. I would have let you go in a week. I'm not such a bad guy."

"You're a mother-fucker," Rebecca said.

"Victoria's coming tonight. Maybe you'll come with her. It would be great to have"—he caressed her arm, and the touch of his rough fingers gave her chills—"one last night."

"Thanks, Mack, but I don't think so." She smiled at him, said "Goodbye" and walked away.

"*Cunt,*" he whispered through clenched teeth, but only when she was beyond hearing.

Victoria was sitting at the make-up table in her old bedroom, applying eyelashes. She was wearing a clinging wine-colored dress low-cut and sleeveless, and the diamond necklace which Beeze had given Rebecca. The burning raw filaments of the bulbs surrounding the mirror made the stones glitter almost painfully. Sensing a presence at the door, she glanced up and was surprised at her roommate's irritated expression.

"Hi, Becky," she said warmly. "Something the matter?"

"Why did you tell Mack Gordon about Beeze?"

"Oh, I'm sorry, dear, I thought he knew. Was it a secret? You should have told me."

"Do I have to say something's a secret to stop you from telling everybody in California about it?"

"Now, Becky, I didn't tell everybody, just Mack, and I only mentioned it because I know how much you hate him and I wanted to make him jealous." She sealed a lash to a trembling lid, then blinked a few times experimentally. "But I guess by this time I should know better than to try to do you any favors. You're so paranoid. Typical Sagittarius. Yes, from now on I promise I'll butt out of your affairs and go my own merry way."

"I'm sorry," Rebecca said. "I didn't mean to get angry."

"You have enough enemies without attacking the people who really love you."

By an odd coincidence, it was the same phrase her mother often used when Rebecca demanded self-respect, the implication being: *How dare you get angry at me, I who have suffered so much for you.* In some recess of Rebecca's mind it occurred to her that whenever she was angry at Victoria, Victoria turned the anger around, just as her mother did, and used it against her. Now Rebecca was stricken with panic that she would lose Victoria's love —or was it her mother's love?

"It's true," she said quickly. "You're the best friend I have— and the most beautiful," adding the compliment Victoria liked most to hear. "You really look sensational." Then timidly, "But do you think it's safe to wear that necklace?"

"Sure," Victoria said, darkening her lips. "They'll think it's paste. Nobody would really wear a necklace like this, except maybe to the opera. What are you going to wear?"

"A nightgown."

"Really?" Victoria looked up from the mirror, saw she was joking.

"I'm going to bed early. I'm exhausted."

She rose from the chair. "Rebecca, you can't! You're the guest of honor! Mack's having the party just for you."

"He'll have to have the party without me."

"But—but all week I've been looking forward to spending some time with you. We've both been on such crazy schedules."

"Have you really?" Rebecca felt a glow inside; she had been forgiven.

"You're going to the desert tomorrow. Who knows when I'll ever see you again?"

"We'll be moving to L.A. . . . ."

"Will you? Or will you decide to go to New York or the South of France, or buy a villa in Majorca? With Beeze's money you'll be able to do anything."

"No, no. I'll come back to L.A.—it's the only place I feel normal. And if we did buy a villa in Majorca, I'd send you an airplane ticket and you could visit for months."

Victoria faced her friend, crouching slightly to minimize the difference in their heights, and allowed herself to look Rebecca in the eye.

"You know how you're always complaining about men having all the fun and women getting a raw deal? Well, here's a perfect example. If you were a man, and you were going away tomorrow to see the woman you loved, and maybe get married, you would spend your last night of freedom raising total hell! You'd have a bachelor party and get drunk, watch blue movies. Maybe the other guys would even give you a hooker! That's what they used to do on the base, when I was a kid in San Diego. I remember the stories I'd hear about those parties. They were blowouts, total insanity! But since you're a proper young lady, you decide to go to bed early, have pure and chaste dreams about your beloved, into whose arms you will flee first thing in the morning." She dropped the hearts-and-flowers voice and continued in a more sincere tone. "I don't want to be obnoxious, but I'd like you to come tonight so we can spend a little time together. And I'd like to see you have a little fun, because for all the nice things you've said about Beeze, something tells me the first couple of years together won't be easy. They never are, even with normal men who have faces. Am I making my point?"

Rebecca hesitated; then she said, "Give me ten minutes for a shower and five to change," and she ran into her room.

"Wow," Victoria said when Rebecca reappeared an hour later. She was wearing the red velvet dress Beeze had given her for her birthday. Her hair was braided in front and held in place with the pearl combs, while in back it fell free and luxuriant.

"You look like Glinda of Oz," Vicky said. "One last touch." She took off the diamond necklace and fastened it around Rebecca's neck. Then they both inspected her in the hall mirror.

Finally Rebecca shook her head. "Too glitzy."

"I hate to agree," Victoria said, "but you're right."

"You wear it."

A brief argument ensued, and Victoria was persuaded, without too much effort, to wear the necklace. That settled, they prepared to leave. Among the last-minute overlooked details that are always so numerous when one is trying to leave the house, and that seem to increase geometrically in proportion to the number of people trying to leave, their desire to go, and their tardiness, was a phone call Victoria had to make, a quick one, she promised. Rebecca stood at the door, tapping her foot impatiently, waiting for her roommate to be done. She could overhear most of it, even though the phone was in the kitchen:

"Yes . . . Sure . . . Oh, that would be great! Can you drop off a copy of the script before you leave? . . . Tonight? But I was just on my way out! Oh, Roy, it's special, it's Rebecca's last night in L.A. . . . Could you get it here in the next hour? . . . You're a dear. Bye-bye."

Victoria ran to the door, saying, "I'm sorry, Becky, it's an emergency. Roy Gleason, this writer I've been seeing, well, he's got a script and he thinks I might be right for a part in it, but he's got to fly to New York tonight and he wants to drop it off at the house, and I promised—"

"Say no more, I understand completely."

"But you go ahead. I'll meet you at Mack's in an hour or two."

"Why don't I stick around?" Rebecca offered. "Give us a chance to talk."

"Darling, I'd absolutely love to, but Roy and I need to be alone. We have some very important matters to discuss." She raised her eyebrows meaningfully.

"God, Victoria, your life is so full of men."

"I'd trade them all for one good one," she said, touching the necklace. "A man like Beeze. Think he's got a brother?"

They pecked each other on the cheek, and Rebecca let herself out the door. Victoria stood in the middle of the living room, stood very still listening for the sound of Rebecca's Mustang. She crossed to the window and watched the headlights move down the driveway and sweep the street. Only when the taillights were like distant embers did she move, first to the icebox, where she removed the insulin from the butter tray, then to her bedroom, where she dropped the vial into her evening bag, then to the hall, where she dressed herself in Rebecca's cape, then out the front door, across the lawn, down to the curb. There she waited, hugging the cape tight around her to ward off the chill December night, consulting her watch with growing anxiety as the hour approached nine.

She had observed, from the day of Rebecca's return, Beeze' long black limousine passing the house at all hours of the day and night. Rebecca never noticed the pattern because she worked all day, but Victoria, who was sitting home with nothing better to do, except perhaps envy Rebecca's employment, timed the limousine, and found that it passed every three hours, as regularly as a commuter train. Nine A.M., noon, 3 P.M., 6 P.M., 9 P.M. and midnight; she had not yet stayed awake until 3 A.M., but she was almost certain that if she did she would see the car pass then too, silent as a phantom.

Five to nine now; crickets chirped, slowed by the cold, and a few houses away a clever raccoon overturned a garbage can. Beverly Hills stretched out below her, its pools like turquoise gems in the moonlight. Victoria stiffened at the sound of an approaching car. A moment later the limousine turned the corner. She stepped into the street and raised her hand, trying to move as Rebecca did within Rebecca's cloak. She feared the car would pass her by, but then it was gliding to a stop beside her, and then she was settling back in the plush interior.

How wonderfully satisfying to have stepped into Rebecca's life this way, to be finally the main character of the drama and not the supporting player, the dumb brunette, the bad girl, the foil. Samson turned his head and stared at her, monstrous and green in the light of the dash. The sight of him up close for the first time evoked a strange combination of joy and terror.

"I don't know how to tell you this," she began, "but Rebecca changed her mind. She really felt awful but she decided that her art comes first and she has to start shooting a film in a couple of weeks. Anyway, she apologizes. She gave me the insulin"—Victoria rummaged through her purse and brought out the vial—"and a special message for Beeze, and I promised to deliver them both personally. I'm busy too, of course—I've got lots of film commitments—but Rebecca's my best friend in the world, and when she asked me to do her a favor, I couldn't refuse. She's a wonderful person but she can be a little self-centered at times. Would you believe it? She wanted to give the insulin to you and let you bring it back. And I said, '*Becky, you can't do that! Beeze loves you, his whole world is at stake.*' You see, she told me all about it. And Becky said, '*Well, Victoria, if you want to go, that's your decision. I'm too damn busy.*' So here I am."

She waited and Samson simply stared at her.

"What I'm saying is, I'm all ready to go. This is it, no baggage. I travel light." She laughed.

Samson didn't move.

"I said I'm ready to go." Victoria was growing impatient. "Don't you understand? Rebecca's not coming. She sent me in her place. I've got the insulin. Without it he's going to die."

And still he didn't move.

"Please," she said, "please take me. He'll fall in love with me, all men do. And I'll be good to him, really. He'll be happier with me than he ever would have been with Rebecca. She'd get tired of him in a week—that's the longest her relationships ever last—but I'd stay with him forever, I swear I would. I'd be there for him day and night. I'd give up acting if he wanted, I'd give up Los Angeles and my friends and spend the rest of my life in the desert with him if that was what he wanted. Oh, please take me, please."

Samson stared at her, then, almost imperceptibly, shook his head from side to side.

"Damn you, you ugly freak!" she hissed with sudden fury. "If I can't have him, no one will!"

She left the limousine, slamming the door behind her, hurled the insulin vial into the grass and ran back to the house.

That night the beach in front of Mack Gordon's house was illuminated with Christmas-tree lights strung on poles, and more lights could be seen twinkling from the branches of a seven-foot spruce at one end of the glass-enclosed gallery that overlooked the sea. Inside and out people milled about the Mediterranean-style villa, talking, laughing, dancing to the disco music which blared from the loudspeakers. They walked in the moonlight, shook the sand out of their shoes, rolled up their designer jeans and waded in the freezing surf. From a distance it appeared to be the height of romance. If one moved closer, however, the illusion was shattered. One discovered that most of the couples were men discussing business, the film business naturally, trying to impress one another with how much their latest film had grossed in the hope of raising their own reputation in order to gain financing or employment for future films.

Of course there were women too, and at Mack Gordon's parties they fell into two categories: women who were highly successful within the industry, whom one treated more or less like men, since someday one might be working with them, and women who were less successful in the industry, whom one tried to fuck since the idea of a person who could not be utilized in some way in the most capitalist of capitalist societies was repellent.

Mack Gordon himself was at present occupied in this latter pursuit. All in white, but for his high-heeled cowboy boots, shirt open to the navel, salt-and-pepper beard trimmed close and eyes red from drinking gin and smoking grass, he had cornered a fashion model whose hair had endorsed a dozen shampoos but whose face, while rather pretty, remained unknown. He was standing with on arm on either side of her, pressing her back to the wall while whispering propositions with a breath so high in alcohol content it was nearly flammable.

"Let's drive down to Ensenada tonight. We'll swim naked in the ocean and watch the sunrise."

"Sounds lovely but I've got a six A.M. call tomorrow."

"Six A.M.? On a Saturday?"

"It's a fashion spread for *Playboy*. They rented a tugboat out of Long Beach and they want me to . . ."

The doorbell was ringing, over and over, and nobody was bothering to answer it.

"Shit," Mack said. "Excuse me while I get that—and don't move till I get back!"

"Depends on how long you take," she teased.

Mack stumbled, disgusted, down the hall, opened the door and saw Rebecca standing there.

"Come in, come in," he said. "The star has deigned to drink with the riffraff."

"Mack," she said, warningly.

He straightened out immediately. "Sorry, Becky. I'm glad to see you, you know that."

"I can only stay for an hour or two. I've got a big drive in the morning."

Mack peered into the darkness behind her. "Did Vicky come with you?"

"She had to wait at the house. Roy Gleason's coming over to drop off a screenplay."

"Funny." Mack's brow creased. "Roy Gleason's here. What are you drinking?"

"Perrier with a twist of lemon."

"Come on, this is a celebration! I know you're a Margarita freak. Prepare yourself for the best Margarita you ever tasted."

"Mack, I don't want to . . ."

But she was too late; he had already started for the bar. While she was waiting for him to return, John Guilford, her costar in *Web!*, came up, kissed her hello, and placed a joint in her mouth. She tried to give it back.

"No thanks, too much to do tomorrow."

"You'll be sorry if you don't, Becky. It's the best grass I've ever tasted. It comes from a small valley in Mexico where the farmers spread the manure in psychedelic patterns. They put phonographs in the middle of the field and play Grateful Dead for the plants, to encourage them to grow crooked. When it's time for the harvest, they bring down truckloads of aging hippies from Marin and dress them in headbands and love beads. In other words, it's the very best. Take a toke, that's all."

"Oh, all right," Rebecca said, charmed by his patter. She took a deep breath and held it in, and because she was exhausted, it hit her like a hammer, made her head spin, made her grab the table for support. "What's in this?" she asked, suspiciously.

"Just what I told you. It's from a little valley in Mexico where—"

"Spare me." She took another drag, held it in.

"There's only one bad effect from the grass," he continued. "It makes you see giant spiders with little men inside them."

Rebecca spit out the smoke, coughing and laughing hysterically. "And Mack Gordon," she added, when she could speak again, "it makes you see Mack Gordon."

John made a serious face. "Becky, I've got a plan. When *Web!* opens, I'm going to buy a McDonald's franchise—I figure I'll be washed up as an actor. Want to go into business with me? You can fold the cardboard boxes for the hamburgers."

"Only if I can wear one of those cute little uniforms and smile like a cheerleader." Suddenly Rebecca's face fell. "Do you really think we'll be ruined?"

"Are you kidding?" he said lightly. "Think of the great actors you know, and the garbage they've done. Sir Ralph Richardson in *Tales from the Crypt.* Jack Nicholson in *The Raven.* Sir Lawrence Olivier in that Harold Robbins movie. Rebecca, you'll come out of this like a diamond on top of a shit heap."

Diamond reminded her of necklace, necklace of Victoria, Victoria of Roy Gleason.

"John," she said, "do you know Roy Gleason, the screenwriter? Is he here tonight?"

John pointed out a kindly-faced man, graying and stoop-shouldered, yet youthfully dressed in white ducks, a blue blazer, yachting shoes and a Lacoste shirt.

Rebecca excused herself, walked over to the group he was standing with, and listened politely for a while. He was telling them about a screenplay he had written, a wonderful screenplay, the piece of work he was proudest of, and how such and such a producer had hired hacks to rewrite it, ruining it forever, and how he had no recourse but to turn to the writing of novels, where the work was his and his alone. It was a speech she had heard before, from other screenwriters, but the man was so gentle and kindly and paternal that she felt his dilemma deeply.

When he had finished with the story, and everybody was done commiserating, Rebecca stepped forward and introduced herself.

"It's a pleasure," he said. "You're one of my favorite actresses. *Land of Lost Dreams*—what a performance!"

"Thanks," Rebecca said modestly. She returned the compliment, naming the screenplay he was most famous for.

"So, Rebecca," Roy said, "how did the looping go? I don't know if Mack told you, but I did some of the rewrites with him. Tricky stuff, looping like that. If you're not careful, it can look like a foreign film."

"I think it went pretty well. But there's something I have to ask you. Did you tell Victoria you were coming over tonight?—because she's at home right now waiting for you. I know it's none of my business, but I think when you're having a relationship with somebody and you say you're going to be someplace . . ."

Roy paled and glanced at the woman on his left, who was long and lean and fiftyish, and tanned from hours on the golf links. She returned his look with an expression that seemed to say, That does it, that's the last straw, time to turn the whole mess over to the lawyers. Rebecca tried to cover her tracks, talking quickly to both of them:

"A working relationship, that is. She can't wait to see the script you promised to drop off. Her boyfriend will be there too. He's a writer and when he heard you were coming he insisted on sticking around to meet you."

The improvisation, she noticed dismally, was only making things worse. Roy's wife gave him an icy glance that seemed to say, see you in court, and strode away. For a moment he gazed after her, mouth half open, not knowing what to do; then he pursued her, crying, "Honey, wait. It's not what you think." The group disbursed, embarrassed, leaving Rebecca alone with another woman.

"I know how you feel," the other woman said. She was slight and bony with curly red hair and crooked teeth. "I just betrayed somebody too."

"I didn't betray anybody," Rebecca said defensively.

"Maybe betrayal's too strong a word, but you know what I mean."

"No, I don't." She had met the younger woman before somewhere, but the time and place eluded her.

"What I'm trying to say is, you don't owe your roommate anything. She played a terrible trick on you."

"Who are you, anyway?"

"Flossy McGee. I work for Billy Rosenblatt. I met you when you were testing for *The Other Woman*."

Now Rebecca placed her, and without another word turned away.

"What's the matter?" Flossy asked.

"You know damn well. I don't want to talk to you."

"No, honestly I don't. What are you so mad about?"

Rebecca sighed with irritation. "Do I have to spell it out? You tried to sabotage my screen test. You filled the champagne glass with mouthwash."

"You're crazy! I suggested you for that part. If anybody put anything in the champagne glass, it was your friend Victoria. She ran off with the glass right before you tested. I remember distinctly."

"So that's the terrible trick she played on me?" Rebecca put her hands on her hips and waited for a reply.

"Maybe. I was going to tell you about another one. Billy was supposed to have lunch with you a couple of weeks ago. Victoria intercepted the message and came in your place."

"So, according to you she's spending most of her time dreaming up ways to fuck me over? Boy, talk about paranoia."

"It's the truth, I swear to God. Ask Billy."

"I don't have to ask anybody. Victoria's my best friend in the world and if you say one more bad word about her I'm going to smack you."

With that Rebecca turned her back and marched away.

Flossy wandered through the crowd looking for Billy Rosenblatt, who had promised to appear at some point in the evening. She had business to discuss with him and the sooner she got it over with, the better she would feel. Men smiled and winked at her because she was Billy's confidante, but none found her quite important enough to start a conversation with, or cute enough to stalk as prey. The difference in treatment between the less important and the more important became obvious when, ten minutes later, the doorbell rang and Billy Rosenblatt joined the party. Every guest, it seemed, came forward to greet him, to shake his hand or slap his shoulder, to chat discreetly about an idea for a project or lavish compliments regarding his latest film. Billy dealt with them all politely; yet it was evident to Flossy, who knew him with an intimacy exceeding that of a lover or spouse, that his pale-blue eye was scanning the room for one thing: women. When he saw Flossy, he smiled with relief, and made his way to her side.

"Nice to see a friendly face," he whispered. "I feel like I'm in the shark tank at Marineland. Everybody wants to bite off a piece of me."

"Why, Billy, I've never heard you talk like that. I thought you considered yourself one of the—well . . ."

"Go ahead, say it. One of the sharks. The granddad, old Jaws himself. Maybe I did, once, Floss—but not today. I'm feeling my age. The years are catching up with me."

"Oh, dear. Billy, I'm afraid I'm not going to make you feel any better."

"Nonsense, Floss, you always cheer me up."

"Not tonight, Billy. Let's go someplace where we can talk in private."

She led him up to the second floor, knocked on a door and opened it, then shut it quickly, apologizing, when she saw a man and woman, half-dressed, grappling on the floor. She had better luck with the next room, a guest bedroom with bamboo wallpaper, a green bureau and lots of plants.

"Sit down," she said.

"What's this all about?" Billy wanted to know. "You're not quitting, are you? If that's what you want to tell me, you can forget it right now. I know I've been promising you that raise for months. Well, first thing Monday morning I'll contact the—"

"Billy, it's not that. This has to do with Angela's novel."

"You told me on the phone that you clinched the deal."

"We did, but—" Flossy hesitated, screwing up her courage. Then she blurted out, "But I'm not selling it to you."

"I didn't hear you right."

"You see, I've been giving it a lot of thought, and I've decided that I want to produce it myself. I've talked to a couple of studios and they're interested . . ."

Billy had turned red, and his silver hair seemed to be standing on end, as though charged with static.

"You ungrateful little pipsqueak! I gave you the money to buy it!"

"I know, but when I decided what I had to do, I kept your check and spent my own money—everything I've saved up over the years."

She dug Billy's check out of her handbag. He grabbed it from her, shredded it with such fury that he might have been shredding Flossy herself instead, and jammed the wadded pieces into his pocket.

"Jesus Christ," he muttered, "after all the years I spent teaching you, training you . . ."

"That's exactly the problem, Billy. You trained me to snap up a good property when I saw it, even if it meant hurting the feelings of an old friend."

"I never taught you any such thing!" he shouted. "Or if I did, didn't mean you should turn it against me."

"I'm not turning—"

"Betrayed by my closest associate. It's unbelievable—like Brutus slipping it to Caesar. McGee, I'll sue you, I swear to God I will. I'll ruin you, I'll make sure you never work in this town again."

"I've got a better idea," Flossy said gently. "Why don't you co-produce it with me? I need your help, Billy, I really do."

"Make myself the laughingstock of the film business?"

"Not true! People would be overwhelmed with respect that you could do a film that pokes some innocent fun at yourself."

"Innocent fun? Salacious slander if you ask me."

"Not when you see the screenplay," Flossy said. "Roy Gleason's going to write it. You know how warm and human his characters are."

"Gleason, eh? He's good. What does he want, an arm and a leg?"

"Fifty grand and one point of the gross."

"Holy hell. How'd you get him to agree to that?"

"I told him the truth. That it was my first film. That I didn't have any money. He was very sympathetic. Apparently he's got a daughter my age."

"Good work," Billy said, pleased with her despite his anger. "What about a director?"

"Well, I sent it out to a couple of people and I'm waiting for a reply."

"You know, Jay Matthews owes me a favor. This might be a perfect project for him."

"You mean you'll coproduce it with me?" Flossy said, so happy she could scarcely believe it.

"I'd better. They'd eat you up alive without my protection. Flossy, let me give you a piece of advice: It's a jungle out there and it takes an experienced guide to find the way. Yes, I think Jay Matthews would be perfect to direct. Floss, make a note for me to call him."

"Billy," she said gently, "I'm a producer now. I don't make notes."

"Why, you little . . ." he began, then he smiled and nodded. "We'll hire you a secretary first thing Monday morning."

It took a while for the bartender to mix the drink, and a while longer for Mack Gordon to find Rebecca in the crowd. "Best Margarita west of the Pecos," he said, slipping the cold glass into her hand. "I was looking all over for you. I thought you'd left."

"No, but I should. This is not my night for parties. First John Guilford gave me a joint that ruined my mind, then I wrecked Roy Gleason's marriage, next that little bitch who works for Billy Rosenblatt tried to tell me malicious gossip about Victoria." She looked at her watch. "I'd really better go—it's almost eleven."

"Not a chance! I haven't had a minute alone with you. Now, relax and drink your medicine while Poppa Mack takes you for a walk on the beach."

"I don't think so . . ."

"Come on! It'll clear your head for that long drive back to town."

They took off their shoes and walked barefoot, feeling the sand slip through their toes, inhaling the cold night air, watching the distant lights of Catalina Island twinkle through the smog. The ocean was peaceful, endlessly folding in upon itself with a sound that covered all sins.

"Ever been out to Catalina?" Mack asked her. "It's all wilderness except for one little town. And there are herds of buffalo roaming wild. Honest to God. The stupidest damn animals in the world. In the Old West white men would stampede them, then guide the stampede into a circle and pick 'em off with a rifle, pow, pow, pow. Or else they'd chase 'em toward a cliff and the damn animals would jump off and land in a pile at the bottom, all dead and ready to get cut up."

"Oh, Mack, that's horrible."

"That's survival of the fittest, Becky. The weak knuckle under so the strong can live. That's what Hollywood's all about. They fire a couple of shots and see if they can scare you into running off the side of the cliff."

"And what are we, Mack? The strong or the weak?"

"We're the strong, Becky. That's why we're here. We see what we want and we take it."

He grabbed her and tried to press his gin-stinking mouth against hers.

"Get off me," she said, and she broke loose and ran toward the house.

He caught her hand and flung her to the sand, down beside the wooden fence that bordered his property, where sprays of bougainvillaea would hide them from sight. Straddling her squirming form as though she were some kind of calf to be branded, he wrapped his fingers around her slim neck and whispered, "Scream, and I'll kill you."

Rebecca looked into his lifeless eyes, and saw a drunken madman staring back at her, and feared for her life.

He ripped her dress down the middle, exposing her small breasts, so the nipples shriveled and cowered from the cold. Then he rose to his knees and struggled with his zipper, grunting with frustration, finally freeing his cock. It was a blunt club with a head the size of a plum. Grabbing a handful of her hair, he yanked up her head and shoved the end of his organ into her mouth, working it deeper and deeper until she began to gag.

"Bite me, cunt," he whispered, "and I'll crack your fucking skull."

Now he hiked up her skirt, pulled down her panties and jammed his cock into the dryness between her legs, making her cry out from the shock of it, the pain. Four deep strokes—five perhaps—before he pulled it out and held it before her eyes for inspection. It was purple, trembling with tension. He yanked on the foreskin and it exploded, spewing ribbons of jism across her face. She gasped. He rolled off her and lay on his back. She ached to cry, but she wouldn't give him the satisfaction.

"Pig," she said, and spat on him.

"You loved every minute," he gasped, still trying to recover his breath.

Suddenly she could no longer contain the tears, and her body was wracked with spasms of pain and misery and fear.

"You hurt me," she sobbed, "you tore something." He thought she meant the dress, but then she touched herself between the legs and showed him the bloody fingers. She tried to stand up and cringed with pain. "I can't walk."

He pulled what remained of her dress around her, picked her up in his arms and climbed the steps to the house.

"Where are you taking me?" she said, panicking.

"To bed. There's a great doctor here tonight. Doc Rosen, my neighbor. I'll bring him upstairs to look at you."

"But I've got to go home!"

"You can't go anywhere right now. You're hurt and you need a doctor. So just relax and enjoy it."

He took her around to the side entrance to avoid attracting the attention of too many guests. Those few who did notice decided it was some kind of game, or if they guessed the seriousness of it, chose not to get involved. After all, one never knew when Mack Gordon's career might take a turn for the better, and one wanted to keep on his good side just in case. He carried her up the stairs to his own bedroom, which featured white leather furniture and a whole wall of windows overlooking the sea, and put her down on the bed, covering her with a quilt. His manner was gentle enough, but his eyes remained cold and dull as lead. Then he left to get the doctor. She tried to stand up, and the pain made her cry out loud. She was cold, yet she was sweating. All she could think was, I've got to get out of here, I've got to get back to the desert. When I see Beeze I'll tell him about this and he'll have Mack Gordon killed. And I will piss on his grave—if I'm ever able to piss again.

Doc Rosen was darkly tanned, with curly black hair, thick lips, glasses with black plastic rims. He was boyishly handsome, unctuously smooth in his bedside manner. He smiled at Rebecca before going into the bathroom to wash his hands, and Rebecca thought, This man isn't a doctor, he's an actor playing the part. I ought to know, I'm an actor myself. Takes one to know one.

He came out, drying his hands with a towel. "All right," he said gently, "let's have a look." He pulled back the quilt, then drew aside the pieces of torn dress, the shredded remains of her slip, as though he were peeling back the petals of a wilted flower. He frowned at the blood pooling on the bedspread.

"I'll need something to raise her pelvis."

"What about a book?" Mack said.

"I didn't know you could read," Rebecca said, her voice choked with pain.

"Good," the doctor went on, ignoring her, "and a spoon, some cotton, iodine or hydrogen peroxide. Maybe you'd better bring an ice bucket too, a couple of clean washcloths." He gazed thoughtfully at her face, which was chalky now and beaded with perspiration. "Do you have any tranquilizers?"

"Valium," Mack said.

"Get me that too."

While Mack was gone, Dr. Rosen felt her forehead, took her pulse.

"Why bother," she said. "I know you're not a doctor. You're not a very good actor, either. Too kind and serious. A real doctor would be angry that somebody took him away from his party."

Dr. Rosen smiled at her. "What would convince you? An illegible prescription? A huge bill?" He wiped her forehead with the towel he had brought from the bathroom. It was blue velour, "M. G." embroidered on it in gold. "When did you last menstruate?" he asked.

"I don't know. Two weeks ago, a month. Sometimes I don't menstruate at all. Can't spare the blood."

Mack returned, looking a little scared now, with the items the doctor had requested. Together they raised Rebecca's pelvis and placed a fat dictionary beneath it. The doctor swabbed the spoon with iodine, then used it as a speculum to hold back her labia.

"Lower," he said to Mack, who was pointing a table lamp in such a way as to illuminate this dark passage; and to Rebecca: "This will hurt just a little."

It was not as bad as any of them had feared, at least in terms of bodily damage. A minor laceration of a vaginal wall was responsible for the bleeding; he stopped it quickly by pressing a piece of cotton against it. As for the hematoma that had formed in the labia, engorging it, turning it the color of rotting fruit, he instructed Mack to apply ice packs until the swelling subsided.

The Valium took effect quickly and the last thing she remembered before sleep was Dr. Rosen telling Mack that if they hadn't been neighbors for eight years, he'd go straight to the police.

She woke to the glare of the sun reflected off a slate-gray sea. Mack was pulling back the curtains. For a moment she mistook the ocean for desert and imagined she was back at the Furnace Creek Inn shooting *Web!* But then she remembered the events of the previous night.

"I have to go," she said, climbing out of bed. The pain was less than before and she hoped to walk, but when she was standing upright, the room began to turn like a merry-go-round, and Mack had to catch her before she hit the floor.

"I brought you breakfast in bed," he said proudly.

Overcoming some slight resistance, he guided her back under the covers and set the tray on her lap. There were three fried eggs, a dozen sausages glistening with fat, two toasted bagels spread with cream cheese and strawberry preserves, hot coffee.

"I'm going to be sick," she said, looking at it, smelling the overpowering smells.

"Boy, that's gratitude. I spent a half-hour fixing . . ."

"Take it away, I'm going to be sick!"

He pulled a chair to the bedside, sat down with the tray on his lap and began to wolf down the eggs.

"I want you to drive me home immediately," she said.

"What's the rush? Becky, you need a vacation. You look like hell. Why don't you stay here for a couple of days? I'll take care of you. We'll go for long walks on the beach."

"I don't believe it," she said, astonished. "Last night you raped me and today you want to take care of me."

"You know, I have a reputation for being a man who never apologizes, but this time I'll say it. I'm sorry. What happened was I got a little crazy. You do that to me, Becky. There's something so sexy about you. I had to have you last night and I didn't know how to ask, so I took what I could, robbed you like a thief. I was drunk and stoned and out of my head. I'm sorry."

"If you could have shown a little patience and tenderness everything might have been different."

"Let me try. Give me a couple of days to show you how can be when I'm not drinking. Please, Becky. We could be so happy living here, making films together. Maybe having a kid."

"If I'm not sterile after last night."

"Damn it, stop rubbing it in. I said I was sorry! I was so filled with guilt I couldn't sleep. I wanted to kill myself for what I did to you. I wanted to get in my car and drive it straight off the side of a cliff."

"I have to go," she said.

"I'll take you home. But let me get Doc Rosen first and see if it's safe. He's right next-door."

Mack left and Rebecca had time to wonder. Why didn't she just get up and leave? It hurt to walk, but she knew she could make it to the car, she was certain she could drive back to Benedict Canyon. From there on, the journey would be a luxury, sprawled in the back of Beeze's air-conditioned limousine. Yet she couldn't make herself leave the bed; she seemed to be robbed of will. Another question bothered her more: Why had she let Mack Gordon rape her last night? Why hadn't she bitten his cock or jammed her knee into his testicles, as she now longed to do? In all likelihood he wouldn't have killed her—he was not, she thought, *quite* that crazy—and if he had tried to beat her she could have called for help. There had been people everywhere. Yet she had submitted with strange docility. Was it possible that she thought this to be the punishment she deserved for her happiness with Beeze? Was this the final misery of the masochist: to allow herself no lasting joy? Was this her fate—her karma, as Yogi Gnesha would say—or could she overcome it, could she leave this foggy place and return to the clarity of the desert?

This time Dr. Rosen came with his black bag, and examined Rebecca with gleaming instruments.

"Healing nicely," he said. "I'd refrain from intercourse for a couple of weeks."

"I'm not exactly in the mood," Rebecca said. "Can I leave here?"

"I don't see why not."

"She wants to make a long trip," Mack said. "She wants to drive out to the Mojave Desert. That's crazy, isn't it, Doc?"

"I don't think you should do anything strenuous," the doctor said, although he was obviously reluctant to agree with Mack about anything.

"Don't you think it would be better if she stayed here and let me take care of her for a couple of days?" Mack pressed.

"Depends on what you mean by taking care of her," Dr. Rosen said.

"Jesus," Mack said, "won't anybody give me a break? You don't know how I've been suffering over this. The truth is it's hurting me just as bad as it's hurting her."

"I doubt that," the doctor said.

"Can I ask you a question about medicine?" Rebecca asked.

"If you value an actor's opinion," the doctor said.

Rebecca smiled at him. "What I want to know is this: Suppose a man is in some kind of accident and has to have his pancreas removed. Then he takes pills, right?"

"Synthetic pancreatic enzyme," the doctor said, nodding.

"And insulin?"

"Yes."

"But suppose a day goes by without the insulin—would he die?"

"It depends. Probably not. He might be able to survive for some time."

"Really?" Rebecca raised her eyebrows.

"Suppose the guy had enough insulin for a week," Mack said. "Couldn't he make it last longer by taking smaller doses, stretching it out?"

"That would be the smart thing to do," Dr. Rosen agreed. "That way he might be able to survive for a month or more. Why the interest? Is this a movie you're making?"

"That's right," Mack said. "It's a love story, a triangle. There's a millionaire who's playing endless ego games with a terrific young actress, and there's a director who doesn't know why he ever let her get away from him."

"Mack, please," Rebecca said, "you're making me puke." She saw the doctor standing up to leave, and she said, "One more thing: Suppose this man couldn't get his insulin—what would his death be like? What I mean is, how would it feel?"

Rosen considered the question for a minute before answering. "He'd have to urinate constantly. His body would dry out, his eyes, his mouth. He'd drink and drink and never satisfy his thirst. Then there would be nausea, vomiting, shortness of breath, as though suffocating. Finally the heart would stop from the concentration of potassium. Might be very dramatic in a film. Very dramatic."

"See?" Mack said, after the doctor had gone.

"See what?"

"This Beeze character—he's playing games with you, he's manip ulating you. If that's your idea of love, you're more screwed up than I thought."

"Look who's talking about being screwed up."

"You heard the doctor. He might last for a month! But he gives you this whole rigmarole about how he'll die if you're not back in seven days. And how do you know he doesn't have a little extra insulin stashed away someplace? He'd have to do that. It's the only thing that makes sense."

Rebecca remembered standing in the laboratory with Beeze, watching him shatter the insulin vials one by one. It had obviously been staged for her benefit. Would a man as intelligent as Beeze keep all the insulin together like that? Wouldn't he have a reserve somewhere else in the house in case of fire, in the kitchen refrigerator perhaps? Rebecca tried to keep her faith in Beeze, but the seeds of suspicion took root with astonishing speed. Everything Mack had said about Beeze was true, that he was a game-player, a manipulator, a man who doled out justice as though he were God.

She napped for a few hours and when she awoke she asked Mack if they could take a walk. The swelling had gone down, the pain had subsided to a twinge now and then, bearable if she took small steps. Outside, the air was damp, cold. The fog hung like a curtain across the sun, gulls emerging from it and disappearing again as they soared and dived and pierced the water for food. Strands of sea grapes lay scattered on the sand. Mack strolled with his arm round her, protectively; she, with both hands deep in the pockets of some jeans he had lent her, comically baggy. She also wore his blue woolen sweater and his sweat socks, since the high heels of the night before were impossible on the sand. Something about wearing his clothes gave her the extraordinary feeling that her own sensitivities, so fine that life sometimes seemed like a crawl across concrete and broken bottles and barbed wire, were protected by Mack's elephant skin, the armor-plate that let him trample those weaker than himself without a twinge of remorse.

About a mile up the beach some friends of Mack's were playing volleyball. He joined them while Rebecca stretched out on a beach chair to watch. She closed her eyes and the sun became a diffused orange light. The cold salt spray made a sort of crust on her skin.

Pretty soon the excited shouts of the volleyball players were over come by the roar of the sea, and she fell asleep to that rhythmic sound. She woke with a start when Mack touched the base of an icy drink to her belly where the sweater had ridden up. She almost snapped at him; but then she realized that it was his way of ex pressing affection and repressed her anger. They sat on the porch of the house owned by the man who had organized the game, theatrical lawyer and old friend of Mack's, and drank beer and told stories. With the booze and the sun and the charming chatter of the company, the day vanished like a card in a gambler's hand. Before Rebecca knew what had happened, it was night and they were barbecuing steaks on a hibachi. After they had eaten, another guest, a songwriter, sat down at the piano and played a few of his own songs, a few of their requests. Rebecca felt so good, so "mellow" in the parlance of the day, that she sang along and when the song was over everybody complimented her and told her she should put together a night-club act.

"I was going back tonight," Rebecca told Mack as they were walking along the beach, returning to his house, "but it's too late and I'm too drunk."

"Stay as long as you like, honey," he said, pulling her close kissing her gently on the forehead.

The next day was Sunday and they spent it lazing around the house, reading the Sunday *New York Times*, which Mack sub scribed to as a certain sort of snobbism, and eating bagels and lo They watched *A Christmas Carol* on television, and *Miracle o 34th Street*.

"I really have to go," Rebecca said.

"Tomorrow's Christmas Eve. You don't want me to spen Christmas Eve alone, do you?"

"Don't you have any family?"

"Nobody but you."

Rebecca eyed the presents under the tree. "Then who a those for?" she asked, little-girlishly.

"Nobody. They're empty boxes."

"I'll bet," she said, smiling at him for the first time in days.

Next morning she drove down to the Cross Creek shoppi

center to look for a present for Mack. At Fred Segal's she found a three-hundred-dollar leather pilot's jacket that seemed sufficiently arrogant, and wrote out a check for it. She also bought an outfit for herself to wear that evening, some tight-fitting satin jeans and a loose, elegant knit top. After all, Mack's old clothes would hardly do for a Christmas Eve celebration.

At one minute after midnight, she gave him the present and smiled, and whispered, "Merry Christmas, Mack."

He looked a little embarrassed as he took it out of the box, felt the leather, put it on and swaggered in front of his reflection in the *lanai* doors beyond which beat the cold black sea.

"Thanks, Becky, it's great. I'm sorry I didn't get you anything."

"Then you wouldn't mind if I opened one of those boxes under the tree?"

"Be my guest," Mack said, genuinely puzzled.

Tearing the crisp green paper, with its repetitions of candy canes and golden stars, made her a child again. She remembered searching the closets for presents, tiptoeing downstairs in the middle of the night to see the fully trimmed tree, and finally the wonderful morning when nobody was allowed to open a present until her mother had finished her first cup of coffee, the cup that seemed never to empty, like the magic urns of the Hindu saints with their endless supply of holy ash. The warm feeling that spread through her as she opened the presents then—and now—was the feeling of love; for in her family Love was presents. Just as gases under pressure turned liquid, love under pressure turned to merchandise. She tore off the cover of the box—it bore the emblem of one of her favorite shops—pulled back the tissue, and looked up at Mack, confused.

"There's nothing in here," she said. "It's empty."

He couldn't help but laugh at the pitiful expression on her face.

"The tree looked lousy with nothing under it, so I took a few old boxes and wrapped them up. For Christ's sake, Becky, I told you they were empty."

"But I thought . . ."

She looked about, like a person who had just wakened from a trance. "What am I doing here?" she said, more to herself than to him. "I must be out of my mind." She turned her back on him and started for the front door.

"Where are you going?" he yelled, running after her.

He caught up with her outside the house, at the edge of the Coast Highway where she had parked her Mustang. Cars roared by, too fast, too close. She sat in the driver's seat, trying to start the engine, while Mack leaned on the door.

"Where are you going?" he said again, his voice gentler now.

"Where I should have gone days ago," she replied. "I just hope to God I'm not too late."

The motor caught; she slammed her foot down on the gas, trying to get Mack while he leaned on the door, break his arm or something, but he sprang back too quickly, laughing at her efforts. She was tempted to go back and run him down, but instead she drove to town, the accelerator pressed nearly to the floor.

Finding her house keys in the cluttered interior of her handbag, inserting the proper one into the door, turning it one way and then the other—the simple task seemed to take hours. She burst into the house and made straight for the kitchen.

The plastic butter dish was empty.

She fell back into a kitchen chair and started to cry. Empty butter dish, empty presents. Who would have done such a thing, who could have taken it?

Only one person.

Hadn't she known it all along?

Of course.

Then why hadn't she admitted it?

Too painful to give up a mother, a sister, a friend.

Rebecca stood at the door of Victoria's bedroom and flicked on the light. Victoria turned a few times under the covers, then opened one eye, then the other. She raised her head and smiled at Rebecca.

"You back?" she said, silky-voiced. "What time's it?"

"Where's the insulin?" Rebecca said, her voice like cold steel.

"What insulin?"

"Don't play games. I'm in a hurry."

"If you're in such a hurry, why'd you spend three days with Mack Gordon?"

"That's none of your goddamned business. Now tell me what you did with the insulin."

"Oh! You mean that stuff you left in the refrigerator? I haven't touched it. It must have been those men who came to fix the dryer last week. They wanted something to drink, so I told them to help themselves out of the fridge. They probably thought it was drugs. I should have known better than to leave them alone with . . ."

"GODDAMN IT, TELL ME THE TRUTH!"

She pulled Victoria out of bed and threw her against the wall. The women stared at each other, astounded by Rebecca's show of strength. Victoria's eyes grew fearful with the realization of physical jeopardy, then cunning. She grabbed a pair of nail scissors off her make-up table and raised them like a dagger. They faced each other, silent and wary.

"I want that insulin," Rebecca said.

"It's gone. I broke it. I flushed it down the toilet."

"You're lying. You always lie to me."

"You spoiled Jewish bitch," Victoria said, "why should I tell you the truth? You always had everything. Rich parents giving you money, sending you to college, buying you acting lessons, getting people to hire you."

"What are you talking about?"

"They hire you because your father's famous, it's obvious. If it was just a question of talent, you'd never work a day in your life. You look like a rat and you overact so badly it hurts."

"So that's the secret of my success?" Rebecca's voice was very low and trembling with rage.

"That and being Jewish. It's obvious all you Jews are helping one another and trying to keep people like me from working. I can see it whenever you get together, you and Leslie *Horowitz* and Billy *Rosenblatt*."

"Get out!" Rebecca said.

"Make me." Then she stabbed with the scissors.

Rebecca grabbed her wrist and tried to wrest the weapon away. The two women struggled for it, pushing and pulling and panting for breath, overturning a night table and sending a lamp crashing to the floor. Rebecca tripped over the power cord, fraying the wire so sparks flew like fireworks in the darkened room, and fell on her back. Victoria lunged at her. Rebecca rolled aside. They grappled, rolling across the carpet, scratching and kicking, and always aware of the scissors, their deadly curved beak. Victoria pushed Rebecca toward the place where the power cord was sizzling and Rebecca had to grab hold of the bed frame to save herself from electrocution. That freed Victoria's hands; she rose to her knees and stabbed again with the scissors, plunged them, with both hands, at Rebecca's heart. Again Rebecca rolled out of the way, but this time not fast enough. The metal beak pecked her arm and warm blood trickled down her side. Somehow the scissors had become caught in the rough weave of the carpet. While Victoria was struggling to pull them free, Rebecca kicked at her stomach. Victoria gasped, rolled over on her back, unable to catch her breath. Rebecca worked the scissors out of the carpet and held them to the other woman's head.

"Tell me where the insulin is," she said, "or I'll stick these scissors in your face. I swear I will. I'll cut crosses in your cheeks and maybe I'll poke out an eye too. There's no plastic surgeon in the country who can fix that."

"I threw it on the lawn," Victoria gasped. "It's still there i nobody stepped on it."

"First you'll show me exactly where you threw it; then you'll come back here, pack your things and get out. I don't ever want to see you again."

But alas, Victoria could narrow down the area where she had thrown the vial to no less than a hundred square feet of the from lawn. No sooner had she done that than she ran for her car, and took off into the night, engine howling. Rebecca got a flashligh from the kitchen and crawled around in the iceweed, alternatel weeping and raging at herself, giving up in despair and reassertin her search with the conviction of a zealot. She felt like one of thos fools who loses her contact lens on the floor of the hotel lobby. A glitter—was that it? Rushing joyfully, then the letdown, only a shar of shattered Coke bottle half-buried in the dirt. She remembered friend who had dropped his wedding ring while mowing the gras and had hired the local Boy Scout troop to search for it. Could sh do the same? Could she tell them, those shy Scouts, that a man life was at stake, and that her own chances for happiness were growing slighter by the moment? She crawled for hours, her trouser knees sopping from the dew, her eyes aching for sleep, before she felt a smooth shape beneath her hand. The vial was full, as it had been when Beeze gave it to her, and the membrane was intact. She sat down on the grass and cried with fatigue, holding the tiny bottle to her chest, rocking back and forth. When she opened her eyes, the limousine was waiting at the curb. Samson was holding the door. She rose and ran to it.

The front door of the mansion was wide open, as were the windows. In the short time of her absence, the desert had begun to reclaim its own: dust carpeted the marble floors and tumbleweed rolled down the corridors, silent as ghosts; owls had nested in the cornices and kangaroo rats had torn the stuffings from the beautiful gilded chairs. Of human occupation there was no trace. She ran up to Beeze's eight-sided room high atop the mansion and found it empty. She looked in bedroom after bedroom, and in the library, where they had played so many games of checkers, and in the music room, where the harpsichord was closed like a child's coffin. In desperation she shouted his name but the only response was the morning song of a poor-will, hauntingly lonely.

She stood atop the steps that led to the garden and was shocked by the scene revealed to her by day's first pink light: flowers shriveled on the stalk, hedges naked as wire sculpture, lawns of clay, everything brown and dry and brittle. That life had ever survived here—any life more flamboyant than the sage and the thistle—was impossible to believe. For moments she stood there overlooking the skeleton of a garden, the formalized celebration of death; then the rising sun picked out Beeze's form bent limp over the side of the fountain, his head and hand dangling within the empty marble bowl where water once danced and sparkled.

His body would dry out, his eyes, his mouth. He'd drink and drink and never satisfy his thirst . . .

A sound of despair escaped her lips; she ran down the steps, down the avenues once bordered by brilliant sprays of blossoms, down to the fountain where Beeze lay dying, and lowered him to the earth. He was twice her weight, but in the face of disaster her strength had become extraordinary. She knelt beside him and took his head in her lap, and caressed the awful ruin of his face, the scars and hollows, as though it were the satin flesh of a child.

"Rebecca?" he whispered, his voice like a rattle of bones in a parchment pouch.

"I'm back, Beeze. I've got the insulin. Tell me where to find the syringe, and I'll . . ."

"It's too late for that." He gasped for air every few words.

There would be nausea, vomiting, shortness of breath, as though suffocating.

"Oh, Beeze." She was weeping. "You were the only one who ever really loved me and I didn't believe you. I thought it was a trick. And now I've killed you."

"Angina, before you left. Blockages in the coronary arteries. Resnick gave me a month to live. Would have died anyway. No guilt, no blame."

"Then your life wasn't really in my hands?" she asked, strangely disappointed. "Or are you lying to ease my guilt? I don't know what to believe anymore. Tell me I didn't kill you. Please."

"You gave me life. Without you, wouldn't have made sense, none of it."

"What will I do without you?"

"A few months, forget. The desert and the mansion like a dream, a fairy tale."

"No, Beeze, no! I'll never forget you."

Yet despite her protestations, it already seemed unreal. She was light-headed from lack of sleep and emotionally exhausted. A shimmering curtain of heat twisted the garden as though it were fluid. The line between reality and hallucination wavered perilously.

"I love you," she said.

But before Beeze could reply, a tremor passed through his body, as though the soul were being torn loose from its moorings, and then his head rolled back upon her lap and his eyes turned blindly upward.

Finally the heart would stop from the concentration of potassium . . .

"Beeze!" she shrieked. But no human voice could call him back from where he had gone.

She threw herself across his body, weeping, crying his name, tearing her hair and beating her fists against the ground like a woman in a Greek tragedy. Her hysteria led to a loss of consciousness; when she came to, it was noon, the sun blazing overhead. She was seized with a sudden horror at what the heat might do to Beeze's body, causing it to swell and bloat with putrefying gases, to burst with a hideous spray of blood and viscera. She pulled closed his eyelids and tried to lift him by the arms, but now that the first rush of adrenaline had passed, she was as weak as a baby. She looked about for Samson, called his name, but heard no reply. In despair she dragged the body herself, up the avenue, up the steep ascent of stairs.

Gaining the rear of the terrace, she pulled him through the double doors and laid him to rest on the cool marble floor of the great hall where they had first met. She knelt beside his body and remained thus for hours, numb to the pain in her knees, recalling the days since their first meeting. He had tested her love and she had failed him. How could she have stayed with Mack Gordon those few fatal days, how could she have done such a thing? Was her self-hatred so immense?

Or was her mistake returning to the desert at all? Had Beeze, as his dying words had indicated, chosen to use his impending death for one final masterful stroke of manipulation? She could learn the truth, she could hunt down Dr. Resnick and ask her if indeed she had diagnosed a coronary blockage. But such steps were not necessary. In her heart of hearts Rebecca already knew the answer: that even in his last moments on earth, Beeze had been lying to protect her. She was the murderess, she had killed him through her own neglect. The police would never punish her for her crime —she had never succeeded in making them believe in Beeze while he was alive—so she would have to punish herself. The idea of living out her life with her lover's death on her conscience was more than she could bear. How she longed for sleep. If only she had brought her beloved Valium she would have taken a hundred pills and slept for a hundred years, like the princess in the tower waiting for the wakening kiss. But she had no Valium.

She knew what she would have to do.

It was getting dark outside and cold, but she was scarcely aware of the wind whistling through the corridor as she made her way to the kitchen. There she found a carving knife, eighteen inches long and ground to a fine blade. She went to the bathroom of the guest suite, undressed and lay down in the empty black-tiled tub, where once whirlpool jets had loosened her body for sleep. She would cut her wrists, watch the blood spill down the drain until finally her eyelids grew so heavy that she could watch no longer. Samson would discover her and call the police. The press would come and she would finally make the cover of *Newsweek*, assuring her at least a month's status as hottest actress in Hollywood. Hottest dead actress.

Of course being a dead actress was simple; being a live one, far more difficult. She would have to play *The Other Woman* and give the performance of her career. She would have to finally become a star with the power to choose her own roles. She would have to succeed; she could put it off no longer. Artistic fulfillment, professional respect, critical adulation, all the things she had ever wanted would be hers. The idea was unbearable; and that led her to wonder if perhaps this killing of herself wasn't simply another way to avoid happiness, the happiness of professional fulfillment. Certainly Beeze would have wanted her to stay alive and make her film, Beeze who loved art and order so, Beeze who worshiped daily in the dark temple of dreams.

And what about Leslie? Just as she carried the guilt of Beeze' death, her beloved manager would carry the burden of hers. He'd probably finish himself off with drugs in a year or two, or try another jump from a second-story window. Her parents would never recover. Everyone she loved would be drawn into the vortex of grief surrounding her death. Only she herself would be spared the pain. Suddenly suicide, like a Jekyll and Hyde character, lost its nobility and grew stooped and ugly, deformed with selfishness. Rebecca realized, with the clarity that comes at moments of crisis, that it was time for a final decision. She could kill herself, or she could put masochism and self-destructiveness aside forever and begin to make some kind of life for herself. She held the knife to her left wrist, to where the arteries flowed like rivers beneath the ice and pressed, her hand trembling from the conflict raging within

Then she gave a cry, a cry of victory and of defeat, a cry for the death of one woman and the birth of another, and threw the knife so it hit the wall and clattered against the floor. Tears ran down the drain, not blood. Later she dressed and returned to Beeze's body, beside which she was sitting peacefully when Samson found her.

The servant's hands and feet were covered with the dust of the desert. At first she was afraid that he would hold her responsible, but his face showed no resentment, only the sadness and confusion of a faithful dog who loses his master. He touched her shoulder in sympathy. Then he hoisted Beeze's body upon his back and carried it to the door. Rebecca rose and followed.

Now she saw where he had been all day: digging a grave in front of the mansion, a six-foot-deep ditch in the iron-hard earth. He wrapped Beeze's body in a green velvet shroud (one of the drapes, Rebecca realized, from the canopy bed she had slept in) and laid him tenderly to rest in the bottom of the grave. Rebecca threw a handful of dirt over him. She wanted to say something special and beautiful, but all she could think of was "Ashes to ashes, dust to dust."

Samson filled in the hole. He placed Beeze's mask where a headstone would be, and that was the only marking.

Later the helicopter carried them into the moon-bright night, and Rebecca watched the grave grow small below until finally it was no more, and the mansion shrink to the size of a toy. Soon that too had disappeared and then nothing remained but the night sky, the blazing stars.

eauty kneeled beside her beloved Beast and, overwhelmed with love for the fine creature, took his head in her arms and kissed him most tenderly. To her astonishment the Beast disappeared and in his stead lay the handsomest prince she had ever seen.

Oh, where has my Beast gone? she asked.

I am the Beast, the Prince said, or at least that was the form in which I was imprisoned by an evil fairy; and thus did I remain and would have remained for all time, had you not undone her magic with your kiss. Ah Beauty, you have saved me and for this I am ever grateful. Will you be my bride and share my kingdom with me?

And Beauty agreed.

And their happiness was complete forever and evermore.

About the Author

JONATHAN FAST comes from a family of celebrated writers—his great-great-uncle was the Yiddish author Shalom Aleichem, and his father, Howard Fast, is also a novelist of renown.

Born in New York City in 1948, Jonathan Fast attended Princeton University. He has written extensively for the theater, motion pictures and television and is the author of four novels. He lives in Connecticut with his wife, poet-novelist Erica Jong, and their daughter, Molly.

RUTH HARRIS
The Last Romantics

She – the nobody who climbed from poverty in rural France to the dizzying heights of the fashion world. Her daring new clothes revolutionised and liberated the lives of women across the world. And her face revolutionised the life of a man.

He – a rich American journalist of social standing, restlessly seeking to conquer the world and find glory through his words. He was feted by the literary world and was the hero of a generation. He fell in love with a beautiful woman in Paris, 1918 – alive with champagne, joy and hope at the close of brutal war.

Together – Nicole Redon and Kim Hendricks shared a romance so fierce and blinding it threatened to consume them both. Torn by their separate brilliant careers, doubt and jealousy, yet their love remained triumphant – they are the last romantics the first contemporaries.

More top fiction from Methuen Paperbacks

These and other Methuen Paperbacks are available at your bookshop or newsage
In case of difficulties orders may be sent to:

Methuen Paperbacks
Cash Sales Department
P.O. Box 11
Falmouth
Cornwall TR10 109EN

Please send cheque or postal order, no currency, for purchase price quoted and all
the following for postage and packing:

U.K.   45p for the first book plus 20p for the second book and 14p for e
           additional book ordered to a maximum charge of £1.63.

B.F.P.O.   45p for the first book plus 20p for the second book and 14p for the r
& Eire   7 books thereafter 8p per book.

Overseas   75p for the first book and 21p per copy for each additional book.
Customers

While every effort is made to keep prices low, it is sometimes necessary to incre
prices at short notice. Methuen Paperbacks reserves the right to show new re
prices on covers which may differ from those previously advertised in the tex
elsewhere.